As they drove back through the sultry night, she said, "Now if we are to be friends, we must be just friends.
No scandalous propositions.

"Wouldn't dream of it!" he vowed, choirboy innocent.

"No—no kisses."

"Not even your hand?"

Kristen sighed with exasperation and reluctant longing.

"Tressilian, your sort of handkissimg should be outlawed. It is hazardous to the moral quality of the kingdom."

"If you say so." One shoulder rippled in a sullen shrug.

"And you mustn't call me your love." She considered his rakish habit of addressing every woman he met with endearments, and decided banning them entirely might prove too difficult. So she allowed, "You may call me 'angel', however.

© 1997 by Alicia Todd Rasley

Published by: Kappa Books, Inc.
Fort Washington, PA 19034

Manufactured in the United States of America.
ISBN: 1-56682-047-2

# CHAPTER ONE

London, June 1808

The dandy in yellow balanced a silver evening pump on the couch and leaned over to adjust its bow. "Just another smidge," counseled his friend draped along the mantel. "No, to the right— "

At the sound of the opening door, the dandy straightened and raised his quizzing glass, ready to slash the intruder with his razor wit. Then the glass clattered to the floor. "Tressilian! I mean, my lord!"

The lean young man standing in the doorway wore the blue and gold uniform of a navy captain. His expression was patient but somehow threatening. Behind him was a phalanx of four comrades— two cousins and two friends, all of them the trim and muscular Corinthian sort. The cousin in the elaborate cavalry uniform balanced his hand lightly on the hilt of his sword.

As the Earl of Tressilian sauntered into the private parlor, the others fanned out behind him like a well-trained invasion force. Lieutenant Destain vaulted over the back of the couch and stretched his long legs out, dislodging the dandy's foot and nearly toppling him. The other cousin, Jeremy Trevarrick, edged himself onto the window sill and tried to look fierce. Barnabas Abernethy spared an envious glance at the dandy's yellow satin breeches— Barnabas would be a tulip himself, would his friends allow it— then stationed himself with a foot poised belligerently on the stone hearth. And the eldest of the group at twenty-five, Lord Lytten held the door open and smiled ferociously.

Tressilian stopped his pacing directly under the chandelier, its light gilding his black hair. His dark gaze held the dandy fast and then just as coolly dismissed him with a glance at the open door.

"My lord. Lieutenant Destain." The dandy's voice rose to a squeak, and he could manage only a nod to the others. "Didn't know you was in town. We were just leaving—"

The dispossessed dandies retreated in some disarray, the friend breaking his silence only as they crossed the threshold. "We're members of the Bracken too. And we was here first."

"Shut up." The dandy in yellow turned back to bow to the earl. "Don't you know that Tressilian has killed men for less than this?"

Brendan Trevarrick had not, in fact, ever killed a man for usurping this room, but then, no man ever stayed around long enough to fight for it. Once again denied a battle, he bent to pluck a scrap of lace from the faded oriental carpet and flung the little handkerchief into the cold hearth. "Jonny, our parlor smells of scent."

Lieutenant Destain, a slim fair man of indolent attitude, agreed this could not be borne. From his command post on the couch, he directed entrenchment operations. "Jeremy," he ordered the youngest, "open that window. Barnabas, light up a cigar. Larry, find the key to the cabinet— it's there, above the doorframe— and open the cabinet, there's a good lad, and get out the decanter. Bren, do you think it's at the same level as last we were here? Let's remember to mark it this time to make sure no one's stealing our brandy— No, Larry, don't drink it. Just sprinkle a bit on the hearth and leave it open."

Soon the parlor smelled as a gentleman's club should, of fresh air and tobacco and cognac. Mission accomplished, Destain laid his head back against the leather arm of the couch and closed his eyes. "Now, Bren, is that more to your liking? If I loved you better, I'd import some sea air, but I fear the London fog is all you're worth to me."

"If you loved me better," Tressilian replied, taking decanter from Lytten and splashing brandy into glasses, "you'd see about that brass plaque to establish our ownership of this room. We've only been gone eight months, and see who's been abusing it in our absence— Tulip Tillson and Pomade Pettrick."

Destain reached out a lazy hand for his glass. "I was set to order a plaque made, to present to you at Christmas. But I thought to check the wording with you first. Do you prefer The Destain-Tressilian Proprietary Parlor, or the Destain-Tressilian Proprietary Salon?"

"I prefer the Tressilian-Destain Anything at All." Ordinarily Tressilian wasn't one to pull rank, but he wasn't about to let Jonny get away with this. "Precedence, you know."

"What precedence? My name comes first alphabetically."

"But I am a peer."

Murmurs of "Got you there" rose from Lytten and Abernethy. Jeremy kept to his perch and did not venture an opinion. Destain only smiled. "What's a peer, compared to a noted wit?"

"Half of one, anyway," Lytten put in, but Tressilian silenced him with a glare. Only he was allowed to insult his cousin.

"I needn't mention that the navy far outranks the cavalry in significance." He paused to let that sink in, but Destain kept smiling. Goaded, Tressilian added, "Especially since Trafalgar, when we established our superiority over that other service— Barnabas, what is the name of that other service? I forget. Ah, yes, the army."

Barnabas frowned in bewilderment. "I thought it was the French you beat at Trafalgar. Not the thing to fight your own army, is it?"

"And," Tressilian went on, dropping into a chair and propping his feet on the hearth, "I am the elder. By two months. Tressilian-Destain, you must agree, is preferred."

"If I am to pay for the blasted thing, it's Destain- Tressilian."

This was an unanswerable shot, and Tressilian surrendered as gracefully as he could. "It's enough to be back home, both at the same time," he said, reaching across and clapping his cousin on the shoulder. "Both safe from the wars."

"You decorated, and I promoted! What great fortune."

"What a surprise," Lytten added. "You must have been the oldest cornet in the army. How long have you served, Destain? Three years? And even now only a lieutenant. Keep up the pace, sluggard, and you might make captain before century's end."

Jon sighed. "That rank's too dear for my pocket. And you know the admiral'd never spring for it."

The admiral was Jon's father, and Tressilian's superior, and, after Napoleon, the army's greatest enemy. He'd never forgiven his son for breaking four generations' worth of naval tradition, so buying a promotion was the last thing he'd consider. Sympathetically Tressilian said, "I'll buy you a captaincy, Jonny."

"Don't bother. Don't want it. Captains work too hard."

"Work too hard? In the army?" Tressilian scoffed. "As far as I can see, all your captains do is play cards and lose duels. If any of them have led troops into battle in the last few years, I've yet to hear of it."

This at least wiped the smile off Jon's face, though he still didn't open his eyes. "And you sea captains are next to galley slaves, I suppose? I supposed you drove yourself to exhaustion on that cruise to Ceylon?"

"Well," Tressilian had to admit, "we never quite got to Ceylon. Ran into a spot of trouble near Madagascar."

"I might have known," Jon said. They'd been raised almost as brothers, and had no secrets to speak of. "Who was she?"

"She?"

"The woman involved. There had to be a woman."

"Yes, Bren, tell us," Lytten chimed in. "Who was this spot of trouble?"

"The sultan's wife. She wasn't my trouble, you understand," Tressilian hastened to add. "But the sultan's.."

"They have sultans in Madagascar?" Jeremy asked, frowning a little in concentration.

"He was visiting. Traveling light— only brought four wives. This one was number three. I was at the palace, negotiating the release of my second lieutenant from the dungeon. No," Tressilian said, putting up his hand, "don't ask me why he was in the dungeon. It does no credit to the Royal Navy, I assure you." A scowl fleeted across his face and was gone. "And the eunuch rushed in— have you ever seen a eunuch?"

"Only Pomade Pettrick and Tulip Tillson," Jon muttered. "Go on, go on. What did the eunuch say?"

Tressilian responded with an incomprehensible burst of speech, then added, "That means 'Princess Fatma has been kidnapped!'"

"Did you do it?" Barnabas's spasmodic gesture connected with his tankard on the mantle and sent it crashing to the floor.

"Kidnap her?" Lytten watched with disgust as Barnabas grabbed the hearthcloth and began mopping up his mess. "Since when has Tressilian had to kidnap a woman? They've kidnapped him, on occasion, but as far as I can see, he need only whisper some nonsense in their ears and they fall into his lap."

"I didn't kidnap her. I rescued her, though. Some rival royal clan had slipped into the palace through an underground tunnel and plucked her right out of the bath. Took her up into the highlands. I got my marines off the Defiant and we chased them back to their hideout. The muskets were a real revelation to the bandits— they still fight with spears. Or they did, until one of the marines left his weapon behind. Don't worry," he assured them, though they didn't look very anxious, "he only left twenty rounds of ammunition."

"So why did you have to turn back from your voyage, if you rescued the princess?" Jeremy prompted. "Didn't the sultan express his gratitude?"

"Certainly did. Gave me a casket of jewels for King George- - and a bejeweled dagger for myself. Even got my lieutenant set free. The admiral thought I'd best get the jewels delivered before I lost them in a card game, so here I am." His modest shrug caused the epaulettes to ripple over his shoulders. "Nothing to compare to that incident in Borneo last year, of course."

Jeremy, who worshipped his elder cousin, asked eagerly, "You never told me about Borneo!"

There followed another convoluted tale involving pirates and headhunters and a cache of gold doubloons— "Have you ever wondered," Jon said in an aside to Lytten, "why you and I dodge creditors wherever we go, and Tressilian, who has enough to last us all a lifetime, can't walk in the park without gold and silver raining on him?"

Lytten dejectedly splashed more brandy into his glass. "For the same reason I give up a mistress I can't afford, only to see her offer herself free of charge to him. And she still cries his praises when he turns her down. Face it, Destain. Those favored at birth are favored in life."

Tressilian had indeed been favored at birth, unless one put too much weight on his immediate orphaning. A viscount from his first breath— his father having died two months earlier— heir to an earldom and a large fortune, he was born with the sort of dark-angel looks that thrilled feminine hearts ever since. And ever since he had lived up to that heroic appearance, risking death, court-martial, and marriage in pursuit of adventure.

Reckless, restless, Tressilian was adventure-prone as some men were accident-prone.

So a barebones recital of how he came to be proclaimed a god in Borneo led Jeremy to beg another anecdote, and another. But finally as the night grew longer and Tressilian hoarser, finally he broke off with a protesting laugh. "Enough of these dull tales! Jonny, tell me of the adventures you've gotten yourself into without me."

Jon Destain would be the first to admit that without his cousin, he would have no adventures at all. In this, as in most things, he was Tressilian's opposite. He would never even have joined the cavalry had Tressilian not gotten him drunk and dragged him insensate to Horse Guards. Now it took a bit of concentrating before he recalled the highlight of his half-year's campaigning with Sir John Moore. "I won the regimental darts tournament."

"Again?" Tressilian said with gratifying wonder. "I don't know why they don't just retire the trophy and proclaim you permanent champion."

"Billiards too," Jon allowed modestly, for he excelled at all sports requiring no exertion whatsoever.

"Well, I had a victory too," Lytten put in with a leer. He paused until even the indolent Destain leaned forward and urged him on. "I can't in honor mention the lady's name, of course, but suffice to say, she's one of the loveliest in London."

"Who's that?" the naive Jeremy asked.

"Olivia Marchant," Barnabas replied promptly. He had flamboyant taste in women as well as attire, and as usual, Lytten scoffed.

"La Marchant's a Cyprian, not a lady."

Tressilian regarded Lytten speculatively. "Ah, your conquest is a real lady, is she?"

"Not for long, if she's mingling with the likes of Lytten," Jon said with a laugh. "Well, when I was here last, he had his sights on your old flame, Bren. You know, the redhead."

"All of Bren's old flames are redheads, or most of them anyway." Barnabas frowned. "Which was the last one?"

Tressilian shook his head, smiling, but Jon exclaimed, "Now I remember! Daphne Frobisher!"

Lytten's memories of Daphne apparently weren't so fond, for he growled, "You call her lovely?"

"I called her rather more than that, if I recall correctly." Tressilian stirred his brandy with his finger and flung a few drops at Lytten. "It's not Daphne, then, your lady?"

"No, and no other redhead either."

"Blonde?" Jeremy ventured, and Lytten grinned.

"That's my boy. Only 'blonde' doesn't do justice to her crowning glory. Sunlight on snow! That's what I called her hair."

"Blue-eyed?" Jon's was a safe bet, England being full of blue-eyed blondes. He was one himself.

"Blue?" Lytten gazed out the window, as if he could visualize the lady in the darkness outside. "No, 'blue' isn't quite right. Deeper than that. Violet, I'd have to say."

Tressilian's restless hands stilled on his brandy glass, and Jon glanced inquiringly at him. "You feeling well, Bren?"

"Of course. I'm fine. Why do you ask?"

"Because you haven't moved in twenty seconds or so, and that ain't like you."

Tressilian shook his head impatiently and turned back to Lytten. "Violet eyes. Blonde hair."

"And the slimmest little body— must have been designed for embraces. A shame how she keeps it covered up with silks and shawls." Lytten sighed. "And that delicious mouth...."

"You're lying." Tressilian sprang up from his chair, his fists clenched, his eyes blazing with a dark light.

Anyone who knew Jon Destain's reputation as a lazabout would have been surprised how quickly he interposed himself between his cousin and Lytten. With a calm that spoke of long-practice, he took hold of Tressilian's arm and said soothingly, "Easy, now, Bren. Larry didn't mean it, whatever he said. And, Larry, Bren didn't really mean to call you a liar. Trust me. I know."

Lytten prudently moved back towards the doorway. "Never thought he meant it. Friends since boyhood, and all that."

"I do mean it, damnit." Tressilian shrugged off Jon's hand and took a purposeful step forward. "Take it back."

"Take what back?" Barnabas glanced from one to the other. "All he said is she— whoever she is— has a delicious mouth."

"He said he seduced her. And he couldn't. She wouldn't."

"I never said—"

Lytten's reply was cut off by Jeremy, whose confusion had emboldened him. "Who the devil is she?"

Tressilian glared at Lytten, but neither of them spoke the lady's name. Then light dawned on Jon's face, and he said slowly, "Violet eyes? You can't mean Lady —?"

A sharp glance from Tressilian cut off his remark.

"Take it back, Lytten, or I'll thrash you within an inch of your life."

"For pity's sake, Bren, there's nothing to take back." Lytten turned his hands palm up, all innocence. "I never said I seduced her!"

Tressilian's tension subsided just a bit. "You said you won a victory over her."

"Well, I didn't mean that sort of victory." Sulkily, Lytten leaned against the doorframe and crossed his arms. "Hell, I never even tried seduction. I'm not one to tilt at windmills."

"Then what was it you won?"

Lytten flushed. "I wrote her a poem. And she thanked me for it. And later I noticed that I'd spelled a word wrong in the third line, and she didn't even rebuke me for it."

"Probably never read it," Jon said. He was still watching Tressilian, ready to intercept him again if need be.

"She did so! Said I did a deft job with my nature imagery. You know, stars and sunlight and flowers. She wouldn't have known that, had she not read it."

"You mean, all you did was write her a poem? And all she did was accept it?" Tressilian's fists unclenched, and everyone relaxed.

"I told you, she thanked me for it too."

"You call that a victory?" Jeremy had imbibed a bit of boldness with the brandy, and spoke without his accustomed shyness. "Bren could win her in truth, did he wish to."

"Don't be so sure of that," Tressilian said. He was always gentle when addressing Jeremy, but there was a hint of steel in his voice. "The lady isn't one to trifle."

"I never said she was," Lytten repeated. "Never meant you to think that."

"I suggest when you speak of her in the future, you be more cautious," Tressilian said coldly. "I won't have her reputation slandered." Then, noting Jon's quizzical expression, he added defensively, "She's a widow.

Alone in the world. Unprotected."

"Quite gallant of you, cuz, leaping to her defense like that." Jon's tone was respectful, but a light danced in his eyes. "And quite a change for you— defending a lady's honor, instead of undermining it. But then, the lady isn't your usual sort."

"She's not my sort at all." Retaking his seat, Tressilian wouldn't meet Jon's eyes. "I just don't like hearing the name of a lady— a true lady— bandied about like that."

"I didn't bandy her name about," Lytten muttered.

"That's right, Bren," Barnabas put in helpfully. "Never said her name. 'Course we all know who he meant. Violet eyes, strict morals, slender body, poetic— we all know who that is."

"I don't." Jeremy looked beseechingly at the earl. "Won't you tell me who she is? I promise I won't— I won't bandy her name about. I just have to know. Who is she?"

Since it was hard to imagine shy Jeremy bandying anyone's name about, Tressilian took pity. "She, my boy, is Lady Killeaven."

"And she," Jon added, "is not just a lady, but a sensible lady. Too sensible to trifle with the likes of Lytten. Perhaps even with our mutual cousin, who regularly makes other ladies lose their senses."

"A sensible lady," Barnabas agreed. "Too sensible. Once I had a dance with her and told her thinking of her had driven me to drink, and she gave me the name of a tonic she said would cure me."

"Sensible." With a groan, Lytten slumped against the doorframe. "One look in those wine-dark eyes and I knew there was no hope. But," he added, "I shall think of her as my muse. The inspiration for all my art."

When Jon made a rude noise, Lytten regarded him with pity. "How unfortunate for you, to be so cynical, and never to know the exaltation of an unsullied love."

As if on cue, the porter came in and removed their empty glasses and overflowing ashtrays. Tressilian took advantage of the interruption before Jon said something unfortunate and unforgivable. "You'll be more cautious with the lady's name in the future, I presume, Lytten?"

"I will," replied Lytten, chastened. "Didn't mean to cast aspersions."

Tressilian nodded and crossed to the door. The others, as always, followed his lead.

He and Jon walked together down Piccalilli, their heads clearing gradually in the cool night air. By morning an unseasonable heat would once again be wrapping the city in a sultry blanket, and Jon was planning his escape.

"Hate to have to pack my kit again," he said,"but I'm going to spend the rest of my leave at home in Devon. If you're going to Tressilian, you're welcome to ride with me, as long as you promise not to hold up any stagecoaches or take up bullfighting along the way." More graciously he added, "M'mother would love to see you."

Tressilian regretfully declined. "I've Navy business in Dover. Greybourne's invited me to stay."

He could never keep a secret from his cousin, and this time was no exception. "Navy business?" Jon stopped short in the path and regarded him suspiciously. "What have you gotten yourself up to?"

Tressilian shook his head, slightly ashamed. "You don't want to know."

Jon swore under his breath. "You know, it's been a peaceful summer so far, with you at sea and bothering only the French. I don't want to have to rescue you again from some folly— does my father know of this?"

Offended, Tressilian replied, "He would know of it, were he in port. And I won't need your rescue, you may be sure of that much."

"That's what you said the last time."

With dignity, Tressilian turned at the corner near Albany, where Jon kept rooms. "The last time was three years ago. You have nothing to worry about."

"With you, there's always something to worry about. Or perhaps—Greybourne, did you say? Isn't his lady a friend of the countess?"

Jon had a mind like a fishing net, catching up all sorts of flotsam. Tressilian wasn't about to admit he might have caught a tuna this time. "I don't know about what countess you're talking about."

"The same one Lytten was talking about. The one you just played knight errant for, defending her good name and all that. One might think that she was a special flirt of yours—"

"One better not think, does one value his skin," Tressilian said with a scowl. "I'll not have you defaming her either."

"Is it defaming her to wonder if she's caught your eye?"

"She hasn't caught my eye!"

"Then why the gallantry?"

"Because—" Tressilian shook his head angrily, and sought the right words. "Because she's a lady of virtue."

"Oh, you've tested her virtue and found it impregnable, have you?"

Jon was a cynic of the first water, and fearless in his own indolent way. Or perhaps he knew that his cousin wouldn't damage him, no matter what the provocation. Tressilian shot him a furious glance but couldn't give him the thrashing he deserved. "No, I haven't tested it, as you call it. I know virtue when I see it."

Jon choked on a laugh and had to stop and bend over to regain his breath. When he could speak again, he said, "Well, you've certainly seen a lot of ladies' virtue discarded, along with their clothing. Is that why you haven't, umm, tested her? Mayhap you're afraid to find that she isn't quite as stalwart as you imagine? I guess you'd rather be like Larry, and worship her without knowing if she's worthy of it."

There was a limit to every man's patience, and Tressilian's was more limited than most. He strode off towards his home in Berkeley Square, and refused to listen to Jon's last cynical comment, which carried in the cool night, "And if she proves to be virtuous indeed, well, all I can say is what a waste."

# CHAPTER TWO

Near Dover, Kent The sun came brilliant through the seaward windows, and Lady Greybourne entered the solarium squinting. "Oh, there you are. my dear! I could hardly see you for the glare. I wanted to warn you that we'll be having another houseguest arriving."

Kristen Marlowe, Lady Killeaven, shook her head to dispel the last wisps of her daydream. Taking up her neglected needlework, she replied, "I need no warning, do I? You've been so kind, hosting my children and me this month. I can hardly complain if you extend such hospitality to another."

"But you haven't heard who the new guest is!" Lady Greybourne fluttered like a moth through the orange trees, and her voice dropped to a

whisper. "I promised you peace, and there'll be none of that— not with
Tressilian about!"

At the inflammatory name, Kristen looked up, startled. But she wasn't
some messiahs girl, struck dumb by the prospect of a rake's arrival. "I'm
sure you'll make him very welcome."

"Well, of course I will." Lady Greybourne subsided into a rattan chair,
her hand over her heart. "He's a war hero, you know, and Greybourne and
I are very patriotic. But—" she sighed gustily, her faded blonde ringlets
bouncing about her face. "But I know none of the maids will get any work
done, for they'll all be fighting for the privilege of making his bed. And as
for the ladies of the party, they'll be fighting for the privilege of sharing his
bed. Have I shocked you?" she added hopefully.

Kristen laughed, tracing her embroidery pattern with a gentle finger.
"I have been married, recall. I am not so easily shocked — even by handsome rakes."

"He is handsome, isn't he?" Lady Greybourne plopped down on a
nearby marble bench, her yellow skirt billowing about her in the still air. A
couple decades ago, she had been one of a set of fast young matrons who
assembled admirers in their dressing rooms every morning and in their
salons every evening. So she was likely to be in sympathy with women who
threw themselves at Tressilian.

She certainly appeared to be disappointed by Kristen's composure.
"Handsome as sin, don't you think?" she prompted, and with a smile, Kristen
nodded.

"But so disruptive!" Lady Greybourne went on. "Chaos follows in his
wake, I hear. And that is not what you need in your time of mourning."

Kristen smoothed her lilac skirt. The subdued pastels recommended
for the second year of mourning suited her generally quiet mien, but lately
she had been longing for a dash of yellow- - or even scarlet. "Gerald has
been gone eighteen months now, Martha. Our stay here has been a true
respite, but I wouldn't mind a little disruption."

"But at such a time! You know how susceptible young widows are to
the blandishment of men, and you are so lovely— now don't blush, Kristen,
you know it's true— he is bound to make a push for you."

Kristen took up her embroidery again, taking fine stitches to demonstrate how serene she was, even with a notorious rake on the horizon. "I've never been susceptible to blandishment, and being widowed isn't going to change that. And Tressilian is hardly one to waste much time dangling after a reluctant lady."

"Well, he hardly needs to, does he, with all the willing ones about. You know, my dear, I worry about you."

This change of subject startled Kristen, and she realized she was in for a helpful lecture. "You needn't, Martha. I am very well."

"How can you say that? A widowed lady with two children is always vulnerable, and you have no family here to protect you. Sometimes I forget, for you sound just like one of us, no accent at all, but you are a foreigner, aren't you?"

Kristen knew there was no intent to offend here, so she answered mildly, "I was born in Denmark, yes, but I married Gerald at 16, and have considered myself English ever since. It's true I have no family here, but I do have friends, like you and Lord Greybourne. I think it unlikely I should come to any harm, and certainly not in your home."

"You never know," Lady Greybourne said darkly. "Oh, it's been wonderful having you. You've make my duties so much easier, by being so sweet and helpful. You're so good with the younger people, organizing their amusements and quieting their bickering. They behave so much better when you're about. And with the elder ones— Why, even after a month, you listen to General Wittcombe's war stories without yawning!"

"I try to be helpful."

"Well, then, you shouldn't mind if I worry about you! And now, with this new guest.... No one would blame you if you were tempted into a romantic entanglement, especially with the likes of Tressilian!"

Kristen wondered if perhaps Lady Greybourne would be a bit disappointed should Tressilian fail to tempt. At her age, Martha was forced to experience romance mostly vicariously these days, and no doubt she saw Tressilian's arrival as a golden opportunity. Obligingly, Kristen murmured, "He is charming, I hear."

"Charming!" Lady Greybourne made that sound like an insult. "More than that! Surely you've noticed his appearance."

"I'd be blind if I hadn't. In fact, I am struck by the paradox that a man can look like an angel and behave like a devil, all at the same time. But he's not my sort of man."

"Tressilian's not anyone's sort of man, dear, or he's every woman's sort, which is just as bad."

Kristen nodded. "Those passionate eyes— and oh, that brooding mouth! Only one look and any sensible woman knows to steer clear."

"Sometimes," Lady Greybourne said, her mouth turning down mutinously, "a woman doesn't want to be sensible. Oh, I agree, he wouldn't make a very comfortable husband, but for a short but memorable liaison.... Ah, if it were only thirty years ago— even twenty years ago!"

Kristen bent over her embroidery hoop to hide a smile, and replied innocently, "But twenty years ago, Tressilian would have been just a child! No doubt he was precocious, but—"

"I meant, of course, if he were the same age, and I were— oh, never mind." Lady Greybourne shook her head in exasperation. "But you, my dear, are precisely the right age."

"Lady Greybourne!" Kristen set aside her needlework and placed her hand over her heart. "I can't believe my ears! Did you just— surely not— just suggest that I share a careless fling with a notorious rakehell? What would the vicar say?"

As the vicar was due momentarily for tea, Lady Greybourne had to recall her wandering morals. "That's not what I meant at all! Only that you must guard against such an— an understandable impulse! Oh, I must go. I have a thousand details to attend to before Tressilian arrives!"

Left alone, Kristen laid her embroidery on the settee and rose to stand by the open window. The crashing of the waves against the Kent cliffs reminded her of Tressilian. He was the same sort of natural force- vibrant, powerful, and very hazardous.

Kristen had spent her life avoiding danger, so she had seldom allowed herself even to envision the dangerous Brendan Trevarrick. He symbolized everything Kristen disapproved of: recklessness, irresponsibility, instability. He never met a temptation he could resist, so the wits said, or a woman he couldn't tempt.

Well, he was tempting enough, Kristen allowed, with his merry smiles and flashing eyes. But so was the ocean spraying diamonds under the summer sun, and she wasn't fool enough to dive in.

Oh, when her friends gossiped about the charming rogue, as they did interminably, she listened and laughed. Kristen would even admit to reading the scandal rags about his latest adventure, just to keep informed about current events. Tressilian's life was so like a novel that it was easy to regard it as one regarded Mrs. Radcliffe's latest) Gothic— a story designed to titillate, tempt, and thrill the ladies. But Kristen took neither Tressilian or The Demon of Sicily seriously.

Some of the legends that had grown up around the fanciful earl had to be apocryphal— after all, he was only human, however divine his looks, and had not lived long enough to accomplish all the seductions and salvations credited to him. Kristen doubted, for example, that even Tressilian could, on a routine voyage in the South Atlantic, rout a band of renegades, destroy a white slavery ring (in the process freeing and captivating a dozen fair damsels), while recovering the crown jewels stolen from an obscure nation with a suitably grateful queen.

But Kristen had it on best authority (her chambermaid's sister, who was in service to Lady Destain, cousin of his late mother) that on a recent shore leave in Shanghai, Tressilian got involved in a friendly card game with a few Chinese merchants and ended up as bridegroom of one of their daughters. All of the earl's charm and most of his first officer's carefully hoarded cash were required to extricate Tressilian with his bachelorhood intact.

Then there were the other stories, the ones her friends whispered over their embroidery when the children had been sent to the garden to play. Kristen had to admit she enjoyed these stories even more than the sailing adventures. For the tangles Tressilian got himself into with women were always droll. Tressilian preferred a flamboyant sort of lady, the kind who would go to any lengths to entice him. So Lady Gardner posed in the nude for the portrait she delivered personally to his townhouse. The actress Althea McNeill wrote an erotic drama in five acts and sent a script to Tressilian with an invitation to audition for the role of leading man. (That tactic worked, for, as Tressilian told his friends, I have always wanted to be theatrical.)

And when the captain developed a destructive predilection for young wives of old admirals, aging salts suddenly became hot merchandise on the marriage mart.

Even the most successful of these women never succeeded for long, of course. Always the sailor, Tressilian was forever off on other voyages, other adventures, other romances. (Those who knew, however, said that his farewells were almost worth the loss of him.) Still, there was no shortage of women willing to make cakes of themselves over the handsome earl, and they had contrived to keep London— and Kristen Marlowe—titillated for years now.

Kristen settled back in her chair and took up her embroidery again. She had learned long ago that concentrating on taking fine, careful stitches blocked everything else from her mind. But after a while the hoop dropped into her lap and she sat quietly, the needle trailing silks over her skirt, her gaze contemplative on the sea. She asked herself why she always felt so contemptuous when yet another woman let herself be victimized by Tressilian.

It was a petty, cruel attitude, she knew: she should feel pity for his discarded conquests. Instead she felt triumphant, as if their blazing disgrace vindicated her own cautious approach to life. Kristen had even caught herself thinking that any woman who became involved with Tressilian deserved what she got— such an unsympathetic view from a generally sympathetic lady.

Kristen clasped her hands in her lap in an unconsciously penitent gesture. It was lowering to realize how hard-hearted she was toward women who followed the dictates of their hearts. But then, she had been bred to believe such an impulse was a dangerous and wicked one. Her childhood had been circumscribed by rules enacted by grim parents and a series of exacting governesses. Every conceivable situation had its system of rules, and each system amounted to the same guideline: Never let your heart rule your head.

So Kristen learned early to hide her emotions in a serene manner and her thoughts in decorous converse. Her cerebral mother taught her to channel her energy into the directions allowed to a lady: planning tomorrow's menus, counting up linens, perusing a book of sermons by some estimable minister. "Wayward thoughts lead to wayward actions:" little Kristen had learned her letters writing such maxims over and over in her copybook.

She knew these proverbs were inadequate substitutes for real moral values transferred to children by parental love. And long ago she had resolved to raise her children differently. She did not force them to earn her approval, but offered them her love just because they were hers. But she had never been able to advance herself that same approval. Life was still a struggle to conform to rigid standards she no longer really believed in. But those standards were all the evidence she had of her parents' love.

Deep inside, Kristen knew she could not go on living her life according to a book of proverbs. She had only to look at her late mother, so rigid, so controlled, to know that propriety did not bring happiness. And Kristen had become more relaxed and, she hoped, more tolerant since her early wedding to an Englishman. Certainly she had been happier here in England, even if the "perfect husband" her mother chose turned out not to be so perfect for a shy sixteen-year-old girl. But Gerald had been kind enough to consider her wifely duty fulfilled when she presented him with two children only fifteen months apart. Then he was content to let her live in London with the children while he hunted with his horsey friends in Wiltshire.

As long as she was enumerating her many faults, Kristen thought wryly, she ought to include that one too: Since Gerald's death, she had felt a sort of freedom that frightened and intrigued her. Widowhood had liberated her in the same way that leaving Denmark had, opening up new avenues for her to explore.

But the avenues she saw stretching ahead in her liberated future were lined with evening lectures and poetry readings at bluestocking salons. She could never see herself walking down the road with an incorrigible rake, however tempting he proved to be.

The rest of the week was more exciting than she had planned, for Nicholas and Corinna had discovered those treacherous cliffs and begged to explore them. Nick wasn't yet five, but he was old enough to know that an earl had every right to disregard his mother's commands, particularly when they were patently unjust. And little Corinna always had to do whatever her big brother did. So Kristen spent their daily walks dragging them in the opposite direction, wishing Parliament would enclose the entire seacoast in a seven-foot high iron fence.

By Saturday evening Tressilian had still not arrived, and so poor Lady Greybourne's dance began sadly flat. But Kristen was young enough to enjoy the admiration of the three youths who clustered around her begging for dances. Their pursuit was entirely innocent, for these country boys relied not at all on the provocative compliments and witty comments that were the stock in trade of London rakes.

Then her countrified flirtation was interrupted by that master of town flirtation, the Earl of Tressilian. Kristen couldn't help notice his belated entrance, heralded as it was by the sighs and flutters of every other woman in the ballroom. They apparently judged the wait worthwhile, for their faces turned up to him like sunflowers greet the sun. And his appearance, as always, was dazzling: His pantherish form kept barely civilized in the splendid uniform of a sea captain, his dark curls tousled, his smile sunny and his eyes stormy in a golden face.

He stopped to greet his hostess with a kiss and a whispered remark that left the old lady blushing like a schoolgirl. Then he surveyed the field and picked out the fairest flower to pluck Lady Killeaven in her elegant lilac gown flowing open over a slip of cream lace, strewn with tiny knots of silver roses.

With a single black glance he dismissed the three country boys, then flashed a smile at Kristen. "Shall we dance?"

Kristen was annoyed at this easy rout of her protectors— she, at least, was made of sterner stuff. "Certainly not. I'm not interested in enhancing your reputation, or in muddying my own."

Immediately his arrogant face reflected only regret. "How unfortunate then, that I have sent away your other partners," he said remorsefully. Really, she thought, battling the urge to laugh, he was indeed theatrical. "Now all the gossips will be talking about poor Lady Killeaven, the wallflower."

His absurdity made her smile; encouraged, he swept her off into the dance. He was quite a graceful dancer and a virtuoso at the delicate art of flirtation, and she was tempted just to lean back in his arms and let him perform. But after one particularly outrageous compliment, she straightened her spine and corralled her straying principles. "I am not interested in engaging in a flirtation with you."

The charming smile vanished, to be replaced with a thoughtful frown. This caused the most intriguing furrow between his winged black brows, and Kristen held back a sigh. Truly, it was criminal how beautiful he was.

"I recall you said that a moment ago," Tressilian replied, his laugh-tinged voice suggesting that she hadn't yet proved it. true. "You said much the same thing the last time we danced. I recollect, it clearly. The Faversham ball. You wore a silver satin gown with sapphires in your hair. Enchanting. May 10, 1805."

For a moment, he had her fooled, for she did in fact have a silver satin gown and a sapphire tiara. But triumphantly, she caught him out. "I remember the date well too, your grace. For my daughter was born that evening. And even for a dance with you, I think I could not have gone to a ball."

"Did I say 1805?" he said immediately. "Of course I meant 1806. After Trafalgar. And you said, very effectively, I should stop plaguing you or you would present me to the archbishop in the cardroom as a marl desiring to repent his sins."

This time she had to laugh, for it sounded just the sort a threat she would make. "There being no archbishop in attendance tonight, I suppose I will have to find a new strategy. In fact, I can think of three: No, and no, and no."

Tressilian regarded her with something infuriatingly like pity. "You are too beautiful to be so cold, my love—"

With a jolt Kristen fell back to earth. His observation chilled the almost-warm feeling his teasing had engendered, and she responded icily. "I am not now, nor will I ever be, your love. Please return me to Lady Greybourne."

Tressilian looked stricken, his lovely mouth brooding again, his eyes dark with sorrow. Then abruptly he abandoned his wounded pose, shrugging his fine shoulders as if to say it was her loss. His arrogance infuriated her, and she pointedly ignored him for the rest of the evening, unwittingly providing Dover matrons fine fodder for gossip.

Late that night, however. she encountered him again. The night was warm, so she had opened the French doors in her bedroom to let in the sea breeze. She woke in darkness, aware only of a formless fear. There it was again, the sound of running footsteps on the balcony outside her room. She grabbed a vase off her nighttable and listened fearfully to the heavy breathing and muffled curses as two men struggled outside her window. She heard a gasp of pain or surprise, then more footsteps, a fading shout., and finally only the rhythmic sound of the surf.

Kristen was not so foolish as to investigate, but naturally she could not sleep, especially when she realized that one of the combatants remained on the balcony. She was calculating the number of steps to the hallway when her nightmare came true: through the French doors stumbled a dark man.

Her heart caught in her throat, effectively blocking her scream. But when the intruder gazed with interest at her slim figure in the practical cotton nightgown before collapsing into a chair, she found her voice. "Tressilian!" she hissed. "I might have known it would be you."

Already his dynamic presence was corrupting her— she did not scream' as any woman of sense would do. Instead she lit the lamp, pulled her dressing gown on, and inquired frostily what he was doing there.

"I surprised an intruder in my rooms." She didn't bother to ask why he was getting back to his room with only an hour lacking to dawn. "Unfortunately, he had a knife," Tressilian continued, looking regretfully at the dark blood dripping down his lace cuff. "But he's surely in worse shape than I, for I saw him fall from the balcony to the rocks below." "He must have been killed!" she whispered with horror.

"I fear so. Tide's in, you know." He smiled sweetly at her, holding his hand up so the blood wouldn't drip on her rug. "I felt far too weak. to make it back to my room, so I took advantage of your open door. And I'm glad I did, for you are even lovelier by moonlight. No, don't raise the alarm," he cautioned as she started for the door. "We don't want anyone to know about this, angel; national security, don't you know."

She didn't know, and the thought of the body being borne off by the tide terrified her. But somewhere under all Tressilian's velvet charm was the steel of command. Trained always to obey authority, she held her tongue and did as he asked.

"My arm is injured," he observed bravely, examining it through the rent in his sleeve. She averted her eyes as he stripped off his uniform coat and his bloody shirt. But while she dressed the wound on his forearm she could not help but notice how muscular his golden chest was, how the dark hair curled as if inviting a lady to touch it.... Angrily she tightened the bandage and he paled, but gallantly he only thanked her for her aid, calling her angel again.

Too weak, or so he said, to make it back to his own room, Tressilian proposed to spend what remained of the night in her armchair. Kristen agonized over her dilemma. Surely such a strapping young man would not be brought low by a minor fleshwound. But the prospect of his being discovered leaving her room just before dawn terrified her. He cared not that he risked her good name, and, ever irrepressible, suggested that if the armchair didn't suit her, perhaps he should join her in bed. Convinced she would be unable to sleep with such a man in the immediate vicinity, Kristen threw caution to the winds and pushed him out the door into the corridor, fortunately empty of early- rising maidservants and sleepless matrons.

All through breakfast she worried that someone would mention seeing the earl near her room. But her grudging act of charity had not irreparably damaged her reputation. Tressilian sat across from her, heroically pale under his tan and holding his left arm a little stiffly against his blue riding coat. But except for flashing an exceptionally engaging smile in her direction, he gave no hint of what transpired during the night.  When a servant rushed in with the news that a body had been left behind on the rocks when the tide went out, Kristen opened her mouth to explain about the intruder. But Tressilian quelled her with a single glance. She kept her silence, furious with him but somehow unable to go against his wishes. She'd never before witnessed a crime, but she always thought she would be the sort of dutiful citizen who would report such happenings to the proper authorities and let them do their jobs. But now, with Tressilian shaking his dark head slightly, drawing her into a conspiracy, she could not speak, even when the magistrate came and asked if anyone had heard anything untoward the previous night.

Kristen was bewildered by her own actions. She owed the man exactly nothing, she told herself fiercely; bandaging his arm and letting him rest for a moment in her room did not make them intimates. She had no reason to protect him from the consequences of his nefarious activities. But when she demanded an explanation, Tressilian was surprisingly agreeable. "Certainly," he replied. "Let's go for a ride."

Once again, Kristen felt herself drawn into an action she knew to be improper. Her usual policy to avoid riding alone with a man was a sensible one which had served her well in the past. But Tressilian's blithe disregard for such conventions was contagious, and curiosity proved stronger than propriety in the end. As the sun rose high in an azure sky, she found herself on her own chestnut mare, following Tressilian's restless black stallion down a narrow path to a beach near the fatal rocks.

Tressilian dismounted and spent a few moments prowling, looking for footprints or messages left in bottles or some other romantic clue. Kristen waited near her mare, trying not to look at the balcony so high above or to imagine the intruder's fate. Finally the earl drew her to a picturesque boulder and bade her sit. "You have questions, my love?"

"I told you, I am not your love," she snapped, all out of patience with him. "And yes, I have questions." Sudden fear rose in her— she was alone on a remote beach with a dangerous, dark man who might have committed murder. "You killed him, didn't you?"

"Never got the chance. No, as I told you, he fell while trying to climb down the balcony wall." He looked disappointed for a moment, then rallied, raising her slim hand to his lips. "It's just as well. If I hadn't been stabbed, I might never have seen you again, my lo— I mean, my darling." Kristen gave an exasperated sigh and yanked her hand from his, hiding it behind her back. "Will you stop that? How do you expect me to think if you are forever kissing my hands and calling me names?"

Tressilian fell back as if shot, his hand on his heart. He tumbled right off the boulder onto the sand and lay there with his eyes closed, drawing ragged breaths. "You have destroyed me, I think," he groaned. "Torn out my heart and thrown it to the sharks— "

As serious as the situation was, Kristen found herself dissolving into laughter. It wasn't fair that he had to be silly too, on top of being so dashing. She prodded his side with her leather boot. "You are getting sand in your hair," she reproved. "I vow, you are no better than my little boy— now sit up and tell me who that man was."

He complied, twisting to brush the sand off the back of his. coat, shaking his head briskly until his curls were all black again and appealingly disordered. "A French spy."

"A— a spy?" Into her well-ordered life burst chaos— but then Tressilian must always bring that along with him. "But why was he here?"

Tressilian clasped his arms around his knees and tilted his head to study her. His gaze lingered appreciatively on her large violet eyes, then traveled to rest on her slim figure in the slate blue riding habit. He decided to trust her, as far as she could tell, on the basis of the fineness of her breasts, for that was the aspect of her character he examined most carefully. "He was looking for some naval maps he thought I would have in my room."

He was as offhanded as if such things happened daily, and perhaps in his life they did. "There's a whole network of spies here near Dover, and Greybourne appears to be a common liaison point,. So I wangled an invitation and set myself up for the capture. Too bad he went and died before I could find out who tipped him off to my arrival. You understand now, don't you, why we must be discreet? Imagine that frosty magistrate trying to deal with this information."

Tressilian rose and held out a sandy hand to help her to her feet. Still dubious, she asked, "Do the proper authorities know, even if the magistrate doesn't?"

"Don't you trust me, angel?" When she assured him she did not in the slightest, he replied with injured dignity that he was here at the request of the Admiralty, of course, and that he would never, ever do anything unauthorized by the proper authorities.

She could hardly call on the First Sea Lord to inquire if Tressilian was indeed acting under orders. So she worried for weeks that a murderer masked as a earl was free in the land. But then she thought of his boyish grin as he lay there in the sand, pretending she had struck him down, and felt a reluctant trust stir within her. She had never met any murderers, but she felt sure that they were not in the least bit playful.

Still, she was more than a little relieved a week after she returned to Wiltshire to open the Gazette and read of a spy ring uncovered in Dover. The church sexton was arrested as the contact, and Tressilian was lauded again for his valor and ingenuity. Kristen experienced a new feeling of guilt for having doubted him, and a certain elation at playing a role, however minor, in this exciting episode. She scolded herself for her silliness; here she was, a widow with two children, her heart, fluttering like a girl's as she imagined herself the plucky heroine of an adventure novel.

# CHAPTER THREE

Her great adventure over, Kristen retreated to her routine at Killeaven for the rest of the summer. She met with her son's estate manager daily, taught her daughter to count, made morning calls with the vicar's wife, attended dinners and dances at neighboring Wiltshire estates. It was at one such affair, at the rambling Restoration manse of Sir Thomas Culbertson, that Kristen's life was once again disrupted by the Earl of Tressilian.

At first she found some vindication of her initial impression of him as the sort of hero who dominated silly novels aimed at silly pre-debutantes. For the arriving Tressilian, elegant this night in satin as black as his eyes, was immediately surrounded by a horde of seventeen-year-old girls. Kristen hung back, watching him as he laughed and indiscriminately kissed the hands held out to him, tweaking curls and teasing girls and murmuring something memorable to each and every one of them. And suddenly she couldn't dismiss him so lightly.

He takes such joy in life, Kristen thought with an inexplicable envy. And gives such joy too. Even shy Ellie Cahern, bespectacled and bespotted, pressing close to the wall a few feet from him, seemed to bask in his radiance. Then Tressilian glanced over, his eyes full of mirth, and saw Ellie there, pushing her spectacles back up on her nose with her thumb. He broke away from the other girls and held out his hand to the wallflower. When she, unbelieving, edged over, he brought her hand to his lips, gazing meaningfully down into her eyes. Suddenly he pulled off her spectacles. Kristen, faintly alarmed, moved closer, worried that he might embarrass the girl, already so painfully inhibited.

But Tressilian knew women, even very young women, and knew exactly what to say to each. Even from a couple yards away, Kristen could hear his thrillingly hoarse whisper. "You have lovely eyes. Like a fawn's, all startled and clear." He remained still for a moment, as if stunned, then returned the spectacles to their proper place, gently fitting the hooks over her ears. "I shouldn't have done that. Only a lover should know how passion softens your eyes in the candlelight." His hand touched Ellie's cheek lightly, caressingly. "I am sorry. I was carried away. Forgive me." Then he stepped back away from the dazed girl, and with one last, regretful glance, he took himself off to greet his hostess.

It was decidedly improper, what Tressilian had done and especially what he had said. But Kristen could not find it in her heart to censure him, for Ellie was even now surrounded by the other girls, the object of envy for perhaps the first time in her life. And a couple boys straggled over, regarding her with new eyes, imagining she must be something rather special to have caught the attention of the knowing Tressilian. The squire's son even made so bold as to push past the prettier girls and solicit Ellie's hand for the cotillion being struck up. And suddenly Ellie's eyes were indeed lovely, even through her spectacles, and her face was lit by an inner glow as she was led out onto the dance floor.

So much joy.... Tressilian finally detached himself from Lady Culbertson and the eight matrons who had found some compelling reason to join her. And then the earl, as Kristen somehow knew he would, crossed the dance floor towards her. He stopped only once, to gaze longingly at the giddy Ellie. But soon he was taking Kristen's hands, marveling gallantly at her fair aspect in the gown of primrose gauze over a cream slip of silk. She could not even bring herself to protest when he pushed down her lace glove to drop a kiss on her wrist. For a moment, she was as dazzled as poor Ellie, and agreed to let him escort her into the buffet supper.

Only when she found herself alone with him on a bench behind a bank of ferns, a plate of tiny tarts on her lap, her gaze lost in his fathomless eyes, did she wake. She was acting as starstruck as Ellie, and didn't even have inexperience as an excuse.

But she couldn't stand up and spill her plate on the rug, or run away and make a scene. So she wrenched her eyes away from his, took a deep breath, and went on the attack. "Must you charm every woman you meet?"

Laughter replaced the desire in his eyes— how mercurial were his moods, she thought irrelevantly, and all reflected in those brilliant black eyes. "I do my little best."

"Well, your little best is rather good," Kristen allowed grudgingly, remembering Ellie. But then he reached over to tug her silver shawl over her bare shoulder, deliberately trailing his fingertips along her upper arm, and she moved decisively three inches down the bench. "Stop that."

With a resigned sigh, Tressilian crossed his arms over his broad chest and leaned back. "You are so cruel," he remarked mournfully. "And so beautiful. It isn't fair."

That echo of her own lament about his unjust attractions made Kristen smile, but before he could take any encouragement she asked reprovingly, "Why must you charm every woman you meet?"

"I don't know." His brow furrowed again in that thoughtful frown. "I never thought of it before. I expect it's because I love women." "All women?" she echoed unbelievingly.

"Most of 'em. I never get tired of seeing them, or talking with them, or—" He broke off, grinning, then added, "Women are so much more variable than men, don't you think?"

"I haven't your breadth of experience," she replied dampingly, although she rather agreed with him that the average man was so— so average. Not this one, of course, with his perfect straight nose and merry recklessness. "But why are you so enamoured of women in general?"

Tressilian chose to look pensive now, resting his square chin on his square fist. "I imagine it's because I never had a mother." "Everyone has a mother," she said.

"Mine died when I was born. My father had been lost at sea two months earlier. So I didn't really have parents to speak of."

Though he spoke casually, Kristen was struck with unwilling sympathy. Her parents weren't especially demonstrative, but they were at least there for her childhood. "Were you all alone then?"

"Oh, no," he said with a laugh, "I had a nurse, of course. And in the castle, the housekeeper and the maids watched over me. And Lady Destain, my mother's cousin, lived nearby. I made myself free with her home and affection, I assure you!"

Kristen had to look down at her plate to hide her sudden rush of pity. For it was so sad, that he didn't even realize how lonely he must have been. She had to concentrate to hear his cheerful observation, "I expect that's why I love women so much— and so indiscriminately, you would say! Because so many women have been so kind to me."

And, she finished silently, knowing he could never let himself realize this, no one woman ever loved you all alone.

A devoted mother herself, she knew better than he what he had missed— that exclusive, enriching, enfolding love between a mother and her babe. Perhaps that was why he needed to see love in the eyes of every woman he met, because he never got to see it in his mother's.

Bemused by this revelation, she murmured an absent affirmative when he asked her a question. Awakened by his shocked but delighted smile, she stammered, "What— what did I agree to?"

"That you'll meet me at the north side of the house in half an hour to drive out to the abbey ruins. Oh, no, angel, don't draw back now. You promised!"

Seeing in his comic dismay that small orphaned boy's longing, she found herself repeating her assent. As he left her to take his leave of their hostess, she wondered if, after all, she had been foolish enough to let him entice her into a meaningless but memorable affair— and out of pity, of all absurd motives.

At least Tressilian was experienced enough at this to make sure no one suspected their wicked scheme. When Kristen pleaded a headache and took her leave, Lady Culbertson lamented, "Oh, I knew no one would stay once Tressilian left!" but did not otherwise connect the two early departures. So no one noticed as Kristen skirted the waiting carriages and slipped around the corner of the house. Tressilian met her, his eyes alight with moonlight and delight, his hand warm over hers.

"Come, my phaeton's over here," he whispered, tugging her over to a gravel lane used for kitchen deliveries. Hidden in the shadow of an old oak tree, the racing vehicle was daringly sleek and drawn by highstepping chestnuts. With his hands on her slender waist, Tressilian lifted Kristen effortlessly into her seat, then leaped up beside her and took up the reins.

Kristen had not felt such guilty pleasure since she was twelve and stole away from her governess in the middle of Copenhagen's pleasure gardens. "But I don't do things like this!" she cried, as the light summer breeze caressed her cheek and teased a lock of hair from its elegant twist.

"I know," Tressilian said soothingly as they entered the valley where the Benedictine monks had prayed even before the Norman conquest. "I'm a bad influence on you, aren't I? But the ruins by moonlight— isn't it worth breaking the rules just this once?"

She almost agreed, for the familiar abbey ruins were suffused with an eerie glow. She could almost hear the mumble of the monks at their devotions, see them walking heads bowed in the shadows of the crumbling walls.

"I once stayed at an abbey in Spain where the monks still practice the rule of Benedict: poverty and hard manual labor and long silences." As the horses dropped their heads to graze, Tressilian's restless hands were still for a change, holding the reins lightly. "It was so calming. Restful. But I lasted only a week. Couldn't keep quiet. Talkative, I am, you might have noticed." He gave her a crooked grin, and she shook her head, trying to imagine Tressilian in a monastery.

"I would think the chastity rule would have tripped you up." Did I say that? she wondered. Could this really be Kristen Marlowe here tonight?

He tugged a lock of her pale-gold hair from its pin and let it curl around his finger. "You underestimate me, angel. I'm a sailor. I'm used to long stretches of celibacy." His abstraction vanished into laughter. "So I make merry while I can on dry land."

His nearness, his lean figure in the satin evening coat, his muscular leg almost touching hers— these were less threatening somehow, suffused as the scene was in milky moonlight. Kristen felt caught in a dream, drifting volitionlessly through the night. Tressilian seemed captured by the same reverie, gazing out at the tumbles of abbey stone, stroking that stray lock of her hair absently, his hand resting gently on her shoulder.

"Tell me about your travels," she said softly, tilting her head to the side to see his face.

So, while the horses grazed on the old abbey grass, he spun magical tales of velvet African nights and silken Indian dawns, of Turkish sultans and Russian tsars, of the Parthenon and the pyramids and Polynesia. His lazy, cool voice evoked a world of darkness and light, of mystery and beauty, that she could hardly believe in. He was scarcely older than she, but had seen so much more, lived so much more. The freedom he described was like a mirage to Kristen, shimmering and inaccessible, and she listened spellbound.

But then he took her in his arms and kissed her. For a moment the kiss was part of the dream, surreal and sweet. Then she awoke from her reverie and fought free of him. All his lovely vistas were just another seduction tool for a man who already had a plethora of them.

"No! I don't want that!"

He caught both her wrists in one hand, but made no move to embrace her again. "You really don't, do you?"

"No," she admitted, ceasing her struggles. "I'm sorry," she added foolishly.

"Don't be. I'm sure you know better than I what is right."

She shivered a bit, though the night was warm. His manner was suddenly more formal, which ordinarily would have pleased her. Instead she felt absurdly guilty, as if she had hurt him by rejecting his advances. And guilt is absurd, she told herself furiously. The earl might not experience rejection very often, but. he should be gentleman enough to accept it gracefully. Of course, he did accept it gracefully, for he did everything gracefully. "So you don't want this," he said at length. He touched her cheek in an almost insolent manner: a sailor's caress, roughened by rope and saltwater, it was indefinably tender. "What do you want then? You must want something, or you would have sent me packing by now."

The sudden question was one Kristen could not answer, even for herself. So, she only returned, as if in a child's game, "What do you want?"

He tilted his head to the side to study her. For an Instant she saw something in his eyes that fascinated and frightened her— a flash of desire so naked, so intense, that she was left breathless. "Oh, I think you know what I want."

No, I don't, she thought, not really. Afraid of what. he might see in her eyes, she dropped her gaze to their clasped hands. After a moment, he went on, "But that looks to be impossible. I don't, as a rule, pursue reluctant ladies. So as an alternative— I don't know. I want you in my life, I think."

His casual declaration was enough to disarm her, and she looked up into the darkness of his eyes. "You do? Why?"

"I don't know," he confessed. "You intrigue me, I suppose. You are so serene— I'm restless, you see, always so restless, but you make me feel calmer. As if, for a time, I can be peaceful. And you aren't—" his perfect nose wrinkled in a childish portrayal of distaste "—you aren't so dazzled by me as ladies are. Oh, I know, they are only doing what I want, but it's refreshing. sometimes, to find victory difficult, even impossible. Do you understand at all?"

Kristen sensed that he wasn't used to examining his motives; he was a man of action, not of contemplation. But she understood. Even without his blazing good looks, he would have been indulged all his life because of his great charm, not to mention his title and wealth. "You know that I am not in the pull of some superficial attraction?"

Even as she spoke the words, she regretted them, for Tressilian's attraction was far from superficial. But Tressilian seized upon this as if it solved a lifelong dilemma. "Just so! When I think of it, I wonder if any of them really know me, even my friends— Well, Jon does," he said fairly. "He's my cousin, Lady Destain's son. And we've always been best friends. He's never been taken in. He knows the worst of me, and the best of me, and isn't much impressed. So he never worries that he. will offend me by being honest, or drive me away if he isn't perfect. And I know he won't leave no matter what I do."

His candor disconcerted Kristen, and she blurted out, "I'd like that too. I mean—" She bit her lip, not even really sure what she meant. "I would like to be able to be myself. But I must needs be— be so responsible." "And proper," he observed with an improper grin.

"Well, yes. But sometimes I would like to have more freedom— oh, as you do. To meet not-so-proper people. To see strange lands. I've never been anywhere, you know, except Denmark and Britain. But you tell me about your voyages and it's almost as if I am living them myself—"

Usually she was articulate, choosing her words well and carefully. But now she stumbled, unable to explain precisely that Tressilian's dynamic presence had already opened up her circumscribed life. And what difference would it make, could she find the words? She would not, could not, become his temporary light-of-love, and that was the only role that men had open in their lives for women they didn't marry. So in her regret she became brisk. "That doesn't mean I approve of your life, of course."

That experimental intimacy was gone, and Tressilian was outrageous again. "But what is there to disapprove?"

"I disapprove that you insist on throwing your life away, that you drink so much and gamble and create scandals with married women." She had talked herself into righteousness, and finally pulled her hands. loose from his grasp. "Be fair, Kristen."

"I'm willing to be fair, but I haven't given you leave to use my Christian name," she said severely, but that only made him laugh.

"Be fair, whoever you are. I'm only three-and-twenty, after all. I've got years yet to throw away before I needs must get serious. Now you— you have children, and I expect they sober one up quickly."

"Well, I've never been irresponsible, even when I was a child myself," Kristen pointed out, thinking that sounded rather sad. "But since my children arrived, I have had to be very dependable——" Oh, dear, she thought despairingly, and that sounds so very dull.

But Tressilian surprised her again. "Tell me about your children. I collect you have a boy and a girl. Are they close in age? Do they get on well, or do they fight?"

Cannily he had discovered Kristen's weakness. She could talk for hours about the children she found truly exceptional, although she was uneasily aware that most parents felt the same about their own quite unexceptional progeny. Finally she broke off, sure that he was bored and only being gallant by asking a dozen questions about Corinna's vocabulary and Nick's dexterity.

"You should have children of your own," she finished, from long habit adding a moral axiom to her conversation. "They would give your life balance."

"Ah, but I'd have to marry, angel, and that would never do. I like women too much to inflict myself on one for life."

Kristen agreed silently that the prospective Countess of Tressilian would have a bad time of it, with her husband sailing off heaven knew where half the year and wreaking havoc in London the other half. "But surely you'll want an heir."

"Well, I have an heir, my cousin. Not Jon, my other cousin Jeremy. He already takes care of my estates, you see, so he'll do well enough by the title— better than I have, surely."

"You don't care for your own estates?" she repeated, aghast. Her late husband had had his faults, but he had been ever diligent in supervising his bailiff and land agents. Since she had assumed these responsibilities for her four-year-old earl, she had come to appreciate how much work went into being a good landowner.

But Tressilian preferred blissful ignorance. "When would I find time for that? Besides, Jeremy is better at it. He's practical, like you. He likes figuring sums, and buying seeds, and- - and— well, whatever it is he does."

Kristen did not care for his implication that what was too tedious for the high-spirited earl was just right for "practical" people like Jeremy and herself. "You're not taking any responsibility for your own life," she scolded.

"I daresay you're right," he replied, assembling a more sober expression. "And you are determined to show me the error of my ways."

"Don't you think you need reforming?"

"Not yet." Suddenly he was restless again, his elegant, eloquent hands stroking the reins, his fine shoulders rippling in a shrug. "Not yet. I'm too young yet. Later, perhaps, I'll settle down— when I'm thirty, I think." He said "thirty" as if it were some impossibly distant year, too lost in the mists of time to matter.

Then, as she laughed at. his childishness, he grinned and took her hands and made her the most shocking proposition either of them had ever heard. "We shall be friends, shall we? You may try and reform me, and I shall try to corrupt you, and we'll be good for each other."

Never would she forget his lazy voice, the teasing light in his eyes, and her own paradoxical seriousness, as if she were acceding to something that would change her life. And never would she understand why she agreed, except that he had invaded her life as ruthlessly as he boarded enemy ships, tantalizing her with the vision of a life lived without limits. Perhaps, through friendship— safe, circumscribed friendship— with Tressilian, she could experience a little of that freedom without any of the risk.

But even as her heart raced at the prospect, Kristen instinctively reacted against her own desire and made excuses for her precipitous acceptance of his outrageous proposition.

After all, Tressilian's life begged for reformation, and Kristen had a Christian duty to help. As missionaries who made forays into the jungles of Africa had to adjust to their quarries' diverse habits, Kristen could not flinch from her chosen heathen's unchristian behavior. For if he were a saint, he would have no need of her reformation efforts.

Still, missionaries to Africa did not let themselves. willingly become dinner for their cannibal parishioners, and Kristen similarly exercised self-defense. As they drove back through the sultry night, she remonstrated, "Now if we are to be friends, we needs must be friends. No scandalous propositions."

"Wouldn't dream of it!" he vowed, choirboy innocent. "No— no kisses." "Not even your hand?"

Kristen sighed with exasperation and an inchoate longing. "Tressilian, your sort of handkissing should be outlawed. It is hazardous to the moral quality of the kingdom." "If you say so." One shoulder rippled in a sullen shrug.

"And you mustn't call me your love." She considered his careless habit of addressing every woman he met with endearments, and decided banning them entirely might prove too difficult. So she allowed, "You may call me 'angel', however."

He kept his promise. Not once on the trip home did he make a threatening move. But he did startle her when, just as he was helping her down from the curricle, he said fiercely, "I knew you would stay true."

It was such a strange comment, and so intensely uttered, that she puzzled over it much of the night. Then finally, as the darkness was lifting, she gave it up. She did not know enough about men to understand a man like Tressilian.

So thoroughly had she convinced herself that her motives for this friendship were mostly altruistic that even the cold light of dawn did not change her mind. In fact, her determination was reinforced when she learned that Tressilian's inclination was not to boil his missionary in oil, as other savages were reported to do. Instead her morning was graced with yet another act of the gallantry that seemed second nature to the dashing earl.

Her abigail Millson woke her, a reluctant smile on her dour face. "I don't know which of your young men did it, but it ran him a packet, I'll be bound." Maid after maid brought in armfuls of purple lilacs and arranged them in vases around Kristen's blue and white bedroom. The title on the engraved card did not surprise her, for who but Tressilian could procure lilacs in August? "To match your eyes, angel," read the bold black scrawl.

He did, Kristen had to admit, have some redeeming qualities.

That extravagant gesture was the last communication Kristen had from Tressilian for months. Typically thoughtless, he had neglected to tell her that his fleet was leaving that next week for the Indian Ocean. She was left with memories of their odd, moonlight-inspired pact, and the lowering suspicion that when he returned, he would remember none of it.

The winter was colder than usual, reminding her of all the lonely winters she had spent in Denmark, staring out at the bleak landscape, longing for a friend to share the desolate hours. On winter days, she could not easily dismiss her loneliness, for the cold stole right into her heart.

Finally it was March, and she saw the first of the spring flowers poking up through the mud. This was the season of rebirth, when everything was bright and anything was possible. So she packed up the children and journeyed to London for her first social season since Gerald's death.

She was determined to enjoy the pleasures the city offered. At two-and-twenty, she was too young to sink into the melancholy of widowhood. But despite her optimism, the entertainments fell sadly flat... until she walked into her drawing room and saw Tressilian again.

# CHAPTER FOUR

Their golden heads touching, Nick and Corey pressed close to their fascinating new acquaintance, who sat casually on the desk, his booted feet swinging. Entirely at ease with his latest devotees, Tressilian drew a detailed map on her best notepaper. "This is Calcutta," he explained, flicking Corinna's snub nose and leaving a smudge of ink behind. "The men there sleep on beds of nails and eat only three grains of rice a day."

Nick's blue eyes were round with an absolute trust neither his governess or his mother had ever inspired. Corinna let the captain curl her fingers around the quill, and with a little help, she drew the path of the prevailing winds through the Indian Ocean. "A very detailed chart, lieutenant," Tressilian said approvingly, and as she raised her chin proudly, Corinna noticed her mother in the doorway.

Slipping from Tressilian's side, Corey proudly displayed a gold and ebony tiger with rubies for eyes and a wicked smile. "Look, Mama, what Captain Bren brought me."

Kristen's practical mind set to estimating just how much that had run the earl, but Nick was interrupting to show off his present— a magnificent

scale-model sailing ship, complete with canvas sails and tiny whittled seamen clinging to the rigging. "It's Captain Bren's Defiant, and it's seaworthy,
he says!"

"Lovely," Kristen agreed. "But you shouldn't have, your lordship."

Tressilian ignored this, as he did most criticism, and kissed her hand
in greeting. How soon he had forgotten his brave resolutions, she thought
as she took back her tingling hand. But then he gave her a merry smile and
she decided to forgive him just this once. Then Nick and Corey scampered
off to launch the ship in the kitchen tub, and Kristen, suddenly shy, was
alone with the earl.

"Really, Tressilian," she scolded, taking refuge in correctness, "you
needn't bring the children such presents."

"Why not?" he replied easily. He lounged back against the desk as if
he owned it, and the rest of the house too. Even in his casual riding dress he
appeared simultaneously elegant and heedless. "It makes them happy. Me
too. Delightful rascals, don't you think? That Nick will make a good midshipman in half-a-dozen years, if you'd like me to take him up."

Kristen began to protest this alarming prediction, for she'd planned
on Nick spending his boyhood at school, not battling French ships. But
Tressilian was holding out another gift. "I brought you something also, and
for God's sake don't refuse."

Kristen found the badly wrapped box and the red ribbon tied in an
intricate sailor's knot rather poignant. But the delicate bowl inside left her
speechless.

"It's from the Ming dynasty. Reminded me of you— serene and eternal."

She touched the depth of the bowl with a reverent finger, tracing the
blue and white pattern. In her confusion, she became indiscreet and addressed him by his Christian name. "Brendan, this must have cost you a
fortune."

"Devil a bit," he answered cheerfully, working the discarded ribbon
into a series of hitch-knots. "Won it in a card game. I only had to stake my
second lieutenant." At her shocked silence, he looked up from his work.
"I'm only joking, angel. Do you think me capable of anything?"

"Anything." Kristen held the featherlight bowl up to the light to admire its translucence. Her heart twisted as she said what she knew she had to say. "Thank you, but I can't accept this."

Tressilian shrugged, dropped the ribbon on the desk, and held out his hand for the bowl. "Very well then. I'll give it to Ariadne." Ariadne, she already knew from a perusal of the scandal rags, was an opera dancer who occasionally forsook her protector for the earl. "She can always use another ashtray."

"You wouldn't!" Kristen retreated to the settee, where she sat and held the bowl protectively in both hands. "If you don't want it—"

Kristen struggled with her sense of decorum. Ladies did not accept expensive presents from gentlemen, at least if they were really ladies. Still, she couldn't let the little bowl come to such a dire fate. She recalled his lighthearted promise to corrupt her and knew the process was well underway, for this was sure to be only the first in a long series of compromises she would make at his urging. "You mustn't give me anything else." Then she relented. "I do thank you, Tressilian, it's lovely."

"So are you," he returned gallantly, once again forgetting his promise to forgo flirting with her. "We'll have a deal of fun this season, angel. The Defiant is in Chatham for recoppering, so I'm on leave for at least three months. This afternoon, I'll take the children to the sail their ship in the pond at Green Park— come now, they don't really need lessons, they're far too young yet. I'll show them how to navigate the Horn, if you insist on instruction. That's much more practical in the long run than nursery rhymes."

He didn't give her time to respond, only gathering up his riding gloves and heading for the door. He called back over his shoulder, "Tell the children I'll be back at two. And why don't we go to Vauxhall tonight? There's to be a grand fireworks display. The little rascals will love it."

She could only escape the prospect of losing Nicholas in the dark paths of Vauxhall by agreeing to come herself, with, she warned him, a most proper chaperone.

"Why?" He turned at the door, baffled. "Oh, your good name. Well, chaperone or no, it will be in shreds if you are seen with me. Perhaps you should wear a mask," he added helpfully. "Then everyone will wonder who the mysterious lady with Tressilian is."

On that cheerful recommendation, he left. To the dismay of her butler, Kristen leaned against the wall and moaned softly. What had she gotten herself into with this man? But even as she contemplated actually wearing a mask to Vauxhall, as married women did when there for a tryst, she felt a thrill of excitement. He was outrageous, but such fun, catching her up willy-nilly in his escapades. Already the season seemed fraught with possibility, even, she thought with a frisson of guilty pleasure, danger.

Gerald's Great-aunt Helen proved to be a less than exemplary chaperone. After a minute or so of Tressilian's boyish smiles, she declared him "the sweetest lad I've ever seen" and waved them away from the supper box he had hired for the evening. "Go, go. You children don't want an old lady dogging your steps. I'll have no worry for your safety, now that young Tressilian is with you."

Brendan greeted this with an innocent smile, as if he had never before given any chaperone cause to worry. And Aunt Helen's trust was indeed justified, for Tressilian was a complete gentleman as he led Kristen to all the Vauxhall sights. His manner was almost brotherly— he teased her gently and told her incredible stories she suspected were mostly true.

But never did he behave in a manner remotely suggestive, though in the Labyrinth, Kristen was wary. She found it difficult to believe that a sailor could get himself so lost, but Tressilian wandered frowning through the hedges, muttering, "Loo'ard. No, windward," until she got exasperated and led them out herself.

When taxed with this lapse, he pointed to the overcast sky. "No stars. I need stars to navigate, or the sun, or charts." But otherwise, he acquitted himself well, for he never took advantage of their privacy to steal a kiss.

This was only the first awkward moment occasioned by their friendship during that season. Tressilian was used to inspiring vicious gossip, but for Kristen it was a new and unpleasant experience. Since the ton had never been presented with the contradiction of two attractive members of opposite sexes involved in a purely platonic relationship, it chose to believe otherwise-and Kristen found herself the subject of scandal-mongering.

The notion that the goddess-like Lady Killeaven was merely human after all displeased many people. Young ladies struggling to maintain moral values in a corrupt society began to question whether virtue, in fact, was its own reward. Men who had received one of the countess's courteous letdowns could not help but resent Tressilian's apparently easy conquest. And the legions of Tressilian's discarded lovers slanted their eyes in Kristen's direction and wondered if she would last any longer than they.

In the end, the recognition that these two actually were merely friends caused more comment than a flaming affair might have, hotly debated in salons all over London. Was it possible to be in close contact with Tressilian and resist the urge to fall in love? the ladies asked, and men were similarly dubious about the odds of remaining only friends with the lovely Lady K.

But over the years, the talk died down, and Kristen was not forced to surrender her reputation for Brendan's friendship. Eventually, society viewed them as just another London oddity, like Baroness Symington and her trained monkeys, accepted despite their bizarre relationship.

In fact, Kristen enjoyed the aura of eccentricity that friendship gave her. She had always been so conventional, and now people thought her almost radical, a new women of the new century, unafraid of opposition and worthy of respect. Paradoxically, her moral respectability was only enhanced by her connection with the a-moral earl. For if she could resist Tressilian, it was said, she would hardly succumb to any other man's blandishments.

Once the risk to her heretofore spotless reputation was removed, Kristen came to cherish the unique experience of having a male friend, especially one as decidedly male as Tressilian. She had not been fortunate enough to have a brother's scorn as she grew up, so she knew she tended to take life and herself a bit too seriously. But Tressilian could always show her the absurdity in the thousand little worries she was tormented with throughout a day.

He was especially helpful when she wondered if she was rearing her children properly, for Tressilian believed that the two little Marlowes were the finest example of children in the kingdom. "What difference does it make if Nick doesn't eat his porridge? Does he look as if he's starving? Boys hate porridge. When he starts to like it, then worry. And Corey is a credit to you— so bright and brave. Of course she got stuck in that tree, because she had the courage to climb so high. What an heartbreaker she will be!"

Still half-child himself, Tressilian even teased the hidden child out of Kristen. He was just such fun, always seeking the unusual experience and sharing it generously. Under his aegis, Kristen and her children learned all about his vision of the future, visiting the Gas Company, the little dock where experimental steamboats were being constructed, even a few balloon ascensions.

Tressilian's interests were myriad and mercurial, and Kristen's own imagination was fired by exposure. She even defied the advice of her business manager and invested in a few shares of the Gas Company, which promised to light London with clean, radiant coal-gas within the next decade.

Tressilian was also an adventurous escort through the social byways of Mayfair, for he knew all the most advanced hostesses (some, Kristen suspected, rather too well). So she found herself attending the most modern of entertainments, such as plays in which ladies and gentlemen played the leading roles— Tressilian, predictably, made a stirring Henry V and a heartbreaking Romeo. Once Kristen was even persuaded to take over a minor role herself, and when she stopped quaking with stage fright, she enjoyed herself, though not enough to repeat the experience.

Often, Tressilian himself was the most popular attraction at a social occasion, for he only had to enter the room to cause a ripple of excitement— he had presence, and charisma, and a dozen other irresistible qualities. And if Kristen basked a bit in his reflected glow, well, that was just another benefit of their friendship.

But the course of their connection did not always run smooth, for Kristen was never blind to his many faults. She deplored his need for danger and his constant challenges to fate. His impulsiveness could be entertaining, and his restless energy truly a natural wonder, but both were wearing on one with more sedate tendencies.

And of course, Kristen could never entirely abandon her plan to redeem the irredeemable earl. She told him in no uncertain terms, though with little effect, that his romantic inconstancy was offensive, and that his aversion to responsibility appalling. But even as he produced a chastened look and promised to try not to seduce any more admirals' wives or to leave all his duties to his poor overworked cousin Jeremy, Kristen knew she was failing. He will never change, she thought with some despair, for he hasn't any reason. Everyone loves him anyway, as incorrigible as he is.

Sometimes, often, he took shameless advantage of Kristen's own affection for him. The worst occasion occurred one March, when he appeared at her door with a doe-eyed damsel and a disarming smile and asked Kristen to marry the girl off.

"I saved this Turk's life, you see, and he gave me his daughter as a reward. Can't blame him," he added thoughtfully, "for he has fifty-three others, and they must be a trial to keep clothed. Not that they wear much."

Her mind reeling at the vision of fifty-three scantily clad daughters, Kristen could not immediately reply. Then she drew Tressilian aside and, voice shaking, declared, "If you think I'm going to take in one of your castoffs, Brendan Trevarrick—"

"No such thing! I never touched her!" he exclaimed, hand on heart. "I don't believe in slavery, you know that. And she's not my type, really, always swearing that she's my vassal for life." He regarded the Turkish girl with distaste, for at the sound of his voice she had knelt and placed her forehead on Kristen's Axminster carpet. "I like women with a bit more spirit."

Though she railed at Tressilian for his effrontery, Kristen did as he asked, finding Farah a gouty old baronet who appreciated his bride's gift for massage. They lived happily enough, despite the girl's unsettling habit of prostrating herself on the floor whenever she encountered Tressilian.

Kristen imagined she also occasionally tried the earl's patience, although he was too polite to say so. She was forever exhorting him to settle down and get wed. One morning she caught him as he was running up her stairs to liberate Nick and Corey from the schoolroom. She agreed that a visit to Richard Trevithick's experimental railroad in Euston would be instructive, but held him back with a hand on his taut arm. "Just a minute, Brendan."

Recognizing the expression on her face, Tressilian grudgingly halted halfway up the staircase. "This lecture won't last long, will it? For the children are doubtlessly torturing their governess to let them go—"

Kristen sighed, for Brendan's exciting jaunts only encouraged the children's impatience with more structured learning. But they did learn so much from him, and they minded him well too. "You are so good with children, Bren. You should have some of your own."

"I like yours better. They are my sort of children. What if I went to all the trouble of getting married and getting a child— of course, getting a child wouldn't be much trouble, I suppose, except for the child's mother—and he turned out to be— boring?"

"I can't imagine any of your progeny as boring, Brendan. Wild savages, perhaps, but not boring."

"It matters naught," Tressilian said with a shrug, taking the rest of the stairs two at a time, "for any wife of mine would probably jump off a cliff before she had a chance to bear a child."

When she was being very honest, Kristen admitted that she rather preferred Tressilian a bachelor. As a single man, he had ample time to devote to her and her children. Indeed, she worried that Nick and Corey would be hurt if he ever had other children, for they regarded him as their own private benevolent dictator. They obeyed him without question, and he, in return, was ever willing to take them to another puppet show or animal circus.

Of course, Kristen thought affectionately, he enjoyed such displays as much as the children did. His heart was innocent, however deplorable his behavior. How else could such a rake be so kind to children?

That mixture of sophistication and childishness forced Kristen to revise her initial impression of Tressilian as a dangerous, heartless lunatic. She still thought him dangerous, and there was no doubt he was a lunatic. But Brendan was blessed with a loving heart. That was the secret of his great charm, and the source of his worst faults. He loved all too easily, and hardly ever well.

His romantic view of life extended to embrace all the traditional ideals, for wild as he was, Tressilian was oddly old- fashioned. A reference to poor King George III as a madman, no more than the simple truth, could provoke a challenge from the hotheaded earl, who regarded his monarch as a symbol of his beloved Britain. And the name "Horatio Nelson" was enough to reduce Tressilian to incoherence. For the late, great admiral had been kind enough to commend Tressilian's bravery during those last hours of the battle of Trafalgar (calling him "that splendid lad").

But he also choked up at the sound of church bells in the distance (the more distant the better, since he was seldom sighted inside sacred walls) and the thunder of hooves along a racetrack. And he reserved his deepest love for his lovely warship the Defiant, inspired to near-poetry in describing her.

But somehow he always had enough love left over for other beauties, most of them married to someone else. Tressilian fell in love every six weeks or so, wooing and winning each lucky woman before moving on to the next. Kristen realized with some exasperation that he was really in love with love, the heady emotion that appealed to his need for danger. At least the women he chose were usually sophisticated sorts who didn't expect more than a handful of glorious memories and the envy of their peers.

Brendan's warm heart and restless nature also brought him a large and eclectic group of friends, including the famous actor Tate Stanford, the pugilist Bruisin' Bill Hadley, and a chronically suspicious Bow Street Runner named Skinner.

Tressilian House was a refuge for every Corinthian dodging creditors or an angry wife, and its venerable walls echoed with a constant if everchanging party. Beau Brummell might drop by to touch Tressilian for a loan (for every sponge in London knew of Brendan's inability to demand payment on a debt) and stay to argue fashion with the philosopher William Godwin. Or Stanford, after a bottle of the earl's best port, might be prevailed upon to declaim a bastardized, pornographic version of Hamlet, in which Rosencrantz and Guildenstern had their way with the queen and Fortinbras turned the Danish palace into a bawdy house.

Of course, Kristen was not on hand for that performance, but she received an extensive review from Tressilian's scapegrace cousin Jon Destain. He drew her aside at Lady Chambertin's al fresco musicale, and, as the soprano overreached herself, inquired if Denmark was really so entertaining. "For if it is, and all the ladies as lovely as you," he added, his blue eyes sly and sleepy, "I shall have to pay it a visit."

Kristen was secretly amused, but she assured the insolent young man that the Danish court bore no resemblance to either Stanford's or Shakespeare's portrayal. Later she remonstrated with Tressilian. "Don't you care that your house has become a way-station for vagrants and scapegallows?"

"I say, Kristen," he protested, glancing over to his cousin, who was drowsing under a shade tree with a wineglass balanced in easy reach on his forehead. "Jonny's a vagrant, he'd be the first to admit it. But he wouldn't do anything criminal— it would take too much effort."

"I don't mean Mr. Destain. He's a charming young man, and besides, he is one of your family, and you have so little of that I suppose you must cultivate it. I mean those men who drink all your liquor and fall asleep on your floor and borrow money and never pay it back and otherwise take terrible advantage of you."

"Oh, you mean my friends!" Tressilian laughed at her pretty grimace of distaste. "Well, they are my friends, even if you find them a disreputable bunch. And as for the loans, I have too much of the ready as it is, and they too little. I'd only gamble it away, if I didn't give it away. I'd do the same for you, angel."

"Ah, but I'd never ask you. For I wouldn't want to exploit our friendship. Brendan, don't tell me you have never noticed how street beggars follow you wherever you go. They have merely to look at you to know you as a soft touch."

But as he just shrugged and procured the very last dish of Italian ice for her, Kristen knew there was no reasoning with him. That was just the way Brendan was: sunny-tempered incurably generous, quick to rage and quicker to forgive. Yes, he loved too easily, and too often, and seldom wisely. But she realized ruefully that if he were any different, she wouldn't feel such affection for him, or maintain that affection after some of the more extreme scandals he got himself embroiled in as the years passed.

# *Chapter Five*

In the early stages of their friendship, Tressilian was usually on his best behavior with Kristen— charming, lighthearted, diverting. But as the trust between them grew, he sometimes revealed to Kristen the obverse side of his reckless, restless character. He could be moody, even fatalistic, as he was when his cousin died of a fever in the spring of 1812. Then that dark side of the earl took over, and Kristen learned to her dismay how much he expected his closest friends to accept.

Kristen recalled Jeremy as an earnest, conscientious boy, totally in awe of his cousin and touchingly worshipful of Lady Killeaven. Brendan had so little in the way of family, just Jeremy on his father's side and the Destains on his mother's, and this tragic death devastated him.

As Kristen was visiting friends in Plymouth when she heard, she traveled the short distance to Tressilian Castle to pay her respects. Brendan was standing on a balcony, staring out to sea. His greeting bore none of his usual gallantry, and his conversation reflected only his despair.

"It's all so absurd. I've been tempting fate out there for fifteen years, while Jerry stayed home where he could be safe. I wanted him to be safe, you know, for we were the last of the line. Then he took cold on Sunday and was dead by Tuesday."

He turned to Kristen with a weary accusation, as if this last event settled some philosophical debate, "And I suppose you'll still insist there's some logical reason for all that happens in life."

She could not tease him out of his depression, which erupted into fury when it became publicly known that he was the last of the great Trevarrick line. A dozen men presented themselves that summer as the rightful heirs to the title. They arrived complete with solicitors and elaborate, if fanciful, genealogies. Each claimant to his title brought Tressilian closer to the sort of murderous rage that made Kristen fear for the nation's safety.

Parliament's declaration of war against the United States only increased his fury. He threatened to mutiny if his ship was ordered to bottle up American ports. "Bonaparte could regain control of the seas, all because Parliament wants to punish a former colony!" he railed at Kristen, who didn't have the courage to point out that he might have oversimplified the issues just a bit.

His behavior in town, never restrained at the best of times, grew more extreme every month. He had a disastrous affair with the wife of an admiral, and was named as a co-respondent in the divorce. only the need for experienced sea captains kept the Admiralty from retiring him for this impertinence. Kristen grew weary of defending him to scandalized matrons, though she did so loyally, and she was secretly relieved when he was posted to the Mediterranean, where he could take out his bad temper on the French.

She spent Christmas with her late husband's family at Killeaven. His aunt Amelia, a prow-bosomed Amazon who dominated the rest of the

Marlowes, ordered Kristen to chaperone young Becky for the London season. An elfin girl with a mop of dark curls, Becky had already decided to make a great splash in town.

Kristen did not relish the prospect of keeping the impetuous heiress out of the clutches of fortune hunters and rakes. But she accepted the role of chaperone, for she was cowed by the formidable Amelia. It might even be fun, Kristen told herself, trying to make the best of a bad situation. London would be sparkling again, seen through the innocent eyes of a newcomer.

Amelia did not mince words. "As Sir Walter is gouty again, and I can't come with you—" (thank God, Kristen thought) "I rely on you to find Becky a good husband. A baronet, at least, with a good fortune and a comfortable home that I won't mind visiting." And, Kristen added silently, relatives who won't mind being bullied.

Becky had her own requirements, which she presented to Kristen in writing. A heroic lover, the list described in round schoolgirl script, with a stark white horse, curly hair, a gloomy Gothic castle, and a penchant for writing poetry. Kristen despaired of finding a man to fill both these orders, but Becky was a taking little thing and would probably receive several offers.

Kristen's holiday was cut short when she learned from a neighbor that the Earl of Tressilian had been gravely wounded in action in the Bay of Biscay. Fearing the worst, she ignored the scandalized protests of Aunt Amelia and ordered her coachman to drive her to Devon. She was so anxious that she couldn't wait for Great-aunt Helen or any one else to prepare for the journey, so her only chaperone was her ill-tempered Abigail.

She found Tressilian, portrayed by her neighbor as being at death's door, sitting in a sunny window reading Chapman's translation of The Odyssey. He was romantically pale, with his left arm in a sling, but otherwise he looked as healthy as when she saw him last. He even rose with a smile to greet her as she entered the morning room. The anxiety that had accompanied her on her journey fled, to be replaced, perversely, by anger. "I thought you were dying!"

"So I was. Had all the physicians fooled too. And all eleven of my supposed cousins were hanging about ready to claim the castle. I had to disappoint them, don't you see?" He dropped a kiss on her forehead and led her to the leather settee. "You needn't have come, angel, but I'm glad you did. You might have been sent by Providence to cheer me. Did you bring the children?" he finished hopefully.

"No, I didn't want them to worry, so I didn't tell them. They loved your gifts, of course," she answered automatically. During the long carriage ride, she had refused to entertain thoughts of his death, and yet fear possessed her, and guilt also. For hadn't she been happy last summer when he finally went back to sea? Now seeing him alive left her shaken and relieved, but the emotional ordeal of the past two days caused her to burst into tears, even as she castigated herself as a fool.

He put his good arm around her and drew her close. She felt the bulky bandages on his chest against her cheek and recalled small details of the four years she had known this man— his sudden, merry smiles; the way he frowned on the infrequent occasions when he actually thought; the endearing way he had of proposing the most elaborate solutions to the simplest problems.

She remembered moments when she thought no one else could understand her as Brendan did, and others when she wished him at the devil. But now she only knew how empty her life would be without his infuriating presence. She sat up and dried her eyes and found him regarding her seriously.

"I feel better now," she said, managing a watery smile, "though exceedingly silly. Will you forgive me?"

"Always." He brushed a tear from her cheek. "Will you be in London this spring?" "Yes, of course. Why?"

Tressilian rose and went to the window, gazing out at the sea he loved so well and tempted so often. "I'll be on invalid leave. They won't certify me as healthy for months. I'd like to see you."

Kristen folded his monogrammed handkerchief into a neat square and laid it on the marble pedestal table as she considered this. It wasn't in Brendan to request company, hers or anyone else's. He always just appeared at the door, full of plans for fun. "Whatever are you talking about, Bren? You have never bothered to ask before."

"I want to assure myself that I shall be welcome."

The restrained sadness in his voice bewildered and worried her.

As far as she knew, he had never needed such an assurance before. Everyone loved him, after all, and welcomed him into every gathering. She studied the set of his broad shoulders, the tension of his lean body silhouetted against the window, but could find no reason for his insecurity. "Naturally you'll be welcome. Why would you think otherwise?"

When he turned to face her his merry smile reassured her. He was the same Brendan after all, laughing and teasing and more than a bit outrageous. "The last time I saw you, angel, you vowed you'd never speak to me again."

Their last encounter had been so distant, and the occasions she'd made that vow so numerous, that Kristen could not immediately recall what precipitated this particular fit of pique. Finally she chuckled. "Well, it was shameless of you to bring that lightskirt to Lady Melbourne's rout and introduce her as your cousin."

"She's got more claim on me than the cousins I've met recently. But you were right, I came to regret that little show of rebellion quickly. Cherry was so afraid of that old cat Melbourne she clung to me all evening and I couldn't get to the cardtables."

He held out his free hand to help Kristen up, the glint in his black eyes warning her he was about to say something she would have objected to years ago. "And now, angel, speaking of Cherry and other tarts, let's see if cook has any for you. Or do you prefer the raspberry sort?"

Once they had shared a half-dozen peach tarts, Kristen pointedly refusing the cherry ones, Brendan went off protesting with his valet to have his bandage changed. Kristen took advantage of his absence to quiz Tressilian's housekeeper about his recovery.

Mrs. Mitchell, a plump woman with warm brown eyes, assured her that the earl was doing nicely except when boredom made him threaten to take his sailboat out. "Captain Destain came home on leave last week. Said he knew something was wrong with his lordship, just knew it, and he was right." The housekeeper dried a tear from her eye with a pristine apron. "They've always been the dearest friends, for all they quarrel every moment. He comes by every day to play dice and toss darts. The nicest lad, Master Jonathan is, and he was that worried about the earl. And I take good care of him, and all the others in service too, my lady, you needn't worry none about that!"

Though Kristen knew Brendan had the loyallest of retainers, she was glad that Captain Destain was home from the Peninsula. It was so hurtful to think of Brendan alone except for servants in this brooding castle on the cliffs. But of course, that was how he grew up, and perhaps he never saw it as a lonely existence. She wondered if he ever longed for a family of his own, or if he had settled for the more casual ties to his distant relatives, friends, and servants.

But she knew he was in good hands, for Mrs. Mitchell had obviously been spoiling her young master most of his life. So Kristen decided to do the proper thing for a change and start back home before dark. Brendan had no real need of her, and if her coming had been a rash act, her staying would be preposterous. Brendan, apprised of this decision only as she was preparing to enter her carriage, assured her that turning right back would be the preposterous action, and that no one would ever know if she spent a night in the castle.

So as she pulled her gloves on, she replied, "One should always obey the rules, even if one won't be observed, so as to stay in the habit."

Brendan's laughter at this eminently sensible sentiment lighted his shadowy eyes and dispelled the disquiet brought on by his earlier somberness. Kristen felt so much better hearing that merry laugh that she rose on tiptoe to kiss him goodbye. She looked back from her carriage to see him still standing cloakless in the snowy afternoon, staring after her with astonishment.

# CHAPTER SIX

March 1813

"Haven't you heard the latest?" Bunny McCall, a plain young woman who dressed like a governess and talked like a courtesan, slipped off her sturdy walking shoes and stretched out on Kristen's pale yellow divan. She looked to be settling in for the morning, but Kristen didn't object. She was dying for all the gossip, and Bunny, also known as the Morning Call, was just the woman to tell it. "Byron's leaving town. And you've just arrived. How sad for him."

Bunny gazed pointedly at a bouquet of white roses on Kristen's cherry occasional table. It was extraordinary that out of a dozen floral gifts in the lilac sitting room— for many men wished to welcome Lady Killeaven back to town— Bunny knew the exact one sent this morning by the handsome poet. But Kristen only shrugged, "No concern of mine, certainly. Why is he leaving, though, when the season is just starting?"

"Rumor is Lady Oxford is increasing and must adjourn to the country for her health. Byron is supposed to be the latest papa in the miscellany. She has forgiven him for making advances on her daughter— Oh, Kristen, you blush so divinely! It's a pleasure to scandalize you, it is— Of course, she isn't."

"She isn't?" Kristen echoed, pressing her cool hand to her flaming cheek.

"Increasing. Lady Oxford. It's a ruse. She's borrowing a leaf from her rival Caro Lamb's book— not that Caro is her rival, for Byron despises the little lamb. She became too wild even for him— Did you tell your cousin that Byron was an admirer of yours?"

At this reminder, Kristen rose and flung open the door, fully expecting to see her cousin with her ear at keyhole level. But no eavesdropping Becky was there to spoil their grown-up gossip. "He isn't, of course. He simply can't abide being refused, so he takes my every setdown as encouragement."

"I would think your romantic young charge would find Byron just to her taste. Dark, brooding, spouting poetry—"

"Oh, Bunny, I was so brilliant!" Kristen confessed as she took a seat across from her friend. "I knew Becky would fall for him, for he's dangerous besides, and I know I saw him riding a white horse last year. I told her—" her voice dropped to a whisper—"that he thinks waltzing is disgusting. And Becky, of course, thinks the waltz was invented to show her to her greatest advantage. She isn't permitted to yet, but she knows she will be quite the princess of the waltz once she's approved at Almacks. So she has no use for Byron any longer."

"These young girls," Bunny scoffed. "They don't know the least bit about real romance. So, darling, did Byron happen to send a note with his pretty tribute?"

"Only the merest rhymed couplet," Kristen replied with a shrug. "It's there on the desk." She laughed as Bunny sprang up and ran barefooted to snatch up the heavy vellum sheet.

"Almost an insult, I'd say," Bunny observed, scanning the pretty lines. "Last year he sent you a quatrain, I recall, dedicated to your violet eyes. Now you merit only two lines."

"Mind you give me that back," Kristen warned, taking up her embroidery hoop but keeping a sharp eye on her couplet. "Someday I'll publish it and make my fortune— Tressilian said much the same when he read last year's quatrain," Kristen added with a laugh. "He said Byron was being ungenerous, that my eyes deserved a sonnet at least. Now don't you think he's far more flattering than silly Byron?"

But Bunny pointed out, "I don't see any sonnets by Tressilian about. But then, he's the sort to inspire poetry, not pen it. And you keep telling me he's not in the least romantic about you, which seems a sad waste of such a man— No, Byron is, by my count, just slightly more romantic. Although, to be sure, Tressilian broods more handsomely, I think."

"Yes, he does," Kristen murmured absently, recalling the sadness in his eyes the last time she saw him. Surely his usual sunny attitude had returned by now-

"Where is our Adonis?" Bunny asked, pocketing Byron's note.

"Give me that back!" Kristen threatened her friend with the embroidery needle until Bunny ostentatiously returned the poetry to the desk. "Tressilian? I don't know. He's not in town yet, and he left Devon weeks ago."

"Such a shame, that one of our dark heroes leaves, and the other stays away. Did you hear how Caro Lamb compared the two?"

"How?" Kristen asked warily, for last year Caro Lamb had claimed intimate knowledge of both dark heroes. Brendan was too much of a gentleman to deny her tale, except to Kristen, but everyone knew she told the truth as far as Byron was concerned.

"Oh, she wrote in one of those horrid letters that somehow find their way to the scandal rags, 'At least Tressilian doesn't have to roll his hair in papers to make it curly!' I hear that's the real reason Byron is leaving town— too many of his friends are sending him cards of curling papers. I fear he's developed a violent distaste for your friend with the natural curls."

"Bunny, how do you know all this?" Kristen had to ask.

Bunny lay back on the chaise and sighed happily. "Oh, dear, let me see. I know about the flowers because my maid's brother works in a floral shop on Piccadilly frequented by handsome poets. In fact, Joey delivered that bouquet— did you think I hastened over here merely because I love you so? And as for Lady Oxford's little ruse, her physician is attending my cousin in her confinement, and he's not one to keep a confidence— he's told everyone she's expecting twins, and here she had been hoping to drown one at birth with no one the wiser— "

"Bunny," Kristen said in despair, "the things you say—"

"As to Caro's letters and Byron's curls, why, Caro herself sends me copies. She's afraid she will in a fit of pique destroy her own copies, and she knows these could not be in better hands."

"Remind me," Kristen said, only half-joking, "never to write to you, or speak to you, or see you ever again."

Bunny only laughed as she pulled on her sturdy shoes and rose to leave. "Oh, Kristen, you needn't worry. For you've never. provided me with a shred of scandal. But I confess I'd never have made your acquaintance years ago if I hadn't thought you were just being coy about this platonic friendship with the dashing earl. Now I know you are far too sensible to be entranced with poets or sea captains, no matter how handsomely they brood. So dull, you are. I can't think why I put up with you."

As she reached the door, she tossed off smugly, "Now, dearest, if you decide you prefer sober viscounts to brooding poets, I expect to be the first to know. After Stamberly, of course."

As usual, Bunny's information was alarmingly accurate. For lately, cautious contemplation (and of all contemplation, Kristen still preferred the cautious kind) was leading her into involvement with an irreproachable man who never brooded, handsomely or otherwise.

In fact, the Viscount Stamberly's most melancholy activity was giving an occasional speech in the House of Lords, where he might be subjected to the catcalls of Whigs on the back-benches. He was the essence of English virtues— solid, unassuming, responsible— and would no doubt make a fine husband.

Kristen couldn't explain why marriage suddenly appeared as the appropriate step to take after six relatively pleasant years of widowhood. She had always dismissed the arguments of her friends who had been urging her to marry for years now. But this spring their reasoning somehow sounded so much more reasonable. Kristen's experiences in previous years had taught her how uncertain a widow's state was, how vulnerable she was without the protection of a husband. Gerald had left her comfortably fixed financially, at least, but even so she found her position in society rather a precarious one. Widows hadn't as much freedom as she would like, not if they valued their reputations. She could not live alone, for example. Fortunately, Great-aunt Helen spent most of her time gossiping with her own cronies, but her presence at Killeaven House was a reminder that widows weren't safe alone— and weren't trustworthy either.

Widows were prey to rakes and fortune hunters, but also might be predators of friends husbands. Widows were to be pitied because they had no future, and feared because of the men that future might otherwise contain. So even the most respectable widows weren't fully accepted by hostesses. For a woman alone unbalanced the seating at dinner parties and so was regretfully excluded from the invitation lists. Widows were also excluded from much matronly gossip, for they couldn't complain about their husbands or speak hopefully of another happy event in nine months time. Widows were apart, somehow unwanted no matter what their real worth.

And therein lay the real danger. For widows could fall victim to all sorts of inappropriate emotions, mistaking the need for companionship and acceptance for something far more volatile.

Kristen trod the path toward remarriage carefully. She knew what she really needed was stability, and compatibility, and a well-defined place in society. The Viscount Stamberly would provide all of these things. He was a fine man who had pursued her quietly since she had come out of mourning. She admired his unhurried persistence, his eternal calm, and the rational case he presented for their betrothal.

Her friends saw him as a good father for her children, and reminded her that he had a comfortable fortune and a lovely estate in Kent. He had serious brown eyes and prematurely gray hair: rather attractive in a subdued way. He would give her calm affection and provide comfortable companionship for her old age. It was a match made in heaven, assured her matchmaking friends, and eventually she came to agree. Except....

Although Tressilian remained away from the capital, Kristen knew in her heart that he would oppose the match. He had been two years behind Edward at Eton and always recalled with disdain that the viscount had never once been rusticated. As far as Brendan was concerned, such villainy disqualified a man from reception in polite company. He would never approve of Stamberly, regarding him as dull and stodgy and without conversation.

But then, Tressilian would never approve of any man Kristen chose to marry. He much preferred lounging about in her drawing room making her prospective suitors nervous and then ridiculing them after they'd gone. He would not take lightly to being ousted from his privileged place in Kristen's household, and he would never appreciate being replaced as surrogate father to her children.

Of course, he had no right to object. They were friends, nothing more. Their friendship had certainly not curtailed his romantic adventures! So she was not about to hand over the key to her heart to Brendan to vouchsafe. He would only gamble it away in a faro game, or pawn it for a set of rubies for his latest lightskirt.

But even as she resolved to go her own way, with or without his approval, she dreaded the inevitable scene that would follow the announcement of her betrothal. So she kept putting Stamberly off, as she had for years now.

Becky, however, was not as relieved as Kristen at the earl's continued absence from town. At breakfast the next morning, she demanded that Kristen produce her dashing friend. But the countess could not predict when the capricious Tressilian would finally appear to dazzle another season's worth of debutantes.

Corinna had gotten a letter from him a month earlier— she was the only one who could decipher his handwriting, having only just learned to write herself. But the note merely instructed her on the care and feeding of the pony he had sent her as an early birthday present. Kristen found the letter under Corey's pillow and struggled through it again, reflecting with unwilling fondness that Bren was never able to wait for the children's proper birthdays to send their presents. And then, when the great day finally arrived, he always bestowed a second gift tied up with intricate knots of ribbon.

She shook her head and reapplied herself to translating that scrawl into English. As far as she could tell, the letter said nothing about when Corey could expect her riding lessons. She could only hope that his absence was not due to uncertain health. He was ever resilient, but his lucky streak had definitely been halted by that French musket ball.

Fortunately Becky did not allow her time to speculate about anything other than what invitation to accept this evening. This morning was reserved for a marathon shopping trip, to fill in the few gaps remaining in their spring wardrobes.

After they returned, Becky, her arms laden, stumbled into Kristen's bedroom. Boxes emblazoned with the names of London's most fashionable shops spilled on the blue and lilac Aubusson carpet. "I don't think I showed you all my purchases, Kristen," she cried, kneeling on the floor to rip open the packages.

Their morning's colorful bounty was soon spread out on the blue satin counterpane of Kristen's canopy bed. After three weeks in town, their wardrobes were nearly complete and quite impressive. Kristen had indulged in the jewel-like colors suitable for a sophisticated matron, earning her cousin's agonized envy.

But however Becky might long for an emerald-green evening gown, her own maidenly wardrobe suited her well. In fact, with her tumble of dark curls and vivid blue eyes, Becky looked charmingly innocent in the soft pastel shades required of debutantes. Of course, innocent charm was not the effect Becky hoped to present to the world.

She held up a frivolous silver creation and demanded, "Isn't this watered silk the most intriguing bonnet you've ever seen? I look like an opera dancer in it, I think."

Kristen dropped the stockings she had been folding and whirled around in trepidation. But with her dark curls peeping out from under the brim, and the wide ribbons tied under her pointed chin, Becky looked utterly enchanting and not the least like an opera dancer.

"Darling, please don't say such things. It is a very pretty bonnet, however." Kristen forbore to describe the effect actually created, knowing that the word "sweet" would no sooner be spoken than the girl would pitch the bonnet in the trash. After many fits and starts, Kristen was finally learning how to deal with her impulsive young cousin.

So she only added, "We have done a good day's work, and it's only noon! A few more mornings like this, and we will have run through our entire wardrobe allowance. Speaking of pockets to let, did you hear Lady Grantwell's latest on dit about Prinny? He's bought a dozen Arabian horses, only he's too fat to ride them! What will Parliament have to say about that extravagance?"

They settled down there amidst the garments on the bed for a lengthy discussion of gowns and jewelry and the men who came to call. Kristen no longer lamented the family connection that had her chaperoning Becky, for she had become very fond of her young charge.

But the reluctant Duenna could not let affection keep her from the near-impossible duty ahead— keeping the impetuous Becky from finding the scandal she sought so eagerly. When she wasn't terrorizing Kristen, Becky was lighthearted and merry and absurdly romantic. Today she insisted that one of her suitors must be involved in some mysterious plot because he looked so blue-deviled and wouldn't tell her why.

"He's probably got a toothache," Kristen pointed out practically as she kicked off her half-boots and made herself comfortable against the bolster. "But he can't confess that to you, so he must needs be cryptic. I'm sure there is no mysterious plot."

Becky clutched a pillow to her chest and sighed. "Oh, Kristen, you are so unromantic. I suppose you are going to tell me that it's a toothache and not a mysterious plot that's keeping the Earl of Tressilian from town."

"I don't know what's keeping him from town, although," Kristen added with annoyance, "I can guess. He's probably got some mistress hidden away in some cottage by the sea."

"A mysterious mistress!" Becky shot straight up, her eyes alight. "That's it! An emigre— perhaps one of Napoleon's castoffs! And she has secret papers—"

This scenario was entirely possible, Brendan being Brendan. But Kristen thought it politic to steer the subject away from any further discussion of Tressilian's amours. "His presence matters not at all, anyway. For he's not going to be joining your court, Princess Becky. You've enough rakes chasing you as it is."

"I have attracted a shocking crew, haven't I?" Becky said proudly. "I worried I would only entice worthy sorts of suitors— my lineage is so blasted impeccable. But I think I have more roués and fortune hunters in my train than anyone else this season."

"Please don't mention that to your mother when you write to her," Kristen begged, burying her head in her hands. She resorted to such dramatic gestures frequently these days, for Becky's artless behavior brought out the tragedienne in her. "And pray don't tell her if you should meet Tressilian. Aunt Amelia thinks it's shocking I associate with him, as blameless as the association is. I can just imagine her reaction if you—" Kristen couldn't finish her warning, fearing to give Becky ideas.

But there wasn't a shocking idea in existence that hadn't already taken root in Becky's curly head. "But of course I shall meet him! How could I go home and confess I hadn't met the devastating earl? Why, all Wiltshire would call me a failure! And I shall dance with him too— the waltz! I can swoon in his arms and he will carry me to a couch in a remote antechamber—"

Aghast, Kristen sat up and seized Becky's hands. "He will do no such thing! Becky, promise me you won't tease Tressilian that way! For he never pays the slightest attention to debutantes, although they all waste their first seasons mooning after him. And your mother would have my head if you fell in love with such an ineligible and came home without a suitable man to marry!"

But Becky pulled her hands away and tossed her dark head. "I could never fall in love with a suitable man. And I won't marry unless I fall in love." For a moment she contemplated a spinster's existence, then added decisively, "And I will fall in love. With a passionate man who will send me great bouquets of flowers and fight duels for me and rescue me from terrible predicaments."

This ideal man sounded perilously close to Tressilian. Kristen knew him well enough to trust him with Becky— not that he was so trustworthy, only that he had no interest in the infantry. But she did not in the least trust Becky with him. She closed her eyes, imagining the dire straits the girl might get herself into to be rescued by Tressilian. A vision of Becky hurling herself in front of a carriage flashed through Kristen's mind.

"Tressilian is out of bounds, Becky," she declared. "He's not looking for a wife, and I'd kill him if he offered you anything less. Not that he ever would, mind you. So just forget him."

Becky opened her blue eyes very wide, for once taking advantage of her innocent appeal. "But, Kristen, I never said I wanted to marry Tressilian— or do anything else with him either! After all, he is dark, and I was hoping for a golden-haired Adonis. And I understand he rides a black horse, and my hero must have a white horse. And I truly don't want a sailor, for I get seasick. But someone very like him— passionate and wild. Someone I can admire and adore and— and then we will surrender to love."

Kristen dropped her head back into her hands with a moan. When she could finally speak, she implored, "No, Becky, don't ever surrender to love. Please don't surrender to love."

Becky paid her no mind, drawing her knees up to her chin and marveling, "Imagine becoming one with a man and saving him from his own wickedness by your beauty and goodness—"

Kristen straightened up. This had gone far enough. "Now you just stop thinking like that, Becky Marlowe. That sort of man doesn't offer you love. Or he offers it but doesn't give it. Or he gives it but only for a while. You might have a few minutes of exhilaration and months and months of pain."

Hadn't she seen women, experienced women who should have known better, fall under Tressilian's spell? The naive Becky, with her Wiltshire ways and country confidence, would be no proof against a rake's charms.

Becky sauntered to the door with a weary sigh. "I'll try. But I think this caution of yours has very little to do with love."

Becky's last words lingered in Kristen's mind like an evocative melody, teasing her with elusive longing. Kristen had never been so innocent as Becky, even at eighteen. She'd never been foolish enough to consider throwing caution to the winds and trusting a man. She'd never been foolish enough to trust anyone, not since she stopped expecting her parents to unfreeze enough to show affection.

Wasn't that why she was considering wedding Stamberly? Neither of them had habits to overcome to become compatible. Neither would have to change very much to become a good spouse. And that appealed to a cautious woman like Kristen.

Becky might be right, that caution had nothing to do with love. But Kristen was not interested in love. Caution did, however, have everything to do with marriage.

# CHAPTER SEVEN

Meetings with the Clerk of the Admiralty always put Tressilian into a childish temper, and today's confrontation had been twice as bad as usual. So he slammed the clerk's office door, then opened it and slammed it again. Rubbing his chest where the musket wound had scarred over, he strode away down the reverberating marble hall, cursing all civil servants and admirals under his breath.

"Temper, temper, my boy."

His mouth twisting with dread, Tressilian turned to see Admiral Lord Destain looming in the doorway opposite the clerk's office. Destain's benevolent expression did not deceive his former midshipman, who had endured a thousand tongue-lashings during his service.

Tressilian knew he could expect little sympathy for the Admiralty's action dry-docking him and his ship for the rest of the year. In fact, he'd be lucky to get off with an "I told you so." But for once resigned to his fate, he suggested lunch at the Old Ship, a navy haunt on Cockspur Street.

Were the potential sermonizer anyone but Destain, Tressilian would be more likely to invite him for pistols at dawn than a quiet luncheon. But sullen as a boy and just as obedient, he followed the older man through the great oak entry doors fashioned from the hull of a Spanish galleon sunk in 1588. This hard-bitten old salt was the one man Tressilian would never defy.

They were bound by a tangle of family and professional ties: Tressilian's father, Christopher Columbus Trevarrick, had been Anthony Destain's best friend; his mother and Destain's wife had been first cousins. And Destain's son Jon, of course, was Tressilian's best friend. So when young Brendan, expelled from Eton, decided to run away to sea, he chose Destain's ship. He served under Destain only two years— their relationship was too volatile for long voyages— but the admiral would always be, as sailors put it, Tressilian's sea daddy.

So, often at risk to his own career, Destain had championed the brilliant, heedless young captain. There was no better sailor afloat, the admiral avowed to his colleagues, and no luckier one either. It was only in private that he lambasted Tressilian.

The Navy Board porter nodded haughtily as they passed through the entrance hall. For as long as Tressilian could remember, that worthy ancient had ruled here, disdaining to note any officer below post rank. Seven years ago, Tressilian didn't really believe he had made post-captain until he received that cool nod from the porter. But even the indomitable Admiral Destain didn't try to engage the old man in conversation, for the porter condescended to speak only to the First Sea Lord.

Cravenly, the young captain put off the lecture as they walked across the cobblestone courtyard and into the soft April morning. And the admiral maintained an amiable silence all the way up Whitehall to the tavern, his goldheaded cane tapping in light rhythm to the cries of the birds.

"How's Jonny? I haven't heard from him since he went back to the Peninsula in January."

"Haven't you been home lately?" The admiral grunted as he bent under the doorframe of the Old Ship. The underground tavern was designed with low ceilings and cramped booths to make sailors feel at home. "The boy came back a fortnight ago. Invalid leave."

Lord Destain seldom referred to his prodigal son by name, and Jon always called his father "the admiral" or "the old man". But Tressilian did not concern himself now with their chill relations— they had never gotten on. "Was he wounded? Is he all right?"

Lord Destain squeezed his husky frame into a booth and raised an impatient hand. A waiter appeared, costumed like a seaman in a striped jersey and bandana. "Wounded? In what action? His kind of war, the Peninsula is, a battle every six months and naught but slumber in between. Always was an indolent young coxcomb. We'll have some rum and ale to chase it. And beef sandwiches. And—"

"Uncle Anthony," Tressilian broke in, waving the waiter away. "How is Jonny?"

Destain's weathered face darkened as the waiter vanished into the kitchens. "I wanted him to bring me some of that chutney, Jon? Malingering, I've no doubt. His mother says he caught a touch of lung fever, that's all."

"That's all?" A chill seeped through Tressilian, for his cousin Jeremy had died of a lung fever. "Is he recovering then? It's not settled into consumption?"

"No, no, I think not. I haven't seen him, but his mother would have told me if he were consumptive. No, he's just coughing, or so she says. No doubt his hacking disturbed the sleep of those damned horses dragoons bed down with." The efficient waiter reappeared with a tray of drinks, a crock of chutney, and a loaf of bread. "Good man. You remembered the chutney."

The waiter ducked his head at the unexpected compliment. "You always order the chutney, my lord. I'll bring the sandwiches in a moment."

The admiral tossed off his rum, then hefted his ale to his lips. Stifling a belch, he regarded the scowling captain in puzzlement. "Well, now, lad, are you still worrying about your cousin? Don't. He's escorting his mother to town, so I expect he's well enough. Just malingering, as I said."

Tressilian maintained an angry silence as the admiral spread chutney on his bread, taking care to cover every bit of the surface. Destain's antipathy towards his son was truly appalling, and only the knowledge that remonstration would have no effect kept the earl silent. Jon was lazy, no doubt, but no malingerer.

And however undutiful a son he might have been, he had always been the best of best friends. After Tressilian's injury, Jon had wangled leave— and everyone knew Wellington never granted his officers leave— just to keep his cousin from cutting short his convalescence out of boredom. Now Jon was the ill one, and the admiral hadn't even seen fit to notify his best friend.

Tressilian was not one to reconsider the past. But he paid only half a mind as the admiral, between bites, sketched on the back of a letter the route of his last voyage to the West Indies. He wondered now if Lord Destain would have learned to love his actual son better if he hadn't had a surrogate son so close to hand.

Destain had certainly been a surrogate father to the orphaned son of his best friend. And Tressilian had never questioned his right to take up virtual residence at Destain Manor, only two miles down the Devon coast from the castle, and to live as a member of the family. But what if he hadn't been there to sit at Lord Destain's knee and listen enthralled to the stories of great sea-battles? To take lessons in sextant-reading and piloting? To follow the admiral to sea? Perhaps if he hadn't filled the filial role, there would have been room for Jon.

Tressilian didn't like guilt, for if he started experiencing that corrosive emotion, he'd never stop, as much as he had to be guilty about. So he poured the admiral another tankard of ale and rationalized. He was far more tolerant than his cousin Jon, after all. He had never minded the admiral's shouts and threats, or his limited repertoire of conversational subjects— ship maintenance, wind velocity, Admiralty politics, that was about it.

And if the admiral tended toward crudeness, all the old-style salts were the same way. The new generation of sea captains since Trafalgar were more conscious of their roles as national icons and behaved more acceptably on and off the ship. But Tressilian could hardly object to the authenticity of Destain's occasional vulgarity.

Jon had never been so tolerant, especially of his father. For they were nothing like. Even in the spectacular uniform of a vice-admiral, Lord Destain was as rough-looking as a boatswain, with a hard, square body and weather-beaten features. Jon took after his gentle mother with his slender form, patrician features, and fair good looks.

Impeccably tasteful, Jon was, appreciating perfection in everything from his choice of mounts— the finest Arabians— to his preference in women— Lady Elise Winterleigh, an acknowledged beauty, the daughter of an earl and daughter-in-law of a marquess. Admiral Lord Destain, whatever his other virtues, was not by any stretch tasteful.

And Jon, however soft-spoken, was as stubborn as his father. From infancy, he had responded to his father's commands with insolence and disobedience, though he was regarded by the rest of the world as a most charming boy. Joining the cavalry was Jon's last great act of defiance. The admiral would not accept such mutiny from his own son, so now they had virtually no contact.

If I ever have a son, Tressilian resolved, I won't reject him if he's unlike me. In fact, I hope he's different from me, he concluded, considering for the first time what a father might say about the course of Tressilian's life for the last decade or so.

The thought of a son was unexpectedly pleasant to a man who had assiduously avoided such a complication. A boy like Nick Marlowe would be about right, and a daughter just like Corinna- "A son, that's the ticket, my boy."

Tressilian started, worried that the generally obtuse admiral had learned to read minds. But Destain only spread mustard on his sandwich and went on obviously, "Get a wife and get her with child, and we'll have you back cruising the Med by Christmas."

"Admiral, what are you talking about?"

"That musket ball idle your ears, boy? I said—"

"I heard. Would you translate for me?" Tressilian took a deep breath and tried to be patient. He focused on drawing constellations in the chutney with his knife. "What's a wife got to do with my being docked? The clerk told me the physician wouldn't certify me healthy— which is a damned lie, for I'm nearly back to normal, and even at half- speed I'm in better shape than most of the old sots you have commanding ships of the line these days."

Recalling that insult to his strength made Tressilian's fist clench painfully on the knife. He had spent the last six weeks at a secluded lodge in the Cotswolds, running up and down the hills, rowing an hour each day in the lake, preparing for his medical examination. "They're just keeping me home because of that damn Bellingham divorce. And I was hardly the only one named as her lover— I wasn't even the only sailor—"

The admiral looked thunderous, and Tressilian wished he'd never introduced the topic of Admiral Bellingham and his dazzling former wife. "Why can't you keep your hands off Admiralty wives, you young fool? Or at least choose one who won't boast of her conquest! Mrs. Bellingham was the second—" Third, Tressilian thought, but prudently kept it to himself.

"And she made haste to tell Bellingham all about your tawdry little liaison-"

"Tawdry?" This Tressilian had to protest. "Hardly. She cost me a packet in diamonds— exquisite taste, I'll give her that."

"She'll cost you your career too, are you not more careful."

"It's all they deserve, those old toads, marrying girls right out of the dance halls. Why I should be blamed for their late-life incapacities, I don't-"

"That's enough!"

At the admiral's bellow, Tressilian backed off like the veriest midshipman. "Aye, sir," he replied meekly, edging away towards the wall, out of range of the admiral's square hand. The old man's face was pugnacious, and he might forget that he was dealing with a fellow post-officer and not an insubordinate subordinate.

"That's better. I don't want to hear about any late-life incapacities from you, Tressilian. For the rate you're going, you won't have anything left to be incapable of later in life, an you live so long. It wears out from overuse, you know," Destain said with utter seriousness, shaking his finger at the younger man. "I told you that years ago, but I see you paid me no mind."

"I subscribe more to the theory that exercise improves all physical functioning," Tressilian countered, ardently hoping it was true. "I shall let you know in twenty years. But you're right, I'm swearing off Admiralty wives. Except yours," he added wickedly.

"Young scamp. Go ahead. It'd give her the thrill of her life, Lady Destain," the admiral observed, lifting his ale tankard in salute, "to be chased after just like one of those opera dancers."

"Aunt Manda?" Tressilian was aghast at his own joke. "You must be— I'd never—"

"Nice to know you have a few limits, my boy. Any road, Mrs. Bellingham ain't the reason you're being invalidate. We admirals ain't such fools as you post-captains like to think. Wouldn't make much sense to keep you home so you'd have the run of our wives. Bellingham, in fact, was all for posting you to the Hong Kong run—"

Tressilian straightened up, his black eyes glinting with anticipation. Of all voyages, he liked best the year-long run to Hong Kong. "I'd like that, sir. I can outfit the ship in a month—"

"Stubble it, young man. Bellingham hasn't the last word on this. The docking orders come from on high." The admiral sat back with a smile. "Very high."

"Melville likes me." In fact, before Tressilian's unfortunate yen for Admiralty wives surfaced, Lord Melville was wont to speculate about Tressilian rising to First Sea Lord himself in a couple decades— a foolish prediction, even then. "He told me I was nearly as good a sailor as Captain Cook."

"Higher than that."

Tressilian's winged brows drew together in a frown of pure puzzlement. "Who's higher than the First Lord?"

"Prinny."

"Prinny?"

"Have I got an echo? Yes, Prinny. Your old carousing comrade. He doesn't often interfere with naval affairs, but he made an exception for you."

It was true that years ago, at a most tender and impressionable age, Tressilian had caroused with the Carlton House set. Prinny had enjoyed his young friend's boundless high spirits and heroic good looks. And Tressilian's propensity for causing scandal amused the scandalous prince. "But he likes me too."

"Everyone likes you, lad," the admiral noted sympathetically, for he considered popularity a burdensome condition, not that he had ever to worry about it himself. "Even Bellingham likes you. Said he knew it was his tramp of a wife that drew you astray— what a kneeslapper! You've always been astray, since you escaped from leading strings! But it's true. Everyone likes you. Prinny especially. And he was shaken, by all accounts, by your last brush with death. So he gave Melville the word to dock you."

"But I'm fine." Tressilian left off breaking his sandwich into ever-smaller pieces, exclaiming, "I shall go see his highness and show him I am none the worse for that trifling injury. Then he will— "

"Don't wager the house on it, lad. He's worried about the succession, you see. Your family is one of the oldest in the nobility, although I expect you've forgotten about it, and you haven't an heir. If you're killed, the Trevarrick name and the Tressilian earldom will be extinct." The admiral shook his head, his bushy eyebrows furrowing in memory. "I was called in to Carlton House for a dressing-down also. Prinny couldn't understand why fifteen years ago I took you to sea with me and got you started on a naval career. Earls don't sail, he said."

"I was only a viscount, then. And besides, Prinny's own brother is a sailor," Tressilian said sullenly, returning to the demolition of his sandwich. He began building a small mountain of bread crumbs in the middle of his plate.

"The kingdom can spare a prince easier'n it can spare a Tressilian. Especially considering what sort of princes we have."

"Grandfather never kicked up much of a fuss. I expect he was glad to have me gone. Why, he was a sailor too, and my father—" He looked up to see the "just so" expression in the admiral's eyes. Christopher Trevarrick had been lost at sea at the age of seven-and-twenty— A year younger than I, Tressilian thought, diverted momentarily. "Trevarricks are always sailors. The earldom came to us as a military prize, after all."

"All those other Trevarricks, however, managed to secure the succession— even your poor father, though it was a close-run thing, you being a posthumous child." The admiral sighed gustily, raising his tankard. "To our fallen comrades."

Tressilian repeated the toast automatically, his mind unworking this latest coil. "So Prinny been alerted to my lack of heirs, has he? Can't I just name an heir? Jonny! He's my cousin—"

"It doesn't work that way, clunch," the admiral said with rough affection. "Has to be a Trevarrick. And you can't just choose an heir. Were that the case, I'd certainly be making a change in my own succession— But that's neither here nor there. There's no help for it, lad. You have to do your duty and get yourself leg-shackled."

He shook his bulkhead-gray head with rue. "Hard to think of you settling down, but there you have it. Now don't look so miserable, boy. It's not the worst fate in the world. Good for a sailor to have a wife at home, waiting for him with the little ones and keeping his house happy. Otherwise you don't have anyone to think about as you walk the quarter-deck— sailing's a lonely life, as you know. But a wife makes it less so."

Destain cleared his throat embarrassedly and raised his hand for the bill. "Think about it, my boy. You can have your ship back as soon as that refitting's done. Or we can give it to a more obliging captain."

Destain made a great show of taking the bill, then, when the waiter had gone back into the kitchens, he dropped it in front of Tressilian. He rose with a grunt, picking up his bicorne and tucking it under his arm. Then he patted the young captain clumsily on the shoulder. "Come to dinner when your aunt arrives to town. Perhaps that scapegrace heir of mine will deign to visit Destain House if he knows you will be there."

Long after the admiral had gone, Tressilian sat there in the dark booth, his long fingers tracing fifty years of initials etched into the oak table. With abstract curiosity he lit a Lucifer and bent close over the flame to search out one particular carving in the center of the table.

"BDET, 2 Feb. 06, H.M.S. Defiant". Brendan Drake Erikson Trevarrick had made post that day, assigned to the great frigate Defiant. He had just turned one-and-twenty, and he'd dragged a reluctant young cavalry officer to this navy haunt to celebrate. That title of 'captain" had always meant more to him than "earl". He had only inherited the earldom from a grandfather he hardly knew in the place of a father he had never met. He had earned his command. Ever since, leading 300 seamen meant more to him than heading up the Trevarrick family. In fact, he had no family at all. Except for—

Blocking that last thought as unproductive, he took out his penknife and under his initials added the current date and the number 24—the sum of French vessels his Defiant had captured in seven years. He brushed away the woodshavings, staring at the scarred tabletop and seeing instead a vision of his lovely Defiant, her sails proudly snapping in the wind. Now they wanted to take his ship away from him, and then he would have nothing left.

# CHAPTER EIGHT

The Baroness Cannon dazzled London every season with a glorious April ball held in her cathedral-sized ballroom. For such an auspicious occasion, both Becky and Kristen had commissioned new gowns: Becky's was of shell-pink satin, as daring as a debutante's gown could be without giving her chaperone palpitations, with a seed-pearl Juliet cap highlighting her dark curls and bright blue eyes. Kristen favored silk, of a blue as pale as ice, set off by a magnificent set of sapphires, her pale hair caught up in a silver comb. She looked, Becky assured her, not in the least like a matronly chaperone, however advanced her age and dignity.

But Becky's compliments could not ease the tension that tightened Kristen's shoulders into knots as they entered the ballroom. The glittering crowd pressed her like sandwich filling between Becky and Lord Stamberly, leaving her no room even to raise her hand to acknowledge the greetings of friends. The forced smile she had to assume instead only gave her a headache.

These assorted irritations probably accounted for her finding so much fault with poor Edward tonight. He was certainly kind, doubtlessly devoted, but rather ineffectual at cutting a path through the press to the open area beyond the staircase. She had a momentary vision of how the crowd would part were Brendan her escort.

But Edward, not being a military man, would never wear a sword to a ball, and would also never wear the sort of scowl that suggested he might use it, given half a chance.

"Come, my dear," Edward said, taking her arm and following a frigate-sized matron's progress through the assembly. Kristen felt a silent niggling that Edward never addressed her more warmly than "my dear". How irritable I am tonight, she thought, and penitently agreed to save the first waltz for him.

She was gazing over his shoulder, wishing he danced better, when a stir at the arched entry caught her eye. Tressilian sauntered in, resplendent enough in his uniform to put the ladies to the blush. Predictably, the crowd parted with an awed murmur and allowed him free passage.

After that first ripple of admiration, the onlookers fell silent, surveying the conquering hero's latest conquest. For on his arm was Andrea Fabian, a pretty redhead who fluttered her fan and her eyelashes at all the attention. She was queen tonight, if only for tonight, and she made the most of it.

Kristen felt herself go rigid right there in Edward's cautious arms. So Tressilian had taken the time to seduce Andrea away from her safe, secure marriage, a task that preoccupied him so that he could not visit old friends, not even two children who lived for his appearances.

And to choose Andrea, of all people! That was a deliberate

provocation, Kristen was sure. Andrea had been, at least up to now, the contented wife of a nice if dull country squire, and one of Kristen's closest friends. So Tressilian had broken two of his own rules tonight— he never intruded on a placid marriage, and he never, never, under pain of death, seduced Kristen's friends (which had the unintended effect of limiting her circle of bosom bows).

Oh, Brendan knew what he was about, he did, although why he wanted to enrage her Kristen didn't know. But he was angry too, she could see that even as he flashed a dazzling smile at Lady Cannon and brought her trembling hand to his lips.

Lady Cannon, Andrea, they might be too dizzied by his gallantry to notice the rigid bearing of his splendid shoulders, the proud line of his jaw, the brooding set of his mouth. But Kristen knew him in all his moods, and this was a dangerous one. She felt an unwilling sympathy for Andrea, who was merely a pawn in some game of Brendan's and would probably regret this night forever.

But how could foolish Andrea help herself? Even as the violent emotions built up in her, Kristen had to marvel at Brendan's stirring good looks, that had earned him so many otherwise unjustified pardons. He had the enviable ability to look careless and elegant at the same time, as if he had dressed in minutes before the ball but still felt more at ease in his finery than any dandy in the room. His black curls were tousled boyishly, and Kristen was startled by a desire to smooth away the tangles. That wish to soothe him vanished, however, as Brendan pulled Andrea against him to whisper no doubt scandalous things in her ear.

When the music stopped, Tressilian led Andrea over to greet Kristen. "Lady Killeaven, how good it is to see you." He disdained to notice Stamberly, as was his wont with people he didn't like.

Kristen's eyes shot daggers at him. "I'm pleased to find you in such good health, your lordship." She ironically emphasized the title, if only to remind him they had been on a Christian-name basis for five years now, though her feelings now were hardly Christian.

He bowed slightly, a graceful move that caused the candlelight to glance off his wicked silver sword. "Thank you for your concern. Do you know Mrs. Fabian?"

"Of course," she snapped, abandoning any pretense of politeness. "I introduced you."

"Remind me to thank you." He grinned maliciously at Stamberly's embarrassment, while Andrea glowed with a shamed excitement.

"I must talk to you," she whispered to Kristen. "Please." With a lingering glance at the amused Tressilian, she led Kristen off to a quiet withdrawing room.

Andrea was striking in the sort of daring gown that she never would have worn last year, her eyes glittering, her coppery hair gleaming. Brendan was running true to form, for he always did like the redheads best, Kristen thought with a spurt of annoyance. "Andrea, do you have the slightest idea what you are about?"

"No! Oh, Kristen, I'm so frightened!" She seized Kristen's hands imploringly. "What if word reaches Arthur in the country?"

Kristen disengaged her hands from Andrea's frenzied grasp and drew off her right glove. As she suspected, the sapphire on her ring had sliced the adjacent finger. She dabbed at the cut with a handkerchief and shook her head. "I'm sure Arthur will hear of it before the night is over. Gossip travels on birdwings, and Gloucestershire isn't far. But why worry?" she added angrily. "You took such trouble to advertise your infatuation! You were clinging to him as if you were drowning! When did this all begin?"

"Last week." Now Andrea didn't know what to do with her frantic hands. Finally she settled for wringing them in her gold lace skirts. "Back home. I was out for a ride, and met him in the hills. He was in the Cotswolds to regain his health, I gather—"

Automatically, Kristen pointed out, "You're wrinkling your skirt, Andrea, gripping it like that. To regain his health?" Sometimes, she thought, pressing the handkerchief painfully against the cut, he is so infuriating. If he needed to recuperate, he didn't have to spirit himself off alone. What use are all his great friends if he can't turn to us when he's needful?

Kristen's heart ached to think of him all alone, waiting for his blithe good health to return, fearing it would not— Of course, he hadn't been alone. Andrea was there. "He'd been swimming in the lake—"

"In April?" Kristen broke in, horrified. "After he was shot in the chest? He could have caught his death of cold."

Andrea shrugged, too preoccupied by love to worry about the health of her beloved. "He was magnificent," she breathed. "He has a— a tattoo. Don't you think that is deliciously rough?"

Kristen gritted her teeth, vowing she would never ask Andrea the location or description of that delicious tattoo, even if she faced death by curiosity. But Andrea, a star-struck lover, took no notice of her companion's emotions. She fell as if in a swoon onto a claw-footed settee. "Oh, he is so devastating, Kristen! I adore him so! He is the handsomest man on earth, and the kindest—"

"Brendan? Kind?" Kristen scoffed as Andrea draped herself romantically across the brocade with her arm flung up across the forehead. "If he were kind, he would have left you quite alone. Andrea, what on earth are you doing? He's not the sort of man you just flirt with! And you are not up to his weight, Andrea, you are too naive and foolish!"

She knew she was being cruel, but she hated willing victims, and Andrea was apparently as willing as could be, to judge from her abandoned posture now.

"You don't understand." Andrea sat up, a mulish expression twisting her mouth. "Everything is different with Brendan. Arthur is so dull and vacuous— Oh, I don't know what to do! What will happen to the children if Arthur and I divorce?"

"Divorce?" The word came out a horrified gasp. "Divorce? Are you running mad? Do you think he will marry you?" Brendan marrying at all was nigh incomprehensible; marrying a divorced Andrea didn't bear considering. "Another divorce will ruin his navy career!"

Andrea remarked loftily, "His career is over anyway. He's being invalidate out. I overheard Lord Melville talking about it."

A cold fear caught at Kristen's heart. Perhaps he hadn't regained his health in the Cotswolds after all. Perhaps his dynamic appearance tonight was deceptive. For he would never willingly give up his command, of that she was sure. "Is he ill?"

"No, of course not." Andrea's scorn indicated that she had rather too intimate knowledge of Tressilian's robustness. "The regent gave the order, because the Tressilian earldom has no heir. Brendan must stay where it is safe— unless, of course, he marries and gets an heir." She smiled smugly, for if there was any accomplishment Andrea could claim, it was the getting of heirs. She had already provided her current husband with four healthy sons.

Kristen pulled her glove back on, imagining Brendan's savage anger in the face of the navy's dismissal. Being barred from the sea would be more dangerous for him than all of Napoleon's navy, for he loved sailing better than anything. Perhaps he would find marriage a solution of sorts, but—

"Don't be a fool, Andrea. He won't marry you. I know him well enough to tell you he might not mind creating a divorced woman, but he'd never marry one."

Andrea's amber eyes glittered as she came to her feet and grabbed up her reticule. "That's it, isn't it? You're jealous, aren't you? You've wanted him for yourself all along, and all this friendship nonsense was just a ruse. And you can't bear to think I've caught him. You're just as envious as a cat."

"Actually, I don't envy your lot at all," Kristen said coldly, turning on her heel and returning to the ballroom. Jealous, was she? What utter fustian. She could have had Brendan as a lover all those years ago. But she was simply too intelligent to make a cake out of herself like Andrea, to throw away an entire carefully constructed life for a short-lived wild passion.

In her angry musing, she hardly noticed that Stamberly was at her elbow, inquiring if she was feeling quite the thing. What if she hadn't spurned Tressilian's advances so long ago? Would she have lasted any longer than any of his other conquests? Or would he have discarded her too, with only a few memories and perhaps some jewels to console her? Just as well she never found out.

Then she shook her head briskly to dispel such worthless speculation. She wasn't jealous of Andrea's intimacy with Brendan, far from it. In fact, at the moment Kristen wished she'd never again meet the deplorable man or any of his foolish victims.

Unfortunately, her wish was destined to be denied. Even as she gazed around the room, locating Becky in the company of a pair of beguiling fortune hunters, Tressilian strode up beside her and swept her off into the waltz.

She was so angry at this peremptory action she ignored the barely-sheathed tension of his arms around her, so hard that he could crush her had he such an urge. She knew she was in no danger from Brendan, however hazardous he might be to women like Andrea.

So she gave free rein to her fury. "How dare you! I had promised this dance to Stamberly."

"Then you should be happy to be rescued."

They were so well-paired as dance partners that even their antagonism couldn't dispel her instinctive enjoyment of this waltz. She looked up to see his smoldering eyes. I'm the one who is angry, she thought. Why is he so fierce?

Tressilian, always the gallant, let her take the first shot. "Well, go on, Kristen, we have only a quarter hour, and you look to have a half-hour's rant prepared."

As usual, his absurdity made her smile, though she bent her head to hide it. "Don't try to tease me, Brendan. I am, in fact, exceedingly put out by you."

"Don't I know it. Let's start with the worst first," he prompted, his hand tightening encouragingly on hers. Oddly' some of the tension had left him, she could feel it in his embrace. He always told her that he found her serenity relaxing, although she could hardly claim to be serene tonight.

"The worst?" Kristen ran through the list— Andrea, this abduction on the dance floor, his rakehell ways— "Why didn't you tell me you weren't recovered? You didn't even answer my note."

He shrugged and looked away. "What would you have done, had you known? Sent me flowers? I didn't need any help, I only needed time. I am quite recovered now. And I didn't see much point in discommoding my friends."

A flush crept up his lean jaw— she'd never known a man who showed his embarrassment as plainly as Brendan, but then, all of his moods were easy to read on that expressive face. "Jonny came home on leave, you know. I almost had to post him back like a parcel to Portugal before they charged him with desertion. Now he's back, ill himself, and didn't see fit to let me return the favor."

Kristen was diverted enough by this to forget her other grievances. "I've never thought of either of you as stoic. I suppose it's just that male conceit, refusing to admit to any weakness. When I'm sick, I expect bouquets and cool cloths and visits from friends bearing bonbons. Why else would you get ill?" Kristen said practically. "You should have sent me word, after all."

"Point conceded. Let us proceed then to your next item."

Kristen found it hard to maintain her righteous indignation when Brendan was being so conciliatory. But then she saw Andrea glaring at her from the edge of the dance floor and stiffened. "What do you think you are about with Andrea Fabian?"

The glitter was back in his eyes, the tension to his arms. "Only the usual sort of thing. I'd forgotten she was some friend of yours— hard to believe, for she's not your sort."

"She is your sort, however, isn't she? Pretty, redheaded, and married to another man?" Remembering poor Arthur Fabian, an kindly man who took good care of his acreage, Kristen almost yanked herself out of Brendan's arms. But she was not the sort of woman who caused scenes in ballrooms, so she settled for holding herself as far away as she could and still be waltzing. "Such righteousness is inappropriate. I've never forced myself on a woman. I hardly exerted myself." He caught his breath, then grinned. "See what your accusations do to me In my defense, I am tempted to ungallantry, to suggest the lady threw herself at me."

"You didn't have to catch her," Kristen returned hotly. "She's got a family, you know, and a decent enough husband—"

"Well, you'd know more about that than I would."

Tressilian's hard tone indicated a double meaning here, but she refused to take the time to uncover it. "She is raving about divorcing him, you know."

Tressilian shrugged. "I hope you disabused her of the notion that I care one way or another about her marital status." "My God, Brendan, you are so cold!" She withdrew from him, from that harsh face he had always taken care not to show to her. "She's talking about giving up her family, and you act as if it makes no matter!"

"The more fool she, if she builds a dream castle out of exactly nothing. I haven't even bedded her yet. She's a romantic, you see. Wants more wooing than I'm capable of providing at the moment."

From somewhere came a rush of relief at this revelation, then a disquieting doubt. Brendan was a romantic himself. He loved to woo women, to seek out their fantasies and fulfill them. He'd never been one to rush the preliminaries, even with impatient ladies. "Bren, are you all right?"

He leaned back his head and laughed at this, misunderstanding, perhaps deliberately, her question. "Ah, my little puritan, you will be glad to hear that while the flesh is entirely willing, the spirit is temporarily weak. No doubt all your sermons on being responsible have taken some root. I am indeed wary of providing grounds for the Fabian divorce."

"Perhaps you ought to make that clearer to Mrs. Fabian," Kristen said with a return of her usual spirit. "She is quite taken with your tattoo."

They had been friends for so long that Tressilian could interpret that last irrelevant observation. "It's on my arm," he said. "And even you could not object to the subject. No dancing girls. No obscene boasts. Only a tasteful rendering of my true love—" He paused for effect, then added sweetly, "My ship."

"You might make sure," Kristen observed as if she did not care, "that Andrea is not planning to be the next subject for your personal portrait gallery."

"Point number two conceded. You are doing well tonight, aren't you? Routing me left and right. But then, I've never been able to resist those censorious violet eyes of yours."

Tressilian's voice deepened meaningfully, and she felt better despite her anger. At least he wasn't so melancholy he'd forgotten how to flirt. "Are you quite done?"

"Quite. Not another allusion to your beauty, charm, and grace will cross my lips, I promise. But I hope you are not quite done? For there's a few moments left, and I can't think of what we might have to say to each other if you aren't castigating me."

Annoyed again at his silky sarcasm, she turned her head away from him. The sight of Stamberly looking desperately bored next to a chattering matron reminded her of his latest offense. "You know, Brendan, you should ask me if I'd like to dance, rather than just assuming that I am free."

"Had I assumed you were free, I would have asked as politely as you please. I only practice abductions when I know I shall be refused," he said reasonably. 'And you aren't missing much."

"That's hardly a judgment for you to make," she replied, though for a traitorous instant she thought that arguing with Tressilian was in fact more entertaining than dancing with Edward.

As if he had read her thoughts, he demanded, "Are you really going to marry that dull dog?"

Now that the moment she had feared had arrived, Kristen took refuge in correctness. "You've been listening to gossip, have you? And I don't care to hear your opinion of the viscount, who happens to be a very fine man."

"Why would you want to marry him?" Brendan's face was fierce again, and she wished the orchestra would bring this infernal waltz to an end so that she could escape. "You can't tell me you're languishing in love with him. His own mother probably took only a mild interest in him."

An absurd sense of guilt made her grit her teeth. "It's none of your affair if or whom I marry, Brendan."

"Oh, no, of course it isn't." His dark voice dripped with sarcasm. "You've taken upon yourself the right to criticize every move I've made for five years now. Yet you expect me to stand by without comment as you waste your life."

This last left her momentarily speechless. Finally she managed with commendable calm, "Waste my life? How dramatic you are. I can't imagine what you mean."

Brendan closed his eyes for a moment, his long lashes shadowing his expression. When he regarded her again, his gaze was sardonic, his voice level. "You waste your life, my love, when you decide to take— what did you call the breed?— a decent enough husband. But you have always been a consistent sort, haven't you? One loveless marriage would have been enough for most women, but not for you."

This time she didn't check the hot words that rose to her lips. "Forgive me if I choose to disregard your advice on love. For I think you know nothing of the subject at all. A man who has fallen in love six times in a single year, and with the sort of woman you frequent, has no real experience to offer."

"The sort of woman I frequent," he snapped, "has some capacity to love— not wisely, perhaps, but at least well. I don't think you have any right to question that, for it's clear you wouldn't know love if it took hold of your shoulders and shook you dizzy."

His scorn struck her like a blow. That she had never expected from him— anger at the match everyone else applauded, even resentment. But not scorn. She felt a tremble begin inside her, threatening to bring on weak tears. How could Brendan, of all people, accuse her of being unloving? He knew how she loved her children, how much her friends meant to her. And he could'nt doubt her affection for him, for she'd proved it a hundred times.

But she knew without asking that love for children and friends was not what Brendan meant. No, he meant that passion that so enthralled him and his mistresses. Well, it was true she and Edward did not share that, the sort of love that blazed brightly then flared out all too quickly. But they shared a great deal more: common interests, common values, common goals. That sharing would last much longer than Tressilian's sort of love.

With a conscious effort of will, she pushed his brutal comment into a dark secret part of her mind, where it cowered with all the cruel observations her parents and governesses and husband had said to hurt her. Then, having arrested her miscreant thoughts and interned them in her mind's goal, she was able to respond to Tressilian as the orchestra finally faded. Her eyes were serene, her voice low and pleasant. "Thank you for the dance. Now if you'll return me to my seat...."

Her serenity was vindication in itself. He had hurt her, but she would not let him know it. So she took his arm to find his muscles rigid with his anger and was glad.

Becky, her face aglow with anticipation, was bouncing only a few feet away. With a light laugh, Kristen led him over. "Come meet my cousin. As you can ell, she has been longing to boast of making your acquaintance."

But her serenity vanished when, with a curt word Tressilian carried off a joyful Becky to dance.

# CHAPTER NINE

Tressilian scarcely noticed his new partner, so occupied was he in brooding over his exchange with Kristen. He never meant to show his anger to her, but then he d never had much control over his extreme emotions. And lately his emotions were all extreme.

Seeing her with that dead bore Stamberly enraged him quite out of proportion. For Kristen was right. She was an independent woman; she needn't vet her decisions with anyone else. It was just unfair that she never took advantage of this freedom to do anything but the conventional.

Tressilian was unused to considering convention, but he supposed a match with the vacuous viscount was conventionally laudable. Certainly that was what Kristen's boring matronly friends must be telling her. But then those conventional friends must never have noticed how closely Stamberly resembled the porridge nurses forced on innocent children— bland, unpalatable, and lumpy.

Tressilian wished he could deal with the viscount as he had always dealt with porridge, by throwing it out the window. But murdering a peer would probably do what cuckolding an admiral hadn't— truly ruin his navy career. Then again, he thought as he scowled at the peer in question, it might yet be worth it.

Tressilian had felt the same distaste for Kristen's first husband, for Killeaven was also a bore, posing on forever about the hunt. Neither of them had the least amount of spirit, or romance, or passion. And apparently Kristen preferred it that way.

He shouldn't have insulted her, of course. It was just that she deserved better from life, and she could have better, if she would only let herself accept it.

But Kristen had a puritan soul, and no matter how he tried, he had never been able to change that.

Tense as he was, he found the strains of the waltz oddly soothing, as was the elfin figure of the girl in his arms.

For the first time, he looked down at her, noting with distant appreciation the pouting mouth, the dancing blue eyes, the adorable spray of freckles across the snub nose.

She was a gamine girl, with a bright eager air that made him feel old of a sudden. I used to be like that, he recalled, excited by life. And it was his duty, he supposed, to give her a bit to be excited about. "You're very pretty." Unfortunately, her name had slipped his mind, so he compensated by addressing her with the same careless endearment he used with laundresses. "Sweetheart. Especially tonight."

Debutantes generally swooned away helpless in his arms, something that always made him lament whatever meager scruples kept him from seducing innocents. But this girl— Becky! he recollected triumphantly— only grinned saucily. "How do you know I'm not this pretty every night?"

"You couldn't be," he replied with automatic, if sincere, gallantry. "For were you always so radiant, we'd none of us men get any rest. We'd be too busy adoring you."

Becky sighed in utter transports of delight, her face lifted up like a flower to the sun. "Oh, I'd hoped you'd say something like that! But perhaps you could repeat it? I don't think I memorized it word-perfect." She clicked her tongue ruefully. "I should have brought a pencil so I could write each compliment down."

Her doleful frown diverted him from his depressing thoughts. "Why would you want to write anything down?"

For the first time ever perhaps, Tressilian saw pity in the eyes of a dance partner. He decided, on contemplation, that he rather liked it. At least it was a change, and so was this Becky's version of a flirtation. "You are very handsome, you know, but you are not very perspicacious."

"Perspicacious?" He had to laugh at her superior look and her five-guinea words. "No, no one has ever accused me of perspicacity, now that I think on it. But why do you say I lack it?"

Impatience pursed her pretty mouth in a school marmish way he found particularly amusing. In fact, he found everything about this girl amusing, from the Juliet cap tipped rakishly over her ear to her little slippered feet tapping in rhythm even as they danced. "I will explain. But you must promise then to resume flirting with me, for we haven't much time to left in our dance, and I don't want to waste it on explanations."

Tressilian found with some surprise that he wasn't ready to release Becky just yet. She distracted him so well he wished he could bottle her and her effervescent absurdity to take home with him. "I could always ask you for another dance. I'll even find a pencil for you, in case you want to note down my every word— but on what? Your petticoat?"

His audacity made her gasp, but with delight, not horror. "Oh, I could die! You are so improper! Just as I have dreamed!"

Tressilian might pass this nonsense off to the giddiness he often inspired in girls of an impressionable age. Except this girl's blue eyes were bright with curiosity, not coquettry. And her disjointed declarations indicated an impersonal admiration, as if he weren't a person so much as— as a monument. A famous church, perhaps, or equestrian statue. That was disconcerting, but novel enough to intrigue him. "You still haven't explained. Recall my lack of— of what? I forget what you call it."

"Perspicacity. I note a lamentable memory also." Those pretty eyes were full of sympathy; she even squeezed his hand to show she didn't hold it against him. "I want to remember every word you say, for I'm going to write a novel. And you are the model for my hero. Of course, my hero won't be so— so un-perspicacious as you. In fact, I mean for him to be intelligent. But he will look just like you, and say improper things in improper tones to proper girls, just as you do." Her brow furrowed in a frown. "But that sounds more like the villain, doesn't it, trying to seduce the innocent heroine with his honeyed words."

Tressilian was a masterful dancer, but at this last he missed a step. Becky observed this eagerly. "Oh, you nearly stumbled there. It must be a guilty conscience! Oh, I wish I had a pencil!"

"It was not a guilty conscience," he insisted, trying to regain control of the conversation as he regained control of his feet. "And I want it understood that I am not trying to seduce any innocent heroine. Not that you are the least innocent, you little minx. And I'm not a villain. I've always been the hero in the novels that have featured me."

"Then making you the villain would be an astute move, don't you think? It would set my novel apart from all the others." She beamed up at him as if she had just discovered a comet in his eyes. "Oh, you will make a perfect villain, I know. A pirate! Weren't you captured by Jean Lafitte and held prisoner at his island kingdom?"

"A couple years ago. But I didn't become a pirate," he pointed out a little righteously. He bent his head to indicate the white Maltese cross on his collar riband, the symbol of the Knights of Bath, ample proof, he hoped, of his un-villainy. But honesty compelled him to admit, "Lafitte did think I had great potential for piracy. And I suppose, if I'd lost that game of faro, I would've had to hoist the Jolly Roger after all."

"What faro game?"

"It came down to that, you see. The island was pleasant enough, but I was getting restless. So we decided to settle it with a game of cards. If I won, I went free. If he won, I would be given one of his ships and join his pirate fleet."

"You won?" Becky's disappointment was palpable, and Tressilian knew he had been lessened in her regard, Knight of Bath or no.

"I'm sorry." After a little while he rallied, envisioning an alternative outcome. "Your hero— villain— could lose the card game, and take to the Spanish Main."

He was absurdly pleased to find himself back in her good graces. "Oh, how dramatic it would be! Your freedom— your very soul!—lost by the turn of a card! And you eventually overthrow Lafitte and take over his pirate kingdom!"

Loath to corral her creativity, which bordered on the awe- inspiring, Tressilian pointed out gently, "Lafitte is still alive, sweeting, and we do meet occasionally. I should like to keep our relations friendly, if you please. Perhaps you might change the pirate king's name, if I am to usurp his throne."

Becky nodded sagely. "A worthy suggestion. And I will need your help with technical details, like what a pirate boat is like."

Tressilian flinched. "Ship. Pirate ship. A boat can fit on a ship, you see."

Becky shrugged off this essential distinction with the nonchalance of a landlubber. "That's just the sort of item I might need help with. In fact, we should collaborate on the novel! Then I wouldn't have to worry that you would sue me for libel."

Because he knew she would love it, Tressilian let his voice go husky and low. "But I can't imagine anything more appealing than-than litigating with you, my darling."

"Oh, you are so wicked," she sighed, her eyes glowing with renewed respect. "Litigating with me— you are just as diabolical as I'd hoped you would be. It's so seldom that mythical creatures live up to their legends, you know."

"So I've reached the stature of myth, have I? You know, Becky, my very own, I've never met a girl like you before."

"Of course you haven't," she replied with complacent pride. "I'm an original. I've worked very hard at it, and I do think I've succeeded. I must have, if you think so, for I imagine you've known untold thousands of women quite intimately."

"Then you have a lurid imagination," he chided. "Untold indeed. But did they total a million, sweeting, you would stand out in my memory. For none has ever examined me quite as— as speculatively as you have, as if you were a botanist and I some exotic weed."

"No, I suppose you are more used to outright lust," she observed, and he choked on a laugh and started coughing. "Oh, look at the attention we are drawing!" she crowed, as he felt the new scar on his chest ripping apart. "Everyone will think I planted you one in the solar plexus in strenuous defense of my virtue!"

He had to stop dancing and collapse onto a convenient couch, convulsed with laughter and coughing.

Becky perched beside him, patting his hand and assuring him, "You may take me into supper, then, for it's clear you won't be able to complete this dance. And don't worry, Brendan, I shan't put this little episode into my novel, for it really doesn't do you much credit, collapsing like this with half the evening remaining. Of course," she added thoughtfully, "I could portray it as a result of your opium habit."

He decided then he was the one needing a pencil, so that he could note down all his objections to her last comments to be read aloud whenever he managed to stop laughing. First, she shouldn't be calling him by his Christian name, even if he had addressed her far more familiarly— that sort of impropriety was expected of him. And second, he had no opium habit, disappointing as such a confession was bound to be. And third-

But just then he looked up to see Kristen floating by. Stamberly had finally gotten his dance. Becky traced the direction of his scowl and started patting his hand again. "Yes, I know. It's just terrible, isn't it? And you are so much handsomer and more dashing than Stamberly."

Tressilian tore his eyes away from Kristen to regard Becky with his own speculation. She was not just an original, she was also blessed with a superb understanding of human nature. "Is Kristen really going to marry that dull stick?"

Becky scrunched up her freckled nose in distaste. "I'm afraid she is.

And it's just lamentable. She doesn't love him. I think one should always marry for love, unless one is direly poor, or with child by some unscrupulous rogue who runs off, don't you think?"

Tressilian assumed a virtuous expression for the benefit of the multitudes observing them so avidly. "A loveless marriage," he remarked, as if he had not frequently benefited from just such an institution, "destroys the sanctity of the marriage act."

He was rather surprised that she let this pass, for even he saw a bit of humor in hearing Brendan Trevarrick affirm the sanctity of the marriage act. But Becky was just his sort of rogue and did not cavil at a bit of hypocrisy in pursuit of a higher goal. "Just so. But Kristen— well, she doesn't trust enough to love, so she must choose a man who won't demand it of her."

This insight was so brilliant he couldn't absorb it all at once. So he remained unprecedentedly silent until they were settled in a secluded corner of the supper room with five plates of Italian ice— they even had identical taste in supper food. Then he raised an imperious hand and asked of the footman who appeared, "Do you know where Cannon keeps his smuggled brandy? Bring me a bottle, old man." He tossed the man a sovereign. "Wait. What do young girls drink? Lemonade?"

"Champagne," Becky said dulcetly, taking a dainty bite of her ice.

Tressilian shrugged his capitulation. "Champagne then. So you are opposed to this prospective match?"

"Oh, indubitably. Kristen needs a strong man, you see, someone who loves her desperately enough to overcome her fears." She polished off her first dish of ice, dragging her spoon against the bottom to catch up the last drops.

His nerves set on edge by the scraping sound, Tressilian tugged the empty dish from her hand and handed her a full one. "I suppose you have a candidate for that fortunate position?"

Becky hesitated with the spoon at her pouting lower lip. She savored the lemon ice thoughtfully before observing, "Well, as soon as I saw you, I knew you would be perfect for my hero— my villain now— and also for Kristen. You are in love with her, aren't you?"

Those words echoed in Tressilian's mind like the sonorous bells of St.

Paul's, and he welcomed the diversion of the footman with Cannon's superb brandy. But eventually he had to listen to the echoes again and reply reluctantly, "I've never actually thought of it like that. Do you think that's what it is?"

"That would give you a reason to down that brandy in one gulp, at least." Becky watched with interest as he refilled his glass. "Are you foxed yet? I hope not, for I don't want to be so distracted when I observe how a villain behaves caught in the toils of wicked liquor."

"I think you haven't any room to judge, young lady, since you're drinking that champagne as if it were lemonade after all."

Becky, who had been wrinkling her nose delightedly at the ticklish bubbles, finished up her champagne in a single flick of the wrist and hid her empty glass on the bench behind her. Then she adroitly changed the subject. "I knew you were in love with her. I always thought it was havey-cavey, all this talk of friendship. You are surely too hot-blooded for that, aren't you? It does sound just like Kristen, though, to look at you and see only your most virtuous qualities. A sad waste."

Tressilian was driven to defend his friend and their friendship and his most virtuous qualities. "No, no, it was refreshing, actually, for no one else had ever seen any virtue in me before."

With silken irony, he commented, "Most people see only vice— vice and villainy— while she was, shall we say, perspicacious enough to see virtue. Besides," he added prosaically, "I had no choice. We couldn't be anything else to each other, for she wasn't seducible, at least under any conditions I could imagine. I knew I wasn't ready to be— oh, mature and responsible and faithful." He flushed as he said those words, as if they were profanities.

"But now you are," Becky prompted.

"I don't know." He stirred his lemon ice into soupy mess, then set it down on the side table. Becky pounced on it and made it her own. "And if I am, what good is it, for she'll never believe it of me. I've got a reputation as a reprobate—"

"Entirely undeserved, I'm certain," Becky put in.

Tressilian regarded her warily. In his extensive experience, most women only discovered irony on their wedding night. But he suspected the precocious Becky was blaming him. "It wouldn't be any use pretending that. Kristen knows me too well to believe me innocent of any charges at all." He gazed unseeing at the crowd around the supper table, oblivious equally to the wounded pout of Andrea and the enticing smiles of another redhead. "I never cared about living the right way, you know. I used to just live, chasing what ever adventure lay ahead. And I loved it. But that doesn't work anymore. Nothing works anymore. Even the women have become more trouble than they're worth." That sentiment made him wince, for it sounded rather like something Admiral Destain would say. But then Andrea passed out of the room, her head bowed, her hand trailing a bit of lace handkerchief, doubtlessly sodden with her tears. "Either she ruins my career or I ruin her life."

Becky watched Andrea's departure with a definitely ironical gaze. "That could have something to do with the women you choose."

Nothing was that simple in Tressilian's universe, for his was, after all, a life of destiny. He might not be a regular churchgoer, but he had the seafarer's belief in omens. "No, I realize now that it's all Divine Providence. I'm being warned, you see. That musket ball I took last fall— that was a sign from above."

This spiritual revelation inspired Becky right out of her sarcasm. "Oh, that's just perfect! The villain receives a sign from God that he must change his ways, and then he reforms and becomes the hero!"

Tressilian was offended, for, having poured out his heart to this girl, he didn't like hearing his tragedy turned into a morality play. Very much on his dignity, he drew himself up and remarked, "I am pleased that I can provide you with such a plot resolution."

Oblivious to any irony but her own, Becky replied gaily, "Oh, but that's not the resolution! The plot cannot be resolved until you get your reward by winning the heart of the virtuous maiden."

That sounded more the thing, but Tressilian had not read many novels of this sort, and was wary of plot twists. "Kristen?"

"Of course! And you'll live happily ever after. But we will have to come up with a plan. Are you very good at plans?"

Becky's optimism could not fail to infect him, as he was also of a naturally sunny disposition. And the idea of a plan appealed to the military in him. "I've always thought so. But the admiral tells me that my strategies are unnecessarily elaborate."

"So are mine! Think what a scheme we'll come up with together!"

They clasped hands in perfect amity, and Tressilian dared to press a kiss on her little palm. She withdrew her hand hastily and fixed him with a admonitory stare. "Now that's quite enough of that. You will never convince Kristen that you will be a trustworthy husband if you go about kissing women in such a way."

He shrugged without much penitence. "Force of habit. Now what about this plan of ours? Let's start with our goal." "To untangle Kristen from him, and entangle her with you."

It sounded remarkably seductive, put that way, and Tressilian almost smiled. But then reality intruded, as it always seemed to these days. "She doesn't think of me that way, you know. After tonight, she might not even speak to me again."

"Well, we will just have to make her see you in a new light. You must show her you are ready to give up your wild ways and settle down to married bliss. You are ready, aren't you?"

He stared down into the amber depths of his glass. "If I can marry Kristen. Otherwise, I'll probably be wilder than ever."

"Oh, dear," Becky murmured, her piquant little face reflecting her fear of what a wilder Tressilian might be. "I think, for the sake of the nation, we'd best convince Kristen to marry you. And she will, I know. No woman's refused you yet, I'll wager."

"You'd lose," Tressilian said, recalling that distant night near the abbey ruins. "Kristen did."

"You've already proposed to her?" Becky's dismay was comic, for she hated to know the denouement even before the drama began.

"Of course not. I've never proposed to anyone," he replied dampingly. "I'm a rakehell, recall? We try only to seduce ladies."

"Well, then, that's all right. For she hasn't actually turned you down. She could never agree to be seduced, for she has very strict morals. Baffling, isn't it?"

Tressilian found himself laughing again. "Lord, you're a right one, babe," he was driven to observe. "If my heart weren't already torn from its fortress, I vow I'd fall for you."

Becky blushed with pleasure, but replied with unusual good sense, "We shouldn't suit, I imagine. We're both too romantic. Probably the bills would never get paid and we would end up in debtors' prison. Now we must get on with our plan."

Emboldened by his confederate's confidence, Tressilian said speculatively, "You know, I've had some experience with women—"

"So I've heard," Becky interrupted daringly.

"Mind your tongue, young lady. It seems to me that even the most sensible of women— and you'll agree that Kristen is the most sensible of women— is susceptible to jealousy. I don't know why," he added, as if he himself weren't at that very moment rusting away from jealousy himself. "But it's true. Of course, that would only serve if Kristen harbors some fond feelings for me."

"Oh, she does!" Becky cried. "She was simply distraught last Christmas when you were injured."

"She was, wasn't she? Perhaps I should get shot again and linger at death's door for a month or so."

"No, that isn't a very good idea. What if you didn't recover this time? Let's investigate your other idea further— making her jealous by making love to another woman."

"Well, I've been doing that all along, haven't I, with no discernible result." He rose and in a single motion pulled Becky to her feet. They strolled back into the ballroom, both with identical frowns of concentration.

For a moment they watched the swirl of dancers, then Tressilian tilted his head inquiringly to the side. "Now if I were to become betrothed to another woman...."

Becky drew her breath in sharply and dug her fingers into the earl's arm. "Oh, that's brilliant. You will show her then that you want to give up your bachelor life. And that you can be trustworthy and faithful. And that she must start thinking of you as husband- material, if only for someone else. And— and, oh, and you will make her jealous! Oh, what a lovely scheme! She will know you are serious about reforming then! But—" Tressilian braced himself. "But what?"

"But your betrothed would have to know that you

weren't in fact serious."

Higher morality being lost on the earl, he had to ask, "Why?"

"Because it wouldn't be fair to let her think you wanted to marry her truly. Because you will be jilting her when Kristen comes to her senses."

Tressilian had been jilting women since he was twelve and threw over his headmaster's wife for a pert chambermaid. But he agreed that breaking an engagement transgressed even his remote limits. "But I can hardly ask a woman to marry me, then tell her about our plan. She'd never go along with it."

"Oh, I don't know," Becky said admiringly. "I'll wager you car get nearly any woman to do nearly anything you want. But we won't need to test that, for I think I can solve your problem."

Tressilian flashed a smile, feeling immeasurably better now that this minx had taken him in hand. "I think we'll deal very well together. Let me take you driving tomorrow- - about eleven, shall we say? And we'll perfect our plans then. Kristen probably thinks I've abducted you by now, so you'd best go reassure her. Damn, here comes Andrea."

"She," Becky remarked, already with a fiancee's proprietary attitude, "has got to go."

Brendan looked regretfully at the woman's coppery head and agreed. "Don't forget about our drive. I hope Kristen will let you associate with a reprobate like me, or all is lost."

Becky vowed she could work Kristen around to agreeing to anything, and, with a last jaunty wave, slipped off into the crowd.

# Chapter Ten

He broke off with Andrea that night. It was a measure of his charm— or his long practice— that after a storm of tears, she agreed that he was right. Of course he had to marry, and of course her children needed her, but she would always long for her handsome sailor.

The solace of another woman now denied him, he took refuge in brandy. At White's, he ignored the jovial greetings of his fellows and flung open the door of the parlor he and Jon considered their own. With a scowl, he dismissed the buck lounging on his overstuffed chair and the two Corinthians defiling Jon's silver-chased darts. We must see about that plaque, he told himself as he did whenever he found this sanctum occupied.

But even without the plaque, the influence of the two cousins was clear. They had personalized the room over the years to reflect their opposite but complementary characters. A portrait of Marlborough, Jon's favorite bay stallion, replaced the commonplace hunting print over the mantle, and a model of the Defiant graced the walnut sideboard. A cavalry sword hung on one wall; opposite was the pair of duelling pistols Tressilian seldom got to use anymore.

Jon's leather couch angled before the fire, so he could doze without fear of drafts. And Tressilian's chair sat near the window, so he could prop his feet up on the sill and toss ice chips out at the pedestrians below.

The room's most cherished feature, however, was the teak cabinet fashioned in India a century ago, now harboring the finest brandy in Britain. Tressilian felt along the top of the doorframe— dusty, he noted with displeasure— for the small gold key that opened the lock.

The brandy so secured was spoils of war, confiscated from the captain's cabin of French warships the Defiant had taken over the years. Tressilian divided among his crew his lion's share of the prize money their ship earned— one way to keep a company loyal, as he hardly needed the funds— but the brandy he kept for himself. He'd collected a lifetime's supply, even at the rate he was plowing through it these last weeks.

He settled in the armchair, crystal glass in hand, brandy bottle at his elbow, feet propped up on the sill. From the open window he could view the lights of Mayfair and hear the clatter of carriages in St. James Street. It was not as peaceful as his quarter-deck at midnight, but would have to serve for the duration.

His wild hope was wearing off now that he was out of Becky's effervescent presence. She found it easy to persuade him that Kristen could indeed be his. But now, as he stared moodily out at the darkness, her optimism seemed misplaced.

He had no great powers of perception, but he did know how women behaved when they wanted him. And Kristen had never behaved that way. In five years, she had never indicated that she wanted from him any more than the friendship that they had always shared, and that suddenly seemed so inadequate. She would never consider marrying him.

Women didn't marry men like Tressilian, after all, not if they had any claim on sense. Sensible women married men like Stamberly, who were already broken to harness. Tressilian was wild in too many ways: He was reckless, finding his greatest fulfillment in defying death. He was irresponsible, lacking any sense of duty. He was a hedonist, seeking sensuality and sensation. And he was often enough dishonorable, taking other men's wives, fighting and winning duels when he knew he was in the wrong.

He was other things also— a good leader of men, even disciplined in certain situations. But he was at his best only on the deck of a ship, when three hundred men depended on him for their lives. On land he was the man Kristen could not even imagine marrying.

But he could change. He already had, over the years. Perhaps he was growing up finally, contrary to all expectations. Lately he had been forced to consider the consequences of his actions and even, occasionally, to take those consequences into account. He was even looking back at his reckless life and imagining that he might live it differently in the future.

Until this last year, he'd had little cause to regret his life. But now that the most important part of his life, his navy career, was going to be stripped from him, he realized how little else he had. The title meant less than nothing to him: If he weren't a earl he'd be sailing now. His Devon estate held happy enough memories, but would never seem as much a home as the quarter-deck. His friends counted for something, for they kept him entertained, although he wondered how many of them would stay around if he weren't so entertaining himself.

And the women, oh, the women. He'd loved them each for a moment, and none for more than a moment. Not one, he realized, truly knew him, as opposed to the romantic hero each crafted for herself and named Tressilian. Ironic it was, that he could have any woman he wanted, except the one he really wanted, because that one knew him too well to take him.

Jerkily he poured out another drink but only held the glass then, watching the candlelight flicker in reflection in the brandy. Other men had families to give their lives meaning, brothers and sisters and parents and grandparents. But the Trevarrick family was just a bad joke, a dozen men who had filed writs with the Committee for Privileges of the House of Lords, claiming to be long-lost Trevarrick cousins. Of course, he did have real cousins in the Destains. But fond as he was of each Destain individually, he thought now they weren't truly a family, at least not any longer.

The only family he had was the family he built for himself, his ship's company, and they would soon enough have another captain. And then, of course, there was Kristen's family.

He'd claimed them early as his own, though he had never been foolish enough to tell Kristen. She was too cautious to knowingly let him get so attached to her children. But he'd known them since they were babies: the handsome, swaggering Nicholas, and mischievous Corinna. Tressilian had had a hand in rearing them, for he'd taught them to ride and to play hazard and to navigate by the stars. And he felt a stab of jealousy to think of Stamberly calling himself their father, when he was as like them as castor oil was like cordial.

Lost in his melancholy, Tressilian did not hear the door open. But he ducked instinctively as a silver dart whizzed past his ear to impale itself, vibrating, in the window frame. "Had I been a cannibal tribesman, my boy, you'd be stew now."

Tressilian rose, rubbing his ringing ear, and held out his other hand. "Welcome back. Your aim hasn't failed you, I see."

Jon gripped his hand then reached for the brandy. "I've been dreaming of this stuff. The case you brought to the camp in Torres Vedras lasted only a month or so, once Wellington discovered I was hiding it. I'll take some back, if I may. Might inspire the general." He dropped onto his couch, regarding his cousin over the rim of his glass. "You look better than last I saw you."

"You look worse. You are going back to the Peninsula then?"

"In June, if the medicos pronounce me fit. Just a cold, but it wouldn't go away." Jon took a sip of his brandy and sighed as it slid down his throat. "Spent most of February in a tent. The winter was so damp— I couldn't seem to catch my breath, you know. And, as I said, I'd run out of your elixir here."

"But you're better now? You're sure? Let me hear you cough," Tressilian persisted, having seen too many sailors invalidate out with consumption to trust the diagnosis "just a cold".

Jon coughed obligingly, a dry hack that sounded reassuringly like the grippe's last stand. "Do I pass, Doctor Trevarrick?"

"You still look weary unto death. But then you always do."

Destain accepted this without rancor, for he was, in fact, the world-weary sort, though his friends just called him lazy. In fact, his heroic regimental uniform was the most dashing thing about him. For dashing was not something Captain Destain ever liked to do.

Oh, he had all the requirements for dash: the uniform, the looks, the wit. He was a slim, handsome man, with deep blue eyes and well-honed features under a shock of sun-streaked blond hair. And he used that noble face well; he was an expert at raising an eyebrow or quirking the corner of his mouth to express much with little movement. He cultivated a slow drawl and a sharp wit that intimidated more than the sword the Royal Army required him to carry. It was said that his insults were so silken they were prized by men, and his compliments so velvety they were mistrusted by women.

But all the correct equipment for dash couldn't overcome his only fault, that cynical indolence that nearly paralyzed him on bad days. Tressilian used to argue that Jon's life would be measurably improved if he just stirred himself now and again— to avail himself of a few of the ladies who admired his charm and grace, for example.

But Jon preferred to drift along with inertia his only guide. Life changes usually weren't worth the effort when one had no ideal life to change to. So he never bothered to change his long-time mistress Lady Elise Winterleigh, though she bored him outside of bed. Just as well, for, as the admiral once told Tressilian, "I think the sluggard's favorite activities all take place in bed."

Even the admiral's enemy General Wellington, who liked the young captain, agreed that Jon might be too fond of that piece of furniture. He informed Destain that his transfer from a line regiment to the general staff was not due to his brilliant mind, though that didn't hurt. "But it isn't good for the troops' morale to have their squadron commander sleeping till noon every day."

Indeed, had Jon continued on his way eight years ago, he would doubtlessly still be at Oxford, the oldest living undergraduate, aimlessly meandering through lectures, assessing with his jaundiced eye each new tutor's style. But such a prospect had horrified Tressilian, who plied Jon with liquor, dragged him down to the Horse Guards, lent him the money to buy his commission, and even held him up while he signed the contract.

Fortunately Destain was not one to change directions once a course had been chosen for him. He was perfectly content to remain in Wellington's entourage until Bogey was routed. It was, as his father said, Jon s sort of war: an occasional battle followed by months of cardplaying and dart games in camp.

But invalid leave in London suited him even better. For this was the life he had expected to live before Tressilian dragged him into the war. Mellow days lay ahead now for Jon Destain: mornings in bed, luncheons at the club, afternoons showing off his uniform and equestrian skills in the park, evenings in a comfortable chair in front of a card table. After four years of privation on the Peninsula, Destain always longed for a bit of peace and plenty.

So only his enormous affection for his boyhood companion could have brought him here to their old haunt. For Tressilian was the least peaceful of friends with his duels and practical jokes and pre-dawn curricle races to Brighton. Somehow Jon, despite his best intentions to stay in bed, always ended up climbing through windows or seconding duels or clinging to a handstrap while reading the race map. That was, after all, as Tressilian never failed to point out, what friends were for.

Tressilian felt that measuring gaze on him and turned from the window, feeling somehow guilty. He had always sensed that his cousin didn't enjoy their friendship quite as well as Tressilian did, but then, Jon moved slower and thus was the one usually captured by the authorities. And Destain never took adventure with quite the right spirit. Even the war, the greatest adventure of the century, which Jon got to join only with his cousin's help, didn't light much of a fire in his heart.

Tressilian felt a sharp envy that Jon had a war to go back to, however dilatory the army's progress. "How's the war going?"

"Same as ever. We've got back the south of Spain, you know. Wellington's got some secret plan to drive the French the rest of the way out, but he hasn't favored us with it yet."

"Likely hasn't conceived it yet," Tressilian said caustically.

Jon's eyes narrowed. "Don't start, Bren. I don't allow even you to criticize my commander. Wellington knows what he's about."

"Aye, he knows he's boring the French to death. A brilliant strategy, I agree. Worked so far— Napoleon found the Peninsular war so tedious he decided to enliven his life by invading Russia."

"All part of the general's plan," Jon murmured. "Bogey left most of his army there in the snow. See what impatience can do to you?" He propped himself up on his elbow, nodding significantly. "Not that you'll ever figure that out. I heard about your collision with Admiral Bellingham's wife. Now you're on invalid leave, they say, for ever and ever, though you look perfectly fit. I wonder if there might be a connection."

"If you would ever deign to talk to your father, you'd have learned that Mrs. Bellingham and her blasted divorce had nothing to do with this." Tressilian's eyes flared dangerously as he remembered his conversation with the admiral. "It's the succession, you see. As if I give a tinker's damn about the earldom."

"You've never given a tinker's damn about anything but that damn ship of yours. So what are you going to do to get it back?"

"Oh, I'm like Wellington. I have a secret plan." Tressilian's mercurial spirits were raised again by Destain's timely arrival. He cocked his head mysteriously, but his friend was not amused.

"Just what we need, one of your famous plans. I think I'll go back to Spain early; it's safer there than here with you and your plans." Despite his harsh words, Destain made no attempt to rise, only regarding the earl balefully from his sanctuary on the couch.

"You'd never have gotten to Spain if I hadn't hired that orchestra to play 'God Save the King' over and over until you decided to buy your colors. One of my most successful plans, you'll recall, for here you are, still in the 16th Light."

"And still disowned." In unusual accord, they both groaned, recalling Lord Destain's reaction to his son's mutiny. "You might have reminded me how the admiral hates the cavalry. Not that he'd countenance his heir in the uniform of any army regiment, but the cavalry took the crown. No, don't tell me how I've benefited from your plans, Bren, for I think I've always been the victim."

Laughing at his cousin's fervency, Tressilian tried to recollect at least one plan of his which hadn't victimized Jon. Twenty-eight years— surely Jon had benefited at least once from his elder cousin's machinations. "You got to see Casablanca," he finally offered.

"Aye, such a brilliant scheme that was, to stowaway to America so we could make our fortune. Only this frigate was bound for Morocco. And you couldn't keep your mouth shut and got discovered—"

"And you fell asleep and didn't—"

"And— and ten years old, I was, and all alone with those cutthroats." Even now, Jon's voice was disbelieving, and Tressilian realized yet again how little his friend understood about adventure. "Lucky I was the captain knew my old man, or I would've been sharkbait for certain. And the admiral wonders why I never joined the navy."

"Well, I would have loved every moment of it," Tressilian said with utter sincerity. "That was the saddest moment of my life, I think, watching that ship disappear over the horizon." Jon's choking sound recalled him to the present. "So you didn't enjoy it as you should have done. Is that my fault?"

Jon found arguing a worthless activity, but he couldn't let Tressilian's assumption of innocence pass without a fight. "Yes. It's always your fault. You were the one got me bunked from Econ—"

"That's unfair. You agreed every step of the way," Tressilian retorted. "You agreed that we needed a race horse, and you agreed that a casino was just the right enterprise to engender the ready. You must admit, you have always been proud to claim the title of the youngest student ever expelled from Econ."

"Twelve years, two months, and four days old." Grudgingly, Jon raised his glass to himself. "I hold the distinction even today, while you have to content yourself with merely being the second youngest to be bunked. I imagine it's the only time I've ever bested you." Then he shook his head. "But even that was a disaster. I ended up at Harrow." He endowed that name with all the loathing a parson might reserve for the mention of hell. "Of course, Harrow wasn't good enough for you. Oh, no, you had to run off to sea on my father's ship!"

Tressilian shrugged. "I knew he wouldn't send me back. In fact, he was glad, when he stopped throwing grappling hooks at me."

Their acquaintances always marveled that the unsentimental Destain remained so loyal to his very different cousin. And, had he been allowed the choice initially, little Jonathan might very well have foregone the pleasure of little Brendan's company. But Jon was still in the womb when Lady Destain stood over her cousin's deathbed and rashly promised to watch after the Trevarrick orphan. They were doomed to friendship from the first.

But, were they more similar, the two might never have remained friends. For they had never become rivals, having little in common to inspire competition. Instead, each learned to rely on the other's strengths.

Brendan was the more imaginative of the two, so he devised their elaborate games; Jon, the more intelligent, got them out of the trouble those games always caused. Brendan was always the romantic, modeling himself on heroes of old like King Arthur and Robin Hood; Jon was a modern cynic, viewing history as a series of stupid mistakes made by stupid men like those same heroes. He was quick to puncture Brendan's more absurd illusions about the life; Tressilian, for his part, dragged his protesting cousin into adventure and forced him to have fun.

As they entered manhood, their contrary natures led to divergent lives and individual circles of friends. But their childhood affection was strong, and they remained each other's best comrade. Each knew without speaking that their friendship would never wear out, no matter how different they became.

So Jon, however he might complain, knew he would doubtlessly have to arrive in time to save his friend from the consequences of this latest secret plan. And he knew Tressilian knew it too. "I expect it's the price I pay for your charming company. But I give you notice right now, I won't second you in any more duels. Rising at four in the morning is not my favorite way to spend the night."

Hand on heart, Tressilian swore he had no duels planned, although one never knew what might come up. "There's some alligator named Evelyn who keeps telling me he's my cousin. I might have to rid the world of him."

"Why he'd want to be your cousin, I can't imagine. Our connection's never been anything but trouble to me— no, Bren, don't you start looking hurt. You know I didn't mean it; I just forget how sensitive you are." To make amends, Jon kicked his cousin's knee with the toe of one gleaming Hessian and admitted, "I wouldn't trade you for any other lunatic in the entire world."

Such unwonted sentimentality threatened to choke him, so he quickly returned to practical matters. "So does this Evelyn fellow have a good claim?"

Tressilian growled, "So my solicitor tells me. Do you think I should find a more loyal solicitor?"

Jon pointed out that the firm of Lebrett Fane had served the Trevarrick family for three generations and would have little reason to misrepresent the gravity of the situation.

"I reckon you're right. He claims his great-great-grandmother married my great-great-grandfather two months before he died."

"Great-great? The eighth earl then? Alexander?" It was no surprise Jon knew about old Alexander. Nearly a century after his death, Devon gossips still relished tales of the devil earl. Brendan had always taken comfort that no matter how bad he was, Alexander Trevarrick had him beat hollow. "This ancestress wasn't the maid he was sticking when he stuck his spoon in the wall, was it?"

"No. That poor girl went mad the next day and hanged herself in the barn at the Aberdeen estate. Seventeen, she was. Still haunts the place, or so the stableboys there always said. No, this was the housekeeper, as far as Lebrett can determine. Had a penchant for the lower orders, did old Alexander. My own great-great-grandmother started life as the gardener's daughter."

Moodily he rose to poke an andiron into the fire, stirring up a shower of golden sparks. "In any event, this Rutherford has the marriage lines. And the parish registry of the housekeeper's child's baptism. Eight months after Alexander exited the stage in such an enviable fashion. At eighty-four!" Recalling the admiral's warning about the limits of virility, he added defensively, "Makes me proud to be a Trevarrick, it does."

Jon shook his head, less with admiration than incredulity. "Eighty-four and stepping out on his wife. You'd think he'd give it a break— of course, that doesn't mean he was responsible for the housekeeper's progeny. Just because the old rifler could shoot doesn't mean he could still hit the target."

Tressilian rose up in predictable defense of his famous ancestor. "The child was born ten months after the wedding. And his virility had apparently not diminished—"

"But fertility does diminish with age," Jon interrupted sagely. "That's why everyone looked askance last year when that twenty-year- old marchioness gave forth with the heir to the eighty-year-old marquess. Of course, it didn't help that the babe looked just like her childhood sweetheart, and that she married him with unseemly haste once the old marquess hopped off. Did the old earl acknowledge the child?" "He was long dead. Probably never knew it was incubating." Tressilian squeezed his eyes shut, the better to concentrate on the unfamiliar task of cogitating. "Help me here, Jonny. How can I prove that it wasn't his?"

"You can't," Jon said with brutal candor. "You're not going to scare up some footman to claim parentage of the child, for they've all been dead this past century. And his reputation precedes him— no one will believe the old lecher didn't consummate the marriage. And you, of all people, can't make any bacon casting suspicion on it being a posthumous child, being one yourself."

Tressilian jutted out the square Trevarrick chin as the black Trevarrick eyes flashed dangerously. "But I am demonstrably a Trevarrick. You need only compare me with the portrait of the seventh earl. And the eighth and ninth and tenth— we all look alike. This Evelyn character looks more like a giant sloth. Not at all like a Trevarrick."

"It matters naught what he looks like. A child conceived during a marriage is presumed to be the husband's doing, unless you can prove otherwise." Destain regarded his cousin with some sympathy. "At least if he's named heir, you might be able to rejoin your fleet. A high price to pay, however."

"Too high." The words tasted bitter in his throat. "I guess the title means more than I thought. I've got another scheme."

Destain sighed wearily. "Just remember, I'm due back with the regiment in a couple months. So I don't want to know about your plan to blackmail the Prince Regent—"

"That's an idea," Tressilian said with a thoughtful frown. "It worked well last time, don't you think? But he'd probably only make me First Sea Lord."

Jon was perhaps better acquainted with navy politics even than a sea captain, for he had watched his father claw his way up the ranks. "You'll never make First Lord, do you live to be a century and destroy the French navy single-handed. You've enticed too many Admiralty wives away."

"I don't care, as long as I can sail. That's why I decided to take your papa's advice and get married."

Jon choked on his brandy, and what with his throat already raw from his illness, and Tressilian jumping up and pounding helpfully on his back, it was awhile before he was able to stammer, "Married? Married? You? What woman in her right mind would marry you?"

Insulted, Tressilian leaned against the mantle, his arms crossed over his chest, his chin held high. "There are a few."

"Well, you are a earl, and rich as the devil, and I suppose there are some who would disregard all else— But Bren, well, would you really want to marry the sort of woman who would want to marry you? I mean to say, not to insult you, for you know I love you, but if I had a sister I wouldn't let her near you. I can't think of a worse candidate for leg-shackling than you."

With great dignity, Tressilian said, "That's only because you don't understand the redemptive power of True Love."

This last remark posed another threat to Jon's lungs, and when he finally stopped coughing, he croaked, "True love? True love? That's rich. There's no such thing. Lust, that's all it is. Another redhead's caught your eye and—"

"Her hair isn't red," Tressilian broke in, thinking of Kristen's golden waves. Then he remembered that Becky was his fiancee, poor girl, and rushed to defend her against Jon's implications. "Brown. Her hair is brown. Like a walnut. And she's a very nice girl, and doesn't care a rap about me being a earl and wealthy. She— she sees me as a hero, by God. She wants to change my life. And besides, there is such a thing as true love, no matter what you say. You won't be so cavalier when it happens to you."

Jon tossed off the last of his brandy. "Never will. I'm not a romantic, Bren. I don't believe in that fustian you thrive on— heroism, redemption,

True Love. So she's not even a redhead. Do I get to meet her, or are you going to keep her hidden away so I can't woo her away from you?"

The image of Jon exerting himself to steal away a conquest was enough to send them both into gales of laughter, dissolving the tension that had crackled for a moment between them. Finally Tressilian managed to reply, "You may meet her, if you like. But it's all very secret. I haven't spoken to her father yet."

Jon instantly sobered. "You're not going to elope, are you? I'm not going to look all over town looking for a rope ladder for you to climb up to her window. And I don't know the way to Gretna Green, not that you'd ever do anything so dull as eloping to Gretna Green. Egypt, that's where you'd go. Love among the pyramids." He sat up, swinging his feet down to clatter on the floor, and gazed wonderingly at Brendan. "Do you really mean to marry? Really?"

Tressilian knew a moment's guilt, for he'd never before kept a secret from his best friend. He had tried, often enough, but Jon had always ferreted it out with a minute or two of interrogation. But this time he would remain stalwart, even if tortured, for his plans had gotten Jon into enough trouble over the years. Now his cousin deserved a peaceful convalescence. "Really."

Jon rose to stand swaying against the couch, one arm held out for balance. But his rueful voice wasn't a bit slurred. "I can't wait to meet this girl. We could sell tickets and make our fortune: See the courageous girl sacrifice herself to redeem the rake."

They made their way home as dawn was breaking over St. James Park. Jon sought his bed in his rooms at the Albany, but Tressilian felt rejuvenated by the cool spring air and decided it was too late to retire. Instead, he had a new pair of chestnuts hitched up and drove out to Richmond at a spanking pace that caused wonderment, not to say fear, among those fortunate enough to be on the highway so early. He was back in town in time to bathe and change and drive to Killeaven House to breakfast with the children.

## CHAPTER ELEVEN

"No, Chesley, don't bother the countess," Tressilian told the open-mouthed butler as he took the stairs. "I m here for Miss Marlowe, and I'm early, so I'll just visit the schoolroom first."

He was barely into that spacious room when Nick and Corinna assaulted him, dancing about him, grabbing his arms, going through his pockets. "Cap'n Bren! Cap'n Bren! What did you bring us?"

Blessing the selfishness of children— at least they were honest— he gave them their presents in exchange for his watch, his compass, and the three shillings six they had liberated from his pockets. For Nick, who despite his mother's disapproval planned a glorious navy career, there was a tiny replica of a sloop-of-war, carved in ivory. The more mechanically minded Corinna received an intricate little machine whose main purpose was to make growling noises as it devoured coins put into a slot in its side. The earl ran out of silver demonstrating, and since the hand-printed instructions were in German, one of the few languages he had no working knowledge of, he handed the contraption to Corinna and told her to figure out how to open it. That she did, with admirable dispatch, and they began all over again.

Finally tiring of the game, Tressilian charmed their governess into allowing them all biscuits and milk. They spent a pleasant half hour discussing the great victory at Trafalgar, Tressilian using the materials at hand to demonstrate Nelson's strategy.

Soon the round biscuits, representing British ships, had utterly routed the French square biscuits— or would have' without external interference. "Corey, my love, if you must eat all the warships, decimate Villeneuve's fleet, why don't you?" He wrested the biscuit from between her teeth and said mournfully, "Look, Nelson's flagship has a piece missing from its hull now. It will sink do we not return to Gibraltar directly—"

Corinna only laughed and grabbed up another biscuit, causing the earl to exclaim, "Not the Conqueror! I told you that was my ship!" Nick struggled with her for the prize, and gaining ascendancy, presented the crumbs to its grieving former lieutenant. Tressilian rose and snatched a square biscuit out of Corey's hand and ceremoniously crushed it to bits.

Soon the battle was joined, and in a few moments the floor crunched with the debris of war.

Tressilian brushed crumbs off his uniform and headed for the door. "Well. I m off now."

"But— but Miss Purvy—" Nick waved a hand at the mess the earl had made of the schoolroom.

"Just smile at her, lad, and tell her how pretty she looks this morning, and she'll forgive you anything."

Not yet an accomplished rake, Nick doubted the success of this gambit and muttered "coward" as Tressilian set his hand on the doorknob. The earl's face as he turned was a study in rage. "What did you say, Killeaven?"

Nick chuckled nervously, almost entirely certain that Cap'n Bren was only playacting. "You heard me."

"It's true," Corinna put in loyally, standing straight by her brother. "For you're leaving us to face Miss Purvy's wrath, and that's craven." Craftily she added, "What would Nelson say?"

Tressilian smiled suddenly and held out his hand to them. "He would say that retreat is often the best strategy. But I'll tell you what— I'll come back this afternoon and take you to the Bartholomew Fair to make up for my cowardice. Straight deal?"

Nick advanced and took his hand in a manly grip, and Corinna, not to be outdone, grabbed the other hand. But Tressilian gathered them both squirming in his arms and kissed their still baby-soft cheeks. "Don't be in such a hurry to grow up," he advised, releasing them so they could scrub at their faces with their dirty hands. "It only gets worse."

Kristen, fragile in a lavender muslin morning gown, her golden hair tied back with a lace ribbon, was waiting for him as he came down the stairs. She met him with a tentative smile, and suddenly he forgave her all. "Come, Bren, let's cry peace. We've been friends too long to let a little disagreement come between us."

Tressilian belatedly recalled his role and struck an injured pose, one hand on the newel post and the other on the gold lace over his heart. "I would not let even a major disagreement come between us. You may be sure, whatever your actions, I will always stand your friend."

Though taken aback by this uncompromising speech, Kristen made another attempt to make up. "I suppose I was piqued because you hadn't come to visit, and the children and Becky were plaguing me every hour with your absence, as if it were my fault. But now I understand how upset you must have been with the Admiralty's decision, and I know I wasn't in the least sympathetic as I should have been. Will you forgive me?"

He had to remind himself that she still planned to marry her vacuous viscount; else he would have discarded Becky's plan and gone back to being content with Kristen's mere friendship. But the realization that he had to save her as well as himself from an unhappy future added steel to his resolve and injury to his tone. "There is nothing to forgive. Friends need not apologize and forgive, and we shall, I hope, always be friends, even if after your marriage your husband bars me from your presence."

Kristen's brow furrowed prettily. Apparently it had never occurred to her that a husband might object to her friendship with a notorious rake. Then she shook her head as if dispelling cobwebs. "Don't be silly, Brendan. I choose my own friends. Are you free now? Shall we go for a drive?"

The thought of Stamberly had driven any graciousness right out of Tressilian. So he took a bit of pleasure in replying, "Actually, I came for Becky. I mean, Miss Marlowe."

Kristen drew back, startled, whether by his refusal of her invitation, the proposed jaunt, or his use of her cousin's Christian name he couldn't tell. But she was gracious enough to accept all three. "It is very kind of you, Brendan, to take Becky up like this. You must know nothing else would be so calculated to make her an enormous success. Why, after you took her to supper last night, Becky was surrounded by eligible young men eager to meet the girl who had caught Tressilian's eye."

Fortunately, she misinterpreted his flush. "Oh, Bren, I know you hate being caught out doing something kind. But you are always so generous with children, and it is very sweet of you. I'm sure you must be bored with a debutante—"

"On the contrary," Tressilian was able to protest with perfect honesty. "I find her a most intriguing sort of girl. In fact, I've never met anyone quite like her before."

"Yes, our Becky is an original, as she is forever telling me. But do be wary. She is very anxious to fall in love, and you know how often you are the target of such emotions." Kristen cast a quelling eye at the chambermaid leaning weakly against the door to the kitchens, clutching a feather duster to her meager chest and gazing worshipfully at the earl. "Becky assures me, however, that she can only love a man with a white horse, so perhaps, till I get her safely betrothed, you might stick with your black?"

Tressilian promised not to purchase a white horse— "They tend toward weaknesses of the fetlock, in any event"— not to declaim poetry and absolutely not to rescue Becky from any dire peril.

Kristen smiled her relief. "It is good to have you back in London, Brendan. I'm sure the children were thrilled to see you. Will you be at the opera tonight?"

"If you wish." Tressilian forgot his role again and behaved as he might have the year before. "Shall we dine here first?"

Embarrassed, she had to admit that she was being escorted by Stamberly, and that while she would be pleased to see the earl at the opera, she also had plans for dinner. On that misunderstanding they parted, Tressilian with renewed resolution to eliminate the encroaching clod of a Stamberly as soon as possible.

Becky might sympathize with her companion's ill humour, but she was only human and could not help but preen as they tooled through Hyde Park behind the high-stepping chestnuts. In the hour before noon, the lane was thronged by Corinthians and whips out for some exercise before lunch at their clubs. Few passed up the chance to welcome the earl back, to invite him to a prizefight or horserace, and, incidentally, to tip a hat to Tressilian's discovery— a lively little deb in a dashingly cut velvet pelisse, with a rakish hussar-style bonnet cocked over one eye.

Becky, in fact, was in alt, and her enthusiasm could not help but inspirit Tressilian. He pulled up in a pool of sunlight near the gate and with a finger tilted up her chin. He grinned at her bright elfin face, at her conspiratorial wink, at the sunny glint in her blue eyes. Then he took her little hand and tucked it in the crook of his arm. "Shall we become betrothed, then?"

As the three Chantwell girls approached them from the gateway, Becky lowered her eyes in mock shyness. "I do think that will serve, don't you? If I'm constantly reminding her of our connection, Kristen will go mad with jealousy."

The prospect of driving the cool Lady K mad with jealousy could not but please Tressilian. But even one so lost to convention as the devilish earl recognized a few perils ahead. "It will have to be a secret engagement, of course. Think of how complicated it would be if I had to ask your father for your hand. He might even call me out when we break it off."

Becky dissolved into giggles. "Oh, I love the picture of my father threatening you with pistols at dawn! If only you knew Papa! He hasn't been seen outside his study in three years!"

Finally, when Tressilian jerked impatiently at the broad ribbons of her hat, Becky sobered. "But you're right. A secret betrothal, with everyone speculating and pointing fingers at me— that would be of all things the most romantic!"

With sudden inspiration, she said, "You can tell Kristen that you want to wait until the end of the season, so that I can be sure my heart is truly given. That will be sure to impress Kristen."

"It will drive her mad!" Becky said. "You must pay great attention to me, do you hear? She will never be able to ignore that. We shall be at the opera tonight with Stamberly. And you can come to take me riding Sunday— Monday too! And Wednesday we shall be at Almack's with Daisy Grey and her mama. I should love to give Daisy a letdown; she has been insufferable since Sir Tracy Ingram danced with her twice in one evening. Do say you'll meet us at Almack's. You can dance with me three times and everyone will talk."

Tressilian's promise was immediate but rash, for it had been several years since Lady Cowper had withdrawn his vouchers for that most holy of London assembly rooms. She had maintained that his presence was dangerous to impressionable maidens, which was undeniably true. But Sally Jersey told anyone who would listen that this was dear Emily's revenge for the earl's rejection of her advances, which was also probably true. Tressilian decided to call on Lady Jersey before he picked up the children and cozen her into procuring a voucher for him. She'd ever had a soft spot for a navy man, and never minded embarrassing her fellow patronesses.

Their admiration of Harriette Wilson's blue and white curricle ostentatiously parading through the park was interrupted by Captain Destain.

With a fine flurry of hooves, he reined in his bay mare beside them. "Didn't expect to see you here, Bren," he remarked lazily, casting an appraising eye at Tressilian's companion. Becky returned it with an uptilted chin and a mutinous expression. "Thought you'd still be unconscious, considering how much brandy you went through last night."

Becky fixed her betrothed with an accusing stare, and he was moved to protest, "Babe, it's no crime, you know. And Jonny drank just as much—this is my cousin Captain Destain, by the way. Miss Marlowe. He's always been a corrupting influence on me."

Jon laughed so hard his mare looked back in wonder. "Don't believe him, sweeting," he finally managed, "he was a reprobate ere I met him."

"When he met me, sweeting," Tressilian countered, addressing Becky yet shooting a sharp look at his cousin, "we were neither of us crawling yet, so pay no attention to his remarks." Then he took Becky's hand and confided, "Don't let it out, Jonny, but we're betrothed. Secretly, of course."

Destain's laughter stopped abruptly, and his eyes narrowed as he surveyed the intended fiancee. But his scathing words were directed at Tressilian. "Of course. With you, how could it be but secret, for heaven forfend you should ever do anything as you ought." He bent to calm his restive horse, meanwhile rearranging his expression into its customary cynicism. "I wish you all the best, Miss Marlowe," he finally said dryly. "You'll need it."

Becky's blue eyes flashed at this provocation, but she only observed, "But I have the best, haven't I? For I have Brendan."

Tressilian grinned at his best friend. "I told you I could find a good woman to marry me."

If they had been alone, Jon probably would have retorted that it was no credit that Tressilian managed to snare a schoolroom chit who saw him through the romantic haze of youth. But he was fortunately far too used to backing his friend up to stop now. "I should never have underestimated you," he said ironically. "Good day, Miss Marlowe."

Becky watched him gallop away, her eyes widening as he expertly threaded his bay through the traffic. "What a splendid rider he is."

"He ought to be; he's cavalry. They're good for naught else. The uniform's a bit excessive for undress, don't you think?"

Becky did not answer directly, only glancing significantly at Tressilian's own undress uniform, with its two hundred guineas worth of gold lace and fringe. "Captain Destain looked rather tired. Is he very dissipated?"

Once again, Tressilian had to disappoint her. "No, love, he's no opium smoker either. He's just been ill." Tressilian noted her swift look of concern— a sympathetic girl, his new fiancee— and sought to reassure her. "Not seriously, but it wore him out. Of course, he always looks weary. He was born tired of life, you know. I keep trying to show him all the possibilities of adventure, but he just yawns."

He took up the reins and jerked back into the lane, clearing Harriette Wilson's curricle by at least an inch and earning from her a provocative smile and an inviting gesture. With a rueful inclination of his head, he indicated his innocent companion, who waited until Harriette was nearly out of earshot to exclaim, "She must be very good at her job, for she's not beautiful at all!"

"What job?" Tressilian inquired innocently, then turned the subject before Becky could favor him with her answer. "Jonny thinks I'm going to ruin your life. He's probably right. He's known me forever, you know, better 'n I know myself." He negotiated a sharp turn, steadying Becky with a firm hand on her knee. "If we really were betrothed—"

"But we're not. And I have not forgotten that this is all for True Love. I shan't awfully mind if my life is ruined, if it's for a Higher Good. But I do think my life will be immeasurably improved, for it's been monstrous dull so far. Wiltshire is truly disspiriting for one with my sense of adventure. Oh," she cried, gripping his arm with both hands, "it will be so exciting! I've never been betrothed before, have you?"

"No, but I shouldn't imagine it to be very difficult." Never taking his eyes from the road, he brought her hand to his lips in a lover-like gesture, to which she responded with a most unlover-like giggle. "If we just make sheep's eyes at each other, and you can contrive not to laugh at my more abject declarations of worship, no one will be the wiser."

Becky settled against him with a happy sigh, so that everyone who passed would realize she was secretly betrothed now. "Oh, I promise you, I shall be the world's most ecstatic fiancee. Kristen will be positively green!"

## CHAPTER TWELVE

Kristen was as tense as the veriest debutante as she entered the brightly lit ballroom at Almack's. But while the husband-seekers in their insipid pastel muslins had reason for anxiety, Kristen could find no excuse. Her sophisticated deep blue silk gown testified to her established rank as a society matron.

And while she might incur the interest of a few men, not one would dare to assess her like a horse at Tattersall s, considering her bloodlines and her breeding potential. Her future did not depend on whether a man asked her to dance, or expressed a desire to visit her upon the morrow, or requested a meeting with her guardian. But still she had to grip her sandalwood fan to keep her hands from trembling— the serene Lady Killeaven, shaking like a leaf, and without any reason at all.

The debutante Becky, of course, was paradoxically composed. Only three weeks ago, she had been so daunted by the prospect of displeasing one of Almack's strict patronesses that she had bitten her nails to the quick. She had even listened intently to Kristen's suggestions for her comportment, and obeyed one or two.

But now Becky was a seasoned veteran, chatting desultorily as she drifted along with her friend Daisy Grey. She disdained even to notice the effect her mint green gown with its bodice bordered in antique lace was having on the assembled multitudes. Magnanimously she offered her hand to one young gallant, promised she would try to save him a dance, then waved him away. "Such a sad squeeze," she remarked with commendable languor.

She dropped her world-weary air only when Daisy stopped short so that Kristen nearly collided with her. But the girl took no notice of the traffic tie-up she had caused by the refreshment table. "Oh, look, Becky, there's the earl! Mama said they would never give him vouchers, but there he is with Lady Jersey. Oh, isn't he the handsomest thing. Mama said I mustn't on any account ever dance with him. I think she did once and has never recovered from the experience."

She glanced back guiltily. But Kristen, already weary of playing chaperone, gazed out at the dancers and pretended not to have heard Daisy's indelicacy. "I can't imagine why he's here. Almack's can't be his usual haunt."

Becky arched a sophisticated brow. "Perhaps he finds the company to his pleasing this season." She regarded Tressilian with a proprietary expression that set off alarms in her eavesdropping guardian. "He does look splendid in uniform, don't you think? Although I think he would look splendid in anything—"

"Or in nothing!"

"I heard that, Daisy." With a jolt, Kristen resumed her chaperone role. But the blonde girl's shock at her own joke was too amusing after all. "Oh, stop blushing, dear. You shouldn't say such things if you are the one most embarrassed by them."

Aware of the narrowness of her escape, Daisy peeled her hands away from her burning cheeks and listened gratefully to Becky's timely interruption. "Tressilian came to our box at the opera the other night. He was most charming, but then, he always is, you know. But you don't know, do you, never having met him."

Daisy retaliated by reminding her friend that the wealthy Sir Tracy Ingram had favored her with two dances only a week earlier.

This endless rivalry was so irritating that Kristen disposed of the combatants expeditiously, steering Daisy into the arms of a lancer and Becky towards an eager grenadier. With them out of the way for the entire waltz, Kristen would have time to talk privately to Brendan and ask him what the devil he was about.

With misgiving, she watched him cross the dance floor, ignoring the importunate gazes of other ladies. He had entered the opera hall Saturday night with the same arrogant disregard, heading straight for Stamberly's box. She had feared a scene, but instead Tressilian was at his most charming, making polite conversation with the viscount and gently teasing Becky that the despised spray of freckles on her nose was utterly adorable. In fact, he had shown Becky particular attention, paying her such extravagant compliments that they both ended up laughing helplessly while Kristen and Stamberly tried to watch the stage.

Brendan had treated Becky with a big-brotherly attitude that was hard to fault, but Becky had reacted less like a sister than a favored flirt, finagling him into taking her for a drive the next afternoon. Then all the way home she had extolled Tressilian's undoubted virtues, the way his black hair curled above his forehead, his reckless spirit, his sweet smile.

Occasionally she looked to Kristen, waiting for agreement, as if she were trying to convince his old friend that Tressilian was indeed a worthy sort. Was she measuring him to see if he fit her model for a husband, or, God forbid, a lover?

Tressilian stopped at the refreshment table to pick up two cups of lemonade, and Kristen had time to consider what she would say to him. She could not accuse him of any deliberate violation. He'd had so little converse with young girls that he probably did not realize that he was on dangerous ground when he paid such marked attentions to Becky. He was only being kind, helping her succeed in society. Once he learned that the world was imagining him as husband material for Becky, he would probably set sail for Polynesia and never look back.

"How fortunate to find you without your watchdog," Brendan said, coming Up beside her and offering her a cup. "He's usually such a conscientious cur. Has he gone to bury a bone?"

Kristen laughed in spite of herself. There was something of the faithful animal in Stamberly, especially in the way he had of worrying a problem, examining it from all sides as if it were a bone. "He's talking with the Dowager Duchess of Melchiore. As you say, he is very conscientious, especially about the Tory Party. She's an important hostess, you know."

Tressilian's black eyes glazed over. Kristen had never been able to convince him to take an interest in his country's governance. She doubted he had sat in the House of Lords a dozen times since he had given his maiden speech— a stirring tribute to the fallen hero Admiral Nelson that had the upper chamber awash in tears and inspired a forty-percent increase in the navy's budget for the next annum.

Considering his personal charisma and potential power, his defection from this duty was all the more censurable. But Kristen had given that fight up for lost. She had long felt that the rights to vote and hold office were wasted on male landholders, and Tressilian's example did little to change her opinion.

Even now, like a naughty schoolboy, he was diluting the insipid lemonade with a clear liquid from a silver flask— vodka, no doubt a gift from a grateful tsarina. He grinned irrepressibly as Kristen tried to appear scandalized. But it was no use. She was so happy that he had gotten over his mad she didn't even mind he was still reprehensible, even after years of exposure to her example.

"Stop drinking and dance with me," she demanded with the familiarity of long friendship. And with some show of reluctance, he tossed off his drink, replaced the flask in his pocket, and took her in his arms.

He danced expertly, effortlessly leading her in the waltz, his arm positively tight around her waist. She fought back the nagging thought that Edward had never made her feel so hazardous and so secure all at the same time.

She tilted her head back to see his face, the abstraction in his fatherless eyes, the slight frown between his brows. Then he glanced down at her, and she caught her breath at the sadness in his gaze. But it was gone in an instant, vanished into the laughter she knew so well and hadn't seen for so long.

"Bren, I want to talk to you about Becky." He inclined his head graciously and, encouraged, she added, "You've been very kind to take her driving with you so often, and to join us at the opera Saturday. But you recollect I told you she was ripe for infatuation? Well, she seems to have fastened on you as a candidate. I'd best warn you, for I'd hate for her to be embarrassed later."

Tressilian asked easily, "Why should she be embarrassed? She's a well-behaved girl, after all. I've found no cause to lament her behavior."

Kristen forbore to point out that his approval was perhaps not the most proper goal young girls could seek. But he was taking this rather too lightly— when it came to understanding headstrong girls, he appeared alarmingly naive. It would serve him fair if Aunt Amelia descended on his doorstep demanding to know his intentions.

Only, of course, it would be Kristen's doorstep Aunt Amelia would descend upon, and that was a prospect worth avoiding. "I'm worried that she will fancy herself in love with you. And she's supposed to find herself a husband this season, and if she spends two months mooning over you, there won't be any eligible men left, and—" she finished on a childishly petulant note— "and I shall have to explain to her dragon mother why."

Brendan loosed her hand and flicked at her snub nose, wrinkled now in distaste. "Well, I can't let you be devoured by a dragon, so I'll tell you what— you may consider my intentions to your little cousin entirely honorable."

With a sigh of relief, she took his hand back. "Well, I never supposed otherwise, of course, but it would help if you moderated your charm just a bit."

"Oh, I can't do that." Tressilian's eyes widened innocently. "I can hardly convince her to accept my suit by being only moderately charming."

"Accept your suit?" The words made no sense, even in echo. "Accept your—" Dismay spread through her as she realized finally what he meant. Brendan— Becky— "It's out of the question."

"Really?" he inquired in tones of polite interest. "Why? You said you were in need of a husband for her."

"Not you!" Kristen struggled for coherence as her words caught in her throat. But none of it made any sense— Brendan, Becky— "Her parents would never allow it."

"They wouldn't?" Brendan tilted his head to the side, puzzling this over. "Oh, I think they will. I'm a earl, after all. Every mother thinks her daughter will make a fine countess."

Kristen knew he was right: Aunt Amelia would love to have a earl in the family. Of course, she would never force Becky to marry some horrid septuagenarian just because he happened to own a earldom, but the Earl of Tressilian, well, he was young and virile and— and unacceptable. "And I won't allow it."

Of course, Kristen would have little say if it came down to cases, but perhaps Brendan would back down if she made her opposition clear. For he wouldn't want to defy her wishes, would he?

"Why ever not? Do you doubt my ability to provide for her?"

"Of course not. I know you're as rich as Croesus. I wouldn't object on such paltry grounds anyway," she replied, forgetting Amelia's proscriptions on men of no fortune. "There are more important things than wealth to recommend a husband."

The music had stopped sometime during her speech, and she thought distractedly that she had best search out Becky and Daisy, and hadn't she promised this dance to Lord Braden? But her legs wouldn't answer the weak signals from her brain, and she could not resist when Tressilian led her to a corner behind a large arrangement of ferns. Trust a rake to find a concealed spot even in this most public of rooms, she observed with distant humor.

"What objection, then, do you have?"

Recalled too suddenly to the dreadful subject, Kristen could only stare at him. Though his manner was easy as he lounged against a window sill, she saw the tension in his fine features. Was he so eager, then, to gain her approval of this mismatch?

She stepped backwards, and, encountering a low couch, sat carefully on its edge. Just as carefully, she said, "I know you expect me to be honest, Brendan, so I shall. I love Becky, and I want the best for her. And marriage to you is not the best for her."

"Surely you know my wife will have whatever she desires."

My wife— He spoke those words so gently, as if they were very precious, and Kristen shivered involuntarily. How often she had told him that was what he needed, a wife. Why did the tender words sting so when he spoke them?

She struck back, hardly knowing what she was saying. "All she desires, perhaps, unless she happens to desire your love." "She will have my love."

At that simple statement she faltered. Could it be true? He hardly knew Becky, but she was a darling girl, easy to love. "When is this supposed to have occurred?"

He reached down and took the abused fan from her nervous fingers. He opened it, his mouth quirking sympathetically at the broken blades. "You would only laugh if I told you. For I know you don't believe in love at first sight."

"Not when it happens to you." Kristen stiffened, recalling all the women who might testify to the transience of Tressilian's love. Becky wouldn't join their number, if her guardian had anything to say about it. "Love without fidelity is a pretty poor bargain, and you can't promise her fidelity." "Can't I?" Tressilian continued studying the fan, tracing with a calloused finger the elegant Japanese figuring on the intact blades. "I've never tried it before, but if that's a promise I must fulfill to make my wife happy, I will fulfill it."

"And a leopard can change his spots," Kristen shot back. "I'll believe that when you lose Andrea."

"Already lost. Never found, really, for I wished her farewell Friday night."

Friday night. The night he met Becky. "And that opera dancer you stable in Earl Street?"

"Oh, I'd forgotten about her. You, of course, never forget anything." Regret struggled with resolve on his handsome face. "She's lost too, and that alone should convince you of my sincerity, for she— oh, never mind," he added with a sigh. "That sort of thing is all in the past. I mean it, Kristen. I'm determined to do this, and to do it right. You know very well her parents won't object. But I want your approval too."

"Give me back my fan," she demanded with helpless, irrational anger. Silently Brendan handed her the broken fan. "And I can't approve of it, not yet. For you've a deal of years to live down. I know you very well, and as you say, I don't forget anything. You'll have to do more than pay off your mistress to convince me you'd make a good husband."

Brendan took her hand and helped her up. "I understand. I also understand that Becky is very young and naive and might not be sure of her own mind. So whatever private agreement we might have come to will be kept private, if you like, until June. That way she can cry off if she changes her mind."

This was so sensible, so sensitive, that Kristen could only stand there, wondering if her dangerous friend's body had been possessed by some virtuous daemon. "And if you change your mind?"

"Oh, I'm not eighteen. I know my mind— and my heart. And that's given irrevocably." His fathomless eyes held hers, and she saw utter sincerity in the darkness there.

The realization that Brendan was telling the truth when he spoke of love was so shocking she forced it from her mind. Into the void left behind flowed a hundred comfortingly mundane considerations. "Then you mustn't speak to her parents yet. They will doubtlessly hear about it, however, so let me deal with that. And Brendan, I mean this. Don't do anything that complicates matters irrevocably." Irrevocably— his term. He had given his heart irrevocably.

Tressilian offered his arm, all amused elegance again. "Then I'd best get back to Becky, for if I'm with you any longer, she will think I'm trysting with you. And that would complicate matters irrevocably, wouldn't it?"

He left her with the other matrons and sauntered across the room to Becky's little circle. With a jerk of his proud head, he dismissed Becky's other swains as he had so often dismissed Kristen's dance partners. He frowned as he spoke to the girl, doubtlessly telling her about Kristen's opposition to their betrothal. Becky laid a comforting hand on his arm, an intimate gesture that troubled Kristen. It was far too early for Becky to form a preference— and such a preference.

Tressilian more than surpassed Becky's desire to best Daisy Grey, dancing with her three times— tantamount to a declaration- - and watching jealously whenever he had to release her to other partners. The news spread through the ballroom like the plague. Tressilian was courting Lady Killeaven's cousin!

The responses were varied, and Kristen was gifted with every one. The old cats who had always distrusted this platonic business were quick to poke little needles of spite at the woman they believed scorned. "She's a pretty girl, your cousin, but hardly your equal. And yet after only a few days, she walks off with the prize of the year!"

Another woman asked sweetly Kristen wasn't planning a double wedding, for surely Stamberly must have gotten an affirmative answer, he looked so pleased with himself lately. Not one person, however, suggested that this match was anything but heaven-made, and not one believed Kristen when she said there was no match at all.

Only Tressilian's cousin seemed to share Kristen's doubts. Captain Destain had come late with Lady Elise Winterleigh and her pallid daughter Amarinda. But he soon deserted them to beg a dance from Kristen. Afterwards he led her to a quiet seat and procured her a glass of lemonade. His patrician face was cynical above the inspiring blue uniform. "It's clearly midsummer moon between our cousins, wouldn't you say?"

The contrast between his romantic words and his ironic tone did not startle her. Captain Destain was no idealist, and he no less than she would have reason to doubt Tressilian's latest profession of love. But then Jon hadn't seen Brendan's eyes when he spoke of giving his heart. "I don't know. He's never before spoken of marriage."

Destain stretched his long legs out far enough to trip any unwary pedestrians. "He's never before been threatened with retirement if he doesn't produce an heir. He as much as told me that was his motive in this little courtship." His eyes narrowed coolly, and he regarded Kristen from below half-closed lids. "Not like our Bren to be so calculating in love, but then, he's never had such reason before."

Kristen knew the captain to be remarkably acute despite his indolence, and had always counted Brendan lucky to have one other friend blessed with common sense. She also knew Tressilian told his cousin things that were too raw or scandalous for her own prim ears, so no doubt Bren had made such a claim.

But much as she would like to, she couldn't believe that Brendan's sole or even primary motive was so unfeeling. "You don't think he could really care for her? Perhaps he had to be forced into considering marriage, and only then became vulnerable—"

"To Cupid's darts?" Destain laughed shortly. "He should be as bristly as a porcupine, then, so often as Cupid has targeted him. But a little slip like your cousin bringing him down? Not that she's not appealing, for she is. But hardly his sort."

"I will kill him if he hurts her," Kristen vowed, and he drew back in mock fear.

"Such a glare from those lovely eyes! Why, I've never seen such ferocity, even behind a French rifle! Were I Bren, I'd be quaking in my boots contemplating my fate." Then his gaze traveled across the room to Lady Elise, whose always splendid bosom was enhanced by the famous Winterleigh emeralds. He shrugged as she smiled and whispered into the ear of a young lieutenant. "In any event, she'll have little cause to complain! will she? She'll be the Countess of Tressilian, and she'll get to wear the Tressilian diamonds, and the Tressilian sapphires, which I'm sure will console her whenever she thinks to lament her lot."

"You are a cynic, Captain Destain," Kristen observed, "and I think you have been associating with the wrong type of woman for too long." When he only grinned at this indubitable charge, Kristen addded with fond contentiousness, "My Becky is not a materialist."

"And you are lovely when you so loftily defend one of your own. If only such an honor could be mine." This wish was delivered in the tone of languishing longing that Captain Destain was known for, as he lightly drew his finger along her cheek. It was the sort of lazy flirtation women always allowed Captain Destain to get away with, and Kristen was no exception. He was, after all, far too indolent to press any advantage he might gain from his impropriety, and far too amusing to set down.

Still Kristen felt a flush of embarrassment to have this innocuous gesture witnessed by her would-be fiancee, approaching now with a recalcitrant Becky in tow. But Stamberly was too much the gentleman to make a jealous show. He only looked assessingly at the lavish display of battle ribbons on Captain Destain's braided chest, asked a perfunctory question about the progress of Wellington's troops, and reminded Kristen that it was getting late.

Kristen's headache had blossomed into a headthrob, so she dismissed Becky's automatic protest. "You can't dance any more with Tressilian anyway," she pointed out with a touch of annoyance, resolving to confront her cousin as soon as they were alone. "A fourth dance and they will be publishing the banns."

Becky only opened her blue eyes very wide then let her lashes sweep flirtatiously as she slanted a look at the captain. "There are other men I haven't danced with even once."

"Minx," Destain murmured appreciatively. Before Kristen could protest either his familiarity or Becky's flirtatiousness, Destain was bowing over her hand and wishing her good night, averring he was about to leave himself.

"Only drudges leave a ball before two," Becky observed truculently, as if insult might work where coquetry had failed.

His eyes cooler than ever, Destain hid a yawn behind his gloved hand. "Just so. Your servant, Miss Marlowe. Stamberly."

Kristen rounded on her charge as Stamberly went to call for the carriage. "What are you doing?"

Becky was scowling after the departing captain but roused herself enough to stammer, "Wh—what do you mean?"

"I mean that you might rest on your laurels for a short time, Miss Hardheart. Having already attracted one serious suitor tonight, must you start in on his best friend also?"

"Suitor?" Becky gazed uncomprehendingly at her for a moment as the master of ceremonies laid a velvet evening cloak over her shoulders. "Oh! Oh, you mean Brendan." She palmed her cheek in an unconvincing show of naiveté. "You don't mean Captain Destain thought I was— I was flirting with him? Oh, no, surely not. For anyone can see he is not the sort of man I admire. He is too world-weary. You know I prefer the passionate sort. And he as much as admitted to being a drudge, didn't he?"

As she followed Becky out to the carriage, Kristen found herself uncomforted by this assurance. For Becky had indeed been trying to flirt with the captain. Of course, she was one of nature's coquettes, and had been flirting with young men all this month.

But tonight of all nights, Kristen would have supposed that Becky might moderate that tendency. Instead the girl seemed little changed by her great achievement of landing the biggest fish in the matrimonial pond. In fact, she was a moment remembering even the identity of her glorious catch. How very callous— how very strange.

And Kristen felt a breath of disquiet brush her. Even now she could envision the light in Brendan's eyes when he spoke of his love. When she spoke of him, however, Becky's lovely blue eyes had never burned with a matching fire.

## CHAPTER THIRTEEN

A week later Kristen finally accepted the obvious: Brendan's pursuit of her cousin was not a short-lived impulse. One afternoon she sat down at Gerald's heavy oak library desk (her own delicate rosewood escritoire not being up to such a disagreeable task) to compose a letter apprising Becky's parents of the courtship.

She could imagine their responses— Amelia would demand an immediate meeting with her ducal future son-in-law, while Sir Walter would retreat to his study to contemplate another disruption to his existence. As

Kristen had no wish to deal with Amelia's presence on top of all her other problems, she added the clever warning that Tressilian was notoriously fickle and would bolt at the least interference. "Trust me," she wrote, "to bring this courtship to a satisfactory conclusion." Amelia, no fool, would trust that the more diplomatic countess had things well in hand.

Kristen sealed the letter and rang for a footman to post it. Then she crossed to the window overlooking South Audley Street, lately thronged with friends calling to felicitate her on her recent betrothal to the Viscount Stamberly. While Kristen had been preoccupied with her cousin's romance, all London was vowing that Lady Killeaven deserved the best, and Stamberly, a solid, sensible man of wealth and virtue, was unanimously regarded as the best.

Well, the regard perhaps was not unanimous. Brendan, of course, disdained to offer his congratulations, and Becky was similarly cool. But they were so caught up in their own romance they hardly seemed to notice the rest of the world. Even now, pulling back the pearl gray drapes, Kristen could see them driving up the shady street in Brendan's phaeton. Brendan was laughing, his head tilted to hear some of Becky's nonsense, and Becky

Incredulous, Kristen squeezed her eyes closed then opened them again. But the impossible vision had not wavered. Becky's pink-gloved hands were clutching the reins of Tressilian's prized chestnuts. And Brendan, though he rested one hand lightly on Becky's, looked perfectly accepting of this extraordinary event.

Kristen dropped onto the damask windowseat, letting her shawl fall from her shoulders to the floor. She could no longer cherish any doubts about Brendan's affection for her young cousin. For never before had he trusted a lady with his treasured horses.

She hardly had time to compose herself before the door slammed downstairs and Becky came running up. She stuck her curly head into the room, calling gaily, "Oh, Kristen, there you are. Bren's taking me to Gunther's for an ice. Shall we take the children too? But if we do, we shall have to walk, for we won't all fit into the phaeton. Though I should love above all things to have Nick see me tool along holding the reins. Did you see? I drove all through the park and even here on the street! Bren says I have a natural talent—"

Kristen finally broke in. "Take your maid. But leave the children, for Edward and I must speak to them this afternoon. And do put your bonnet back on before you leave the house."

Obediently Becky jammed her silver-trimmed poke bonnet back onto her head and retied the broad pink ribbons. "But there's no room in the phaeton for a maid, and Flossie worships Brendan and stares at him constantly. It is most disconcerting, I assure you."

"You'd best get used to such stares, for Tressilian is ever receiving them," Kristen assured her dryly. "And if Flossie can't ride, then you must walk. You will need the exercise, do you consume your usual number of ices and pastries at Gunther's."

Becky took herself off to find Flossie, wondering aloud why she needed a maid when she was with dear Brendan who was able to protect her against any peril at all. And Kristen knew a moment's guilt, for she supposed the presence of the goggling Flossie might put a damper on the high spirits Becky and Brendan shared on their jaunts together. But then she told herself it was just as well to insist on propriety, for already this secret betrothal was the most widely known on dit in town, so devoted a swain was Brendan.

Kristen would never have predicted Brendan's unprecedented resolution in this pursuit. Uncomplainingly he escorted Becky to any amusement that caught her fancy— Venetian breakfasts and musicales and picnics out to Richmond. Instead of spending his evenings gambling and wenching, which Kristen imagined he'd still prefer, he waited to take his beloved and whatever little friend she favored to the theatre or the opera. For Becky, apparently, he would abide even the simpering and giggling of debutantes and their mamas.

Now, through the glass, Kristen saw him shake his head and grin as Becky emerged from the front door, Flossie in tow. He leaped down from the phaeton and tossed the reins to his groom. Then he offered an arm to Becky and the other to Flossie, who was so shocked she actually accepted. Kristen was obscurely relieved to see Brendan flirting outrageously with the breathless blonde maid— he was still as bad as ever, at least a little bit.

Coming up the other way past Grosvenor Square was Edward. Kristen smiled slightly to see him progress sedately up the street, avoiding horses and carriages and tipping his hat to the strolling ladies. He was such a courteous man, so well-respected about town. No one would ever accuse him of instituting scandal or behaving rashly. He would be a good, steady husband and a constant father to her children. Nick and Corey, when they were told of the upcoming marriage, would no doubt accept it with equanimity, if not joy.

But instead Kristen received an object lesson in the impossibility of predicting childish behavior. Once Edward had handed his gloves and hat to the footman and the children had been summoned to the drawing room, Kristen knew a sudden apprehension. There was a mulish look on Nick's face, mischief in Corey's violet eyes, as Edward cleared his throat. "Children," he began, "I am pleased to inform you that your mother has consented to make me the happiest man on earth."

When the children showed no sign of appreciating Edward's delicate euphemism, Kristen added gently, "Lord Stamberly will soon be your new father."

This announcement produced a more immediate response. Corinna flung herself at her mother's skirts and burst into tears; Nick drew himself up to his full height and declared, "Never!"

Preoccupied with soothing her daughter's angry sobs, Kristen could not halt Nicholas's elaboration. "You'll never be my papa, never! I won't let you marry my mother!"

Stamberly, nearly speechless with affront, could only stutter, "Wh— What a thing to say, young man! What a thing to say!"

Kristen spoke sharply to Nick and set Corinna back on her feet, explaining to Edward that the children needed time to get accustomed to sharing their mother with someone else. "Now go to your rooms," she told them sternly, "and think about how rude you have been. And when you are willing to apologize, you may come out."

"Then we'll be in our rooms till doomsday!" Nick stomped out, Corinna marching straight-backed in his wake.

Helplessly Kristen wondered what had become of the well-ordered life she had so painstakingly built. Nothing, nothing was going according to plan. Becky was betrothing herself to Brendan, and the children were resisting this eminently suitable new father

"And what, my dear, are you planning to do about that?" Edward's voice, as usual, was level, but she heard the hint of accusation and flushed.

"They are usually much better behaved. It was just the shock; I might have prepared them better. But they will come around soon. For certainly they had no objection to you before this."

Stamberly was eventually pacified and left with the recommendation that Kristen remonstrate with her children about their rudeness to their future father. Finally she was able to go up to her daughter's yellow gingham bedroom to investigate. "Now what prompted that shocking display?"

Corinna stuck out a mutinous lip and pulled at the embroidery on her daffodil comforter. "You never said you would marry him. You never asked who we might like to have as a new papa."

"Whom, dearest," Kristen corrected automatically. She was frankly baffled by this daughter of hers, sitting so small and rebellious in the big bed. "But you liked him well enough before."

"We didn't know he was going to be your husband. He's a dull old stick, he is, and he will never take us to Mexico or Peru and we shall have to stay forever in boring old Kent."

Kristen hid a smile at this— it was nothing serious, then. "You mustn't call people names, Corinna, especially not Lord Stamberly. Mexico and Peru! No one goes to those places! You are English, after all, and Kent is a particularly lovely part of England."

"But he'll make us stay there forever, I know," she said stubbornly. "And you'll live in London and we will never see you. And his mean old housekeeper will not give us enough to eat and I expect we'll probably starve. But you won't know it because he will tell you it's not proper to spoil children by seeing them everyday."

"I shall never again read those German fairy tales to you at bedtime." Kristen tugged the ringlet out of her daughter's mouth and tilted her chin up to see her own violet eyes looking sulkily back at her. "For they've given you the oddest notions. Nick is not Hansel and you are not Gretel, you know."

But a trace of truth in this absurdity gave Kristen pause. Edward, like most childless men, had strong theories about successful child-rearing. He had indeed once lamented the unlimited access some modern parents (Kristen perhaps one of them) allowed their children, suggesting such indulgence made them think the world was at their beck and call— as Nick and Corey indubitably believed, now that she considered it.

But even that recommendation hardly argued the sort of villainy that Corey imagined. "You will be with me, just as always'" Kristen said reassuringly, "even when you are exceptionally naughty, as you were today. I won't ever send you away, no matter what Edward says. Besides, he loves you both already and only wants the best for you."

Corinna greeted this with a dubious frown, but offered no more objection. Satisfied that she had muted if not eliminated her daughter's resistance, Kristen visited Nick, who sat in the corner of his room, holding the ivory warship Tressilian had given him.

Over the years, Nick's room had evolved into a shrine to his favorite human being (after his mother, Kristen liked to think). Nick was the grateful recipient of every small memento or castoff Tressilian could remember to send him.

So a walnut shelf ran the length of one wall, displaying a dozen models of the H.M.S. Defiant in a dozen different styles. Tressilian liked to keep his sailors' hands busy, so he bought every ship model they carved or constructed. A tattered flag signaled "engage the enemy" from one of the bed posters, and a chart of the currents jamming the Drake Passage adorned the bedstead. Nick's prize possession, the wheel discarded after the Defiant's last refitting, leaned against a wall papered entirely in nautical charts.

Kristen could never enter this room without the despairing realization that one day Nick would follow his mentor off to sea, and that Corinna would stuff her golden curls under a cap and go with him if she could.

But that worry, at least, she could postpone for a few years. Now she perched uncomfortably on the authentic seachest spotted and warped by saltwater and stenciled "Tressilian HMS DEFIANT".

Like Corey, Nick had a profusion of blonde curls, but his eyes were a clear blue like his father's. He owed his slimness and fine features to the Danish side of the family, but the squared-off chin was pure Marlowe, as was the stubborn set to his mouth. For Becky Marlowe was wont to put on that same pout when she didn't get her way. No Andresen, Kristen was certain, was ever allowed to sulk.

Nick would not meet her eyes as she repeated the assurances she had made to his sister. "So you may be sure I shall keep you with me always, at least until you go away to school."

"I shan't go away to school, for I'm to join the navy," Nick declared, dragging in that other irresolvable argument for good measure. "I shall get my own ship as soon as can be and come and take you and Corey away to other lands. I shall take care of you, so you may tell Stamberly that you don't need him to marry you."

Kristen had long since learned the value of selective deafness, and simply ignored her son's provocative announcement of his professional aspirations. The assertion of responsibility for his family was more touching, showing the courage of a boy who had never had a father. Though he was only nine, Nick liked to think of himself as the man of the house. Naturally he was reluctant to have another man take the place he saw as his own.

"I know you'll always take care of us. And when you grow up, you will take care of your estate and be head of the family besides. But in the meantime, Edward will just help us with some of the more difficult tasks."

"Captain Bren can help us," Nick replied, cradling the ivory ship against his Eton jacket.

Captain Bren was hardly able to handle his own affairs, much less anyone else's, but Kristen could not bring herself to deny the boy his hero-worship. "Captain Bren can't be expected to take a hand in our matters. But with Stamberly living with us, we will be a real family with a real papa."

Nick only lifted his chin at this, disdaining to reply that Stamberly was entirely unnecessary to their little family. And Kristen was at a loss to explain why she had so felt the lack of a husband lately, especially since she wasn't entirely sure herself. She just knew she didn't want to be alone anymore.

But Nick would never understand that, because he had never been alone. He was surrounded by people who loved him; in fact, he saw himself as the sun around which all revolved.

But his mother had lived long enough to realize that she was not particularly essential to the continued activity of the cosmos. In fact, she was essential to no one except her children, and they would be grown and gone soon enough. She could not face a return to the loneliness of her childhood; Stamberly would give her a life's companion without the risks inherent in another sort of marriage.

So she only kissed her son and told him no matter what, his and Corinna's welfare would always come first. As she left the room, she turned to see the speculative glint in his eyes and realized her mistake. Now he would challenge this prospective marriage at every turn by claiming that he and his sister would be hurt by it.

Edward would no doubt tell her again that she was too lenient with her children, and no doubt he was right, for she had never been able to counteract their willfulness. But she secretly loved to see that trait in them, knowing that their headstrong natures would help them succeed at life.

Her own childhood had been circumscribed by rules and regulations that often still restricted her decisions. She didn't want her children to be forever living by someone else's rules of conduct. Perhaps they would grow to be more aware of what they needed from life, and more insistent on acquiring it.

Brendan Trevarrick had never been one to abandon ship, but beyond a bottle of brandy at his club, the horizon looked bleak. In fact, affairs were worse now than when he and Becky had first conceived their clever scheme. A week ago, Kristen had announced her betrothal to that clod Stamberly.

With the pragmatic despair of an admiral surveying his fleet after a battle, Tressilian totted up his score. On the debit side, Kristen was planning on marrying her dead dog, but it was a credit that she resisted setting a date. Stamberly's attempt to limit the earl's access to the Marlowe children— a bad influence! Me! Tressilian raged— was reason to call for the dueling pistols.

But Kristen's resistance to this mitigated the outrage a bit. Still, she appeared to accept his own betrothal with disturbing equanimity. But then she never let a day go by without reminding Becky that an unofficial betrothal could easily be broken— "And you know how proper she is, she doesn't truly believe that! She just wants me to jilt you for her own reasons!" Becky had explained gleefully.

Well, even if the worst occurred and he gained no bride from this scheme, Tressilian could at least count himself one friend up. For Becky had proved to be the best of conspirators, making sure Kristen heard about Tressilian's every act of gallantry and teasing her about how luscious life as a duchess would be.

Privately, Becky confided that she loved this role as the secret fiancee, for everyone wanted to meet the girl who had reeled in the season's prize catch. Beau Brummell had even condescended to dance with her, pronouncing her "refreshing".

"Of course," Tressilian had told her, "he owes me a thousand pounds, so he knows better than to try to set you down."

Now that she was safely attached, other beaus had declared themselves Becky's faithful knights, knowing she could not demand their rings as tokens of their esteem. And with this betrothal she had incurred the envy of many women— and the pity of quite a few others, of course.

Becky heeded none of the warnings of these helpful souls, for, after all, she had no intention of marrying the notoriously notorious earl. Indeed, she professed not the slightest qualms for the future, when presumably she might be left husbandless as her erstwhile groom waited at the altar for another bride.

Tressilian was not so sanguine about her plight, and resolved to find her a mate from among his friends before the season was up. Of course, when he actually considered his comrades as potential husbands for the girl so dear to his heart, he drew back in horror.

Kristen was doubtlessly right about the lamentable racketbrains he called friends— who among them would be good enough for his Becky? Not Barnabas, he was too thick, and Larry Lytten was too poor, among a host of other failings. Charlie Makepeace smoked opium, and Erlander started a brawl whenever he got foxed, which was near every day. Chelten would gamble against the sun rising in the morning, were the odds good enough.

Choosing a replacement fiancee for Becky was such a futile quest that Tressilian turned with some relief to his most successful strategy— one he had conceived on his own, he thought proudly, for Becky took credit for everything else.

The Marlowe children were heartwarmingly glad to join forces to outwit the hapless Stamberly. They, at least, preferred Tressilian as their papa. They were simply inspired at demonstrating their opposition to their prospective stepfather, and the price to keep them in line was reasonable-marzipan smuggled in every evening by a saucy kitchen maid, and the promise of Mexico if and when Tressilian became their father. In return, they performed masterfully.

At first, Becky had been piqued that Tressilian had not consulted with her before enlisting reinforcements. But soon she was reporting every triumph the children scored. Corinna, a graceful little monkey who scrambled up towering trees, always grew clumsy at the sight of Stamberly. Cup after cup of tea she dumped accidentally into Stamberly's lap; beaver hats by the dozen she destroyed by sitting on; intricately tied cravats she ruined by tugging at them to see how they were tied. Even the stolid Stamberly was losing patience, inquiring of Kristen if her daughter wasn't the least bit, well, odd. That, Becky vowed, provoked a major disagreement, and Stamberly now kept a careful distance from his prospective stepdaughter.

Nick took a different tack, making impossible demands upon the viscount as a condition of his acceptance. "Teach me to shoot," he commanded. "I want to be a highwayman when I grow up." "Take me to a cockfight. My real papa loved cockfights." "Buy me a giraffe. I want to start a menagerie at Killeaven, and it's my estate so I can do as I please."

It was a mark of Stamberly's desire for the match that his resolve did not falter under this barrage. Rather he spoke obliquely of how Eton would be the making of Nick, and that Corinna might benefit from a stricter governess. Kristen countered tartly that only she would make decisions about her children, no matter who called himself their father.

Accustomed to her children's temperaments, Kristen did not suspect that their mischief was influenced from without. Deny it as she liked, Kristen was secretly proud of their independent attitudes. She was not a very forbidding person, Tressilian thought lovingly, despite her rigid upbringing. In fact, sometimes he thought she might break down and become human instead of the goddess she so resembled. She was always ready to bend her rules for someone she loved— and perhaps that meant she loved him, for she'd certainly had to bend a lot to remain friends with him.

He scowled as the door opened and a couple gamblers stumbled in. When they caught sight of him in the leather chair, they held a whispered conference and then bowed their way out. At the door one turned back and said hesitantly, "Join us for a game, Tressilian?"

His reputation as a boon companion would never survive this

melancholy season. "Perhaps later," he temporized, for Garber, once master's mate on Nelson's flagship, was ever a scintillating conversationalist. Lately he had been assembling a book of reminiscences on the battle of Trafalgar. I must get a volume for Nick, Tressilian thought, signed to him by the author.

If that great victory had been the highlight of Tressilian's life, this looming defeat was definitely his lowest point. He was not yet ready to surrender, but he was beginning to get discouraged. It was not just the cold black print of the Gazette announcement that troubled him; that smug look that so frequently marred Stamberly's fatuous face enraged him. At the same time, playing the ardent lover in public to Becky served its purpose, but it was torturous when he wanted to be addressing those tender words to the fragile golden lady nearby. Only hope that soon he could speak his true feelings kept him from admitting defeat.

Brendan Trevarrick had never been given to contemplation of the future. Usually he just catapulted ahead, expecting events to fall into place around him, and if they didn't, he would just catapult off in another direction. But he could not be impulsive now, when faced with losing Kristen forever to a man not fit to kiss her hand. Any mistake could be fatal, dooming them both to a lifetime of disappointment. For he realized now, if Kristen didn't, that they would never be happy apart. Kristen needed his love to free the love she kept locked inside. And he needed her, for she was the one woman he would be content to love for life.

Tressilian did not regret his past, but with the advantage of hindsight he could see that his romantic affairs had been essentially empty. Probably the women had felt some affection for him, and in the thrill of the chase he too regarded each warmly. But that feeling soon faded and he moved on to find another woman to quicken his pulse.

In all that time, however, only Kristen continually challenged him, with her serene eyes and quick wit and independent spirit. Only Kristen could he imagine loving forever; only she inspired in him a desire to be better, to be faithful and constant. If only Kristen would give him a chance to prove that she had, in fact, succeeded in reforming him.

A year ago he might have dismissed marriage as a trap for the unwary. Now he saw its rewards— constant love, a refuge from care, the presence of children. That it would also enable him to resume his navy career was no longer an overriding concern. He would marry Kristen regardless, just to have her as his own. And if he couldn't marry her, he'd marry no one, and become a pirate like Jean Lafitte.

He found himself smiling, for piracy was Corinna's ultimate ambition. Nick, less ambitious, just wanted to he an admiral. They're mine too, he thought fiercely, and I shan't let Stamberly have them.

He lingered over the last of his brandy, uncertain what to do next now that he had no mistress to fill his nights. He didn't want to go home, for surely one of his alleged cousins was camping out on his doorstep. He was safe, at least, inside the exclusive environs of White's. Jonny would be arriving eventually, to groan and complain whenever he or Garber happened to mention the word "Trafalgar". In the meantime, he might as well take Garber up on the offer of a game. Tonight might well be his night to win a fortune, for everyone knew that good luck in cards followed bad luck in love, sure as day followed night.

# CHAPTER FOURTEEN

The next afternoon, Becky waited alone in the drawing room of Killeaven House, dressed in her jaunty new riding habit. Of a military cut in green velvet, the jacket clung to her slim figure and flared slightly at the hip over the mannish skirt. It was braided in black across the front, just like a rifler's uniform, and made a very patriotic statement.

At the gilt mirror she adjusted the hat, tilting it daringly over one eye. They will say I look adorable, she thought modestly, if Bren ever comes to take me riding. She flitted back to the window, peering down South Audley Street to Grosvenor Square. She could just see the stone steps of Tressilian House, where a portly man waited patiently. One of Bren's "cousins", no doubt, ready to spring on the earl whenever he should leave his townhouse.

It wasn't enough that the woman he loved was betrothed to another man; he also had to deal with the spurious legal claims that one of these impostors was his heir. And then their scheme required that he spend his time taking Becky riding in the park and doing the pretty at Almack' s. It was enough to drive a sensible man mad, and no one had ever accused Brendan of being sensible.

So Becky could not blame him for drinking late and playing deep at White s, although she believed he'd do better to channel his restless energy into uncovering spy networks and rescuing maidens from peril. Now he was champing at the bit, talking wildly about challenging Stamberly and abducting Kristen. These threats were an improvement, she supposed, over his previous despair. But she would be very happy when their scheme succeeded and Kristen could take charge of the volatile earl.

Becky, at least, was optimistic about their eventual success. She had the advantage of seeing Kristen everyday, of observing her cousin's unusual abstraction. Kristen was not inclined to moodiness, but for one contemplating her nuptials, she was uncommonly unhappy. Beneath the placid waters of this betrothal, Becky thought gleefully, a whirlpool was being stirred up, mostly by Nick and Corey. Kristen was deeply troubled by their resistance, and by Stamberly's corresponding displeasure.

But more than this mutual antipathy disturbed Kristen's serenity. This morning, when Becky announced in her usual blithe way that Tressilian was coming to take her riding, Kristen had said wistfully, almost to herself, "Brendan never comes around anymore, except to take you off somewhere." You see how much she misses you, Becky would tell Tressilian when he arrived.

If he ever arrived. Much as she loved Brendan, Becky had lately been forced to acknowledge a few of his faults. He was charming and his appearance quite took one's breath away, but did that make up for his lack of punctuality? He knew she was longing to try out her new habit on her legions of admirers in Hyde Park, but no doubt he had been detained by some prizefight or hazard game-something much more important than keeping a date with his conspirator.

Becky pressed her forehead to the window, determined to see Tressilian come cantering up on his black stallion. But only a butcher's delivery cart clattered up the street towards her. She laughed bitterly, recalling that in the beginning she had been just the least bit afraid she would fall in love with Tressilian despite her brave resolutions. After all, he was really disastrously good-looking, and his life rollicked with adventure. But that fear seemed absurd now. She loved Bren as the brother she never had. (Not that she didn't have a brother, for she did. But she had long since disowned the bullying Lawrence.)

But occasionally even the adventurous Becky felt a traitorous longing for peace. Knowing Brendan was like trying to harness a hurricane. His moods were so variable, his whims so powerful. For the first time in her life, Becky had met someone who was more impulsive than she, and the combination frightened her.

Suddenly she was the rational one, pointing out the need for caution— not a role she was accustomed to perform! Just last week, for example, Tressilian had responded to her offhanded request to attend a prize-fight by procuring a set of boy's clothes in her size and tickets to the vaunted Hadley-Rains match. She shuddered now to think what might have happened if she hadn't had sense to refuse.

No, this secret betrothal was not the picnic it once promised to be. Of course, the last weeks had been thrilling, but the excitement was beginning to pall. While a dozen men were paying court to her, none ventured very close, for everyone knew her secret fiancee's predilection for pistols at dawn. In fact, the girl unanimously counted the toast of the season had not received one proposal of marriage.

So no matter how delicately the end of her betrothal was handled, Becky had a dark suspicion that she would appear slightly ridiculous. There she would be, bravely declaring she had broken off the engagement, while everyone else believed she'd been thrown over for her own cousin.

She was a willing martyr, of course. Aiding True Love required a few sacrifices. But even if everything worked out as they planned, Brendan would be happy with the woman he loved, while Becky— Becky would be alone.

She stamped her foot so hard the windowpane shivered. Bad enough that she would be jilted practically at the altar. It was altogether insupportable that she should have to spend this beautiful afternoon waiting for her irresponsible fiancee.

Suddenly she pushed back from the window. Kristen was out at the dressmaker's being fitted for a ballgown. The children were in the school-room terrorizing their poor governess. Great-aunt Helen hadn't emerged from her room in a fortnight, not since her elderly beau eloped with an opera dancer. No one would notice if she left the house a little bit alone. So she cocked her little hat and picked up her gloves and walked casually down to the entry foyer. "Have the groom bring my mare around, will you, Chesley?"

"But, miss—"

"Just get my mare," she said sternly, and Chesley complied, muttering to himself that the groom was going along whether she liked it or not. The intimidated groom trailed Becky by fifteen feet as she entered the park, so she appeared to be quite alone. She gloried in the reproving glances of the older ladies safely guarded by their men. They hadn't the sense to enjoy this delicious freedom that made the world a limitless arena of play. And without the dangerous earl by her side, she would be free to carry on a delicious flirtation with some delicious young man.

Unfortunately, the first man to reach her was Captain Destain, and Becky had already determined that flirting with him was a waste of time. Several times lately she had directed a speaking glance in the captain's direction, even unfurling her fan and peeping over it in the manner her beaus found so enchanting.

But Captain Destain had only regarded her out of those half-closed eyes and smiled in that ironic fashion that said he saw right through her poses. If his uniform weren't quite so striking, and his lazy drawl so compelling, she would not pay him the least mind at all. For such a cynical, indolent man obviously hadn't a romantic bone in his body. Certainly no romantic would carry on a fleshly affair with that married lady, whose charms were all too apparent.

That irrelevant consideration made it easier to ignore Destain's slow, sweet smile as he approached her. He wasted none of his precious energy greeting her, only wheeling his bay with a decidedly military briskness into line with her mare. That soft drawl did not enchant her either, coupled as it was with the biting sarcasm she had come to expect of him. "Deserted by your fiancée?"

"Certainly not," she retorted, urging her horse forward. But without any visible effort, Captain Destain kept pace with her, and she was forced to elaborate— and fabricate. "Brendan is doubtlessly off on some splendid adventure— ferreting out some more spies, I imagine." She didn't know why she lied, except to taunt the superior Captain Destain, who was so cynical about heroics. Unfortunately, Brendan was not living up to her expectations of a hero lately, so she had to be especially inventive.

She had forgotten, however, the unlikely friendship between Captain Destain and his cousin. "Such exceptional powers of recuperation, Tressilian has, to be routing spies after last night at White's. I'm surprised he can raise his head."

Foreboding filled Becky. "What did he do now?"

"Ah, do I hear a bit of trepidation in your voice?" She flushed under Destain's amused regard. "Now you know the fix I've been in for nearly thirty years, never knowing what mess he's going to land himself in next, whether he'll survive the night— he did, by the way, though most men would have had the sense to crawl away and die after all he drank. Instead he restored himself by losing six thousand pounds at faro."

"Six thousand— he's not ruined, is he?" Bleakly Becky recalled her Uncle Rupert's flight to the colonies after he couldn't make good on his vowels. Her father never mentioned that name without warning Becky about the evils of gaming.

"Ruined? Bren?" Destain scoffed. "He could lose that much a dozen times and still have more than most of us. But then he won a pony back from Chelten in one of those drunken wagers the two of them can never resist." A reluctant grin lightened his sardonic expression. "We all had to adjourn to the courtyard to watch Tressilian shoot out the coal of a cigar held in Chippingham's mouth from twenty paces."

"Did he do it?" Becky demanded.

Destain was amused at the anxious excitement that had her bouncing in her saddle. "Well, of course he did. I imagine Chippingham was grateful for that marksmanship when he woke up this morning and realized what a fool thing he'd done."

"Oh, famous!" Becky tossed her head back in a laugh, envisioning the dark courtyard, the cigar clenched in the man's teeth, Tressilian in shirt sleeves taking casual aim— Captain Destain watching it all through narrowed eyes. She turned to him with the accusation, "You don't approve, do you?"

Destain leaned back in his saddle, his gauntleted hands resting easily on the pommel, and the sun caught his dark gold hair under the black shako hat. "I don't approve of any purposeless activity, my sweet. Waste of energy. But then, so much of what Bren does is a waste of energy. All those foolish heroic endeavors, all those endless romantic interludes—" His smile turned a bit malicious as he added in afterthought, "At least that's behind him, all the wasted gallantry, isn't it? Now he will concentrate that on you."

Becky flushed and looked away in to the line of trees at their right. She didn't know why Captain Destain was so angry with her after all, he was the one who had been so cool to her friendly overtures. "I don't consider heroism and romance a waste of energy," was all she could trust herself to reply.

"Of course you don't. He's all you've ever dreamed of, isn't he?"

Actually, if Becky were dreaming, she would make Brendan more reliable and divest him of one wicked-tongued friend. "Yes, yes, of course," she replied impatiently, wishing someone else would approach and interrupt this infuriating conversation.

But somehow, effortlessly, Destain had maneuvered her down a secluded lane towards the rose garden, and they were alone, except for the abashed groom a dozen yards back. An illicit thrill ran through her. Whatever would Kristen say if she knew? If anyone but Captain Destain had guided her here, Becky would have suspected he harbored dishonorable intentions. But naturally she was not to be so fortunate. The captain's only intention was to taunt her.

She risked a haughty glance to find him watching her speculatively.

"One of the lowering realizations of adulthood," he advised her with weary wisdom, "is that dreams are never as delightful in their fulfillment as in their conception. Rather like babies, I expect."

Ordinarily, Becky would have been gratified to hear a young man use such an improper metaphor as the conception of a baby. But she would not accept even the most scandalous of speech when delivered in that top-lofty tone. "You've learned that from painful experience, have you?" she snapped, hoping she was scraping some inner wound left by an adolescent heartbreak.

"God, no. If you know nothing else of me, know this— I don't dream. I have, however, observed this phenomenon among those who do give their lives over to that useless activity. They are inevitably disappointed—as you will be soon enough."

Becky knew she should punish him for his attitude by galloping away. But she hated to cut short an interlude so fraught with decadence, and she found Captain Destain oddly stimulating, enough to wonder what lay beneath that cynical shell.

Was he a disillusioned romantic, perhaps, despite his denials? She shivered a bit, intrigued in spite of herself. So she only answered loftily, "I think you will be the one disappointed, when my dreams come true and I am as delighted as may be and you must confess you were wrong."

"You are right, I shall be disappointed then." The dark look Destain slanted at her invested this statement with more significance than she expected. But then he grinned. "But you will be disappointed if you expect me to confess I was wrong!"

Becky had never been shy, but now she smiled shyly at him, attracted more than she liked by his self-deprecating wit and the spark in his dark blue eyes. He apparently took her smile as some encouragement, for he swung down easily from his mount. "Come, let's look at the gardens."

Becky hesitated, looking down at him, imagining all the dangerous things they might get up to on foot that they could never do on horseback. Not that she was in any danger—Captain Destain wouldn't even exert himself for a simple flirtation; he would hardly go to the bother of seducing her.

"Afraid?"

That careless accusation was all she needed. She slipped off her saddle so quickly that he hardly had time to catch her. Nonetheless she felt the hard grip of his hands on her waist, the scratch of his coat's military braid as she slid down against him. Suddenly breathless, she spun away from him towards the famous gardens while he secured their horses and waved the groom away.

"Not very impressive," Captain Destain, coming up behind her, observed of the careful rows of staked plants. This early in the spring, there were no blooms on the spindly rose bushes and the earth around them was raw and dark. Becky resolved to come back in May, when the roses would be blooming. Perhaps Captain Destain would be more congenial then. Now she could only take the arm he offered and tread down the spongy path beside the bare bushes.

She had removed her gloves and could feel the rough wool of his uniform jacket, and beneath that, the easy muscularity of his arm. She was more aware of her scant inches than usual, for Destain's lean form evoked a lazy power as they strolled. For once she kept still, afraid to disrupt this fragile peace with some provocative statement.

He finally broke the silence. "Did you really think that Tressilian might be ruined in a night's play?"

His return to an earlier subject was puzzling, but then, much of Destain's conversation confused her. She sensed he was amused by her ignorance, so she retorted, "Why shouldn't he be? My Uncle Rupert was rolled up on the turn of one card."

"Well, even Bren's not that reckless," Destain observed fairly. "If he were, I'd find a way to stop him, you may be sure. But I meant did you really think six thousand was the limit of his fortune?"

To a girl limited to fifty pounds of pin money each quarter, six thousand pounds was a fortune. But she knew better now than to admit to such naiveté, and only shrugged.

"You know," he said slowly, guiding her back towards their mounts, "for a mercenary little baggage you certainly don't know much about your fiancee's finances."

"Mercenary little—" Words failed Becky, for perhaps the first time ever. But the wicked light in Destain's eyes fired her into eloquence. "If you think Brendan Trevarrick's greatest attraction is his fortune, Captain, you must be blind as well as foolish. No, I don't know anything about his finances, nor do I care. I would never marry for money, and I wish I could call you out for suggesting it." She suited action to threat by pulling her riding glove out of her pocket and slapping it challengingly against her palm.

He drew back in mock fear. But his next words were just as challenging as her gesture. "Then I acquit you of being a mercenary little baggage. It is clear to me now that you are instead a starstruck little fool."

That was, if anything, worse. "Wh—what gives you the right to judge me at all?" she demanded when she got her breath back.

"As Bren's best friend, I claim the right." His arrogance was breathtaking, particularly when he stopped near their horses and seized her arm in an imperious grip. "You are being a starstruck little fool if you think he'll make you any kind of husband. He's too wild— and you haven't the strength to rein him in."

Becky yanked her arm free, furious on behalf of Brendan, who had his faults but would never behave in this unchivalrous manner. "You call yourself his best friend, and yet you call him wild and stupid and— and all sorts of other insulting things! And he is so— so boastful of you, telling me how clever you are, and how good at games, and— why, he would never insult you so!"

Destain had the grace to look ashamed, but strove to explain himself. "We've been friends all our lives, so I don't have to defend my treatment of him to you. I know him better than anyone. And I know what sort of wife he needs, and that's not you. I can see why he's enchanted your high spirits and innocence. Any man would be. But you're too inexperienced and too idealistic. And too much like him. In a month, you'll both be in disaster, because neither of you can see straight enough to know where you're headed."

That in a soberer time she might have agreed did not dispel her outrage. So angry was she that she did not even linger on that promising "I can see why—" She merely drew herself up to her full sixty-two inches and with all the haughtiness of a would-be countess, replied, "Brendan thinks otherwise."

"Such an endorsement!" Destain mocked. "He can always be counted on to think rationally, can't he? And even he, sweeting, has expressed a few reservations about this marriage. He does recognize the likelihood of ruining your life."

"Only because you keep harping on it, I wager." His flush told her she had launched a home arrow, and she followed with another shot. "And it isn't the slightest bit your affair, in any event."

"Of course it is. It's my duty, in fact. I've spent my life keeping Brendan out of trouble, and I'm hardly going to stop now when he's about to make the biggest mistake of his life."

Becky hid her angry tears by turning to untie her horse. "You are so certain that marriage to me would be ruinous, are you?"

He hesitated behind her, and for the first time she sensed he was considering his harsh words and the effect they might have on her. Then she felt his hands gentle on her waist, lifting her into the saddle. "Only for him," he finally replied, gazing up at her rigid in the saddle. "And only for you."

If that was his idea of apology, Becky was unmollified, and didn't wait for him to mount before she spurred her mare back towards the public path. But he rode up beside her and grabbed the mare's bridle, easing her to a stop. A typical female, Sherry ignored her mistress's command and gazed adoringly at the cavalry officer. Becky was not so easily cozened; she pretended fascination with a gnarled oak and gave him only her back to address.

But his voice was low and unwontedly urgent. "Do you know, when Bren gets himself embroiled in a duel of honor, as he does every fortnight or so, it seems, he invariably names me his second. The vestiges of conscience, I daresay, for he's so often in the wrong in these affairs. He knows I'll be able to persuade the other party to retract the challenge. For Bren never misses, not if he's of a mind to win. And they usually retract. The ones who don't would, if they had it to do again."

He let her consider that, her bonny Bren, so gentle, so kind— so ruthless. Then he echoed her thoughts. "He's a dangerous man, my girl. A good man, but dangerous. All I'm doing is playing his second again. You are not up to his weight. This marriage will be bad for him, but worse for you. Let it go."

She still stared at the gnarled tree, hearing his words echo in her mind. He was right, of course, Brendan did need another sort of woman. In fact, if Tressilian made only one sensible decision in his life, it was to fall in love with Kristen, for she was truly a woman strong enough and wise enough to love him well.

But Captain Destain's wisdom, as usual, was edged with a malice she didn't understand. He had made it clear that he viewed her as a foolish girl whose only consequence was that she might ruin his best friend's life. Hurt and angry, she retaliated as she had learned from her elder brother, attacking what she sensed was his weakest point.

"Are you jealous, Captain Destain?" she inquired sweetly, tossing a bright smile over her shoulder. "It must be irritating always to be Brendan's second."

Her emphasis on that last word gave it special insult, and he responded hotly, "If I had the least desire to live like Tressilian, I would. But I don't intend to start behaving according to the standards of heroism some half-formed chit has imbibed from lurid novels!"

Becky's standards of heroism were, in fact, gleaned from the sort of Gothic novel she hoped to write. But none of the men she had met in London were compelling enough to make her change her mind. Even Captain Destain, so dashing in his regimentals, so striking in his anger, persisted in naming her a naive schoolgirl, too shallow even to merit his contempt.

"But I don't expect you to behave as a hero, Captain Destain," she retorted, "as it is apparent you haven't the least capability of doing so!"

He released her reins then, his patrician face set with rage at the dimensions of her insult. And Becky galloped off back to Rotten Row, oblivious to the disapproving stares of park matrons. Encountering her anxious groom near Stanhope Gate, she turned home, assured that she had neatly routed the cavalry officer. But for some reason, this victory, secure as it was, felt somehow hollow.

# CHAPTER FIFTEEN

Only the annual May Day masquerade of the Marchioness of Drayton could induce so many people to make the onerous seven-mile journey to Richmond during the height of the season. By noon the sundappled formal gardens, the expansive lawns unfolding to the river, and the flagstoned piazzas were thronged with satyrs, monks, fairy princesses, and witches.

Tressilian characteristically disdained the tradition of costume, for once with official approval— military men were expected always to make a military show during this tense time. Still, in his naval uniform he was more theatrical than Stamberly, costumed as Shakespeare, or any of the other men who had been forced by custom or a wife to submit to the indignity of masquerade. Brendan had left off his dramatic bicorne hat, so his dark hair glinted blue-black in the sunlight.

Kristen, a medieval lady-in-waiting in flowing rose gauze, ran a finger under the tight band of her wimple and wished she d followed Tressilian's example.

But he was more concerned with Becky's apparel, or at least one accessory she had insisted on bringing. He cast a wary look at the lamb that added just the right finishing touch to Becky's shepherdess costume. Like all children and small animals, it was drawn to the earl, but he did not return the affection. He took Kristen's elbow and guided her back a few steps onto the velvet lawn, so Becky was between them and the lovestruck lamb planted squarely in the middle of the busy path. But to no avail, for the little lamb followed him slavishly.

"If I remember my ancient history, this sort of nonsense got Marie Antoinette beheaded," he told his fiancee, who only wrinkled her nose and tugged at the stubborn animal's leash.

Kristen wondered if the irrepressible Becky's antics were beginning to pall with her betrothed. That malicious thought made her guilty, so she compensated by urging, "Oh, Brendan, don't spoil her fun. You look adorable, darling," she told Becky, "and Tressilian will help you find some place to tie that creature."

"I?" Tressilian arched one skeptical eyebrow. "I think not. I have no affinity for sheep." He pulled his boot away from the lamb's tongue. "Stamberly now," he added, as the viscount arrived with lemonade, "he looks the sort to know a great deal about sheep. Don't you agree, my love?"

Becky assented with a giggle, replacing the lemonade in Stamberly's hand with the lamb's leash. Kristen cast the viscount an apologetic glance, but it was true, he had four thousand sheep on his Kent estate and doubtlessly knew better than the negligent Tressilian what to do with this animal. With grudging courtesy he inclined his head to Becky and dragged the recalcitrant lamb away.

Becky turned her back on both hapless creatures and took Tressilian's arm. Swishing her sky blue skirt under the lacy apron, she asked flirtatiously, "Do you like my costume, darling?" But her mischievous glance was aimed at Kristen on Brendan's other arm.

"Very much. I am impressed that you have contrived to show more ankle than any other shepherdess here. Of course—" Tressilian stopped and surveyed the area in question with an expert eye "—your ankles are prettier than any of the others in evidence."

Becky crowed delightedly. "I'd hoped you would notice that! Mary Callison's are rather plump, and Lois McDale's are so bony. And of course, I was the only shepherdess who thought to bring my own lamb. That is the touch that makes the whole costume authentic."

She glanced across Tressilian's gold-braided chest to Kristen and added with innocent wickedness, "I shall make a wedding present of the lamb to Stamberly, as he gets on so well with it."

Kristen found much to take issue with in her companions' conversation—the bantering tone, Brendan's outrageous appraisal of Becky's ankles, and the implied insult to Kristen's fiancee. But she was weary of playing gooseberry. She wasn't old enough to be the damper of high spirits chaperones were expected to be.

And her disapproval made no difference anyway. No matter what Kristen did, Becky's behavior showed no improvement, Becky's parents still approved the match, Brendan showed no desire to cry off. Kristen was, in fact, nearly irrelevant to this glorious romance.

Becky and Brendan were too involved in giving absurd names to the costumed guests to notice the approach of one particular partygoer. But Kristen recognized the heavyset priest and said with a touch of malice, "Look, Brendan, there is one of your cousins. He must have sneaked in here— Lady Drayton is so lax in such matters."

"Evelyn Rutherford, madame," the florid intruder interposed with a bow. "At your service." He turned with another bow toward the earl. "How are you, cousin? Completely recovered from your little accident, I trust. I often came to visit during your convalescence, but I was told you were not receiving."

"We are not acquainted." Tressilian detached his arm from Kristen's hand and rested his fingers lightly on the hilt of his sword.

"Not acquainted?" Rutherford had some justification for his incredulity, for no one had been able to leave Tressilian House lately without stumbling over that bulky figure, and the earl's desk was buried under petitions from Rutherford's solicitor. "Why, we are cousins! Your grandfather was my mother's second cousin, so that makes us—" he ruminated happily for a moment— "cousins of some sort. My mother's middle name was Trevarrick. I have the family tree right here."

With a flourish he withdrew a scroll from a pocket in his voluminous priest's robes. He stabbed at a branch on the pen-and-ink tree with a fat finger. "There! Cornelia— my grandmother— was the daughter of Eliza-beth Trevarrick, the second wife of the eighth earl. It's all here in black and white."

Tressilian disdained to accept the proffered scroll. "I have never ac-knowledged any kinship with you. Of course, I've seen you any number of times, camped on my doorstep, and have often considered running you through." His fingers encircled the hilt of his sword, and, alarmed, Kristen laid a soothing hand on his fist. He looked down at her, his eyes opaque with anger. But then he took a deep breath and nodded in answer to her tacit plea.

Rutherford was oblivious to his narrow escape. "But I visited Tressilian Castle as a boy. Mama and I enjoyed our stay so much— say you cherish the same warm memories!"

The earl's fist clenched again under Kristen's hand, but his tone was level. "I recall some overbearing, underbred woman thrusting her son at my grandfather. The boy was fat and smelled of sausage. Grandfather took one look and said, 'Trevarricks breed true, and that's no true Trevarrick.' Is that the happy visit you remember?"

Mr. Rutherford struggled to assent to this unflattering description but only succeeded in stuttering. Becky intervened helpfully, "If anyone said that about my mother, I'd call him out."

"No need for that, no need for that!" Rutherford said hastily. "There should be no animosity among cousins. After all, I'm the earl's only surviv-ing Trevarrick relation."

"If that's true, and I beg leave to doubt it, it's only for the moment. For I intend to set up my own nursery soon. What do you say, sweeting, would five sons be enough to ensure the succession?"

Becky clasped her hands and smiled blissfully, like a Madonna whose child had just been put to bed. Kristen felt an odd twist, her imagination balking at the vision of childish Becky as a mother to five Trevarrick boys. But the anguish was gone in a moment, and she could concentrate on

Rutherford's blotched face.

"We shall see," he said darkly, and Kristen shivered in spite of the warmth of the sun. He was an absurd creation, a corpulent villain from a farce. But there was something chilling in his protuberant blue eyes. Her apprehension did not abate when he regained his unctuous composure. "That will not affect the great feeling I bear for you, cousin," he said fervently.

"Oh, get him out of here," Tressilian exclaimed, and a hovering footman took Rutherford's arm and dragged him, still smiling, away.

"What an awful man," Kristen observed, chilled by the encounter. "Is he really your cousin?"

"Of course not. Trevarricks never run to fat," Tressilian said haughtily.

"But he couldn't inherit anyway, could he?" Becky asked, her pretty brow furrowed. "I thought the connection had to be through the male line. Even if his grandmother was a Trevarrick, he would be descended from a female."

"Military title," Tressilian observed with lowered brow. "Henry VII granted the title entailed on heirs males whatsoever, so even the distaff line can inherit. That was meant to ensure that the title survive no matter what. But if he'd gotten wind of Rutherford there, he'd never have done us the favor." He shook his head to dispel his anger. "Never mind. Let's apply ourselves to making merry. What's your pleasure now, sweetheart?"

Kristen opened her mouth to answer before she realized the endearment was addressed to Becky. She was further humiliated when Becky, secure in her privileged position, condescended to include Kristen in their little magic circle. "Stamberly seems to have vanished, so let's not leave Kristen all alone. We can stroll about until the luncheon tables are set up. I do want to give everyone a chance to admire my ankles."

"Becky, you rogue, I do adore you." Tressilian smiled down at his fiancee. "You never fail to divert me from my ill-temper. What an amusing wife you will be! Now lift those skirts just a bit, give me a glimpse of dimpled knee— ah, my heart, my heart—"

"If you'll excuse me," Kristen said glacially, dropping her hand from Tressilian's arm, "I'll leave you two to your flirtation."

"No, no, we'll be good!" Becky grabbed her arm and tugged her to the side. "Brendan, tell her we'll stop. I imagine such silliness must be annoying, don't you think? We don't find our love talk maudlin, but we mustn't inflict. it upon poor Kristen."

Kristen found herself installed between the two lovers, an even more uncomfortable position, as it implied they needs must be separated or their passion might overcome all decorum. At least for the moment they were good to their word and ceased the teasing interplay that scraped like a file across Kristen's nerves. Love talk— yes, it was annoying to hear the two of them cooing like doves. Still, Brendan's laughing voice made even maudlin words absurdly appealing. But then, he was an expert at appealing to women, wasn't he?

Soon enough, Tressilian resumed his flirtation right across the head of the reluctant chaperone as they strolled towards the great Palladian house. "Did I ever tell you, my own, that once before I was felled by Cupid's arrow?"

"Only once?" Becky had to twist to grin at Tressilian around Kristen's towering wimple.

"You are a rogue, aren't you?" Tressilian replied appreciatively. "But yes, only once before have I lost my heart— oh, stop me, Kristen, before I get started again."

She shook her head wearily. "I never traffick in lost causes. You are, I fear, incurable."

"What a dire prognosis! In any event, Becky love, I shall in a moment or so reveal to you the woman who first stole my heart away."

He added as Kristen stopped short in the path, "No, angel, I shan't introduce her to any former mistresses, I promise."

"Then half the women here will be forgoing the pleasure of her acquaintance, I fear," Kristen muttered under her breath.

But Becky had heard and squeaked. "Half? Brendan, you amaze me!"

"Not half, not half of half of half." He turned a censorious look upon the countess. "Kristen, what are you thinking, to say such a thing? You know the girl is already too impressed with my checkered past."

A shamed color crept up Kristen's cheeks. She wasn't accustomed to being reprimanded by Tressilian, and it was lowering to realize he was right. Her remark was reprehensible, especially as Brendan's checkered past appeared to be entirely past.

Penitently she held her tongue as they strolled towards the tent that sheltered a circle of society matrons in low chairs. She noticed absently that Elizabeth I seemed to be the favored role of these queens of the ton, although a puritan and a nun were also imbibing champagne under the pink and white awning.

As Tressilian continued his teasing, Kristen wondered if he were trying to make Becky jealous. She also couldn't escape the sense that there was a message to Kristen in his rhapsody to lost love. "She was a goddess, as lovely as Venus and wise as Minerva. And as powerful as Juno." He raised his voice slightly so that the matrons in the tent could hear him. "I never did get over the terrible trauma of learning that another man had claimed her first."

For a dizzying instant Kristen imagined she might be the woman he described. She hardly had time to rebuke herself for that absurdity when they stopped before one Queen Elizabeth, who looked up with feigned surprise before glancing triumphantly at her friends.

"Yes, dearest, here is the lady who stole away much of my heart. I thought she took the entire of it, until I met you and realized I had a fragment or two left." Brendan released his two escorts and bent to drop a kiss on the lady's round cheek. "My first love— my Aunt Manda."

Vertigo again shook Kristen as Brendan smiled at Becky. "And this is my second love, Miss Marlowe."

Some secret betrothal, Kristen thought helplessly as the matrons all sat up straighter in their chairs and waved their fans, anticipating a rare show.

But Lady Destain saw nothing amiss in this declaration, only sighing luxuriously and reaching up to take the earl's hand. "Oh, Brendan, dear, you have simply made my afternoon. Now sit down; you're so tall you make me feel quite faint looking up at you. You too, Lady Killeaven, and you, dear child, right here by me."

Tressilian sprawled gracefully on the grass next to Lady Destain's chair, and Becky and Kristen took their more sedate seats in nearby chairs. Still a bit dazed, Kristen had a sudden vision of a profusion of ears turned in their direction, for every one of Lady Destain's friends wanted to be privy to this conversation.

And Brendan, who never failed a lady, leaned back on an elbow and bestowed a languishing gaze on his aunt. Of course, there was nothing he liked more than to be at the center of a group of adoring women. "Even today I remember how bewitched I was when first I saw my magnificent Manda."

"Well, you can't remember it, you scamp, for you weren't an hour old yet. And you wouldn't have been bewitched by me, huge with child as I was. For my son Jonny," she told Becky, "was born exactly two months later."

"Hush, Aunty," Brendan said sotto voce, "you are spoiling my ballad."

Lady Destain reached down to ruffle her minstrel's dark locks. "Go on then, but do speak a bit louder, for I most especially want Irma Caruthers to hear this, and she is behind you."

Tressilian raised his fine voice. "Can you hear me, Irma my love? Yes? I am so glad. For three years, near enough, I lived in blissful ignorance, dreaming of the day I would make my lady truly mine. Then I learned that the big lout—" he broke off, glancing around warily. "Uncle Anthony isn't here, is he?"

Lady Destain joined the rest of his audience in laughter, for everyone knew Tressilian feared no man, except perhaps the fierce Admiral Destain. "Don't tell him I said that, if you love me, ladies."

"Oh, we do," Irma cried from the back, and Brendan tossed her a smile over his shoulder before taking up his story again.

"That the big sailor who clumped around the house clanging his sword had already wed her. I thought to challenge him to a duel of honor— rapiers, of course— but he refused, the villain."

"That you weren't yet as tall as the rapier might have had something to do with that, my dearest boy," Lady Destain observed.

"That was merely his excuse. He worried that I might win and take you away from him. Instead I had to be content to worship from afar, and I vowed I would always be faithful to the goddess who first taught me about beauty, wisdom, and truth. And I have always kept my vow. Well, I have," he protested as a few ladies gave way to unladylike guffaws. "In spirit, at least."

"Of course you have, darling," Lady Destain said soothingly. "But now my most faithful— in spirit!— acolyte is deserting me for another." She reached over to tweak a curl from under Becky's lacy shepherdess cap. "And such a pretty successor as I have."

Brendan sat up, clasping one knee, and said with melting sincerity, "Oh, I'd hoped you'd think so. For I chose her with you in mind. In fact, I know my last sweetheart will not be surprised to hear how very much I think she resembles my first sweetheart."

As she watched the first and the last sweethearts assess each other, Kristen realized he was telling the truth. Lady Destain was fairer, her golden hair fading to silver now, and plumper, as befitted a matron. But her blue eyes danced with the same innocent fun that made Becky so lovable. And everyone knew Lady Destain in her youth had been a merry sort of girl, the perfect bride for a rollicking sailor....

Brendan rose smoothly to take the hands of his two sweethearts. He smiled reassuringly at Becky, for in this den of gossiping goodwives she had fallen silent. "Yes, you two are just alike. Enchantingly pretty with those big blue eyes, and happy as larks, and most of all—" He bent to whisper in his aunt's ear, then dropped both hands and laughingly dodged away from her rapping fan.

"You rascal, you!" Lady Destain aimed another blow at the unrepentant Brendan, but he had taken shelter behind Becky's chair, resting his hands lightly on her bare shoulders. "Why, Irma, you should have heard what he said to me!"

"What?" chorused the ladies, including Becky but excluding Kristen, who could very well guess. But Lady Destain only flounced a bit and waved her fan as if to cool her blushes. "I can't say," she announced, looking pointedly at Tressilian, "in mixed company."

"Oh, Brendan, go!" Restored to her usual high spirits, Becky pushed her fiancee away. "Or I'll never hear what scandalous compliment you paid me! And take Kristen too, please, for I know she will try to persuade Lady Destain to hold her tongue, and we'll all be so disappointed!"

Brendan looked stricken as only he could do, with his hand on his heart and his dark eyes full of hurt. "You are sending me away? All of you?" He drew a ragged sigh and limped out of the tent. "Come, Lady Killeaven. You must convey me forthwith to the river, then you must come back and report to them how I hurled my heartbroken self into the torrent."

Kristen bade a more restrained farewell to the assembly and followed the broken man out of earshot. "The limp was an inspired touch," she observed fairly.

"Quite Byronesque, I thought." He took her arm and guided her down the lawn to the river, just in case any of the ladies had doubted his suicidal intent. "I must go back and rescue Becky soon, I think. When Lady Destain starts recounting my childhood scrapes, she will never run down."

"There is an endless store to choose from, I imagine." Kristen felt a traitorous wish that he would forget about Becky, just for a few moments, and concentrate on his current companion. They were so seldom alone anymore, and she missed the easy hours they had together before he began to spend all his time with Becky.

As if he read her mind, Tressilian steered her along the path where willow trees trailed fronds into the water. Soon they entered a secluded arbor framed by trellises of rose bushes.

Even if Brendan had reformed, he retained the instincts of a rake, Kristen noted gladly as she sat on a rustic log bench. She arranged her full gauzy skirts around her, irrelevantly happy to be with him again, here under a brilliant blue sky with the light scent of flowers everywhere. With a relieved sigh, she pulled off the tight wimple and rubbed her forehead.

"Why, Lady Killeaven, you cannot go bareheaded in the sun," Tressilian said in a shocked tone. "It isn't proper."

"Fainting dead away from the headache would be even less proper," she replied, twisting her hair into a simple knot at the nape of the neck.

"I shall be your milliner then, to save you from both disgrace and swooning." Tressilian plucked three pink roses from one of the trellises, then carefully broke off every thorn with a calloused thumb. He took a seat beside her and, frowning judiciously, inserted the blooms into her hair. Kristen held her breath as he took her chin in his hand and turned her head to see the effect.

"There," he said with satisfaction, moving back for a comprehensive appraisal. "May I say, my lady, you nearly do justice to my brilliant work. Your lovely fair skin almost complements my color scheme, and the golden tresses add rather a piquant touch, I think. That will be thirty guineas."

She laughed at his imitation of a fop, incongruous as it was from such an overpoweringly masculine man. But then his gaze grew somber and she had to drop her eyes, for his expression was at once too revealing and too veiled. "Have I told you today how lovely you are, even without the roses?"

She was both relieved and disappointed that he had fallen back on his familiar flirtatious patterns, and she followed suit. Just to tease him, she lowered her eyes demurely. "No, you were too busy admiring Becky's ankles."

"I was not the only one." He leaned back against the bench, stretching his legs out lazily. "I cannot believe you let her out in that rig."

This reproof, coming from a belted rakehell, raised Kristen's hackles. "She had threatened to come as Robin Hood, in doublet and breeches. I thought this the lesser of two evils. But you are right," she added with a sigh. "I am an utter failure as a chaperone. She is relentless. She is always so logical, in her absurd way, and when logic fails she just pretends not to hear my objections."

"She is extraordinarily persuasive, isn't she?" Tressilian remarked proudly. "I don't know why the foreign office hasn't snapped her up to conduct the peace talks. Even I succumbed and let her drive my horses, after she begged and pleaded for three days. It's easier to surrender at the start than waste all that time telling her you will never allow it."

As he smiled to himself, Kristen bit her lip pensively. She no longer doubted Tressilian's affection for Becky, but somehow the certainty gave her no comfort.

Weary of Becky and this unfortunate courtship, Kristen decided to divert Tressilian's attention. She smoothed down the flowing rose gauze of her skirt with an unhappy sigh. "I feel like an ugly duckling in a pond full of swans in this undistinguished costume. All the other ladies are so elaborately done up, and without my wimple, why, I'm nothing special at all."

Tressilian laughed aloud at this blatant fish for compliments. But he was always willing to play these romantic games, and gratifyingly hyperbolic, he set her violet eyes sparkling with his words of admiration. She counted herself no more vain than the next woman, but lately she had been starved for flattery. Edward was so sparing in his praise, preferring to reserve it for special occasions. During their short engagement Kristen had almost forgotten how lovely it was to have a man pay court to her with every evidence of sincerity.

Tressilian was so skilled that the game seemed entirely harmless, just a diversion at a long afternoon party. Only later, when they were strolling back to the piazza where couples danced to a small orchestra, did the game become tantalizingly serious.

He stopped in the middle of the path, a curiously intent look in his dark eyes, and touched her silken curls with a gentle hand. Then he took one of the pink roses from her hair and pinned it to his lapel. It was only a gallant gesture, she told herself, but her wildly beating heart told her it was something else entirely. It was a token of possession, a signal that they were somehow intimate.

But it was all wrong. Brendan, in love with Becky, should not be making such a loving gesture to another woman, and Kristen, planning a loveless marriage to Stamberly, could not justify her breathless longing for another man.

# CHAPTER SIXTEEN

Becky produced a creditable blush for the older ladies when Lady Destain repeated Brendan's compliment in a stage whisper. I don't really think it was so shocking, she thought, proud of how sophisticated she had become in only two London months.

But Lady Destain found Becky's new sophistication less intriguing than her new status. "Now tell us all about this secret romance of yours. I confess I'm dying of curiosity about the little innocent who caught my rascal nephew."

Becky colored becomingly, but she felt oddly empty as she disclaimed any secret romance. It was absurd keeping up this charade of secrecy when everyone from the Prince Regent down to the lowliest chambermaid knew that she and Tressilian were betrothed. Except that they weren't, and the fortunate Miss Marlowe wasn't so fortunate after all.

But Lady Destain needed little encouragement to keep the conversation going, regarding Becky's reticence as charming in a naive young lady. "Well, I do understand your parents' reluctance, if that's the fly in the ointment. Brendan does have a lamentable reputation, and it's not at all exaggerated, I'm afraid."

Becky cast her eyes in pretended shyness down as Irma chortled, "No, thank the stars, for what would we have to talk about were he not such a wild one?"

"But there's not an ounce of meanness in the boy, is there, dear? Why, he was always the most charming child, with those dark eyes and dark curls. But such a handful!"

Lady Destain fanned herself more vigorously now, as if the very memory overheated her. "He was walking at seven months— oh, not walking, running!— and never stopped moving. His nurse always lamented that he never slept, not even as an infant. Why, he might miss some excitement if he closed his eyes! I expect," she addressed herself to Becky again, "he has told you he virtually grew up in our house. His mother— my cousin— died when he was born, and he found the castle too big and empty. And he and my Jonny are just of an age, although they aren't at all alike. Surely Brendan has introduced you to my son, for they are still the dearest of friends."

Becky nodded, then, when Lady Destain seemed to expect some comment, she added, "Captain Destain is so dashing in his uniform."

"Oh, yes, those dragoon regimentals are quite splendid. Of course, it sends the admiral into a spasm every time he sees his son in an army uniform." Sadness flickered in Lady Destain's eyes. "Anthony has always thought of your Brendan as another son, as they are both sailors. Jonny is the dearest boy, but not at all the sort of son Anthony expected."

Becky's hasty words accusing Captain Destain of jealousy came back to shame her. How hard it must have been for him, to be rejected in favor of his best friend. He must have been tempted either to cast Brendan aside or to be content in his shadow. Captain Destain had done neither, however, going his own way while remaining the earl's friend.

But Lady Destain gave her no time to reflect on this revelation. "Now, I too adore Brendan, but only in small doses. All the drama, all the emotion! Why, an hour with him and I'm exhausted. And the mischief he makes! Oh, he was forever getting into scrapes, and Jonny was forever getting him out— I think he still does, only they don't tell me about it anymore, and that is a shame, for I'm sure the scrapes are much more interesting now.

I recall when Jon was arrested for climbing into Lord Crayton's window to steal those love letters to Lady Crayton— now wouldn't you think Brendan would know better than to pour out his heart on paper? Such a passionate, foolish boy he is! Now he will be your responsibility, I fear." Lady Destain pressed Becky's hand and smiled kindly. "I don't envy you, dear."

"I do!" called out the irrepressible Irma as she led the other ladies out in search of more champagne. Becky managed another blush, wishing she could politely make her escape with them. All this speculation about her nuptials made her quite blue-deviled.

Lady Destain went so far as to pinch Becky's cheek— if we were men, Becky thought, I'd call her out for that. "I can't say you're the sort of bride I expected Brendan to take. I thought he'd prefer a more experienced kind of wife. Not that you aren't adorable, but you're so young! And so lively and high-spirited! Oh, just thinking what your children will be like wearies me!"

Now Becky quite intended for Brendan to have a more experienced bride, and should never have taken offense at Lady Destain's blithe observation. But the viscountess, like her son the captain, insisted on judging Becky as if she were a racehorse, finding her untrained and not yet up to the rigors of the course.

Fortunately, Lady Destain did not expect a reply to her most improper speculation about Becky's future progeny. "Now you'd be just perfect for my Jonny."

Becky greeted that alarming statement with a stare, but Lady Destain went on cheerfully to blacken her son's name. "Of course, he thinks he also prefers the most experienced sort of woman— and believe me, Elise Winterleigh is the most experienced sort, if you don't mind my saying so, and you shouldn't. But truly he needs a lively young girl to drag him into enjoying life instead of just lying back and observing. Not to say he isn't perfectly content with Elise, for I'm sure he is. With a woman like that, he needn't stir himself, for she doubtlessly does all the work!"

Becky firmly shut her mouth, which had been showing an alarming tendency to spring open in silent shock. And Kristen thought associating with Brendan might sully Becky's innocent ears!

But Lady Destain only smiled a sweet, matronly smile and patted Becky's cheek. "I dread the day Lord Winterleigh meets his maker, for Elise will no doubt catch Jon when he's feeling listless— much of the time, I fear!- - and push him right to the altar. I regret to say it, but I don't think I could ever accept her. You, however, you would make a delightful daughter, I just know it! Already I can talk to you about anything! Now if only Jon would come to his senses and find a sweet girl like you. Why, here he is now! You just missed Brendan, dear, but here is his blushing bride-to-be."

Becky raised her head to stare coolly into Captain Destain's eyes. After Lady Destain's monologue, Becky felt not the least sympathy for him. If his feelings were hurt because his father thought him an inadequate son, Captain Destain could seek solace in Elise Winterleigh's arms.

But Lady Destain ignored the antagonism blazing between the two young people. "Oh, Jon, take this darling girl away. I'm about to adopt her, for she is truly the dearest thing, sitting all this time listening to my tedious talk when she could have been off exploring secluded paths with your handsome cousin."

"Would you like to explore the refreshment tables instead, Miss Marl?" Now Captain Destain was all smooth civility, as if they had never exchanged insults in the middle of the Hyde Park rose garden.

So Becky responded in kind, silently accepting his arm. Like Tressilian, Destain disdained the theatrics of costume and wore his regimental colors with casual dignity. He led her to the white-clothed tables stretching a hundred feet along the yew hedge. A liveried footman bowed and offered chilled china plates and blue damask napkins wrapped around silverware.

Becky dropped her cool air at the delectable sight before her. "Oh, crab cakes! Lobster patties! Chicken tartlets! Champagne punch!" The footman exchanged an amused glance with Captain Destain as Becky held out her laden plate for a serving of mushroom fritters. "I do love al fresco meals," she sighed as they retreated behind the hedge to a white iron table set up in the formal garden.

Captain Destain's plate looked a little lonely, with only one lobster patty and a handful of apple fritters— an insubstantial meal for one who had been recently an invalid. So Becky generously speared one of her six macaroons and held it out to him.

Surprised, he accepted it off her fork as the peace offering it was meant to be. "I expect I should enjoy such bounty while I can. The menu on the Peninsula seldom carries macaroons."

Becky looked down at the plenty on her plate, obscurely guilty. It wasn't her fault that young men had to suffer deprivation in war; in fact, were she in charge of the world, she would probably do away with war altogether, although she would require all handsome young men to wear military uniforms. But she wondered if this lovely party seemed frivolous to the captain, who had been so long at war and would so soon be returning to it. "Have a raspberry tart," she insisted, dropping the pastry onto his plate.

"You are just like my mother," he said with amusement. "She is ever trying to feed me also, although her offerings run more to roast beef and mutton pie."

For the second time in an hour, a young man in a position to know was comparing her to Lady Destain. Becky was not sure she liked that, as she preferred to think of herself as incomparable. Doubtlessly this was meant as a compliment, for Brendan doted on his aunt and Captain Destain probably thought the world of her. Still, Becky could not quite approve of Lady Destain, who looked so sweet and spoke so wickedly—rather like her son, in fact. "Lady Destain is very entertaining," Becky said with careful understatement.

"Oh, Mother's an original," Destain observed with a grin. "I'd love to know what she said to make you blush as red as that raspberry tart."

Recalling the romantic connection Lady Destain proposed, Becky blushed again. "No, you wouldn't want to know. Believe me."

Captain Destain assessed the display on her plate and chose a sugar-cream biscuit. "If it concerned Bren, take it with a pinch of salt. She's always enjoyed embellishing tales of his mischief. Not that they need embellishing, of course. I mean to catch him sometime today, by the way. Where is he?"

"Somewhere about," Becky answered, deliberately vague. She was determined to give Tressilian an hour alone with Kristen, and if Captain Destain intended to impede this goal, she would just have to keep him otherwise occupied.

Destain smiled with deceptive amiability. "Leaves you alone a great deal for such a devoted lover, doesn't he?"

Becky yanked her plate out of his reach. "We don't live in each other's pockets. But I have no complaints about his devotion, I assure you. He squired me about to all the exhibits, the Chinese pagoda, the little grass hut the pigmies live in—" In her excitement, she quite forgot her pique and let Captain Destain steal another pastry. "Why, he even introduced me to Lord Byron. He is back in town again, did you know? Although all he did was sigh and look pensively at Kristen."

"You expected, perhaps, he would rattle off a few heroic couplets in homage to Tressilian?"

"Of course not. Everyone knows Byron's too jealous of Brendan's curls to write a poem honoring him. I did rather hope he would say a few words about my curls, however," she laughed, fluffing up her dark hair under the little lace cap and slanting a beguiling look at the captain.

But he only grinned at her latest foray into flirtation. "You'll catch cold waiting for me to rectify Byron's lapse, kitten. I don't versify on demand." He forestalled her angry response to his candor by inquiring, "So which of the exhibits did you like best? The Egyptian pyramid on the terrace, no doubt."

He was a master at diversion, if not flirtation. "Oh, not that dull pyramid. Why, everyone has pyramids. Lady Ellismore had one constructed in her dining room. No, I was most intrigued with the American Indian house. It was constructed of leather! In a cone shape, like Kristen's wimple. And inside, there was a fire laid. Imagine having a fire in a leather house!"

Destain agreed that seemed rather dangerous, to the suppleness of the leather if nothing else. For a short while they conversed happily, as if there were no barriers between them. But the amity could not last when Becky sighed dreamily, "I would so love to travel throughout Indian country visiting the tribes, learning their customs and languages. Don't you think that would be fascinating?"

"No," Destain said with the certainty of a man who had spent most of the past five years in a foreign land. "Foreigners aren't any more interesting than your nearest neighbors. And those Indians are forever making war on each other— and you only think that's fascinating because you've never been to war. Besides, they only have the most rudimentary of dining facilities. I understand they eat with their hands from a common pot."

His disgust at this practice was perhaps excessive, considering he had just plucked a mushroom fritter from Becky's plate. "And one wouldn't travel in comfort, there in the wilderness. Pack mules would be the only mode of transport. No well-sprung carriages of the sort you are accustomed to. No, after a few days of it, I'm sure you would wish yourself back in gentle Wiltshire."

Becky crashed to earth with a painful thud. Captain Destain had evidently made it his mission to puncture her every illusion, to ridicule her every dream. Her voice shaking, she declared, "Now I know why I love Brendan so dearly!"

She saw him flinch, but rushed on oblivious. "He would understand! Why, he would offer to take me to America with him! He would never laugh at me! But you— you wouldn't know adventure if it came up and bit you on the nose! No, you value your comfort and ease more highly than anything else!"

Belatedly she remembered that comfort and ease must have been infrequent companions since his regiment left for the Peninsula. But before she could take back her words, Captain Destain shot back, "Oh, yes, the two of you will make a great pair! Is that what you think life as a countess will be— smoking peacepipes with the Cherokee before launching your raft on the Amazon? Grow up, infant! For you may be sure Brendan won't, not with the likes of you beside him!"

Becky jumped up, spilling her plate with its forgotten treats onto the ground. "At least Bren and I embrace life! We don't push it away, as you always do!"

The tears that threatened whenever she encountered the captain finally spilled over onto her cheeks. "And Brendan may be— may not be as mature as can be, but at least he can never be counted a coward like you!"

The accusation echoed in the lambent air, even after the accuser had gone. Destain was ordinarily slow to anger, but there were some challenges he could not ignore. People were taking advantage of his good nature, he brooded as he watched Becky run out of the garden into the small ornamental forest. But no longer.

Only last night Elise had made a startling proposition— call it a demand, for she never expected him to refuse. He had to marry sometime, she reminded him, why not now? And Elise knew better than anyone how he hated fuss, and how idiotic he would find the typical sort of courtship. So she had saved him the trouble of finding a bride.

He could marry Amarinda, her sixteen-year-old daughter. She was a compliant girl who would make no trouble even when she discovered that her husband and her mother intended to continue their long affair. Elise took for granted that he would be grateful for her attempt to run his life, and she was astonished when, with rising disgust, he told her the whole idea was incestuous and that he wanted no part of it or her or her daughter either.

Now this starry-eyed girl was making the same mistake, assuming that because he had not a fiery spirit he had no spirit at all. In her ringing taunts, her scornful blue eyes, he felt the sting of contempt, the same contempt he d known all his life from his father. She had measured his mettle and found it lacking, without any more knowledge of him than the admiral had ever had. Coward, she called him, never wondering why a coward might join a cavalry regiment famous for its combat performance, never noticing the battle ribbons on his chest.

But even as he plunged into the forest after her, he knew her accusation had nothing to do with his war record. We embrace life— that was her motto, and her challenge— you will be a coward until you stop observing life and start living it. Even her attempts at flirtation were a taunt to him— Is your best friend's betrothed too dangerous a temptation to taste? Are you so certain to lose you won't even attempt the game?

She was standing before the artificial lake, the setting sun silhouetting her defiantly rigid figure and casting rubies of light on the water. As determinedly commonsensical as Jon was, he could not but be affected by the poetry of the scene. Becky's dark curls spilled wantonly from her cap, her creamy breasts rising from the white muslin costume. She was so very pretty, so disastrously appealing, so entirely forbidden—

So she wanted romance, did she? She wanted danger and adventure and excitement? In one fierce moment he pulled her to him, taking her initial resistance as a challenge and her eventual surrender as a triumph.

It was worth the effort after all, he thought dizzily, imprisoning her in a savage kiss. But his romantic flight could not last. Becky tried to pull away, her sweet face streaked with tears, and Jon knew the mingled shame and pride of a man who had conquered his woman. Fiercely he tightened his arms around her, possessively he tangled his hand in her curls and brought her closer for his kiss. Mine, he whispered against her mouth.

But even as her lips melted under his, Becky worked a hand loose. Then, with all the strength in her slim body, she swung her fist round and punched him in the jaw.

The blow was sufficient to distract him momentarily, and Becky broke free and began to run. When Jon's vision cleared, he saw her destination. Suddenly the full import of his impetuous adventure was revealed to him. This was why he never did things impulsively, for then he did them so badly. A more experienced adventurer would have thought to glance about to make sure the girl's fiancee was nowhere in sight.

As Jon gazed at the lovely tableau something twisted inside him. So this was romance— the fierce protector, the weeping girl, silhouetted against a tawdry azure sky. No, it was cheap melodrama, and he was cast in the role of the vile seducer. As if he had rehearsed it, Jon knew precisely what the next scene would bring. The girl would avail herself of the hero's comfort as she had availed herself of the villain's kisses, and all his precipitate dreams, not to mention a life's friendship, would be ended.

Jon acknowledged this was mostly his fault, for making such a fool-hardy scene and doing it so badly. But it wasn't until Becky Marlowe came into his life that he began betraying friends and abusing schoolgirls. Now he couldn't tell which hurt most— seeing Becky take shelter from him in another man's arms, or hearing his cousin's icy words: "Jon, if we hadn't been friends all our lives, you'd be dead before breakfast."He could feel Tressilian's fury crackling across the beach like heat lightning. And he answered with the same frozen despair, "Don't bother, Bren, this isn't worth the bullet." Refusing to apologize for this insult, or any other, refusing to look at the girl he had injured, he strode away and kept going until he reached his rooms and the oblivion of brandy.

## CHAPTER SEVENTEEN

When Kristen entered the breakfast room, she was startled to see Becky already up and dressed in a lavender morning half-dress, her prim chemisette buttoned to the neck. But the girl made only a pretense of eating breakfast, cutting up her sirloin and hiding it under the eggs then breaking bits of toast over the whole mess. Her wan face and red-rimmed eyes testified to the cause for her distraction.

The poor thing must have cried herself to sleep, Kristen thought painfully. Guilt made her solicitous. "Are you feeling better now, darling? Would you like to talk?"

"No, thank you, Kristen. I'm fine, truly I am," she declared with palpable untruth. She, ordinarily the most consummate of liars, could not meet Kristen's eyes.

But Kristen did not press the girl. She had no desire to receive Becky's usual artless confidences. For she didn't want to learn that she was to blame for Becky's sadness. Did Becky suspect? More to the point, was there anything to suspect?

Only a single rose, a gentle caress, a curiously intent expression in Brendan's eyes. A moment of longing, an instant of hope. And then they rejoined the rest of the world, Tressilian taking himself off to find Becky, Kristen intercepted by the neglected Stamberly. A short time later a footman brought her a note from Tressilian, telling her tersely that Becky was feeling ill and that he would escort her home. The note was a reminder that whatever they had shared in that brief moment, Brendan was engaged to Becky.

When Kristen arrived home and looked in on the girl, she found Becky was not ill, only exhausted with weeping. Could she have witnessed that ambiguous episode and broken off her betrothal? Kristen's always-active conscience overcame the bud of hope before it had a chance to bloom. Her good sense was just as swift. Becky was depressed, but her anguish was not directed at Kristen, nor at Brendan.

In fact, when Kristen suggested a shopping trip, an activity that usually raised Becky's spirits, she only replied, "Thank you, but Bren is coming by later, and I'm sure he'll cheer me."

Disappointment mingled with relief in Kristen's thoughts.

The romantic gesture was just that, a romantic gesture, of the sort Bren performed so expertly. She was not instrumental in breaking her young cousin's heart. And she was not, after all, in any danger in the presence of the man she had befriended so long ago. "Then it's not Tressilian who has made you so upset?" she inquired gingerly. "It wasn't anything Lady Destain told you?"

At the mention of the viscountess, Becky looked up startled from the remains of her toast. "Lady— Lady Destain? Uh, no. She only talked about Brendan's childhood. She said she felt sorry for me, for he would be so hard to control."

"Well, that wasn't very kind, considering how dearly he holds her in his heart. And to say such a thing to you! No wonder you're upset! Now you mustn't pay her any mind, for you know Bren would never hurt you—"

Becky shook her head wearily. "I haven't the least worry about that. She only meant for the best, I think, but Lady Destain doesn't know him as I do, not as he is now, at least."

Kristen hardly had time to react to this casual assumption of intimacy before Becky went on, "It hadn't the slightest thing to do with Brendan, so pray don't rip him up or Lady Destain either."

"I would not dream of ripping them up," Kristen said, very much on her dignity. "But if either of them hurt you, I would—"

"They didn't." In a rush, Becky added, "Oh, Kristen, thank you for your concern, but truly it is nothing. I expect I'm only being silly, as young girls are sometimes."

This deprecating statement from a girl who guarded her dignity like the crown jewels alarmed Kristen so much she declared her intention to remain home with Becky all day. Only repeated assurances that such solicitude was entirely unnecessary soothed Kristen's anxiety.

"You must promise to tell me if you are still blue-deviled after you see Brendan. For if you are, I shall override all your objections and drag you to Bond Street and force you to accept a delicious bonnet utterly unsuitable for a debutante. I am prepared, you see, to be very ruthless."

Becky's smile was weak but true, and Kristen, reassured, added, "The children won't be annoying you, for Edward is taking them to see the Elgin marbles. Oh, I do hope Lord Elgin saw fit to insure his statuary. I know they've stood fast through hurricanes and wars and invasions, but they haven't met Nicholas Marlowe yet!"

Becky contrived a brave laugh, and Kristen bent to embrace her frail shoulders. Their cheeks touched just for a moment, and Kristen felt a fierce wave of anger at whoever had hurt this sweet girl. That she herself was not entirely innocent only made her feel more passionately protective. "There's Edward now. Do promise me you will rest. I'll be back for luncheon."

In the drawing room, she made a careful inspection of her children. Nicholas stood straight in his handsome blue Eton suit, a sweet little cap perched on his dark-gold hair. Corinna was meltingly precious in a blue gingham pinafore, with her curls caught up in a blue ribbon. Anyone unacquainted with them would not hesitate to describe the little Marlowes as angels. "Now Nicholas, you must hold your sister's hand and follow Lord Stamberly. There's quite a crush at the exhibition, and we don't want you to get lost." Her angels exchanged a significant look, but she was too busy straightening Corey's apron to take much notice. After a last kiss, she sent them both out of the room.

As he left, Edward promised, "I'll show them only the statues which are properly clothed, have no worries on that score."

Kristen mused that only Edward could have said such a thing. Once she would have repeated the remark to Brendan, and they would have shared a laugh. Conventional Kristen might be, but she could see the absurdity of protecting children from two-thousand-year-old nudity. But she could hardly criticize Edward, for he was her fiancee, and Brendan was only her— her what?

He was surely not her friend any longer, at least not as he used to be. She felt constrained in his presence, and so often he became remote and ironic with her. And yesterday, when she felt them on the brink of some new and dangerous intimacy, what did that mean? Nothing? Everything? She didn't even want to investigate that. All she could let herself know was that she missed him in some absurd way, and feared he might be lost to her forever.

Pushing such chaotic thoughts to the back of her mind, Kristen shrugged on her amber pelisse and gathered up a maid, a footman, and four baskets of charity goods to distribute before lunch.

The tenements near the parish of St. Martin in the Fields were hardly the worst slums in London. But the vicar's wife focused her charity in her own neighborhood, organizing a group of ladies to distribute charity to worthy but needy families living in the shadow of the great government buildings of Whitehall.

A widow herself, Kristen always volunteered to visit those ladies who lost their husbands in the war with Napoleon. In the last of these homes of mourning, she sat on a rickety wooden chair and pulled a woolen shirt over the plump shoulders of a baby boy. "How chubby he is!" she told the mother, a careworn woman of her own age. Babies provided a conversational bridge between them, for they were both mothers, if they had nothing else in common.

"He's been eating well, thanks to you," the mother said with gruff gratitude. "I couldn't bear it if he did poorly, for now that I've lost my Ned, this boy's the only child I'm like to have."

Kristen guided the baby's arms through the long sleeves, admiring the dimples where his knuckles should be. "Oh, but perhaps you'll marry again, and have another, a girl perhaps. One baby is a miracle, you know, but two give additional joy."

Mrs. Cowley busied herself making a pot of the tea Kristen had brought in her basket. "What of you, Lady Killeaven? Now that you are marrying again, will you be having another child?"

The baby chortled, catching the brown ribbon of Kristen's poke bonnet in his fist. Automatically she worked it free and retied it, and finally replied, "I expect so. That is the way of nature."

"Your husband will surely expect it too," Mrs. Cowley said wisely, handing her the tea in a chipped mug. "I remember Ned—" her voice broke, then she shook her head and added brightly, "Men do love to see themselves reproduced, don't they? And your new husband will be the same."

Kristen murmured something affirmative, suddenly aware that she had no idea what Edward thought about the prospect of children in their marriage. In fact, they had never discussed much of anything about their marriage, for they were so compatible, surely they felt the same way about all important matters. Edward, like most men, would probably be happy to claim a few heirs.

But she realized that he was likely to limit his involvement in their lives to rare outings like the one he made today with Nick and Corey. Most men were like that, she knew, for her father and Gerald had been just so remote. But that brand of fathering seemed so inadequate now. She had just been spoiled by Brendan, who would far sooner attend a circus than a musicale. He and Becky would probably have half a dozen little black-eyed devils....

"Little Barry looks just like his papa." Mrs. Cowley held out her hands to her son, who slid off Kristen's lap and toddled over. "Do you think all mothers want sons to look like their husbands?"

Suddenly Kristen wasn't at all sure she wanted to bear tiny duplicates of Stamberly. But she did not voice her thoughts, knowing the blunt Mrs. Cowley would ask her why she would marry a man if she didn't want his sort of children.

This conundrum was still battering her aching head when she returned home to find Chesley wringing his hands with anxiety. His lordship, the Earl of Tressilian, had arrived. And Miss Marlowe was entertaining him in the garden. Alone. Chesley invested that word with the most sinister of intonations.

Kristen sighed and handed him her pelisse and bonnet and headed for the door to the back garden, knowing she had failed once again as a chaperone. She should have told Chesley to roust Great-aunt Helen from her self-imposed exile on the second floor as soon as Tressilian arrived, so that the young couple could be adequately supervised. But this season had been a salutary lesson in the limitations of principle. All Kristen's ironclad strictures had just melted away in the radiance of Becky's sunny disobedience.

But the tender scene awaiting Kristen was punishment enough for her laxity. If she had had more backbone, she would have avoided this searing pain of discovery.

For on a bench under an arbor of roses— so like the arbor she and Brendan had shared yesterday— the young couple sat with a casual intimacy that dashed Kristen's vile hope of conflict. Becky rested her head on her fiancee's broad shoulder as if to draw support from him. And he offered it, his voice as gentle as if he were soothing a child: "But what man could help loving you, baby?" In a gesture as tender as a kiss he stroked her cheek. "Don't worry, it will all turn out right for us."

Kristen abandoned any attempt to impose propriety on the scene and retreated to her bedroom. She sat there on the bed, shaken and confused, until she heard the heavy door slam. Only when she was certain that Tressilian was gone could she return to her duties.

# CHAPTER EIGHTEEN

When Tressilian arrived to Killeaven House at noon, he had been greeted by a frigidly formal Chesley. I must have forgot to tip him the other day, Tressilian thought, but even the dexterously palmed sovereign failed to improve the butler's demeanor. He only took the earl's hat and riding gloves and intoned, "Miss Marlowe is alone in the garden. If you would wait for her ladyship—"

"Devil a bit, Chesley," Tressilian replied with a grin. "Miss Marlowe won't mind seeing me alone. Send out some Madeira, will you? And something for the lady too. She likes champagne."

Chesley's disapproval followed him like a cloud into the garden, already misted over from Becky's dejection. The sunlight faded around the drooping girl; even the birds had stopped singing in this sad bower. Tressilian took a seat beside her on the stone bench, hoping he had not been so joyless a companion these last few weeks.

"Come on, sweetness, smile for me. Or if not for me, for Chesley, who's peering out the window at us." He nodded up at the morning room window, and Chesley's head was quickly withdrawn. "He thinks I'm the one who stole the roses from your cheeks."

Becky, sagging back against the brick wall, admitted, "Kristen thought so too. She was sure you'd hurt my feelings somehow."

"You are ruining my reputation as a source of light and joy in women's lives, my pet. Now come, just a bit of a grin for me." He tilted her chin up, smiling sympathetically at her woeful expression. "You aren't even trying to smile. If I weren't such a kind man, I'd say you were reveling in self-pity."

"You're a fine one to talk!" Becky straightened up militantly, her blue eyes sparking again. "Lately you've been glooming about as if your favorite dog died."

"And you never failed to cheer me with your bright smiles and laughter. I merely seek to return the favor." He pulled a red bloom from the vine-laced brick wall and jammed it into her curls.

Becky squirmed under his attentions, complaining, "Oh, Bren, red clashes with my gown."

"Matches your eyes, though," he retorted, putting an arm around her shoulder. "Now relax and tell your Uncle Bren everything."

With a languishing sigh, she settled against his chest. Her voice came muffled by the concealing curtain of her hair. "I am probably crushing your lovely gold lace."

Tressilian had a dozen uniform coats in his armoire and was reconciled to sacrificing one in a good cause. "I'm trying to ignore that. But before you weep all over it, do consider my valet."

"No tears," Becky promised, raising her tearstained face to him. "Though I'm utterly miserable. Oh, Bren, I'm so distraught! That cousin of yours— why, I wish I could call him out, I do!"

"I think you've already visited enough violence upon his person, cherie. That was quite a jawbreaker you threw! Did you learn that from Gentleman Jackson?"

"From my elder brother. He's a monstrous bully— but Captain Destain is the real bully! First he insults me, then he assaults me!"

Tressilian's fist closed spasmodically against her arm, then he reminded himself that Jonny was a reasonable man, so he had to have a reason for what he did. "I'd lay him out myself, Becky, were I not convinced he wouldn't have put himself to so much trouble except under the direst of circumstances. Start from the beginning. What happened after I left you with my aunt?"

"Oh, she told me that you will probably be a lamentable husband, and that our children will be demons, and that she pities me. Irma feels otherwise, you'll be glad to know. Are you certain Lady Destain likes you?"

"Adores me. But she knows me too well. And we probably would have demon children, don't you think?"

"Captain Destain—" The name was uttered austerely— "Captain Destain has also seen fit to warn me about your poor potential as a spouse. I must say, Brendan, with relatives like that, you need no enemies."

Tressilian laughed. "The Destains, all three of 'em, see it as their mission to keep me from becoming too puffed up. I don't complain, for I think it gives them a shared purpose as a family, and God knows, they need one. Now tell me more about Jonny."

A bumblebee buzzed around them and settled on the flower in Becky's hair, so her reply had to await Tressilian's courageous intervention. Then slowly she recounted her conversation with the captain. "We were trying very hard to be pleasant to each other, though I do think I tried rather harder than he. For he began making merry of everything I said, telling me I was silly and immature to want to live with the Indians. Isn't that infamous?"

"Well, I think so," Tressilian allowed distractedly, for the bee had returned to hover longingly over their heads. Prudently the earl removed the alluring flower from Becky's hair and tossed it into the lily-pond, whereupon the lovestruck bee dived in after it. "But no one ever credited me with having any sense. No doubt he's right. It seems a paltry thing to come to cuffs about, in any event."

"But his attitude was so offensive! As if I were so absurd! And I know he's perfectly civil to everyone else— except you, of course. Why, I'm sure he never speaks so cruelly to Elise Winterleigh!"

"Aha." Tressilian was struck by the significance of her bitter words. "So that's the way the wind blows."

Becky ignored his interruption and, tugging her hair loose from his epaulette, sat up straight. "Well, I thought it was unforgivable, and I told him so. And I told him a few other things also."

"Finally we approach the provocation. What exactly did you tell him?"

Becky hesitated, her cheeks flaming. But she tilted her chin up stubbornly as she said, all in a rush, "I told him he was dull and boring and— and a coward!"

Tressilian rested his forehead on his fist, this last being too much for him. "A coward?" he echoed. "Baby, perhaps you haven't noticed that fine uniform of his— although your mouth always hangs open whenever you see him in it, I can't help but mark— That's the 16th Light, you know. A fighting regiment, not the Hyde Park Hussars. Jon's been in nearly every engagement on the Peninsula. Talavera, Fuentes de Onoro, Salamanca—

nasty little affairs, you know. Men got killed at one or two of 'em. And Wellington's aides are always in the thick of it, don't you see, scouting and evaluating and moving brigades about. Jon won't boast of it, for he's not that sort, but Wellington thinks the world of him. So don't let his demeanor fool you, Becky, a coward's the last thing he is."

He took her by the shoulders and shook her gently. "Don't you know better than to fling such words about, especially towards a military man? We take such accusations seriously."

Becky dropped her eyes, chastened. "I didn't mean that he wasn't a brave soldier. I would never imply such a thing, for I know Captain Destain must be very courageous in battle. I only meant— oh, that he is too afraid to take his life in his hands and really live! And he is! His own mother said so!"

"Lady Destain is a font of wisdom, isn't she?" Tressilian said ironically. "For all that you're right— God knows I've told him that often enough myself— it's hardly your place to tell him so."

"Then it's not his place to tell me I'm immature and frivolous and flighty!"

Tressilian was so accustomed to accepting his cousin's criticisms he never considered that Becky might not be so amenable. "Point taken. But he's a scout. He stands around and watches. And then he gives the world the benefit of his observations. He only joins in when he's dragged into it— and I think you dragged him into this bumblebroth, sweeting. Coward!" He interrupted himself, shaking his head with amazement. "Did you really call him that? Well, then, what did you expect? After that insult to his virility. he had no choice but to prove you wrong by conquering you romantically. Poor Jonny," he concluded with a crooked grin.

"Poor Jonny?" Becky pulled away and shook her fists at his chest. "I was the one who was assaulted and humiliated and doubtless ruined for life!"

"It was only a kiss, sweetheart," Tressilian pointed out with rare good sense. He caught her fists and gently urged them down to her sides, away from the already abused gold lace at his lapel. "And he's not a blackguard. In fact, he's the best of men. Loyal as a hound dog. You know, I'm not always the easiest of friends—"

"I know, I know," Becky broke in.

"And you've only known me two months!" Tressilian said with a laugh. "Imagine how tired of me he must be after more than a quarter-century! And he's been loyal to the army too, for he could have sold out years ago, and who could blame him, uncomfortable as the duty's been. You're not seeing him clear, if you see some care-for-none. He's only a man who thought he had the whole structure of life figured out. You don't fit into his framework. In fact, you smash it to pieces."

"You make it seem as if it is all my fault," Becky said in a small broken voice.

Tressilian surrendered to the misery in her tone and let her rest her tearstained face against his coat again. "Of course it's not. But he must be questioning every value he's ever had. He prizes detachment, yet he's anything but detached with you. He values our friendship highly, he really does, I know it, and yet he's stealing my betrothed. He values rest, and yet he's chasing after you. And he values excellence— I can't tell you how many years he's been regimental darts champion— and his one attempt at playing the romantic hero was a fiasco."

"I wouldn't call it a fiasco, precisely," Becky said fairly. "He was quite masterful, all in all. And I must say, I'm glad it was a stolen embrace. I would be so disappointed if my first kiss had been an ordinary sort of occurrence."

Diverted, Tressilian put her away from him and asked, "That was your first kiss?" At her shamefaced nod, he shook his head disappointedly. "I can't imagine what all those rakehells nipping at your heels have been about all these weeks, if not one of them has pressed the issue even that far."

"They all fear you will put an end to their existence do they more than kiss my hand," Becky said darkly, for the timidity of her admirers had been a sore trial to her.

He said triumphantly, "And yet Jon disregarded the danger and charged into the breach! Not that I would have killed him, you understand, though I was tempted to rearrange his face a bit."

But Becky only turned a stubborn face away. "You will not persuade me that Captain Destain has courageously fallen in love with me in the face of all the barriers between us. He hasn't the least inclination or capacity to do something so romantic. And I wouldn't want him to, in any event. For he's far too cynical to live up to my heroic ideal."

"If that's what you wanted, you would have fallen in love with me and been done with it," Tressilian exclaimed with exasperation. "But you didn't. So perhaps that isn't what you want. And God knows it isn't what you need."

"I don't need a man who makes mock of everything I believe in," Becky said obstinately. "He never loses an opportunity to tell me I am a silly dreamer, and that if my dreams come true I shall only be disappointed. If he cared for me, he wouldn't be so cruel to me. No," she said sadly, "he doesn't love me."

Tressilian drew the bent little head back to its accustomed resting place and brushed a tear from her cheek. "But what man could help loving you, baby? Don't worry, it will all turn out right for us."

Becky let herself be comforted, but looked up sharply when Tressilian remarked, "Now we'll have to handle this very carefully."

Loath to surrender command to her capricious conspirator, Becky inquired suspiciously, "What are you planning?"

"Don't you worry, I shall take care of it all." When that assurance only enhanced Becky's anxiety, he added, "You and I, my sweet, are going to break off our engagement."

Becky frowned in automatic rebellion, but soon her brow cleared. "I do think that will do the trick." She smiled up at him through a haze of tears. "It has been my very great pleasure being betrothed to you, your lordship." Gravely he kissed her cheek, as if in final farewell.

As he drove down Oxford Street, the Earl of Tressilian felt very cheerful for a man who had just broken off his engagement. His innate optimism had resurfaced; they had turned the corner, he was sure, and were in the homestretch striking for the finish line.

Yesterday Kristen had fallen so easily into flirtation with him that Tressilian was convinced she seldom thought of Stamberly when he was out of sight. Indeed, she even demonstrated a little jealousy of Becky, just as they had planned so long ago. And just as Becky had prophesied, Kristen was impressed, not to say astonished, by Tressilian's newfound stability. She had always held him in affection; now he let himself hope that her regard was deepening as she imagined losing him altogether.

And his fears for Becky's future were unfounded after all. She would not have to marry an opium addict or an unregenerate gambler. She could have Jonny, his best friend, and the best of his friends. Her profession that she did not want him he dismissed as the pitiful squeaks of her rational mind. Becky, like Tressilian, followed the dictates of heart, and her heart, he knew now, belonged to Destain. If they could stop arguing long enough to finish what they started on that beach, they would realize that they belonged together.

He was mentally tying up the loose ends of the package of the future when childish shouts intruded upon his reverie. "Captain Bren! Stop!" With misgiving he obeyed, reaching out a hand to help the disheveled young Marlowes scramble into his curricle.

"Where did you two demons come from?" he demanded, maneuvering a U-turn on the crowded street. "Where is Stamberly?"

"We lost him," Corinna bubbled, settling in comfortably at his side. "Can I take the reins like Cousin Becky does?"

"No. What do you mean you lost him?"

"Because we went to the bazaar! And we saw a dancing bear, and a monkey! And Nick won me a puppet at a booth!" She held up a shabby puppet, exposing a rent in the sleeve of her pinafore. Her crushed bonnet hung by its ribbons from her grimy neck.

Nick leaned over the back of the seat to shake hands with his idol Pierre, the gaptoothed groom perched behind. "We ran away from Stamberly, you see. He was taking us to see some crusty old statues, but we fooled him. He stopped at the park entrance to let a lady drive past and we jumped out!" Tressilian's eyes squeezed shut, for he was stricken with a splitting headache. A shout from Pierre revived him, and he swerved in time to avoid a collision with an ice wagon. Too weak to go on, he pulled into a mews road and stopped in the shadow of a haberdasher's establishment. "Damn it, Nick, you were supposed to vet all your plans with me! You could have been kidnapped—" "I wish!" the boy returned fervently. "No, you don't," Tressilian said with unprecedented sternness. "If you ever pull such a rig again, Nick, or you either, Corey, I shall— well, I can't think now what I'll do, only know that you won't like it very well! The town is too dangerous these days, with all the footpads and youth gangs. So never again, do you hear?"

Heads bowed, the children both assented, chastened by the only display of anger the earl had ever shown them. "Then we shan't speak of it again," he concluded, already regretting his harshness. "Now tell me about your adventures."

Corey perked up immediately. "We just dashed away like sloops of war, Captain Bren, and Stamberly rolled and foundered like an old yawl! He got stuck in traffic and couldn't follow us. So we went to a Punch and Judy show, and Nick bought me a lemonade—"

"I did have some funds, sir," Nick said penitently. "We planned on taking a hackney home, once Corey'd had her fun."

"I said to forget it, son. Let's don't worry about what didn't happen." Tressilian pulled Corey's bonnet back up and expertly tied the ribbons into a dashing bow under her ear. "I like Punch and Judy too, sweeting. Did they make merry with the Prince Regent?"

"With all the princes. Punch strangled his valet with a cravat. It was very chilling, and so amusing. Did the Duke of Cumberland really kill his valet, or was Nick telling faradiddles?"

"There are those who say he did," Tressilian observed fairly, "and those who say he did not. I understand that the real cause of death was a slit throat, though were I to kill my valet, I think strangling with a cravat would be poetic justice."

Corey shivered deliciously. "In the show, the valet came back to haunt him."

Tressilian approved of that ghoulish touch. 'I should come back, were I murdered. But I should cause the scoundrel to walk in front of a speeding carriage. What else was on the program?"

"Oh, just the usual silliness about Caro Lamb and Lord Byron. I wish someone would strangle them with cravats!" Nick reached over Corey to stroke the reins, but his current credit was not high enough to rate more than a touch. "We saw a fight between a greengrocer and a coachman—vastly entertaining! And a pickpocket got taken up by the Watch. What will happen to him, Captain Bren?"

"Nothing much. He'll spend a fortnight in Newgate, and then they'll release him to join the navy, where he'll probably lead a mutiny against me, or transport him to Australia. I've no doubt you're destined for a similar fate," he added without censure.

Recovered from his moment in the dock, Nick grinned cheekily, and with his grimy face and torn clothes he surely resembled a pickpocket. "We know what to do now, sir. We'll tell Mother how scared we were and how bad boys tried to hurt us, and how Captain Bren saved us."

Tressilian struggled with his conscience, and, as usual, found it an easy victory. "We'd as well make some pie out of the mincemeat you've made of Stamberly. But don't do this sort of thing again. It's one thing to smear jam on Stamberly's coat, but quite another to lose yourself in the middle of London. I'll have your oaths on it, if you please."

In unison, Nick and Corey spit on their dirty palms and held them up to the breeze. "We swear on the Union Jack and the anchor of the Defiant."

"Now give me the puppet, darling. It wouldn't do to have your mother thinking you enjoyed yourself." Corinna surrendered the toy only after he promised to return it soon. Then she let him take up the reins and drive them back to Killeaven House.

Theatrical himself, Tressilian could only admire the children's performance. They might have been born for the stage instead of the staid lives awaiting them. Corinna was masterful, hurling herself into her mother's arms, crying incoherently of falling from the viscount's curricle and the bad men who chased them and dear Captain Bren who saved them.

Nick swaggered a bit, just as he ought, describing how he had leaped from the carriage to rescue her sister and then protected her from the dangers of the city.

Thoroughly shaken by her children's brush with danger, Kristen held them close for a very long time. After they were bathed and fed, she put them to bed, though they had made a miraculous recovery and protested they weren't in the least bit tired.

She finally returned to the drawing room where Brendan waited with Becky. Humble, unable to look at him, Kristen repeated her murmurs of gratitude. She was brought up short by his angry question, "Is this the man you want as father to your children— one who loses them in the middle of London and doesn't even bother to inform you they are missing?"

Kristen protested feebly that there must be some explanation, that

Edward would surely not abandon them.

But Becky roundly declared that Stamberly should be shot for exposing her darling cousins to who knew what dangers, and Kristen made no further attempt to defend her fiancee. She only murmured again that Tressilian had been most kind, and ran upstairs again to look in on her alert and unrepentant children.

Becky trailed him to the door. "You are the most unscrupulous man I've ever met," she remarked admiringly. "Using her own children against her that way."

"It was Nick's idea," he admitted, dropping a kiss on her forehead. "But all's well that ends well."

"All's well that ends well? Oh, what a brilliant line!" Becky exclaimed. "Where's my pencil? That would make a lovely title for my novel!"

# CHAPTER NINETEEN

In the morning, Kristen's usually neat desk was as disordered as her thoughts; heedlessly she shoved unanswered letters and unopened invitations into pigeonholes. Then she sat, pen in hand, trying to compose a letter to Edward.

Her anger at him had dissipated, but not her dismay. When Edward had arrived the previous evening at Killeaven House, his cravat askew, his face flushed, he had told her the children had leaped out of the curricle and vanished. He had not wanted to worry her with the news until he had searched for them. He regretted that this had occurred while the children were in his care, and recommended calling in Bow Street.

Icily Kristen had assured him that the children were safe, thanks to the intervention of Tressilian, and that they had not jumped from the curricle at all.

Edward, patently relieved, still had to make a demurral. "I distinctly saw Corinna turn the handle of the door and jump out, with Nicholas right behind her. It was deliberate, I am sure. And as for Tressilian, I have no doubt it was his reprehensible example that incited the children to such mischief. Perhaps now you will understand why I say that he is not a suitable companion for you or for the children.'

Kristen, outraged, had ordered him from the house. That he would blame this on the children— and Brendan!— passed all understanding. Why had she never before remarked that rigid, self-righteous attitude, that inability to accept fault? Brendan was right; she could not trust her children's future to such a man.

Of course, her children's gleeful faces in the clear light of morning suggested that Edward's accusation might well have been true. Jumping out into Oxford Street was just the sort of mischief those two would get up to.

They were very bad to do it, of course, but Kristen recalled her own escapade in the Copenhagen pleasure gardens and could not entirely blame them. However she might suppress it, Kristen often felt the same urge for independence and adventure. And Edward seemed to think quelling such improper urges was the first duty of a husband and father.

Eventually she struggled through a terse note, summarily breaking off the engagement. It was over, this shortest of all betrothals, and she felt only relief. For once she cared naught that the gossips might speculate about her inconstancy. She had done it finally, broken off with the fiancee who was no longer acceptable as a husband or father.

Kristen knew she was being unfair, rejecting Edward for the very qualities she had first appreciated in him— his stability, his respectability, his conservatism, all of which seemed to tally so closely with her own values. But if she had learned nothing else from this short engagement, Kristen realized now that sharing those undoubted virtues wouldn't be enough to make a marriage.

Even as she enumerated them, Kristen thought how trivial were may of her complaints about the man the world predicted would be her perfect mate. He was ponderous in speech, and inexpert on the dance floor; he laughed little and flattered even less. That last was the silliest complaint, but somehow telling. After Byron wrote a quartet extolling her amethyst eyes, how could she be content with Edward's customary, "You look very well, my dear?"

She hated to think herself so vain, demanding compliments as her due. But lately she had wondered if Edward recognized his good fortune in engaging Lady Killeaven. It wasn't just that she had been courted by a

German prince and had last year turned down one of the wealthiest men in the kingdom.

Even if Edward had been her only suitor, she hoped he might count himself fortunate to win the lady of his heart. But he never whispered that they were destined for each other, that he would adore her all his days. He preferred to tell her how well-suited they were, how pleasant their life would be together, much the same import, perhaps, but so very different in effect. He claimed no wild passion for her. Indeed, the thought of Edward in a passion was absurd.

Restlessly Kristen began to tidy her desk. She paused with her letter-knife halfway through an engraved envelope with a royal frank. She saw not her name inscribed on the face of the letter, but a vision of that tender scene in the garden the previous afternoon. Edward would never speak of love in a voice husky with emotion. Even when he proposed, he never spoke of love, only of warm regard and suitable affection. She hadn't taken much note of it at the time, but suddenly Kristen needed a little more enthusiasm from a man with whom she would spend her life.

But then, she certainly didn't feel any passion for Edward. She had agreed to his suit for several calculating reasons: because everyone wanted her to, because she was weary of being a widow, because she feared that in her loneliness she might do something rash.

In fact, agreeing to marry Edward was the rashest thing she had ever done. She should have realized that she was too independent to submit to Edward's authority, and that he was too conventional to allow her freedom. They would have battled constantly, if in a civilized way, over Kristen's supervision of Nicholas's estate, over her choice of friends, over her child-rearing decisions.

This last incident brought these issues to the fore. Even if Edward was not to blame for the children's disappearance, he had taken too much on himself by not informing her immediately. Then he was so self-righteous as to blame the children's rescuer! After Tressilian had been almost one of the family for five years!

But every man had faults, every woman too; the trick of marriage was to overlook them. But she knew that her affection for Edward would never be strong enough to blind her to even the most minor of his flaws. Kristen's second marriage would have become a mirror of her first, with separate residences and separate lives. Now she understood Brendan's angry accusation: "Wasn't one loveless marriage enough for you?"

No, she needed more than stability and respectability in a husband, and more than compatibility and commonality in a marriage. But the realization that at last she was seeing clearly left her bleak. Indeed, she felt that she had lost control of her life, that her emotions were escaping from the carefully proscribed boundaries she had set so long ago. If she knew now that love was something she had lacked all these years, where was she to attain it? The answer to that dilemma she could not even allow herself to imagine.

# CHAPTER TWENTY

"His lordship is not in charity with the world this morning, Mr. Hastings." Lansing, the earl's valet, bestowed a smug smile on the butler as they met in the vast entry hall. Lansing was always the first to see their volatile master in the morning, and liked to lord his superior knowledge over his arch-rival.

But. Hastings was no slow-top himself. Brushing an invisible bit of lint from the valet's pristine sleeve, he murmured, "No doubt his mood has something to do with the letter from his solicitor that I sent up with his morning coffee."

Their exchange of steely smiles was interrupted by the earl, who, hand on bannister, vaulted down the last five steps in his usual tempestuous fashion. "Oh, Lansing, there you are. One of the buttons came off my sleeve. Come into the library and sew it back on, for I've work to do and can't be bothered to change."

Lansing caught the tossed button and examined it minutely, finally accepting from the Royal Navy insignia that this had most likely come from the earl's coat. "All those buttons were secure this morning, your lordship," he observed in chilly accents, "else I should never have let you wear the coat. Of course, after you spoiled the gold lace on the coat you wore yesterday— "

"It's my coat, damnit," Tressilian reminded him, striding across the marble floor. "I can spoil the gold lace if I want. And I can yank on the damn buttons if I want. Stupid idea, it is, to hang them on with thread anyway. Iron nails, that's what's needed to keep buttons from falling off in your hand. Hastings, come in here too. I want to know about my parents."

Hastings and Lansing at once put aside their differences and held a hurried conference outside the library's double oak doors. "His parents?" Lansing whispered.

"Most unusual," Hastings agreed. "His lordship taking an interest in his family history— unheard of."

But soon Lansing was settled on the leather couch with his needle and thread and the earl's coat, while Hastings, declining a seat, stood at attention before his employer. The shirtsleeved Tressilian lounged behind his grandfather's massive mahogany desk, deep in thought, occasionally taking a sip of coffee from a heavy china mug.

Finally he looked up with a frown at his butler, who, he had learned long ago, knew nearly everything there was to know. "Did you know, Hastings, that I was a posthumous child?"

Hastings did not betray with the flicker of an eyelash that the question was in anyway unusual. "Yes, your lordship. A terrible tragedy, both your parents dying so young, and you being orphaned." The butler drew a sepulchral sigh. "It was said your mother had no reason to live once she heard your father had been lost at sea."

Tressilian frowned, for he had always thought himself sufficient reason for any lady to go on with life. Then he dispelled such unfilial sentiments. "Did no one question that I was my father's son? After all, he wasn't around to confirm it."

This last raised a gasp from Hastings, and he drew up in flushed affront. He had never known the former son and daughter-in-law of the house, having been rescued from Newgate not ten years ago by the current earl. But he had retroactively adopted all his employer's forebears, and took personally any aspersion on the family. "The idea! That the late marchioness would— Why, she was a Barrington! And your mother!"

"Yes, yes, I'm certain that she was all that was sterling. But what if she weren't a Barrington, but some lesser sort he had run off with?

Would anyone have been sure I was a Trevarrick?"

Hastings decided, not for the first time, to humor his mad employer. Soothingly, he said, "It was apparent from the first, your lordship. So I heard when first I came to the castle, for I had the whole story from poor Mistress Linden."

Poor Mistress Linden had been Tressilian's nurse until she retired before his second birthday claiming nervous exhaustion. Ever since she had lived on an ample pension in a distant wing of the castle, regaling new servants with tales of her last and worst charge.

"Mistress Linden told me she had assisted at your birth. She said you were a beautiful baby." The dignified butler dashed a tear from his eye, "You smiled at the midwife when she was about to apply her hand to your bottom, and she forgot what she was about and never did spank you."

"I presume I managed to take my first breath unprovoked then," Tressilian said dryly. "This is all fascinating, Hastings, but you haven't answered my question."

"I am coming to that, sir." Hastings shot a sharp look at Lansing, who was just the sort to repeat the earl's rebuke at the upper servants' supper table. But Lansing merely tied a knot in his thread and contrived to remain inconspicuous. "Your grandfather came in then to ascertain that you were indeed the male heir he needed. He peered into your face and observed with great satisfaction, 'The Trevarrick chin!' And your poor mother, in almost her last breath, pointed out to him that you also had the Trevarrick nose. So you see, there was never any doubt."

Tressilian considered this, absently stroking the telltale chin. "But had I the misfortune of inheriting the Barrington nose, and the Barrington chin, would Grandfather have been so sure? My father was a sailor, after all, off at sea most of the year."

Hastings face grew red with choler, but he managed to answer almost civilly, "You were born in November, your lordship. Your father was on leave throughout the preceding winter and spring. Mistress Linden said that it caused quite a furor in the servants' hall, that his lordship and her ladyship took nearly all their meals in bed. Rather trying, to carry trays all the way from the kitchen to the third-floor bedroom wing."

Tressilian almost surrendered to the urge to learn more about these sybaritic parents, but sternly recalled himself to the matter at hand. "So the resemblance, coupled with my father's presence at the appropriate time, was enough to convince even my curmudgeon of a grandfather, who I recall thought only the worst of his fellow humans and of me especially, that I was indeed my father's son, though he had been dead for weeks?"

"And your mother's spotless reputation," Hastings concluded.

Tressilian hoped no mother of his would have had a spotless reputation, but his butler's expression made him keep this to himself. "But if my father had not been available to do the deed—"

"You are verging on the offensive, your lordship."

"All I mean is that the old earl and everyone else thought to count back to make sure my conception coincided with his son's leave. Just to be certain she wasn't palming off a bas—"

Tressilian broke off, for his butler had taken on the alarming shade of a lobster. "Sorry, Hastings. But tell me, hypothetically, if a child born within a marriage isn't the husband's, can he still inherit the title? No, no, don't swarm on me. I'm not talking about myself. I've only to look at a portrait of the tenth earl to know I'm legitimately the eleventh earl."

Hastings relaxed a bit, letting his fists uncurl behind his back. "Just so, sir." He took a deep breath, marshaling his extensive legal knowledge, garnered not merely as a criminal defendant but as a clerk in a solicitor's office during his misspent youth. "Generally, sir, if the husband accepts paternity, the law does not interfere, even when a title is at stake. The assumption of fidelity lies at the heart of a marriage, after all, and the courts would not challenge that if the husband does not."

"But what if, as in my case, the husband was no longer around to accept or challenge paternity?"

At the earl's persistence, Hastings voice shook slightly, for he could not like whatever the earl was about. "Without evidence otherwise, I am certain legitimacy would be presumed."

"But with evidence that the husband was not the father?"

A sigh escaped Hastings. "I just don't know, your lordship."

Nothing daunted, the earl shot back, "Well, then, do you know how far it is from— oh, say, Exeter to Aberdeen?"

Hastings blinked at this irrelevancy, but answered soon enough, "About six hundred miles, I'd say, sir."

"More than a week's drive, certainly, even in modern times."

"Ten days, more like, your lordship," Lansing put in, weary of being ignored. In his capacity as bearer of the earl's wardrobe, he was quite familiar with cross-country travel. "Not as you travel, of course, but in the normal way of things. I have secured your button, sir."

"Hmmm" was the earl's only reply as he shrugged into the coat Lansing held up for him. When the front was fully fastened and fine adjustments made to the stand-up collar, he added, "I want to see my great-great-grandfather's personal diaries. Alexander Trevarrick. A great diarist, he was. Bring the whole cabinet down. It's up there somewhere." He waved up at the second level of the library, accessible only by a spiral staircase far narrower than the cabinet containing the eighth earl's diaries.

All morning, both Lansing and Hastings found reason to report back frequently to the library as the earl perused the dusty but legible volumes. Once Tressilian looked up from year 1689 and, wide-eyed, assured Hastings, "The eighth earl really was much more of a reprobate than I. I can't imagine doing half the things he did, let alone recording them for posterity."

In fact, Tressilian was able to confirm why the castle's master bedroom adjoined two separate lady's chambers. Alexander did indeed keep both his first wife and her twin sister close at hand to serve his convenience, just as he and Jon had always hoped.

Fascinating as the eighth earl's middle years were, Tressilian forced himself to the final volume, year 1725. "Got it!" he declared after a half-hour's assiduous search.

"You called, your lordship?" Hastings appeared magically at the door, Lansing peering over his shoulder. "Send for that tapeworm who calls himself my cousin."

Hastings had had just about all he could take of scurrilous attacks on the earl's family, even if they had all been made by the earl. "There's no call for that, your lordship! Captain Destain might be trying to steal your betrothed, but that's hardly reason to call him a tapeworm. And he doesn't just call himself your cousin, he is your cousin. Your mothers were—"

Tressilian broke in impatiently, "Not Destain. I know he's my cousin. And how do you know he's trying to steal my betrothed?"

"There is little concerning your affairs I don't know, your lordship," Hastings observed loftily, and Lansing, not to be outdone, chimed in, "I either."

"Then I shan't follow the eighth earl's example and write my memoirs. You two may make your fortunes publishing your own accounts of my life."

Lansing had been considering funding his early retirement to Brighton with just such an enterprise, but he joined with Hastings' righteous denial of such an intent. Then, penitently, he brushed a patina of century-old book dust from the earl's sleeve. Tressilian pulled away and repeated his previous request. "The tapeworm who calls himself my cousin, the one in the fuschia coat— and I hope you'll agree that my cousin Destain might have many faults, but a blinding wardrobe is not among them."

"Rutherford, sir."

"What?"

"The tapeworm. Rutherford. I shall produce him directly."

Hastings was as good as his word, for Rutherford, repeatedly evicted from the doorstep, had taken up residence in the square just across the street. For his first visit to the house he hoped to call his own, he was dressed in a lime-green coat and powder-blue pantaloons. He gazed about the library with a discerning eye, as if already measuring it for remodeling.

Tressilian leaned back in his chair, regarding Rutherford as a biologist might regard a particularly repellent beetle, for that was what the dandy resembled in his bright raiments. "Yes, do examine the Van Dyck. That's as close to it as you'll ever get."

Rutherford's obsequiousness was gone; in fact, he laughed rather arrogantly. "On the contrary, cousin. Once my claim is approved, I shall be entitled to inspect all entailed property at regular intervals. The art treasures are entailed, are they not?"

"Not to you. For your claim won't be approved."

Rutherford clapped his hand to his forehead in mock sympathy. "Oh, isn't your solicitor keeping you informed? Perhaps you don't know that the attorney-general has recommended that my claim be presented to the House of Lords Committee on Privileges. I expect the committee to agree with the attorney general that I am as much the great-great-grandson of Alexander

Trevarrick as you are. And thus your lawful heir."

"No, Rutherford, it is you who are ill-informed. I can prove that Alexander Trevarrick was six hundred miles away when your ancestress was conceived by the castle housekeeper. Who did the trick, I don't know, but it wasn't Alexander. And had he lived, he would have denied paternity and thrown your great-great-grandmother and her bastard out of his house."

His equanimity finally shaken by this, Rutherford took a threatening step forward, then stopped as the earl raised his hand. "It's a lie! You can prove nothing!"

"You didn't know, did you, that Alexander Trevarrick kept a diary. Seventy-five volumes. Fascinating stuff, by the way. You'd be especially interested in the year 1725, when he contracted a quickly regretted marriage to the castle housekeeper. After only a fortnight he fled to the estate in Aberdeen, leaving his new wife in Devon. Six hundred miles away. Six weeks later he died, and eight months after that, the housekeeper delivered a bastard."

Rutherford's wattled neck shook as he gasped for air. "But— but there was no disinheritance—"

Tressilian shrugged. "There was no reason for the new earl to make a stir, for he already had an heir of his own, my grandfather. Doubtlessly he paid the woman off and sent her away. Perhaps he told Grandfather of the incident, and that would explain why he was so loath to accept you into the family, as if your loathsome appearance weren't enough of a deterrence." He gestured to the walnut cabinet beside the desk. "The evidence is there, and I'll present it if you do not withdraw your claim." "Withdraw? Never! The earldom is mine, mine by right!"

Tressilian rose, his hands squaring into fists at his side. "It's not yours. And you're a fool to pursue this, for even if you would win, which you won't, I've told you I shall be married soon and produce my own heirs. You'd be cut out of the succession as soon as I could manage it."

Rutherford shut his lips tight and turned his head away obstinately. Tressilian went on in a deceptively soft voice, "Or were you planning to cast a spoke in that wheel also? Establish your claim, then make sure you couldn't be cut out? Were you hoping to do the deed before or after my wedding?"

His eyes watering, the other man protested, "Nonsense, cousin, nonsense. I wouldn't harm you or yours. We're family!"

"You are no family of mine. And know this, Rutherford. If you approach me or my home or anyone connected to me again, I'll take it as a matter of honor. And I'll kill you. Then the House of Lords can do whatever it pleases about the earldom."

His corsets creaking alarmingly, Rutherford whirled toward the door, declaiming like a stage villain, "You shall live to regret this! No one defies Evelyn Rutherford and gets away with it!"

"You try my patience, Rutherford," the earl said casually.

"I'd get out while you still have your skin," a man interposed from the door. "He's dangerous when his patience is tried."

Rutherford transferred his furious glare from Tressilian to the intruder then back again. "You'll be hearing from me," he declared as he stormed from the room.

Destain headed straight to the decanter on the sideboard. He looked as if he had spent a deal of time at the decanter lately; his usual elegance was undefinably impaired, though his uniform was still impeccable. Perhaps it was the shadows under his eyes that gave him that intriguing seedy appearance. "May I get you anything?" he inquired perfunctorily, splashing brandy into a crystal glass.

"No, no, but do feel free to help yourself," Tressilian said, propping his feet on his desk. He took out his watch and checked it ceremoniously. "Starting a little early, aren't you?"

"Making a lot of enemies, aren't you?" Destain returned testily, flinging into a chair. "Don't make one of me too."

"I hadn't planned on it. But I've never been one to ignore insults either, as you know well, having seconded me so often."

Then Jon, gazing morosely into his glass, reminded them both that in twenty-eight years they had never fought— they argued incessantly, perhaps, but they never disagreed when it mattered. "It's not that I precisely mind being killed, Bren, for I've expected it anytime since I embarked for Portugal. But I do mind your doing the killing. I'll burn in hell, knowing I kept you out of the navy forever. For they'll never let you back in after you've killed an admiral's son."

Tressilian was glad he had never been burdened with a conscience, for Jon's haggard countenance showed it to be an uncomfortable possession. He gave up any thought of punishing Destain for his impertinence, for the poor fellow had obviously put himself through the tortures of the damned already.

"Sneck up, Jonny, I'm not going to shoot you. Your mother would never give off blaming me for it, even if this once it really was all your fault. I'm not saying you don't deserve to die writhing in the dust, but you'll have to find someone else to do it." Inspired, he added, "I could give Becky a pistol and let her have at you."

Jon's eyes narrowed. "Far be it from me to make excuses, lad, but that little girl is trouble. She pushed me just a little too far, and damnit, that's pretty far! So I acted like a scoundrel, and frightened her, and angered you— Well, I can't say it's her fault, precisely, but I never did anything like that before I met her."

"I should say not," Tressilian laughed, remembering his indolent cousin of a month ago. "And don't pretend to be the injured party. It wasn't her that assaulted you."

Jon scowled but could not in conscience take issue with that. "She brings out the worst in me. Always challenging me— so if you refuse to shoot me, what do you plan to do?"

Tressilian noted that this elaborately casual question had Destain leaning forward in his chair, an abashed but obstinate look on his face. "Plan? I thought you wanted nothing to do with my plans."

"This concerns me." Abruptly Jon rose and started pacing the carpet. "Look, Bren, we're in a damnable coil here. You know that I would never do anything to hurt you. And I never meant— Even if I'd be of a mind to betray you that way, I know better than to compete with you for a woman. It ain't fair, but that's the way it is. You can always get any woman you want. But—"

He stopped to stare blindly out the window. "But Becky's mine. So she can't be yours. I'm sorry I wronged you, but that's why I did it. I wish I could say I did it to save you from disaster, because she'd be disastrous for you. But I did it because she's mine, only neither of you know it yet."

"Oh, I know it," Tressilian observed, balancing his chair back on two legs and resting his head against the wall. "You'll have to persuade Becky yet, but you've convinced me well enough."

Jon jerked around, staring at his old friend as if he'd changed into a creature beyond recognition. "You know? Then what are you going to do about it?"

"Bow out gracefully. What did you expect? A jousting tournament with her as the prize? No, my boy, Miss Marlowe and I have decided to end our engagement— rather an easy decision to effect, as it was never official anyway."

"That's it? You're not engaged anymore?" Destain echoed incredulously. "You're bequeathing me your bride?"

Tressilian closed his eyes in pain. "Let me give you a word of advice, Jon. Having had the honor to be Becky's fiancee for nearly a month now, I have formed some sense of what pleases her. And referring to her as a piece of property to be transferred will not please her. These modern girls, you know, have exalted notions."

Jon edged himself onto the window sill, leaning back against the leaded glass. He studied his cousin's face closely. "Tell me if I'm ruining your life. I don't know that I'll give over, but it's best that I know."

Tressilian opened his eyes and smiled the old merry smile, and Jon relaxed into confused relief. "Becky's mother will never be the same, I suppose, having lost her earl before she even got him, But I shall survive this blow. I warn you, though, that the friendship Becky and I have will outlast our betrothal. You'd do best to accustom yourself to it."

"It's little enough to ask, I reckon. Hell," Jon said recklessly, "I'll even forgive you for the Morocco voyage."

"I shan't settle for less than all your grievances against me. Say we're quits, or there is no deal."

"We're quits then." Jon raised his brandy glass in salute. "So this is that True Love you were yammering about."

"So it would seem."

"Stupid sort of emotion," Jon observed darkly. "Unhinges the most rational of men. I can't imagine why anyone would go out looking for it." He tossed off the last of the brandy and rose. "But I thank you anyway."

After Jon left, Tressilian smiled to himself, balancing the sultan's dagger on the palm of his hand. The amethysts in the hilt glinted magically in the wan sunlight, like Kristen's eyes.

How confusing life had become for all of them: The most cynical man in London losing his head for an innocent girl; a romantic maiden seeking a hero and finding an aide-de-camp; a woman of sense losing her sense of direction in love. Tressilian didn't even bother to catalog all his own changes; it sufficed to note that the world had been transformed and he too struggled to adjust.

He tossed the knife into the air and watched the blade impale itself quivering into the blotter. This game had become more amusing as the stakes grew higher. He couldn't wait to see how little Becky played her new hand.

## CHAPTER TWENTY-ONE

Becky was halfway through breakfast when Kristen, heavy-eyed, made her way into the sunlit dining room. The younger girl's cheerful greeting was such a contrast to her recent gloom that Kristen grew wary. She interrupted Becky's humming to comment, not without envy, "You certainly seem happy today."

Immediately Becky sobered. "I suppose I am trying to mask my despair," she sighed with her customary melodrama. "I should tell you before the gossips hear of it— Brendan and I have decided not to go through with a formal engagement."   "You're not going to elope!"

"Elope?" Becky echoed in a shocked tone. "Of course not. And if we were, I certainly would know better than to tell you! I mean, we shall not be getting married at all. So there will be no need of a formal engagement."

Kristen could not believe her ears, for only the other day she had heard Brendan avowing his love and his hopes— "Don't worry, it will all come out right for us." But it hadn't, apparently, and, torn between guilt and a gladness she couldn't deny, she asked warily, "Why?"

Becky stirred her eggs and frowned at the resulting mess. "We decided," she finally explained, "that we would not suit."

"What on earth does that mean?" Kristen demanded, for once wishing Becky would speak with her usual impetuosity.

But the girl only shook her head sadly. "We held off any formal betrothal because we weren't truly certain we would be right together. Well, we have decided we wouldn't. As you and Stamberly have also decided you wouldn't suit. At least," she added with a bit of spite, "we weren't so precipitous as to send off an announcement to the Gazette before we knew if we really wanted to marry."

When the only answer was a frown, Becky concluded cryptically, "I imagine that Brendan will be more enlightening.'

Kristen recalled Tressilian's quiet statement that he had given his heart irrevocably, and wondered if, after all, his heart had proved a revocable gift. Had he given it again? To whom?

Kristen's breath caught as she recalled those few tantalizing moments on May Day. But as she studied Becky's elfin face she saw not the slightest sign of a woman scorned. In fact, in this entire betrothal, Becky had never played the lovestruck heroine, a role that should have suited her down to the ground. Indeed, her affection for Brendan had seemed remarkably casual for a prospective bride. Perhaps Tressilian wasn't the jilter after all.

Kristen was persuaded that the answer to this conundrum was in residence at Tressilian House. She could not bear to wait to summon Tressilian; besides, she suspected if given time to prepare he would come up with some nonsense like Becky s. No, she had to catch him unaware and demand to know why he had ended the betrothal. So, after a struggle with her sense of propriety, she ordered her scandalized Abigail to accompany her to the earl's residence.

Fortunately, Grosvenor Square so early was the realm of nursemaids and their mischievous charges. No one noticed the young lady hunched secretively in a dove-gray pelisse as she mounted the Tressilian House steps, her face hidden by the wide brim of a silver poke bonnet.

As she dropped the brass knocker on the great double doors, Kristen heard the echo of her mother's lectures on all the things ladies must never do if they intended still to be ladies. Chief among the restricted activities was visiting a man in his home. Oh, Mother, Kristen thought with a wry twist to her lips, I'll bet you never thought to see me reduced to such depravity.

If Tressilian's butler had indicated how shocked he must have been by such a visit, Kristen would have rushed away, consumed with shame. But

Hastings was sensitive to her plight and dispensed with the creaking formality of morning calls. Taking her wrap, the butler said, "His grace is still breakfasting, my lady, but I've no doubt he would like to have you shown right up." And without further comment, he led her and Millson through the great hall.

Marble-floored, silk-papered, this entry boasted a vaulted ceiling painted with a mural of a battle at sea. But Kristen's attention was drawn to the magnificent double-winged staircase hung with portraits of the ten previous Earls of Tressilian, who bore a striking resemblance to the black-eyed rogue currently holding the title. There was no portrait of Brendan, unfortunately, but she imagined he would never stand still long enough for one to be made.

Kristen gave Hastings a grateful smile as he led her discreetly to the breakfast room. Now she knew Brendan had been jesting when he told her the butler had nearly hanged for attempting to strangle his previous employer, a prominent solicitor. For Hastings was altogether too considerate to be a murderer.

Millson, adjured to wait, vowed to stay right by the door- "within earshot!" Casting a quelling look at the maid, Hastings quietly opened the door. "Lady Killeaven."   "Kristen? What's happened?" Brendan leapt up, dropping his newspaper onto his plate of buttered eggs. This informal room had been designed for a large family, with its long wall of windows and a table for twelve. So Brendan's solitude brought Kristen an unexpected ache. How alone he always was, orphaned at birth, reared by servants, escaping in boyhood to the only family he could truly claim, the navy. He had never had anyone of his very own— not even, it seemed, his fiancee.

"It's not the children, is it?" he demanded, coming to take her hands in an imperative grasp.

His anxiety roused her from her abstraction. "Oh, no. They are fine. I'm sorry to have interrupted you."

"You ought to be," he retorted, leading her to the seat beside his. "You nearly gave me heart palpitations. I thought those demons must have run off again, to warrant your risking social ruin like this."

He raised a peremptory hand and Hastings, who had dismissed the attending footman, came forward to offer her coffee. Kristen cast an apologetic glance at Hastings, who silently withdrew. Such a sensitive man, she marveled again. Returning her regard to Brendan, she noticed with fond exasperation that he was only half-dressed, in his Hessians and riding breeches, a fine lawn shirt open at the neck. Had he bothered to brush his hair? No, for it rioted in boyish curls over his forehead. Her hand opened with a urge to smooth back those black locks, but she gripped her reticule tightly until the desire passed.

How mutinous her thoughts were. Once she had been able to marshal them like Captain Destain's troopers to follow her orders; now her command failed at every turn.

"Kristen," Tressilian prompted her. "Why did you come here?"

Recalled to her role, Kristen jerked up straight and managed quite a militant tone. "Becky said you had called off your engagement. I hope you can offer a better explanation than she did, for you know it does her reputation ill to waltz in and out of betrothals like this." Self-righteous, she accused herself, *as if I haven't just broken off my own engagement.*

But Brendan could not have heard about that disaster and so attempted no counter-attack. Instead, he concentrated on layering a scone with butter and marmalade and finally a dollop of honey. "It was a decision we made together," he replied finally, offering her half of the sweet monstrosity.

She waved away the scone, refusing to let his careful evasiveness get by. "That tells me nothing. You assured me at the start that you were serious, that you would not draw back."

"I haven't." Tressilian dropped his scone on the Wedgewood dish and rubbed his forehead with his fist, leaving a streak of marmalade on one winged eyebrow. "I shouldn't have said that. Why don't you just accept that we wouldn't suit— it's no more than you've been saying all along."

This time she couldn't halt the hand that touched the napkin to that sticky eyebrow. When he smiled at her maternal helpfulness, she colored and hid the napkin away. "You are saying that Becky decided she didn't want to marry you."

Brendan looked ready to demur, so she added impatiently, "Oh, Bren, don't start being decorous this late in life! Now tell me the truth, or I swear I will withhold Becky's allowance until she explains."

Tressilian put up his hand in capitulation. "She's formed a partiality for another man. I released her to let her pursue it." "Another man?" Kristen tried to keep her voice casual as she picked up her coffee cup, for she didn't want to seem too taken aback by this no doubt painful admission. Of course, she shouldn't be so surprised. Becky had been sunk in the blue-devils right up to the end of the betrothal; now she was happy as a lark. As Kristen suspected, she had never loved Brendan, at least not with the passion she claimed necessary for marriage. But what man could have inspired the passion Brendan Trevarrick had not?

As ever, he seemed to read her thoughts. "I shan't tell you his name. That's for Becky to do. But I assure you, if he were not an acceptable sort, I would have done my best to stop her. You will have no objection, I think, does she win her aim."

"This isn't a game, Brendan," she scolded, then cursed her temper as his thick lashes swept down to conceal his expression. He wasn't too blame, for he had behaved admirably, and never so much as now. "Oh, I knew she wasn't mature enough to be betrothed!"

Tressilian leaped to Becky's defense, only increasing Kristen's admiration. "No, it wasn't fair to push her into a connection she didn't want. She could hardly turn a earl down, and I suppose I exploited that. It was really very brave of her to call a halt to this before it became irrevocable."

That word again. Irrevocable. "I'm sorry, Brendan," Kristen whispered. "She must have hurt you very much."

Manfully he denied it. "Surely it's the best for us both."

She covered his hand with her own, aching for him. He was saying all the right words, accepting all the blame, when in truth he must be suffering the loss of the first real love of his life.

A wicked voice whispered in her mind: Now is your chance- Angrily she silenced it, but it echoed even as she determined to do something to ease Brendan's pain. Now is your chance— "Perhaps you can win her back."

Tressilian's hand tightened into a fist under hers. "Kristen, you just said this isn't a game."

"No, Brendan, listen. Becky's like any other woman, you know, susceptible to jealousy."

Tressilian's dark eyes glinted with a strange, eager light. "What are you suggesting?"

Embarrassed, Kristen released his hand and looked away. "Must I spell it out for you?"

"Yes, I think you must."

"You can try to make her jealous. She may come back to you if she sees you with someone else." Her hands gripped painfully in her lap, Kristen added shyly, "I could help."

Tressilian buried his head in his arms, his shoulders shaking, and she drew back in shamed affront. "You— you think it so amusing that an association with me might provoke jealousy?"

"Certainly not," he said hastily, raising his head. But his eyes still brimmed with laughter, and in that dear, familiar expression she could take no insult. "But it is amusing that my principled Kristen could be so duplicitous. Such a novel scheme! But doomed, I think. For what's-his-name won't take kindly to your participation in such charade."

"Stamberly has nothing to say about it." Kristen hated to admit the enormity of her mistake, but she knew the news would be out any moment now anyway. "We are no longer engaged."

"No?" Tressilian was less surprised than she had expected, only taking up his coffee cup and raising it in ironic toast. "You and I, angel, aren't very good at this engagement business, are we? Well, then, if you are free again, how can I refuse? Wellington himself could hardly contrive a more enigmatic strategy. I myself," he added sardonically, "prefer a more direct approach. But you see where that has gotten me— jilted in my first betrothal."

He sighed sorrowfully, and she along with him, then he squeezed her hand lightly. "But you mustn't tease Becky, promise. If she's not interested, no amount of persuading will do either of us any good. She shouldn't have to feel any guilt, and I shouldn't like to be known for my slavish pursuit of a reluctant lady."

He was so good, Kristen thought as she left after extracting the promise of a riding date later that afternoon. She had never realized before just how unselfish Brendan was to those he loved. He felt only compassion for the authoress of his heartbreak, hoping that everyone would say she had made a lucky escape from an unhappy marriage to a belted scoundrel.

But Kristen, at least, knew that his behavior had been beyond reproach. The knowledge shamed her, for she had once been so certain that inconstancy was as much a part of him as his black eyes and restless spirit. He had proved her wrong. It was a shame that he had expended all that effort for a girl who could not appreciate his many special qualities.

## CHAPTER TWENTY-TWO

Kristen had promised not to upbraid Becky, but she could not but act a bit coolly in the next week. As Becky responded by withdrawing, their former intimacy deteriorated into the cordiality of acquaintances who just happened to share the same house. They exchanged pleasantries over dinner, but their camaraderie was gone.

Kristen thought longingly of the days— not so distant!— when she had been privy to Becky's confidences, when they had happily traded gossip and fashion information. Now she saw little of the girl. She was always off riding with one of her newly-emboldened swains, or leaving for some jaunt with Daisy Grey and her mother. She took little notice that Kristen was seeing a good deal of the Earl of Tressilian.

So Kristen's bold plan to make Becky jealous was doing little but alienating the girl. Perhaps the engagement was indeed a mistake, and its end best be left in force. But Brendan was so pleased with the scheme, so hopeful of its success, that Kristen could not back down now.

After a week of distance, Kristen took advantage of a brilliant May morning to suggest a shopping trip. Becky agreed with an alacrity that indicated her own desire for a reconciliation. So with a footman trailing behind to bear packages, they set off through the fresh morning air to Bond Street.

Those hardy blades who rose early that day to walk could count themselves rewarded for their virtue. In fact, bowing men littered the path of the two Marlowe ladies, each of whom responded characteristically to the masculine attention. Every inch the lady, Kristen acknowledged the admirers she knew with a pleasant smile; a cold nod dismissed the encroaching strangers. Her pale gold hair swept back smoothly under a Prussian blue bonnet; her slender form was most properly embellished by a gown of pale blue shadow-stripes, the lace inset in the bodice flirting with decorum. Her delicate features reflected serenity, while her violet eyes unconsciously promised something more.

Becky, in contrast, was the picture of pretty exuberance, in her deep rose muslin dress, with a satin-trimmed bonnet framing her wanton dark curls. She twirled her jaunty parasol and smiled pertly at each admirer.

But Kristen was too pleased with Becky's high spirits to criticize this forward conduct. She was a darling, but not right for Brendan after all, Kristen told herself. Soon, perhaps, he would realize that and take back his battered heart.

"Tell me about that young man— Danvers?— who comes to call," she invited breathlessly as they dashed across the busy street.

Becky made a moue of distaste. "I suppose he is handsome, but I have never cared for green eyes. He's fabulously wealthy, of course, but expects to be made up to on account of it. His mother has royal connections, you know, but that has made him monstrous high in the instep."

This casual categorizing of attractions did not argue a passion to cause a jilting. Alec Danvers wasn't the beau ideal, then. "He seems rather taken with you, to judge by all those languishing glances he bestows on you. And surely those massive bouquets he sends each day indicate deep regard."

"So vulgar, don't you think?" Becky trailed her hand along the brick sill of a shop window, smudging her lace glove. "A single rose— cream with just a blush of pink, like a maiden's cheek-stolen from a garden in Hyde Park— is so much more romantic, don't you think?"

Kristen had no time to figure which of Becky's admirers knew her well enough to make such a gesture, for Becky's dreamy sigh faded into a plea. "If Alec Danvers should approach you for my hand, promise me you will head him off before he addresses my father. I don't want to marry him."

Kristen shrank from such a task. It was one thing to discourage Brendan's suit— and what a lost cause that had proved. But she hardly knew young Lord Alec. And besides, Aunt Amelia would love this rich son of a marquess nearly as much as an earl. "If you keep refusing offers," she reminded her cousin uncharitably, "you'll end up on the shelf, and no one will ever believe you were once the toast of town."

In a low voice, Becky retorted, "You needn't tax me again with throwing over the prize of the marriage mart. I've already received word from my mother that I've forfeited every groat of my legacy and that if she weren't too overcome by the disgrace to travel, she'd haul me off home like a dog."

"I know. She wrote to me too," Kristen said ruefully. "She thinks no ordinary mortal will have the temerity to approach you now that you've jilted Tressilian, and she may be right.'

"Oh, pooh," Becky replied, but then they were separated by a ragged band of mischief-seekers. One boy, with bright blue eyes like Nick and the same sort of cocky grin, brushed Kristen's arm as if by accident. Coolly she took hold of his collar and let him squirm until she removed her reticule from his dirty fingers. When he looked up at her, eyes brimming with tears, she relented and gave him a sovereign and sternly urged him on his way.

Becky rejoined her and repeated her comment with a toss of her head that sent her bonnet ribbons dancing. "Oh, pooh, I say. We weren't officially engaged, after all. It's no one's affair if we decided we shouldn't suit."

You decided you wouldn't suit, Kristen accused silently, and Brendan was gentleman enough to let you go. But she turned dutifully to her self-appointed task to reunite the couple, though she was strangely reluctant to succeed too well. "Won't you reconsider, dearest? I'm certain Brendan would be happy to take you back." The words tasted oddly bitter, and she had to stop to gaze blindly into a shop window to hide her expression from Becky.

The younger girl joined her at the window, glancing quickly at her then back to the display of ormolu clocks. Kristen had to strain to hear her soft answer amid the din of the passing crowd and the clattering carriages. "I do want the best for Brendan, for I am truly fond of him. But I shouldn't be the best. We would go crashing through life like two children, for neither of us, as everyone always says, has the sense God gave a goat. And we would end up blaming each other for every disaster. We shall do better as friends, I think, and I hope we shall always be that."

Kristen could not help but be impressed by Becky's newfound perception. She was right, of course. She needed a husband wise enough to abet her romantic flights without getting caught up in them. Brendan was not that man, however he might like to be. "But he cares so much for you."

"I know. I hope he finds a woman who can love him as I can't," Becky replied poetically. Then she spied the reflection of a dark blue uniform in the window and whipped around. Disappointment flashed in Becky's expressive eyes. But then she blazed a smile at the dazzled lieutenant and tugged Kristen away down the street. "Eighteenth Hussars," she said knowledgeably. "A handsome uniform, of course, with all that trimming. But those Hyde Park Hussars aren't much of a fighting unit. They've spent most of the war at Almack's dancing with debutantes."

Since the debutante Becky had never yet refused a dance with a hussar, her scorn seemed a bit misplaced. But the girl went on with arch irrelevance, "Besides, it's nothing like what you and Stamberly have done, breaking off your engagement after it was announced. Or had you forgotten your former fiancee already?"

Kristen wished she might forget, but Stamberly wouldn't hear of it. That most placid of suitors had turned passionate. For the past week he had importuned Kristen with letters, and would haunt her house did Chesley let him in. "But I'm not a girl in her first season. The eyes of every gossip in town aren't on me."

"Oh, no?" Becky's own eyes were alight with mischief. "Well, you just tell me the object of Mrs. Garfield's stare."

Kristen located the noted gossip just across the street in front of Celeste's Hat Shoppe. Mrs. Garfield was, in fact, watching Kristen and whispering something in her companion's ear. Becky flounced her shoulders knowingly. "I overheard her at Lady Harburton's musicale yesterday— such a tedious affair, you were quite right to stay away, for the soprano was sadly out of key— and Mrs. Garfield might be pardoned for preferring gossip to entertainment—" Becky took a deep breath. "The point is, Kristen, she was gossiping about you! Oh, do let's go into Francine's, for I shall die if I don't purchase one of those duck-feather fans, and I think I've ruined these gloves somehow."

Kristen threw a darkling look at the encroaching Mrs. Garfield, then followed her cousin into the elegant glove shop. Becky dashed off towards the wall where an astonishing assortment of fans hung from little gold hooks.

But Kristen paid no mind to Francine's overpriced wares. "Becky, if you don't tell me what scurrilous things that cat said about me, I shan't lend you another groat and you will have to die of lack of duck-feathers after all."

Becky hid her grin behind the flutter of a black lace Spanish fan. "Oh, only that you make a habit of breaking men's hearts."

Kristen caught a relieved breath. The gossip could have been so much worse, for she recalled seeing Mrs. Garfield at that May Day picnic, and it would just be like the nasty witch—for that was the costume she had worn—to secrete herself outside rose arbors the better to provide herself with scandalous on dits.

Absently she held out her reticule and let Becky help herself to a ten-pound note, for the girl pronounced herself unable to choose between lace and duck, and thus required both. "But Becky, that's absurd. I haven't broken any hearts. Stamberly might be making a cake of himself, not that I would ever have predicted it, and I do think he's just doing it for effect, but surely no one else has been brought low by me."

She smiled to herself, recalling how, whenever she had to decline his invitation to ride or drive or dine, Brendan used to exclaim in his theatrical way, "You have broken my heart!" Then she sobered, for she hadn't been the one to do it after all.

Becky asked innocently, "Is it really true what Mrs. Garfield said, that a German prince drowned himself after you refused his suit?"

"He didn't drown himself!" Automatically Kristen held out her hand for the change. "He got foxed on the voyage home and fell overboard. It was entirely an accident!"

Becky held the opinion that there were a great deal too many German princes as it was, so she took this one's loss more equably than Mrs. Garfield. "The ladies did speculate that poor Stamberly was in for a similar fate, for they say he is drinking late and deep and stumbling home near dawn. Think of all the dire fates that await one in those dark streets."

"But whoever would have guessed he would take it so hard?" Kristen asked, genuinely puzzled. "He never even drank before, except when prices on the Exchange fell. And if you could have heard his proposal— well, Becky, I know you would have found it entirely lacking in romantic fervor. Now his notes are so panegyrical they put me to the blush! And what are you going to do with those fans, pray tell? They will do only for evening wear, and as the season's almost over, you'll never get the use of them. You surely won't have much need of them this summer in Wiltshire."

"Oh, I don't think I need to worry about spending the summer in Wiltshire," Becky replied, that silly, dreamy look returning to her eyes. Then she shook her head and briskly took Kristen's arm. "Let's go to Sam's Royal Library before we return for lunch. Daisy told me they laid in a large supply of that new novel Miraculous Nuptials— so appropriate a title, don't you think?"

Kristen was frankly baffled by the turn of the conversation, but put it down to Becky's realization that it would indeed be miraculous if she caught a husband this late in the season.

Sam's was a narrow storefront on Bond Street, filled to its dusty rafters with popular novels and prominent citizens. More gossip was exchanged by patrons leafing through Sam's books than in all the salons in London. Kristen knew that if there was gossip about the broken betrothals at Killeaven House, she would hear it here. So she sought out Bunny McCall, who could be counted on to give her the truth without any bark on it.

Bunny, dressed in her usual governess-gray, greeted Kristen with a sly smile and proceeded to pump her for details. "Come, now, Kristen, I've only heard the barest, that little Becky and the dark Adonis parted amicably, the more fool she, and that you and Stamberly parted not so amicably. Is it true your children conspired to destroy him in your affections? I always said you gave them their heads too much, not that I don't think it best all in all, for now that I think on it, Stamberly is not really your sort."

As Bunny had been Stamberly's chief advocate when Kristen was debating his suit, the countess replied to her a bit acerbically, "Thank you for your timely counsel, my dear. And no, my children didn't conspire— my word, they are mere babies! They couldn't have thought up such a scheme. What else do you hear?"

"Nothing too startling." Bunny idly straightened the volumes on the bookshelf before them and moved on to tidy another set. As much time as she spent in Sam's, Bunny might as well have been an employee, so she always tried to make herself useful. "Only that you and the dark Adonis have been spending a great deal of time together. Misery loves company, I suppose." "We have ever been friends, you recall," Kristen said stiffly.

"Oh, yes, that's right. Friends. Poor Tressilian doesn't seem to make much of an impression on you Marlowe ladies, does he? Why, if I had had your opportunities, I'd be a countess today. Where is the little tormentor, anyway? I hear Danvers is ready to throw his heart at her feet. Will she stamp on that one also?"

Bunny headed off Kristen's predictable rejoinder by observing archly, "Oh, there she is, your Becky. Conversing with Elise Winterleigh. Why, they seem to be arguing! I can't imagine why, unless it has something to do with that charming young captain of dragoons. He's recently given Elise her congee, you know, and she's in utter despair. For Captain Destain is one of those men who likes to take his time, if you take my meaning—"

She threw her head back and laughed at Kristen's furious blush. Bunny was by all accounts a faithful wife, but somehow she knew more about the amatory abilities and preferences of London men than the most popular courtesan. "This breaking off must be contagious, you know. He did it at nearly the same moment your misguided cousin was ending her engagement— to his cousin! Isn't that simply too intriguing?"

Kristen bid her friend a distracted farewell and pushed her way to the table display of Miraculous Nuptials. Becky was at the center of a half-circle of ladies, her back against the table, her eyes wide with fear. Lady Elise leaned toward her, her lovely bosom heaving threateningly, her voice hissing with lady-like rage. With growing disbelief, Kristen heard her accuse Becky of enticing away Elise's lover and her daughter's prospective husband, both of whom turned out to be the same unfortunate man, Captain Destain.

Kristen's protective instincts came to the fore. Becky might have broken Bren's heart, might play the heedless flirt with a dozen young men. But she was only a naive little girl from Wiltshire, no match for the vindictive vixen Elise.

But Kristen was. With the prong of her parasol, she shoved Elise back from her cousin. "Dearest, I wish you would find me that book of sermons by Dr. Winggold. Hurry now, for we've plans for lunch."

Becky only gazed at her, her eyes opaque. But she roused as Kristen gave her a gentle push towards the minuscule section devoted to religious works. Then Kristen turned back, her hand balanced lightly on the handle of her parasol. Brendan was wont to ready his sword hand in just such a manner when he considered attack, she recalled. She raised her weapon slightly to tap Elise on one blue kid slipper.

"My, my, Lady Elise, you have drawn quite a crowd to the display table. Miraculous Nuptials, is it? How vastly appropriate, don't you think, Lady Elise? For indeed it is miraculous, how some nuptials survive the shocking behavior of one of the principals. Have you ever known it to be so? Why, of course you have."

Elise stared uncomprehendingly at her, then rage again twisted her sensuous mouth. "That little tart—"

"Is that what you had for breakfast, Elise? Little tarts?"

A woman in the back snickered as Kristen cocked her head wonderingly. "Now who was it who told me you preferred spring lamb for breakfast? The springier the better, I think she said."

Elise's gasp was followed by waves of giggles from the audience, for her preference for younger men was well known. But all fell silent at the approach of the hesitant Becky. "Dr. Winggold," she whispered, handing Kristen a thin red volume.

"Oh, it's not for me, dearest. I have my own copy at home. Rather I thought Lady Elise might want to study it. Perhaps you've heard of Dr. Winggold's meditations on the Ten Commandments, Lady Elise? He's written a

chapter on each one. You might be especially interested in Chapter Six.'

The regular churchgoers amid the spectators inhaled sharply in unison; their less spiritual sisters had to whisper, "What does she mean, Chapter Six?"

Kristen picked up Elise's limp hand and pressed into it the red volume. "Read and repent," she said in the forgiving tones of a Methodist missionary. "Come, Becky, didn't you say you were engaged to ride with Captain Destain this afternoon?"

With a last flourish of her parasol, she bowed graciously to the stunned Elise and swept Becky towards the door. Scattered applause followed them out to the walk.

Once in the revivifying sunlight, Becky drew a ragged breath. "That was splendid, Kristen! I- - I was so frightened, for she was venomous. But you routed her left and right— what did you mean, Chapter Six?'

"Really, dear," Kristen chided, taking her arm to cross the street. "Have you forgotten your Bible lessons so quickly? What is the sixth commandment?"

Becky's lips moved as she went down the list. Softly, she finished, "Fourth commandment, Honor thou thy mother and father. Fifth commandment, Thou shalt not kill. Sixth commandment, Thou shalt not commit adultery— Kristen!" Becky's eyes widened and Kristen nodded. "Precisely."

"You didn't really— Oh, Kristen, I cannot believe you, of all people! Right there in Royal Sam's! Why, it will be all over town in minutes, that you told Elise Winterleigh to read a sermon on adultery!"

Becky regarded her with a respect bordering on awe, and Kristen was no less amazed at her own effrontery. What had become of the prim Lady Killeaven, who always conducted herself becomingly in public?

But Becky did not lament the transformation of her guardian. She linked arms with Kristen as they turned into South Audley Street. "Oh, everyone will think you are a prime goer. And you are! You were just like St. George, rescuing me from the dragon! And with such devastating subtlety! Beau Brummel must surely look to his laurels as London's greatest dispenser of insult."

Kristen had no time to reckon whether she truly wanted to eclipse the great Beau in that field, for Becky had clutched her arm. "But— but— you said I was to ride with Captain Destain this afternoon. And I'm not! We had a little disagreement, and he swore he'd never speak to me again. Of course," she added, "he didn't mean it. But it will be several days at least before he realizes that he would die without me. Not that I care in the least, for I can't think why I would want to keep alive a man who would— well, you know— with such as Elise, and expect me to pretend it matters naught."

"You'll see him this afternoon, whether either of you likes it or not. I am certain I can persuade him to surrender a bit earlier than usual."

Kristen wished savagely that the captain could see Becky now, blinking back her tears, all her town bronze blasted off by his light-of-love. He would have to be cynical indeed to make light of Becky's distress. And he wouldn't, if he valued his life.

Becky dashed at her cheeks with her glove, leaving a smudge behind.

Then she looked up tremulously. "You are so good to me."

Kristen smiled back absently, still preoccupied with unknotting this latest kink in the coil. So Brendan had relinquished Becky to his own cousin. How unpredictable was love, after all.

# CHAPTER TWENTY-THREE

Jon Destain stuffed Lady Killeaven's curt note in his pocket and embarked on his reluctant way. He blinked as he emerged into the bright afternoon, for he kept his rooms at the Albany dark so his sleep would not be disturbed by the premature sun. The raucous parade of Piccadilly only abraded his tender nerves, but not as much as the gossip he heard from the worthy Fletcher, valet to Lord Byron, who had taken Albany rooms on his return to town.

Fletcher was returning from the tailor with an armful of the poet's shirts, but couldn't resist stopping. "Must be on your way to see the little Miss Marlowe," he observed archly.

Destain regarded his interrogator coldly, but was impelled to ask, "Why would you think so?"

"Lady Killeaven said as how you were riding with her cousin Miss Marlowe this afternoon."

It was definitely beneath the dignity of a Destain to pump a servant for information, but the valet's casual use of the names of the unimpeachable Marlowe ladies was too provoking. And his information was doubtlessly impeccable, for as Byron's manservant, Fletcher always had prime on dits about his master to trade. "You had converse with the countess, did you?"

The scorn of aristocratic young men could not wound Fletcher, who had suffered much worse from his volatile master. But few valets would pass up a chance to discompose a nobleman. "Certainly not, sir. My master, of course, is sincerely admiring of her, so I can do no less. But no, I had it from the tailor. It's all over Bond Street, how Lady K trounced Lady E in Royal Sam's."

Lady E? Destain flinched, then gestured peremptorily. "Go on."

With rather more relish than was precisely called for, Fletcher related the story of the encounter that had Mayfair consulting dusty Bibles. Chapter Six— Destain was better schooled than Becky, and recognized the allusion right off.

Adultery— the sins of his youth, he thought gloomily as he left the grinning Fletcher behind, were rising up to haunt him. And such meager sins as they were, it was scarcely just. Elise's husband, after all, was admirably tolerant, and Jon was hardly her only lover, off at war as he was most of the time. He hadn't the shocking history that so many of his friends did— Tressilian, for starters. Nonetheless he was the one tarred with that ugly brush. Adultery.

He flushed with guilt at the thought of such vulgarity confronting the innocent Becky— for innocent she was, despite her pretense at sophistication. She should never have had to suffered through such a scene, or had to turn to a gentle widow for protection (even if the countess had proved unexpectedly up to the battle). He could hardly blame the pair of them if they greeted him with a rain of musket balls as he approached their home.

Guilt had been an uncomfortably persistent companion for the captain of late. Falling in love with his cousin's fiancee was something he could not have imagined doing a year ago— although he had, in fact, always preferred Bren's toys. That shame would be with him always, along with the fear that, despite his denials, Brendan was suffering silently for Destain's sake. Lately Jon couldn't see his cousin without searching for some shadow of sorrow on his face. And it might all be for naught, for Becky would probably sending him packing for good after this encounter with Elise.

As he trailed a nurse and her four little charges across Berkeley Square, Jon realized that his connection with Elise had come as no surprise to Becky. Her rejection of his proposal had baffled him at the time, with her heavy emphasis on trust and sacrifice and death- defying love— all of which he assumed he had offered along with his name.

She was talking, in her melodramatic way, about Elise, but he had been too dense to understand. He had never considered discussing his former mistress with Becky, for a man simply didn't speak of such things to a girl he hoped to marry. And he had expected that Becky, did she learn of the connection, would ignore it, as most girls had sense enough to do.

He had forgotten that Becky was not like most girls, but an odd mix of the practical and the romantic. Committed to a dream of ideal love, she was prepared to pick and choose to get it. She must have been disillusioned indeed to end her betrothal with Tressilian, and to refuse to begin one with Destain.

He could just envision Becky lying in her innocent bed, tears trailing down her round cheeks, recalling the gossip some malicious matron had seen fit to impart. No doubt Becky worried that Jon would be as careless with his own marriage as he had been with Elise's. And any protestation that Winterleigh minded not the least, or that no emotions were engaged, would only be dismissed as more cynicism. There was, after all, an ideal at issue.

Destain murmured an abstracted apology to the maid he collided with on Adam's Row. He would just have to explain that he had been changed utterly, as impossible as that was even for Destain to believe. The cynicism that had allowed him to disregard his mistress's wedding vows had gone fleeting the instant he imagined saying those vows himself. Marriage— his own— would be perhaps the only ideal he would hold sacred. He had only to prove to Becky that he would never hurt her, or allow anyone else to hurt her either.

But before he could do that, he had somehow to survive this interview with Lady Killeaven.

So he prepared his most disarming smile as he was ushered into her drawing room. The countess was disarming herself, like a pale ray of sunshine in a gown of jonquil crepe with a froth of lace along the puffed sleeves, and yellow ribbons in her hair.

Always observant, Destain noted that her pretty mouth was trying to assemble into stern lines but showed a distressing tendency towards laughter. She is proud of herself, he realized, taking a seat across from her and accepting a cup of tea. He almost felt sympathy for Elise, who could be no match for an avenging angel.

Suddenly he recalled that night at White's so long ago, when poor Jeremy Trevarrick had asked Tressilian to name the loveliest lady in England. Tressilian had run through a dozen or so names, deliberately avoiding Lady Killeaven's, or so Jon had thought. He could never have imagined then that she would have any use for the wild Bren's with his pantheon of beauties. Or that she would now be turning those censorious violet eyes upon the man who had championed her own beauty on that summer night. The silence made him nervous, so he broke it as she plucked a sugar cube from the bowl with silver tongs. "I hear I am to take Miss Marlowe riding this afternoon."

"Unless you intend to make me a liar. Sugar?"

He declined, piqued by her chill tone. Despite his penitent resolutions, he felt a bit ill-used, for he had, after all, offered Becky his heart and his name and been sent off smarting. "Have you received Miss Marlowe's acceptance on this assignment? For she has been less than welcoming of my presence recently."

"She will go along, I assure you." The steel in the velvet voice indicated that Becky had better go along, if she knew what was good for her. Then the countess took note of her guest's truculence and switched tactics, adding gently, "Perhaps I should explain."

Apparently marshaling her thoughts, Lady Killeaven absently added a fourth sugar cube to her tea. One yellow ribbon was in imminent peril of coming loose and spilling pale gold curls on Kristen's shoulder. And the dainty gold unicorn pin holding her fichu— Destain noticed such details— was upside down. Fascinated, he wondered what had happened to the usually impeccable countess. Did her slight deshabille indicate great inner turmoil? Or simply a new insouciance to go with her new role as protector of the innocent?

"You have heard, I take it, of Becky's encounter with your—" She frowned, searching for a proper term, her association with Tressilian having taught her only improper ones. But it was a lost cause anyway, for there were no proper terms for Elise Winterleigh. "With Lady Elise."

Impatiently she pushed a wayward curl behind her ear with her teaspoon. "I believe it is in Becky's best interest to be seen in public with you, for then the censure and impudence will be directed elsewhere—where it belongs. Of course, you will get off lightly, but then men usually do."

Stung by this, for he did not feel that he had gotten off lightly at all, Destain retorted, "And if I refuse this commission of yours? As I ought, for Becky has made it clear that my presence is burdensome to her."

"You mustn't take her so seriously," the countess chided. "She has been waiting for you to call. Every time she caught a glimpse of a cavalry uniform she thought it was you coming to apologize."

Apology was indeed what Destain had been set on only a few minutes ago, but as was natural with penitents, learning it was expected had him perversely self-righteous. "I can't think what I have to apologize for, when she's the one who rejected my suit."

The countess set her teacup down with a clatter. Too late Destain realized that he probably should have consulted Becky's guardian before he had offered that suit. But inexperienced at this sort of ritual, and none too confident of success, he had wanted to get it over with. So he had never considered the time-consuming and humiliating preliminaries of gaining permission first. Just as well, since Becky had refused him. To be scolded now for rushing his fences would truly add insult to injury.

But Kristen only picked up her cup with a fine show of unconcern. Gratefully he realized that she was loath to admit her charge had not confided in her, and so she ignored his revelation altogether.

"I am not asking for apology, only your presence at her side. I can't think what I can do to persuade you——" She shrugged with appealing helplessness, which fooled him not for a minute. "There's always blackmail, of course——"

He had only a moment to curse his cousin's inability to keep a secret before she continued with a beguiling smile, "But I prefer to rely on your good nature. I have always had the highest regard for your better qualities, else I should never have considered you worthy of my dear Becky. I should so hate to be proved wrong."

So she had resorted to blackmail after all, but so sweetly. Destain raised his teacup in ironic toast. "I have oft admired General Wellington's tactics. But had he your skills, madame, he'd be dancing at a victory ball instead of pacing around in a tent in Spain. You have my unconditional surrender, not that you expected any less."

With a faint smile she rose to draw the bellpull, and when Chesley appeared, she said, "Inform Miss Marlowe that Captain Destain is here for their riding engagement."

Kristen's smile faded once Becky and her captain had departed, hardly looking at each other. The girl had been shy, but covered it up with a defiant air, and poor Destain translated his embarrassment into a remote elegance of bearing and speech. Kristen hoped they would work out their disagreement during their ride. In the meantime, the denizens of Hyde Park would witness Becky's triumph in the battle for Captain Destain.     The news of Destain's proposal came as a shock to Kristen, for she would have hoped Becky would disclose such a exciting event. But their easy intimacy had been another casualty of Becky's broken betrothal. Kristen determined to restore that closeness, if only because she was dying to hear if the cynical captain actually went down on one knee and vowed eternal love like the most starry-eyed Romeo— and if Becky would accept him the next time.

Though she would never have chosen Jon Destain as the ideal match for little Becky, Kristen admitted it made some peculiar sense. Destain was a strong man despite his indolence, and would probably do a better job controlling Becky than Kristen had. He was sensitive too, a close observer of human nature, his cynicism only a guard around a vulnerable heart. Becky's gift of happiness would draw him into a real participation in life. Already she was affecting him: The pain in his usually cool eyes when he spoke of Becky's rejection suggested he had experienced more real emotion in the last weeks than in his entire life.

They would deal well together, and Aunt Amelia would just have to forgo her dreams of a earl and settle for the heir to a viscount. For a delicious moment Kristen envisioned the first meeting between Amelia and Admiral Destain. They were well-matched to engage in endless in-law squabbles. And they did deserve each other!

Kristen decided on a subtle strategy to persuade Becky of the rightness of this match. She would speak admiringly of the captain's heroism on the Peninsula, of his romantic appearance in uniform, then decry the despair that must have led him to take a dissolute like Elise to mistress. What dire fate might await him were he to suffer real tragedy, Kristen wouldn't like to imagine. Becky would swiftly envision herself as the shining savior of the jaded hero, and dash off an announcement to the Gazette.

Lost in speculation, Kristen started when she heard Tressilian in the hall. That insidious, insistent little whisper rasped, "Tell him. It will break his heart, but then—"

She shoved the traitorous thought away. He would hear soon enough. Until then, Kristen would make an effort to cheer him. So she greeted him at the top of the stairs with a welcoming smile. "How nice of you to call! Do let's take a walk in the garden. It's such a lovely afternoon and my flowers are all in bloom."

Tressilian agreed absently and turned back down the stairs. His mind was clearly elsewhere— with Becky, she thought with a spurt of annoyance, and a little of her pleasure seeped away.

Fortunately the garden, in full spring splendor, was enough to cheer the saddest heart. Kristen had laid out the neat, color-coordinated rows herself for maximum effect. But then she had to turn it over to her gardener, a secret tippler, who had some objection to pruning. So her roses and tulips and hyacinths grew untamed, their petals scattering the flagstone path with color.

Tressilian, however, managed to ignore the gaudy display. He focused his opaque gaze at the brick wall ahead and unconsciously twisted a gold button on his uniform front. Round and round the button turned, until Kristen wanted to seize his restless hand and make it stop.

Instead, she said carefully, "I haven't any good to report. Becky has been seeing a good deal of Danvers— and Destain." From under lowered lashes, she assessed his reaction-brave and generous, as always.

"Jon would be good for her, don't you think?" he asked quietly. "He's the best of men, better'n Danvers, by far."

"Yes, but hardly her ideal." Kristen halted in the middle of the Shakespeare plot, amid the rosemary for remembrance and pansies for thoughts. She began to argue against the match she had just determined to promote, because Brendan looked so subdued, so lost. "He isn't given to romantic gestures—"

"He's learning. Becky's not close with her expectations, you know." Briefly a smile flickered in his eyes. "I thought she might write a manual— what every aspiring hero needs to know."

With an encouraging tone that sounded hollow even to her own ears, Kristen maintained, "But perhaps, when she lists the requirements for heroism she will realize that you are the only one who fits them. For you are, you know. Every girl's dream."

"Don't." His voice was harsh, his gesture jerky. Then he looked blindly down at the button in his hand. "I keep doing that. My valet is ready to dismiss me, I think."

Alarmed, Kristen took the button from him and stuck it into his breastpocket. That automatic, intimate gesture brought color to her cheeks, but she stilled the nagging of her conscience and captured his hand. "Bren's, you mustn't worry so. You'll make yourself ill."

Tressilian gently turned her hand over, studying her open palm as if he might find an answer there. She wondered if he might press a kiss there, as he used to when he wanted to annoy her with gallantry. But instead he only gave her a crooked smile. "I have never been ill in my life."

Disappointed, she took her hand back. "Last winter you were not in top form, I recall."

"That was an injury. I am not entirely invulnerable, only nearly so," he retorted with a trace of his usual arrogance.

"Not nearly."

She spoke softly, as if to herself, and just as softly, gazing down at her, he echoed, "Aye, not nearly."

For an instant their eyes locked, and Kristen ' breath failed. In the darkness of his gaze, she glimpsed something frightening, alluring. She was the first to break the exchange, to look back towards the house for witnesses. But they were alone except for the rioting flowers. Now's your chance, came the whisper again.

After a moment, Tressilian said, "I gather your grand scheme to make Becky jealous has been fruitless."

Becky again. Anger passed through Kristen like a shudder, and left her determined to make him forget Becky, if only for a moment.

But her manner was demure as she raised her eyes to his. "Oh, I don't know if it's been so unsuccessful. She's watching us from her bedroom window right now. No, don't look," she said hastily.

She slipped closer, until they were close enough to waltz— closer even than that. Then she entwined her arms around his neck, meeting his fathomless eyes with unusual audacity. The intoxication of touching him made her dizzy but bold. "I told you she was watching. Do you always expect ladies to instruct you how to go on from here?"

That roused him out of his trance. His hands at her waist, he pulled her closer than she thought possible, so her body met his at every juncture.

There was little tenderness in this kiss, but she felt no fear at his barely leashed power. This is Bren, she thought hazily as her fingers slipped into his hair. He will never hurt me.

She imagined that this was no different from that single kiss by the moonlit ruins so long ago. His arms were as strong around her, his mouth as demanding. But she was different, as if the fragrance of the flowers and the heat of the sun had weakened her resistance to that treacherous longing.

Finally some instinct for self-preservation, if not self- respect, asserted itself, and she shakily drew away. He loves another, she thought in anguish, turning from him as if to leave. But no instinct could preserve her when he caught her back into his embrace. Helplessly she surrendered, her head spinning with impossible thoughts and her heart full to the breaking.

# CHAPTER TWENTY-FOUR

Thomas Chesley inspected the house every evening, running a finger along the baseboards to test the maids dusting, looking for his distinguished reflection in the polished tabletop in the small salon, stooping to search for elusive dustballs. Tonight he proceeded through this duty with a distracted air, most of his attention focused on determining what had gone wrong with his household.

Years had passed at Killeaven House without any event more dramatic than the downstairs maid running off with the Earl of Tressilian's groom. But this season all Hades had broken loose. Chesley might admit he had initially been excited by all the activity, but now he longed for the peace and quiet of the old days.

Once he had been able to visit his club and exchange complacency's with the other butlers, speculating how long this governess would last with the Marlowe children, boasting discreetly of Lady Killeaven's charity work. But now no sooner did he enter the varnished portals of the Myrmidon Club than he was accosted by his fellows avid questions.

He could hardly blame them, what with engagements being made and broken off four weeks later, the children vanishing into the maw of the

Pantheon Bazaar, the Viscount Stamberly haunting the doorstep, and the daredevil earl trying his luck with both the Marlowe ladies. The whole house had tilted sideways, following the lead of its once straightforward mistress.

Lady Killeaven had changed, Chesley mused as he inspected the brass mirror for spots. When he had stopped by for afternoon tea, the Myrmidon Club had been abuzz with her morning's rout of the scandalous Lady Elise. Most of the talk was admiring— the Winterleighs had dismissed four butlers in the last two years— but one major domo had observed archly, "Lady K certainly has become the bold one." Chesley had had to become very stiff until his adversary backed down and added, "I mean, the courageous one."

Once Chesley might have blamed his employer's rash behavior on the example of the earl. But for five years, Lady Killeaven had withstood the corrupting influence of Tressilian, and Chesley could not imagine why she would falter now. In fact, Chesley's attitude toward the earl had quite mellowed over the years, due only in part to the sovereigns he passed out like candy. He was, Chesley had to admit, a generous man.

Stamberly was another sort—tight as a tick; even farthings stuck to his fingers. The entire staff was glad when the countess threw him over, though his eccentric behavior the last few days had made them all want to put the poor dog out of his misery.

At least the earl had responded amiably to his jilting, not even forsaking the Killeaven household with its welcoming children and grateful staff. He hadn't even forsaken Miss Marlowe, to judge from the note he left for her when he departed this afternoon— "for her eyes only, Chesley, you understand," he said confidentially as he slipped another sovereign into the butler's hand.

Lady Killeaven was too busy with her own intrigues to worry about her cousin's anyway. Clad in a brown cloak that would have been undistinguished even on a maid, the countess had left a quarter hour past, airily declaring she was just stepping next door to Mrs. Pesham and needed no escort.

Her inexperience at falsehood showed in her eyes, however, and when Chesley probed, she told Chesley quite sharply to go about his business. If he didn't know any better, he would think she was going to an assignation with a man. But that, even in these untoward times, was most unlikely, he told himself as he mounted the stairs. Lady Killeaven had always been a most proper lady.

Unusual activity on the landing above him halted Chesley in his tracks. Was one of the maids calling out the window to her lover? No, it was those two little scamps in their nightclothes, leaning precariously over the sill, their golden heads touching. Corinna called out in her clear treble, "Even if you have been jilted, Stamberly, you needn't make a cake of yourself."

Young Lord Nick chimed in with a jeer, then they picked up a large water pitcher. Chesley watched helplessly as they dumped the contents out the window. Suddenly the caterwauling he had dismissed as a catfight ceased, replaced by a howl of pure rage.

Giggling, children slammed the casement shut. Their laughter faded as they turned to find Chesley, all dignified authority, waiting for them. "It was only Stamberly," Corinna offered.

"He was trying to serenade Mama. Didn't you hear?" Nicholas added in a man-to-man voice, "Don't you think he's an ass, to stand in the middle of Audley Street bellowing Italian love songs?"

Chesley could not but agree, especially as the countess had left before Stamberly and his violinist arrived. But Chesley imagined love had brought down more exalted figures than Stamberly. His lip twitching, the butler said sternly, "I am persuaded you two should be long abed. Why, it's almost nine o'clock!"

Corinna's enchanting little face turned up to him. "You won't tell Mama? She might not view this as we do, you know."

Chesley found himself agreeing to keep this escapade secret along with all the others he'd been privy to over the years. All they needed, he thought as he sent them scurrying off to bed, was a father to give them a bit of loving discipline....

The knocker sounded. Such a night! Before Chesley could make his way down the stairs, Miss Marlowe dashed past, dressed for the outdoors in a blue velvet cloak. "Daisy Grey and her mama have come for me, Chesley," she called back.

Miss Marlowe, unlike her virtuous cousin, was a most accomplished liar. The butler suspected nothing from her careless words and innocent expression; no, he was tipped off only by the navy blue and gold liveried footman at the door. But they were gone before he had time to protest that the Greys were unlikely to send a Tressilian House footman to collect their guest.

Chesley sighed and headed back into the servants' wing to his own chamber. Was it so odd, after all, that the young lady was making clandestine appointments with her former fiancee? No odder than other recent events in this sideways-tilted house.

Kristen was hardly to the end of the street before she regretted her sharp words to Chesley. Of course, he was concerned about her safety, but she could hardly tell him she was just going down the street to Tressilian House. She couldn't believe it herself. She had spent so long designing her life, making all the right decisions, thinking all the right thoughts, that it hardly seemed fair to find herself in the middle of a maelstrom.

She pulled up the concealing hood of her brown cloak as she crossed the street to Grosvenor Square. Although the square was thronged with carriages headed for the Holts' musicale, the dark afforded her anonymity. She walked past Tressilian House, which stood stately and grave in the soft light of the street lamps. Then she slipped into the shadowy service path to catch her breath and to gather her courage.

How could she have lied so boldly to Tressilian this afternoon? She might have been some brass-faced hussy, long given to deceit, so easily did she persuade Brendan that his former love was watching them. She might vow she had engaged in the charade only to keep Tressilian's hopes up. But however persuadable he was, Kristen could not deceive herself. She had lied so that she could feel his arms around her, his mouth on hers.

And from this little flirtation with sin, she had learned— what? That he was reluctant— ah, that had hurt. That he was adept— but then she had expected no less. That she had longed for more— that was the worst. Her little experiment had worked, for she had proved herself a fool.

Two men sauntered up to the entrance to Tressilian House, and she melted back into the walkway. Her heart stopped, for the one who greeted Hastings was in navy uniform. But he was slighter than Brendan, and his hair gleamed golden in the lamplight— Derek Lanier, Bren's first lieutenant. He had a navy officer's voice, quiet but clear, able to cut through the clamor of an ocean gale. So Kristen easily deciphered his words as the door closed discreetly in their faces.

"Not home now, and dining in alone later? I sensed a definite not-to-be-disturbed message there, didn't you? I'll wager he won't be alone at all. Shall we return and ruin his little tryst?"

The other man laughed, while Kristen's cheeks burned. Was the young officer right, that Brendan was entertaining a new mistress? Not in his own home, surely— proper Hastings would never allow it.

"I haven't such courage. Who knows what Tressilian'd do? The way he's behaved of late, he might shoot us out of hand."

All Tressilian's seamen were intensely loyal, and young Lanier reacted with predictable ire to this slur. He seemed entirely willing to stand there in front of the earl's house for the rest of the evening, spiritedly defending the honor of his superior officer.

But Kristen could wait no longer, for her courage was a fragile thing. Her gloved hand trailing along the brick wall, she ventured back down the service path. The narrow passageway to the back garden was dismally dark, and Kristen braced herself for an assault by rats or goblins. But her previously exemplary life had apparently earned her a bit of credit with Providence, for unaccosted, she achieved her aim: a dark window at the back of the house.

Brendan was a typical Englishman and ascribed miraculous powers to fresh air, so she was able to wedge her fingers into the space between the sash and sill and push the window up. Clambering through the chest-high aperture proved a more difficult task, ruining her stockings and a new manicure.

But Kristen was inside the room before she allowed herself to realize just what she had done. She had spent the morning shopping, the afternoon deceiving and kissing a man, and the evening housebreaking. Her descent into evil was certainly a precipitous one.

She deduced from the dim outlines of a massive desk that she was in the library. That was all for the best, for the library was Bren's favorite room (next to the bedroom, she thought with a flash of amusement). If he was truly dining alone, he would probably take his brandy in here, and then— and then she could talk to him.

What she would say, she hadn't precisely determined. As she stumbled against a broad book cabinet, muttering unladylike curses under her breath, she wondered if she had become overset by a nervous ailment. Ladies were forever being stricken with brain fever after spoiled romances, so no one could blame her if she had become a little demented.

She was certainly exhibiting a trend towards lunacy tonight— coming here in the first place, climbing through a window rather than walking in the front door, crashing around in the dark rather than lighting a candle, set upon saying something to Brendan yet having no clue what.

She regarded herself with a curious fatalism as she dropped into a sidechair. She was obviously no longer responsible for her actions or even her thoughts. It was a reasonless woman who sat in this library, seeing Brendan's eyes in the darkness that surrounded her. How nonsensical— but how fitting— that she had fallen like so many others for this daring rake with flashing black eyes. All her experience with Tressilian had taught her nothing.

But perhaps she had learned after all, Kristen thought, untying her bonnet and dropping it on the table. If Brendan's patented charm were all that had attracted her, she would have been infatuated from the start. No, the qualities she loved best in him were ones known only to his intimates— his disregard for dust and dignity when the children wanted to play on the floor; his generosity to his friends, as if he ran a charity especially for unemployed actors and impoverished peers; his endearingly skewed perspective on life's priorities; and the sudden, sweet smiles he reserved for those he loved. Of course, she confessed, if only to herself, it couldn't hurt that he was also breathtaking, and that his kisses left her dizzy.

"I love him," she whispered experimentally. The words lingered in the darkness. She couldn't recall when this had happened. When she thought he was going to marry Becky? She had been jealous then, however she had tried to hide it from herself. But this breathless fear, this unnamed anticipation, had come earlier than that. Last Christmas, when she thought he might die? Did she realize then how empty her life would be without him?

She had reacted so stupidly against that vulnerability, engaging herself to a man she didn't love to protect herself against the man she did love. She had wasted so much time, missed so many opportunities. She had lost him by lying to herself. She could win him only by telling them both the truth now.

She was very bold in the darkness. Could she actually look into Brendan's fathomless eyes and tell him that she loved him? Especially knowing that part of his heart— surely not all!— was given to another?

How ironic it was that she had once challenged him to prove his fidelity to Becky. His reluctance to return Kristen's kiss— how that rankled!— was proof enough to torment her. But he had responded, and she was damned if he didn't enjoy it too, enough to kiss her again and again before she had sense enough to pull away.

But then if she hadn't been so sensible, she would know now if she had a chance to make him love her after all these years. She tried to assemble her jumbled thoughts into some coherent form, but she was dreadfully afraid that as soon as she saw Brendan she would blurt out some tumultuous declaration. She would have to be calm, present a rational case, remind him how well they got on, how friendship was the best basis for affection— oh, no, she sounded like Edward!

Rationality and calm had no place in her emotions, and friendship didn't begin to describe her affections. She only wanted to hurl herself into Brendan's arms and tell him the truth and never worry about the consequences.

Her brave resolve to do just that faltered as she heard the heavy front door open and Hastings greet his employer. "You are just in time, your lordship. Here comes Miss Marlowe with Irving, just as you said."

Kristen was struck with panic and a strong sense of outrage. Becky was supposed to be with Daisy tonight! Since when was she making surreptitious visits to men's homes? Applying that question to her own predicament, Kristen sought feverishly for a solution. Meeting Becky here would never do, and she didn't need to hear Brendan's rich voice raised in welcome to prove it. "Becky, baby, I have missed you so!" And her cousin's excited laughter was trailing right to Kristen's lair-

Almost too late, she remembered the huge book cabinet, so awkwardly placed next to the desk. It was deep enough, surely, to conceal one slender housebreaker. She clambered in and crouched between two piles of books, her back pressed against the back panel, her knees wedged to her chest. She pulled the door shut, forgetting to check if she could open it from the inside.

At least she was hidden, though terribly cramped. Elise Winterleigh could never hide here, she thought with obscure pride. But the dusty books on either side of her made her want to sneeze. She thought intensely of the heavy, cold, fresh snow of Denmark, drifting up against the walls of the palace, burying landmarks in white, until her nose stopped twitching. She couldn't afford to alert anyone to her presence-bad enough to be discovered sitting in the dark library, but to be found cowering in a cupboard would be disastrous!

A few minutes of silence convinced her that Tressilian must have chosen another locale for his quiet dinner. She forced a sigh of relief, strangely disappointed. Now she would have to return home, having failed ignominiously to seduce the stalwart earl. And she would have to face the deceptive Becky without revealing that she had learned of the deception. Oh, she would never have the courage to tell the truth, to Becky or to Brendan.

She felt along the interior of the cabinet with a hand wary of splinters. The handle remained somewhere beyond her grasp, on the other door, but she feared she would bang her head on the ceiling if she stretched. She was trying to think of a graceful way out of this coil when the door opened with a shocking squeak.

She didn't breathe for a moment, unable to decide which was worse, being discovered by Tressilian or by one of his servants. The horrible question was soon resolved. It was by far the worst to be discovered by someone she didn't know.

The man's body filled the entire door across from her. The pallid light from his candle allowed her a moment's reprieve; he was concentrating on the other side of the cabinet, filled with dusty volumes. She could hear him muttering to himself as she shrank back against the wall, "1699, 1701, 1686—" a random collection of numerals. Just as she realized he was identifying years, he espied her halfboot of Moroccan leather and flung open the other door.

They held suspended for a moment, both staring. Then his evil gaze traveled from the telltale boot up to her face. "Rutherford!" she breathed. In an instant she felt a cold steel blade against her throat and fell silent.

"So it's the lovely Lady Killeaven, is it?" he murmured unctuously. "How nice of you to stop by. You may be just what I need." He tilted the blade against her throat, ruminating. "The volume's not here. He's hidden it somewhere, don't you think?"

She could not answer him, for she was utterly baffled and frightened to death. She opened her mouth to scream, but he twisted his wrist so the knife point dug into the soft flesh above her larynx. "No, don't do that. I should hate to kill you, for then I can't trade you for the diary. Vastly clever, don't you agree?"

Her fulminating eyes showed she did not, but she kept silent, for the knife stung cold against her skin. The florid face swooped down at her. "We'll go out the way I came in, through the window. Rather awkward for a lady, but under the circumstances— Now come out of there, but don't forget the knife."

Kristen did not think she could ever forget the knife, not in a thousand years. But she had read enough of Becky's gothic novels to know what to do in this circumstance. Bracing herself against the back of the cabinet, she knocked the blade aside and butted her head into the massive stomach of her assailant.

Her first thought was relief that instead of slitting her throat, he only grunted and smashed the heel of his hand against her temple. Her second thought, as blackness closed over her, was indignation. She should have known such paltry tricks would work only in novels.

## CHAPTER TWENTY-FIVE

"Sixth Commandment?" Tressilian repeated blankly. "What's that?"

They were supping in Becky's favorite room, the Cylinder Saloon, so styled for its twenty-five-foot diameter and thirty-foot high dome. Jon Destain would doubtlessly be intrigued by Becky's preference for this room above all others in Tressilian House. He liked to call it the Phallic Saloon, assuming its designer, the infamous eighth earl, modeled it after his most cherished body part. The nubile figures entwined in gilt and plaster on the soaring dome also attested to Alexander's primary preoccupation, although only the artisans assigned to clean it every decade could really appreciate the erotic masterpiece.

Unfortunately scaffolding was not available, so Becky's education remained incomplete. Still, she knew more on some matters than Alexander's great-grandson.

"Kristen always claimed you were a pagan at heart, and now I know it's true." Becky sucked the Rhenish cream off her spoon to complete her second supper of the evening, and bestowed a superior look on her erstwhile fiancee. "The Sixth Commandment. Thou shalt not commit adultery." That last word echoed ominously in the great dome, and Tressilian joined in.

"Adultery?" He fell back against the cushioned brocade in shock, his hand clasped to his forehead. "Kristen said adultery right in front of you?"

Becky made a great show of picking up her tulip glass and turning it over and shaking it. Not a drop spilled onto the drawing room's gray and navy Axminster carpet. "She didn't say that. She was far more subtle. As I said, she just told Elise to take particular note of the chapter about the Sixth Commandment. Those of us who understood her allusion were quite impressed. More, please."

Tressilian sat up to pour Becky another half-glass of champagne. "Mind you drink this one slowly, love, for that's all you get. What had Elise to say to this impressive Biblical insult?"

"Oh, she only opened and closed her mouth like a fish. But I think I shan't have any further trouble from that quarter."

"Good, for Elise isn't at all the sort of lady you should be associating with," Tressilian observed in his new big-brother voice.

But Becky was unimpressed. "Oh, Brendan, I hope you are not going to get all stuffy and sedate just because you think Kristen might marry you," she said cuttingly. "It really is not becoming in a rakehell, and I can't think that she would like you to start imitating Stamberly and his ilk."

When she had him properly chastened, Becky edged a bit closer along the couch. "Bren's? What does spring lamb mean? Not the animal, I know that. But Kristen said that she heard Elise likes spring lamb for breakfast. I don't think I was supposed to hear that."

"Good lord, I hope not. I think Kristen has gotten carried away with her subtlety. And I think I shall have better sense than she and not explain that little metaphor."

Tressilian winced as he saw the obstinate set to Becky's mouth and her paradoxically pleading gaze, but he waited until the footman had cleared the supper dishes from the low table and left before he surrendered. "If you must know— promise you won't ever use that term or any other scandalous euphemisms your guardian might let slip. I don't know what's come over Kristen lately. Spring lamb— well, it is said that Elise is developing a taste for rather young men. Just down from Oxford, or even better, just up from Eton."

"Oh!" In his comfortable presence, Becky didn't bother to hide her blush. "Jon— I mean, Captain Destain— how old is he?"

"Eight and twenty. Two months younger than I."

"Too old, then! Elise won't have any use for him very soon, do you think?"

"I think," Tressilian said gently, "that Jon has no use for Elise even now. I would hope he has made that clear to you. Surely you understood that Elise's behavior was that of a scorned woman."

Becky couldn't help but preen at her victory, for Elise Winterleigh was one of society's great beauties, no matter how vulgar her conduct. "Well, I did ask Captain Destain while we were riding today, but he became top-lofty and told me I shouldn't know about such things. As if I'm some naif who never heard of the Sixth Commandment! So I told him—" she flounced her shoulders in dudgeon, and Tressilian dropped his head into his hands, "I told him that he and Elise deserved each other, for they were both shallow hedonists consumed with their own wicked pleasures."

"Wicked pleasures— Becky, what am I going to do with you?" He yanked the glass out of her hand and set it on the kingwood table, then took her by the shoulders and gave her a shake. "If you don't start behaving, you are going to end up marrying me after all, for no one else will abide this melodramatic nonsense of yours! Most men of our age have had a few affaires—"

"Some rather more than a few," Becky broke in, jerking away from him. "I know that. But it's not nonsense to expect an assurance that those wicked pleasures— and adultery is wicked, Bren's— that they are at an end before one consents to join one's life to another's. And it is altogether too provoking to be told that one's ears are too innocent for such adult matters, as if a proposal of marriage isn't an adult matter which one is supposed to—"

"Wait a minute. Did one receive a proposal of marriage, and if one did, when, and what did one say?"

"Yes, I suppose," she admitted. "I mean, yes, I received a proposal, not I said yes. Yesterday, in fact. In the garden at Hyde Park, where we had our first fight."

"How fitting," Tressilian murmured. "You sent Jon off denied and defied, I take it. And he didn't tell me!"

"I imagine he didn't want to disappoint you, with the honor of your family at stake."

Hastings had come in to close the drapes to the moonlight he had not a quarter hour ago opened the drapes to let in. He lingered there at the soaring window, carefully examining the drapery cord for frays. Tressilian cast him a nettled glance. "Taking notes for the memoirs, Hastings? My butler and my valet," he added to Becky, "are collaborating on my memoirs."

"Vastly amusing, my lord." Hastings tugged the gray satin drapes smooth and then moved with stately grace to the exit.

When Hastings had closed the door behind him with a decided click, Tressilian asked, "Now what's this about the honor of the family? Oh, because you have already thrown one cousin over, the other must succeed or we are disgraced for generations."

Taught to regard himself as a person of epic possibility, Tressilian could not but admire this Wiltshire girl who saw herself as Helen of Troy. "But, baby, I'd hoped you'd formed an affection for my poor cousin. Why deny him what you both want?"

Becky's face took on that mulish Marlowe look. "Because he doesn't want it enough. Not as I do. At least he's given no evidence of it. He hasn't made the slightest push to win me; in fact he's been nonchalant— why, when he proposed he didn't even go down on one knee!"

"Perhaps he didn't want to sully his uniform breeches on the garden dirt. The proposal itself— did it possess the requisite intensity?" "Oh, he said all the proper things—" "Another mistake, of course."

"Well, I did like to hear that he adored me, but the rest was simply insulting— he thought I'd make a wonderful wife, and an exemplary mother! I ask you, Brendan, can you imagine anything more deadly?" Even now Becky's bosom heaved with the outrage of it all.

Tressilian, much moved, took her hands in supplication. "Becky, darling, you mustn't be so cruel."

"Look at you! And you aren't even trying!"

Tressilian, bewildered, looked down at his hands, clasped fervently around hers.

"And your eyes— how smoldering they were as you accused me of cruelty! You'd never tell me what a wonderful wife I would make!"

Tressilian cast her hands scornfully away, a gesture that had her sighing again. "Only because I think you will make the most impossible wife in the three kingdoms! Poor Jonny will be tormented beyond measure trying to please you! He'll never get a moment's peace, wondering what crazy invocation will win your approval now."

"Just so," Becky answered with a firm nod. "And such an entertaining life, he must earn."

"But, sweetheart, that's not his way. I can't help being ardent and all that, for it's my nature. But Jonny's nature is to be wary. And when he's wary he becomes remote and arrogant and acts as if he doesn't care very much."

Becky's eyes softened at this close reading of Captain's Destain's character. "That's true, isn't it? Perhaps that's why he frowns so fiercely when I'm about, because he's terrified of my power over him." She pursed her lips thoughtfully. "Well, I do like that, although I would like it much better if he would admit it."

"You must learn to look beneath the surface, Becky. You are falsely impressed with my fervency, for I don't adore you— " at her outraged gasp, he added hastily, "as much as Jon does. You might consider that his expression is excessively cool precisely because his emotions are so uncontrollable."

Pensively Becky replied, "But if so, will he ever show those emotions? For I think he doesn't truly want to win me. I think he would like to keep his distance from all the anguish I'm likely to bring him, and all the joy. So he makes only a half-hearted effort and his failure will only confirm his cynicism with love and all it entails. And considering the sort of love he's had before," Becky concluded with a twist of her lips, "I suppose I shouldn't be surprised."

Embroidering freely, Tressilian declared, "You wouldn't call him cynical if you had seen him here last week, vowing that you were his and that he would kill me before he would let me have you."

Becky was gratified if not entirely credulous. "Now if you just would have made a stand, Bren, so he would have had to make good on that threat—"

"Becky, I love you both, but not that much. The fire in his eyes—" Tressilian shivered, as if undone by the memory. "I wouldn't risk defying him, even for you."

Then, theatrics over, he rose to tower over her in an almost-threatening way. "Come, Becky, you know he loves you. But he's changing the habits of a lifetime for you. He's not used to all this intensity and passion and so he isn't very adept at it. But he'll get better at it with practice."

"No, he won't." Becky rose too and stood defiant before him. "He'll fall back on his old habits, does he not break them soundly now. If I accept his suit without forcing him to win me, he will think he need only do the minimum to keep me. He'll be minimally loving, and minimally faithful— when I'm in town he'll curtail his visits to his mistress— and we'll have one of those dreary ordinary minimal marriages, instead of the epic love we could share."

Tressilian, knowing his cousin's predilection for taking the easiest course available, could not but agree, although he was loyal enough not to say so. "Well, give him a hint what sort of effort you require. Has he tried the wildflowers that he picked himself at dawn while whispering your name? The gypsy love wine? I think I have an extra bottle about. Rescuing you from great peril?"

"That would be sufficient," Becky allowed.

"I could impress you into His Majesty's Royal Navy. But knowing you, you'd like it monstrously and be furious when he saved you." Tressilian glanced up at the elaborate grandfather clock and exclaimed, "It's after eleven, sweeting, we'd best get you home. Or perhaps you can stay here, and to save your honor— what a joke!— Jon will have to challenge me, and I'll delope as I am in the wrong, and he'll kill me after all. Think how happy you will be then."

Balling up her small fist, Becky punched him precisely on his still-tender musket scar. As he groaned and she giggled, the door opened and an agitated Hastings entered.

His nostrils flared with offense, the butler intoned, "There is a— a messenger, your lordship. He insists you will see him if I give you this."

From Hastings' extended hand, Tressilian took a delicate gold pin— a unicorn done in filigree. As he held it up to the light, Becky gasped. "That's Kristen's. She was wearing it this afternoon, don't you remember?"

"I wasn't paying attention to details, love— send him in."

The ragged urchin who sauntered through the door wouldn't be worth a second glance, resembling as he did a hundred orphan boys who prowled the bystreets of Westminster. But his cockiness was a thing of wonder. Appraising at the splendor all around him, winking approvingly at Becky, he took his time before addressing Tressilian. "You're a flash one, ain't ye? Be you the earl too?"

At the sharp answer, the boy wiped his grimy hands on his pants leg, then pulled from a hole in his jacket a folded piece of paper. He held it tight while gazing speculatively at the earl. "'E said you'd be giving me a sovereign for delivering it, but 's far as I come, and spooky a night as it is, happen I need more."

Tressilian caught the boy's wrist and pried the paper out of his hand. "Give him a fiver, Hastings," he said absently as he scanned the message. Then his fist closed spasmodically on the note. In a voice that shook slightly, he said, "No, Hastings, wait. Lad, do you want to earn a pony?"

Twenty-five pounds was more than the boy could expect to see all at once in his lifetime. He could only nod.

Tressilian's voice was level again, almost calm. "Tell me who gave you this note, and where, and when. Every last detail you can recall."

The boy lived by his wits, and they didn't fail him now. He furrowed his brow thoughtfully, then rattled off, "Oxford Street, near Great Titchfield, 'arf an hour ago. Some flash cove called me over. A yellow waistcoat, he had. Climbed out of his carriage-hired from Garritty's, I reckon, for the wheels were picked out in red. Reg'lar job horses— plodders. The coachman wasn't in Garritty livery though. Big feller, broken nose, an old pug.

Punch-drunk, and gin-drunk too, I'd wager."

"Did you see anyone in the carriage?"

"Never got close 'nough. And even under the street lamp, it weren't light enough to see through the windows."

Tressilian nodded, dismissing him. "Hastings, get the boy a pony. And then get that diary I was looking at last week. I hid it next to Dr. Johnson's dictionary in the bookcase near the library door."

Much mystified, Hastings went out, trailed by the eager urchin. A moment later the butler returned with a slim volume and a tan high-crowned bonnet. "I found this, sir, on the table in the library."

"Kristen's!" Becky watched bewildered as Tressilian seized the book and strode to the door. Then she ran after him and clutched his arm. "What is it, Bren? Is Kristen all right?"

"I knew something would go wrong," Tressilian said distractedly, thrusting the note into her hand. "All day I've been wound tight— I sensed it." Then he left her alone.

Becky could not immediately grasp the import of the intricately worded paragraph, although she recognized the signature as that of Brendan's spurious cousin Rutherford. "If you value the dainty owner of this dainty pin, arrive alone at the Greenwich house with the item we discussed previously."

Becky closed her eyes, as if blindness might make the evil words and their evil author vanish. But she opened them when Tressilian returned and took her cold hands in a hard grip. "Babe, you've got to help me. Now listen carefully. My coach will be ready in a moment. You go find Jon. He'll be at White's, and you won't be allowed in, so send the coachman to get him. Tell him to get hold of Skinner— he's from Bow Street— and bring him to my house in Greenwich. Jon's been there, but remind him it's the one I won from Chelten, that's being made into a rest-home for sailors. It's in the close by St. Alfege's Church. Make sure he understands this isn't a cavalry charge— no blazing guns."

He had gone before she had time to voice her agreement, her support, her fear. She stood there for a moment, breathing deeply, gathering her courage. Then, still clutching the note, she ran out to the waiting carriage.

Summoned from his winning hand by the coachman, Captain Destain flung open the door of the coach and bit back an oath as he saw its occupant. Becky felt relief wash over her at the sight of his face, and didn't grudge his angry demand. "What are you doing here, in Tressilian's coach, at this time of night?"

Becky pulled him into the carriage and kept hold of his hands. "Oh, Jon, the most horrid thing has happened! Kristen has been kidnapped by that Rutherford man, and Bren's gone to rescue her, and he needs our help!"

The captain regarded her suspiciously in the dim light. "Is this a joke? Not that it doesn't sound just like the sort of thing that happens to Bren, but it also sounds just like the sort of thing you would invent—"

Furious, she shoved the note at him. "Read it for yourself," she retorted, although there was not enough light for reading. "Now this is what he told me to tell you— listen closely, for we haven't the time to go over it again."

Captain Destain absorbed the information and immediately sprang to action. "I'll take my curricle— it's already hitched up, and we might need to transport Kristen back—"

Before Becky could wonder what condition Kristen might be in for the ride, Destain added briskly, "The coachman can search out Skinner and bring him after me; I'll give him the runner's direction. And you can go home and wait."

"Go home and wait?" Becky exclaimed, scrambling out of the carriage after him. "Certainly not! I'm going with you."

Destain had no time to argue, so he only ordered curtly as he tossed her into his curricle, "Then keep out of the way. If Tressilian's involved in this, there's sure to be shooting."

Gathering her cloak around her, Becky shivered, from fear, not, from the cold. The very efficiency of Destain's motions, checking the pistol he kept under the seat, yanking the reins to send the horses cantering towards the Strand, testified to the gravity of the situation. For he was entirely the soldier now, cool, analytical, prepared for any peril.

They were crossing the Tower Bridge before Becky found her voice. Almost to herself, she said, "We never meant for the plan to hurt Kristen. We only meant to make her happy."

Jon glanced at her, his eyes narrowed against the pale moonlight. "We? Who is we? And what is this plan?"

"Bren and I— we only planned to make Kristen jealous." It was so distant now, that delicious conspiracy, that lofty goal.

After he took a gulp of the cool night air, Destain murmured, "Bren's secret plan. I should've wormed it out of him. So this great betrothal of yours was all a hoax? Bren doesn't love you?"

"Well, of course he does. And I love him," Becky replied distractedly, peering ahead at the Surrey Commercial Docks. The city's congestion was thinning out; moonlight, not oil lamps, lit the rutted road, and between the low dock buildings were occasional stretches of scrubby field. Greenwich lay only a few miles east along the Thames.

Becky suddenly recalled her companion and turned to see his guarded expression. "But we don't love each other," she added with an exasperated sigh. "I would think it apparent to all that he worships Kristen. It's a puzzle to me how we've gotten away with it this long, with him threatening to throttle Stamberly, and gazing so soulfully at Kristen whenever he thinks she's not looking. Why are you laughing?"

Jon shook his head, smiling despite the seriousness of the evening. With his free hand he pulled her closer. "Oh, I don't know. I can't believe Bren could keep such a secret from me. I must have been caught out sleeping. But I should have known the two of you romantics would come up with such a foolish scheme. When I think how guilty I've felt, stealing you away from him, thinking that he was just the best damned friend in the world, and all along it's been a little game— oh, he'll pay for this, he will."

Becky pulled away, remarking with great dignity, "There's nothing to pay for, and nothing to steal. I'm not some snuffbox to be traded back and forth between you. And this wasn't a game. It was a sacrifice for True Love. But you'll only scoff at that, won't you? You'd never sacrifice for anything so foolish as that."

She felt his hand close into a fist against her thigh, saw his face likewise harden, and knew a sudden regret. She cried impulsively, "I'm sorry, Jon. I shouldn't bait you. I know you don't even know what I mean. And perhaps falling in love at first sight is romantic enough. But I just think we can't settle for that. We won't value it if it comes so easy."

She looked away into the darkness that lay ahead, into the danger that awaited them. Then his gloved hand slipped under the hood of her cloak to lie smooth and warm against her cheek. "Did you really fall in love with me at first sight?" he inquired.

"You looked so very dashing, there on your horse. The uniform was so heroic—"

He drew his hand away, and she felt the sting of the wind on her cheek. "How disappointed further acquaintance has left you," he drawled. Before she could protest, he added, "We're coming into Greenwich." The outskirts of this river town were silent, the road deserted, the houses dark. "There's the spire of the church. The house is a hundred feet or so behind it. Not another sound, Becky."

Obediently, she held her breath as he reined in the curricle in the mews beside the church. As he secured the horses, he pointed to a sprawling house half-hidden off the tree-lined lane.

Becky's unwonted obedience vanished when she realized he meant to leave her behind in the carriage. As he came to the side to bid her farewell, she jumped over the side, sliding against the lean strength of his body. His arms circled her. "I might have known you'd have to— Well, stay back and stay down," he whispered. "And stay quiet."

He kissed her hard on the mouth. "Whatever you say, whatever you do, you'll always be mine."

# CHAPTER TWENTY-SIX

Tressilian had vaulted over a brick wall to approach the house from an oblique angle, along the overgrown hedges. He knew this village well, for Greenwich on the Thames was a navy port, home to the Royal Hospital for seamen. But he'd visited the house only once a year ago, along with an architect, to determine its suitability as a sailors' rest. He couldn't recall enough of the floorplan, or how it might have been modified, to guess Rutherford's defenses.

The lawn beneath Tressilian's feet gave way to brick as he came abreast of the half-timbered facade. He walked quietly across the dark courtyard, skirting the ghostly dolphin fountain in the center.

The elm-lined vicarage lane was behind him, beyond an open iron gate. Above the peaked roof of the old Elizabethan manor rose the spire of the old church. A few hundred yards north was the beautiful hospital designed by Wren, and beyond that the river. Tressilian wanted to call out a contingent of marines from the ships anchored there and storm the house, ripping Rutherford apart with a volley of musket balls.

But the bastard would kill Kristen before the marines crossed the brick courtyard. No, Rutherford held all the cards, and Tressilian could only bluff, and pray that he still had a bit of credit with his indulgent Creator.

Most of the windows were dark, but light spilled from one room along front. She was being held in the parlor, he realized. He estimated the distance from the front door to the lane, wondering how Rutherford had learned of this place. Probably Tressilian's always helpful solicitor had listed his extensive holdings, just to keep the putative heir salivating over his prospects.

A ladder leaned against the ivied side wall, leading to a second-story window. He could climb in and sneak down and grab Rutherford from behind and garrote him. But that would leave the coachman to take Kristen—

The hardest thing Tressilian had ever done was dispense with his heroic dreams of rescue and walk, empty-handed, through the front door. In the foyer strewn with paint buckets and dropcloths, he offered no resistance as the bulky coachman pinned his arms behind his back, or when Rutherford's efficient search turned up the diary in his pocket and the pistol in his boot.

Constraint of any kind drove him mad, and Rutherford's leering face completed the job. But Tressilian forced his hatred down, thinking of Kristen, helpless and bound in the room beyond. "I want to see Lady Killeaven."

"Certainly," Rutherford said, scanning the last pages of the diary. "I've been hoping for a touching reunion between you. You came alone, I hope. Or I will kill her before your very eyes."

"You won't have a chance," Tressilian said softly, his muscles straining against his will to break free. "I'll kill you first."

Rutherford's smirk vanished under the glare of those black eyes, and he made an abrupt gesture to the coachman. The burly prizefighter twisted

Tressilian's right arm, and they all waited to hear it snap. But at the last moment, Rutherford lost interest and flung open the parlor door.

The room was only half-refurbished. Plaster from the demolished ceiling dusted the oak floor. A twelve-foot scaffold was anchored precariously to the wall, supporting the bare rafters. Kristen was slumped under the scaffold on a pile of Holland covers, her hands bound at the wrist, her golden hair spilling over her cheek. Her eyes were closed, her breathing shallow and hoarse.

"Lady Killeaven, how lively you look!" Rutherford swept low into a bow before the unconscious woman, his laughter echoing in the rafters above the razed ceiling.

From within the white heat of his rage, Tressilian felt the coachman loosen his hold as he joined in the joke. Twisting away from his captor, Tressilian hurled himself at Rutherford. All his brave resolutions of restraint vanished as his hands closed over Rutherford's throat. He saw himself reflected— savage vengeance— in the man's small, terrified eyes and slowly tightened his grip.

But, as he knew it would, the blow came from behind, and he hardly had time to curl away from it when the dimness claimed him.

"at'll cost ye extra." The coachman nudged Tressilian's shoulder with the toe of one muddy boot. "Strikin' a peer's a hanging offense. But ye got what ye came for— let's pike it, guv'nor, and leave these two lay."

"Tie him up." Rutherford rubbed at his bruised throat through his scarlet neckcloth. "I said, tie him up! I'm not going to leave him lay, not when he and the fair lady can lay witness against me."

The coachman ruminated as he pulled a rope out of a canvas bag and began binding Tressilian. "Do as you please, but hear this— I won't kill no earl. Ye'll do that yerself, if 'tis to be done."

"Oh, it will be done," Rutherford predicted grimly as the coachman shoved Tressilian's body against the scaffolded wall. "And if you want your pay, you'll give me aid." He cut off the reinforcements. You check the lane out front— I'll look in back."

Behind the lacy curtain of her hair, Kristen closed her eyes again as the door closed. As soon as she had awakened among the eerie shadows the scaffold cast, she had realized her likely end. She didn't know what ransom Brendan had paid, but she knew it could not be enough. Rutherford wasn't foolish enough to pike it as the coachman urged him, for he would not be safe as long as his two captives were alive to press charges. He'd probably kill the coachman too, while he was at it, to guard against future blackmail, although his confederate was too dull to figure that out himself.

Even as the despair closed over her, Kristen took some comfort in the solid press of Brendan's shoulder against her side, the even tenor of his breathing, the peaceful cast of his features. He was unconscious, but still alive. She cursed herself for having dragged him into this situation, for being unwittingly responsible for his injury. But as long as he was here, she could not lose hope.

She struggled to a sitting position, her back at the wall, her hip pressed painfully against one of the wooden struts of the scaffolding. She might strike her head against the board nailed to the frame above her, were she able to stand. But her ankles were bound, and her knees weak, and her head spinning, so she thought she would not put her assumption to the test.

Instead she bent her elbows to reach across her knee and with her bound hands touched Tressilian's face. Her fingers caressed his wind-rough jaw and trailed to his hard, beautiful mouth. She closed her eyes, wishing absurdly that she had thought to do this years ago, under different circumstances. Then she felt his teeth close lightly on her thumb, and her eyes flew open to his roguish wink.

She couldn't help laughing as she drew her hand back to safety. "Brendan," she murmured gratefully as he sat up.

He grinned wryly at her before turning his attention to the ropes at his wrist. "Angel, I'm sorry you got involved in this."

"It was my fault," she corrected penitently. "I can't believe I was so racket-brained to climb in that cupboard."

He gave her a curious look, then brought his wrists up and began to gnaw at the knot. She watched in astonishment as, with a combination of white teeth and long fingers, he contrived to free himself.

"How on earth did you do that?" she whispered as he next applied himself to his ankles.

"I'm a sailor, recall? There's not a knot in the world I can't undo.

" He took her wrists and, with professional contempt, made short work of her bonds. "You see the value of a Navy education. Nick could tie a better sheet end than that— Corey too."

"Please don't tell them that. They'll decide to practice their knots on poor Miss Purvy, and she'll give notice again."

She hardly had time to flex her aching wrists before he began wrapping them up again in the hated rope. "They'll be back in a moment. Contrive to look confined."

"Then what?"

"I don't know. The element of surprise is our only weapon— that and my cousin, who I hope will be arriving momentarily."

Now the danger acted on her like champagne, making her reckless. "Well, if you are here, and the cavalry on the way, Rutherford will soon learn his lesson," she said with a toss of her head.

Brendan did not share her optimism, only muttering, "I'd rather we were none of us needed to teach him."

Rutherford returned alone to find them sitting silently together on the floor, to all appearances still bound. He barely spared them a glance as he lowered his bulk into a Holland-covered chair. Then, pistol at the ready, he addressed his captive audience. "Much as I pay Purcell, you'd think I'd get some loyalty from him. But you just can't get good help these days."

Kristen felt laughter bubble in her. Here she was, held at gunpoint by a madman who made the same complaints about the lower orders her friends did.

But Brendan, uncharacteristically, took a less humorous view of their circumstance. "I can't commiserate with you," he said coldly, "as I take it he balked at the task of dispatching us to our Maker."

Rutherford was uncomfortable with such candor; he squirmed as if the chair had become too snug for his posterior. "So you guessed, did you, cousin?"

"I am not your cousin."

"Precisely why I must kill you," Rutherford said reasonably. "I do hope you understand that this is nothing personal. If you had accepted me as your heir, of course, we would not have had to resort to this— I would have had to kill you soon at any rate, before you sired a son, but I could have left the lady out of it. But that's all water under the bridge. Just as well, for now I'll inherit the title and estates immediately."

"Let her go." Even pleading for her life, Brendan couldn't keep the arrogant ring out of his voice, and Rutherford stiffened as if he'd been threatened.

"Well, I can't, unfortunately, for she knows too much." He looked almost penitent for a moment, gazing at Kristen. "It's a pity that such loveliness must end, isn't it? What a fine duchess you'd make! If only—" he halted suddenly, his eyes narrowing speculatively. "You know, a wife's testimony can't be used against her husband. You could marry me—"

"I'd rather die," Kristen declared, as Brendan went rigid beside her.

"Then you'll get your wish." His face contorted, Rutherford pulled himself to his feet. He jerked the gun up, pointing it directly at Kristen. "High in the instep, ain't you, for a chit. trussed up like a Christmas goose. Well, we'll see how proud you'll be when you're found dead in this room, and the whole world thinks you were killed by your lover Tressilian. He, of course, then turned the gun on himself in a fit of remorse!"

Kristen despaired at the disgrace her children faced if his ruthless scheme worked. Then she straightened her shoulders. Brendan had been in worse fixes before— though none sprang immediately to mind— and had come out unscathed. She would have to stay alert and optimistic, and trust in his survival instincts.

"It won't happen. Don't you know that?" Tressilian taunted him. "Nothing you try will ever succeed."

Rutherford whipped the gun to point straight and true at Tressilian. "All right, cousin, if that's the way you prefer it, I'll kill you first, so that I can have my way with your lady here."

Kristen's every nerve was ablaze with tension, and she flinched at the slight pinch on her arm. Oh! she thought with a start, and tried to look relieved. "Well, it's about time you got here," she said with exasperation, looking toward the door.

As Rutherford half-turned toward the entrance, Kristen hunched down under Brendan's urgent hand. He sprang up then, grabbing the board above and one of the wooden supports and pulling the whole scaffolding and part of the wall down. Just like Samson, she thought admiringly as the contraption crashed down on the flailing Rutherford. The gun discharged harmlessly into the wall behind him.

Brendan's black hair was frosted with plaster dust, she noticed as he extended a hand to help her rise amidst the rubble. Brushing impatiently at her own hair, she glanced at the insensate Rutherford, sprawled under a trap of wood and plaster. Then she looked up with wary relief into the emptiness above. "I hope the ceiling doesn't cave in."

Brendan added, "I hope Purcell didn't hear the racket."

Kristen clutched his right arm, then released it when she heard his stifled groan. "But Rutherford said he ran off!"

Tressilian kicked a board out of the way and went to press his fingers on Rutherford's temple. "Still alive," he reported regretfully. He scooped up the empty pistol and made a quick and fruitless search for more ammunition. "Put out the lamp, Kristen."

As he crossed to open the window a crack, he pointed out, "Rutherford said only that Purcell refused to kill us. He's not so fastidious he will leave without his pay. No, my darling, we are not out of danger yet."

She picked her way through the debris and the darkness to stand beside him at the open window. She was cooled by the evening air, warmed by his endearment— silly girl, how many others has he called his darling? Still she nestled close to him, and he put a comforting if dusty arm around her shoulders.

But his words weren't so soothing. "I'm also worried that Jon and the Runner he's bringing will walk right into Purcell."

Hoping to console him, she said with mock severity, "A Runner! Oh, Bren, I knew if I associated with you, Bow Street would come looking for me eventually."

His scowl relaxed into laughter and he caught her up in his arms, kissing her lightly on the lips. "I couldn't hope for a better cellmate than you, angel."

He turned her, still bemused by the kiss, to face the window. She leaned back against the length of his body, resting in the circle of his arms. Then, following his gaze to the inoperative fountain, she saw the bulk of the coachman looming up beyond.

Amidst the soft buzz of the dead of night, she heard the lonely cry of an owl and shivered. Brendan's arm tightened around her then dropped. "The cavalry has arrived," he whispered.

Startled, for she had heard nothing but that lonely owl, she trailed after him into the foyer. "Stay here. I'll take care of Purcell."

"I am not staying here with that toad," she hissed. "And you are not going to face that criminal holding an empty pistol, at least not alone. Remember, I was the one who provided the diversion you needed a moment ago."

"Must you always be so stubborn?" She was about to retort that she was never stubborn, only sensible, when he pushed her behind him. "All right then, just stay behind me. He'll think I'm Rutherford, at least until he sees I lack three stone or so of bulk. And then we'll just have to see how well General Wellington has taught our favorite dragoon."

Like a barnacle, Kristen stayed close to his back, so that Purcell would see only the one figure he expected. The coachman's bulky silhouette turned as they emerged from the house. "Is it done, guv'nor? Ye've done 'em, have ye?"

Tressilian continued to move forward, Kristen in his wake. Confused by the silence, Purcell repeated, "Is it done, guv'nor? Ye'll pay me now?"

"With a penny's worth of lead," Tressilian said calmly. "Slowly, now, drop your pistol. I never miss, you know."

Unfortunately, Purcell was unacquainted with the earl's dead-shot reputation, and too slow-witted to realize his apparent danger. His arm jerked, and Brendan reached back and shoved Kristen down against the rough bricks.

Time held still for a moment, long enough for a half-moon to emerge from behind a cloud and illuminate the courtyard. Kristen raised up on her scraped elbow as the moonlight glanced off the barrel of Purcell's pistol, and she knew a final sadness, that she would never know Brendan's love.

Then, unbelievably, she heard a light, imploring voice call her name. "Kristen, oh, are you all right?"

The glancing moonlight swerved off towards the source of the voice, in the shadows near the iron gate. A curse tore loose as Tressilian launched himself across the ten yards to the coachman, but he was too late. There was the crack of a shot, then another, and Kristen had an instant to think clearly, "He must have two pistols," and then despairingly, "Oh, Becky."

But then the courtyard seemed to shake as Purcell fell. Tressilian reached him a second later and stooped to fling him roughly over. Then he ran on into the shadows, calling, "Jonny!"

Kristen scrambled to her feet and ran after him, hardly noting that one half-boot pulled off and the bricks tore her bare foot. She reached a tangle of bodies just as Brendan knelt down and gently eased the captain onto his back. Becky, dazed and breathless, struggled to a stand, then fell back to her knees as she saw Destain's face, pale with pain in the wan light.

Kristen dropped down beside Becky, slipping an arm around her. But the girl was oblivious to that and to Brendan's calm, admiring observation as he slipped off one sleeve of the cavalry coat, "And I thought I was a marksman. Twenty yards at least, in the dark, and on the dive— Jonny, you got him right between the eyes."

Darkness stained the shirt over the captain's shoulder, but he only murmured, eyes still closed, "The trick is imagining him a dartboard."

Kristen took Becky's shawl and used it to stanch the blood flow. But when the captain's eyes opened, they went right past her to focus on Becky. His voice was husky with pain. "Was that heroic enough for you? Will you marry me now?"

Becky stopped ripping up her petticoat for bandages just long enough to vow tearfully, "After you rescued me from dire peril? How can I refuse?"

Gratefully he closed his eyes. "I reckon that's worth getting shot," he concluded lazily.

## CHAPTER TWENTY-SEVEN

Kristen's abduction ended less dramatically than it began. The Bow Street Runner arrived just in time to see Captain Destain shot, and he lost no time arresting "the one that kilt his lordship's cousin."

Fortunately, his lordship's cousin wasn't actually kilt; in fact, during the nightmarish trip to London he occasionally roused to remind Tressilian that they had started a whole new ledger and the earl was once more deep in debt.

His slender form notwithstanding, Jon was a sturdy young man and took the ball in his shoulder without much fuss. In fact, the surgeon who visited him at Destain House predicted Jon would recover in time for his wedding— "although," Becky said gloomily two days later, on one of her infrequent respites from the sickroom, "he told me not to expect much of a wedding night. I can't bring myself to ask Jon about it, but I— I wouldn't want to interfere with his convalescence if he thinks—"

Kristen could only hug the girl and assure her that young men tended to recover certain abilities rather quickly. "In fact, I wouldn't doubt if such— such an incentive wouldn't encourage a quicker return to health."

Becky sighed and pulled a fresh morning gown out of her wardrobe. "We'll have a whole week after the wedding to find out, before he rejoins his regiment in Spain."

For Captain Destain, having won his true love, was now intent upon winning his war just as expeditiously. With the sort of bravado he might be expected to deplore, he had refused to ask the physicians at the Horse Guards for an extension of his invalid leave. And Becky, having demanded heroism from her lover, could hardly now aver that she'd rather he stay home and raise orchids.

"He told me he's been through all the marches and retreats and he's not going to stay home when they're about to force the French out of the Peninsula for good. Isn't that heroic?"

Kristen, playing lady's maid, was buttoning the back of Becky's gown and couldn't see the girl's face. But she heard the forced cheer in Becky's voice and ached for her, wondering how the young couple would bear being separated as soon as they were joined.

"Well," she replied briskly, tying the pink sash around Becky's trim waist, "if he offers any resistance on your wedding night, tell him the honor of his regiment is at stake. Surely he wouldn't want it bruited about that the 16th Light Dragoons might like to fight, but they aren't so enthusiastic when it comes to love!"

Becky's giggle was a bit watery, but she turned and hugged Kristen with renewed strength. "I must learn to count my blessings, mustn't I? I'm determined to be more mature about such things, for a soldier's wife must always be brave. He's going to live, and be well, and we shall have seven days before he leaves. And the war will be done soon, he promises me, and we'll be together forever. Until then we shall write the most affecting love letters and when we're old I'll publish them and scandalize our children."

As Becky debated which bonnet would make a convalescent's heart beat faster, Kristen asked casually, "Have you seen Bren?"

Becky glanced back from her hat shelf, surprised. "Haven't you? Well, of course, he's been by to see Jon. He's taken to skulking about the backstairs until Lady Destain leaves, for as you can imagine she's quite put out with him for getting Jon shot. Jon isn't so uncompromising; he has decided to settle for Bren's new phaeton and that matched set of chestnuts. It's to be Jon's wedding present to me, although I haven't quite persuaded Jon of that yet."

Kristen hated to criticize the hero of the hour, but such exploitation of Tressilian's guilt seemed rather un-cousinly. "And it's all my fault," Kristen murmured miserably.

Becky shook her head. "Oh, no, don't say so. After all, this Rutherford fellow was Brendan's problem. Why, if we are going to assign blame, you might just as well say it was my fault for calling out to you and alerting the gunman to our presence. And," she added decisively, "no one would dare to say that. Brendan is quite used to taking the blame for Jon's misfortunes, so you needn't worry about his feelings. Once he turns the phaeton over to me, he will feel he has paid his penance. Now I bid you farewell, dearest Kristen," she called as she skipped out the door. "Jon gets so restless if I am not there to bathe his forehead with cool water and read to him from Miraculous Nuptials— it is miraculous, isn't it? But I'll be back before tea."

Without Becky's brave cheer as an example, Kristen gave into melancholy. She wandered through the house like a sleepwalker, replying absently to the housekeeper, unable to concentrate on the newspaper. Finally she stopped at the drawing room window and stared moodily out into the street, empty except for one unfortunate maid who clung desperately to her straw hat. For the balmy weather of the last few weeks had vanished, replaced by a whipping wind and torrents of rain.

Brendan, like the sun, had deserted her. She hadn't seen him since that dawn when he kissed her lightly and handed her over to her furious Abigail, who naturally suspected the worst. He hadn't even sent a note round to explain his absence, but of course, he never did that. She supposed Eton, unlike girls schools, didn't offer courses in etiquette.

Kristen couldn't bring herself to cross Grosvenor Square again and demand his attention. She had been bold before and it brought only disaster. No, she would wait for him to make the first move.

Finally she stopped her restless pacing and settled on the couch with a book of verse. A page or two later, however, her thoughts returned to the tender moments they had shared. What a dizzying feeling it was, to love such a virile man, so like a young god in his dark beauty and passion. She no longer cared about reforming him into a responsible landowner, a respectable churchgoer. She didn't want to change him at all, except to make him love her. But if she hadn't done it in five years, the cause was surely lost.

It was poetic justice, she supposed, that after repressing her feelings for so long she had fallen headlong in love almost without noticing her descent. Once she had controlled her thoughts, held a hammerlock on her emotions; now she didn't care that her cheeks burned at the memory of his embrace, or that her heart leaped when she heard his voice in the hall outside.

Still when Tressilian, with his customary disregard for the formalities, entered the drawing room without being announced, some vestige of pride made her rise to greet him with the most serene expression she could manage. But he was not fooled. He crossed the room in a few strides and took her hand to lead her back to the couch. Cavalierly consigning her book to the floor, he wrapped her in his arms, and she felt his rain-wet hair against her cheek. "What's wrong, angel?"

Kristen no longer tried to resist her need for him. In the circle of his embrace, she felt safety and comfort— and a dangerous, leaping hope. Nonetheless, she dissembled. "Oh, I just haven't felt secure lately, not even in my own home."

"You'll never know how sorry I am that you became involved in this. But it's over. Rutherford's already on his way to Australia, and in his condition, I can't imagine he'll survive the voyage. Now don't give me that shocked look, Kristen Marlowe, for I know you would have killed him barehanded after Jon was hurt, and Becky, well, she would prefer to have tortured him slowly first—bloodthirsty wenches, the two of you. Now what was I saying?" he added in some confusion.

"You were about to explain," Kristen murmured against the crisp linen of his cravat, "why you haven't called on me in two days."

She didn't look up, but she knew well that puzzled frown of his. "I was? Oh, I've been too busy making the world right again, bribing magistrates right and left. I want to keep your name out of it, and Jon was adamant that his great heroics be kept secret, for he'd passed his physical exam last week and didn't want to alert the medicos that the results were no longer valid. He didn't used to be such a savage warrior, you know. I think he intends to impress Becky once and for all with his courage and lust for adventure."

Having lost his train of thought once again, Tressilian released her and, studying her closely, resorted to the question Kristen dreaded. "But I've also spent two days wondering what you were doing in my library in the dead of night. And why didn't you call out when Rutherford came?"

She evaded the first question by answering the second. "He was holding a knife to my throat," she retorted, then, incurably honest, added, "And I didn't want your servants to find me there."

A demon of laughter danced in his dark eyes, but he persisted. "That doesn't explain what you were doing there in the first place."

"In a way it does," she explained, avoiding his amused gaze. "Hastings is so upright, you know, and I hated to shock him by coming to your home so late."

"I assure you, he's seen more shocking things in his time," Brendan replied. "And I can't think how you got by him and the two footmen at the front door."

Kristen sighed, figuring he would pry the truth out of her eventually. "I climbed in the library window."

"You climbed in the window? You climbed— Kristen," he exclaimed, "did it never occur to you that breaking and entering is far more improper than walking in the front door?"

Kristen sat up very straight and haughtily began to repair the damage his embrace had done to her blue lutestring gown. Finally, dignity restored, she answered, "Of course I knew it was improper. But no one was looking." When he bent his head to hide his laughter, she assured him, "I checked."

"Well, I'm glad you weren't so lost to common decency as all that," he said with mock severity, tugging at the satin ribbon that held back her curls.

She quickly regained the offensive and the untied ribbon. "You, however, didn't seem to mind that your butler and your footmen and every passing coachman knew that you were entertaining Becky alone for dinner." With jerky motions, she gathered her long hair at the nape of her neck and tied the ribbon into a neat bow.

"Missed one," he told her, pulling a strand of pale hair out of place and letting it curl around his finger. "It was entirely innocent, you know. I'd never do anything to hurt Becky."

Kristen was warmly aware of his hand resting on her shoulder and the utter ease of his smile. "Is that why you are so complacent about her betrothal? I worried that you might avoid her."

"Avoid whom?" His surprise was genuine, and Kristen knew a gathering peace.

"Becky. Surely you remember her. The one you gave your heart to? Irrevocably?"

Brendan had the grace to look ashamed, an oddly appealing expression on that wicked face. "Oh, yes. Well, you'll recall that I did not specify the recipient of my meager gift. I meant you."

Unwilling to question her fortune, Kristen tilted her head to take his kiss— "Becky! Oh, that little minx. You two planned this!"

"Ingeniously, if I do say so myself," Brendan answered modestly, stroking the gentle line of her jaw with a calloused finger. "And we felt our brilliance ratified when you proposed nearly the same scheme yourself later."

"And you let me think Becky had cavalierly broken your heart, and I treated her so coldly! Not that she doesn't deserve it, mind you, but I thought such cruel thoughts of her!"

"I did tell you that I was entirely to blame."

"But you said it in such a forbearing way, as if you were making a manly sacrifice— Oh, Brendan, you are such a rogue!" she finished despairingly.

Tressilian's mouth drooped sulkily. "And I thought I was being so good all this time." "If this is your idea of being good— conspiring against me—"

"Not against you," he protested. "For you. For I knew— and you know too, now, I think— that you'll never be happy without me."

"So you proposed to Becky."

"Actually," he corrected, kissing the tip of her slightly imperfect nose, and then kissing it again, as if he had been longing to do so for a very long time, "I think she proposed to me. She was born for the stage, either that or perdition. At any rate, it worked, did it not? For you were indeed driven mad with jealousy."

"I was not driven mad," she protested, smoothing back that wayward curl on his forehead, as she had also been longing to do for a very long time.

"Oh, no? Then what, I ask again, were you doing climbing through my library window like a thief in the night?"

Even now the memory brought a flame to her cheeks. But Brendan's honesty was so clear, if rather belated, that she could offer no less. "I was resolved to tell you that I had been hiding something from myself. But I never got the chance." "You have the chance now."

He was waiting, his body tense, his eyes wary. But she was still frightened. "Kiss me first," she whispered, closing her eyes to the darkness in his. And he gathered her close, his kiss insistent, his arms demanding. Finally she drew slightly away. "I discovered that I—"

The drawing room door slammed back against the wall. Cursing under his breath, Tressilian released her to catch Corey, who hurled herself into his arms. Nick, however, adopted a stern stance before them, arms crossed over his chest. "Another new papa, I suppose," he observed scornfully. "I do hope you marry this one, Mama."

Kristen's happiness was too new to tempt, so she only replied demurely, "Well, I don't know. He hasn't asked me yet."

"Of course he hasn't." Nick had a fair grasp of protocol and a firm sense of his own importance. He squeezed in to sit between the two lovers. "Captain Bren knows that he must first ask me for your hand."

"Me too!" Corinna cried, not to be ignored.

"I don't need any permission from you little demons," Tressilian said severely. "And the sooner you scamper out of here, the sooner I'll be able to address my question to the only person whose answer I do need."

He picked Nick up and set him firmly on his feet, then repeated the process more gently with Corey. But the children weren't quite finished. "Just a minute," Nick said. "We haven't discussed the wedding trip. The West Indies, I think we agreed?"

"And Mexico," Corey chimed in. "To stroll in the shadows of the Mayan pyramids and watch the panthers at play in the jungle."

"Brendan, you don't mean you enlisted my children in this horrid scheme?" Kristen bent her head in helpless laughter, her righteous outrage somehow dissipated into a sense of inevitability.

"They enlisted me. For they, if not you, understood who would make the best father. Isn't that right, Corey? Nicholas?"

Nick did not second his sister's enthusiastic endorsement. "That depends," he said austerely, "on how the wedding trip goes."

"I did rather promise them," Tressilian explained apologetically, "that they could come along. In return they promised not to cause an ounce of trouble between them, but I shouldn't like to rely on that."

"Brendan, I can't believe you actually enticed my children into such a deception. Oh, no, Stamberly was right, wasn't he? They did jump out of his curricle just to incite dissension—"

"That wasn't my idea," Tressilian said just as Nick averred, "That was my idea." He ruffled the boy's golden curls and said proudly, "Now you see, Kristen, how these two would simply be wasted on a father like Stamberly. No, they need someone who can appreciate their innovation and high spirits—" "And lead them into a life of crime. Oh, Brendan," Kristen sighed despairingly, "what is truly reprehensible is that I agree with you. You see, you accomplished your aim after all. You have finally corrupted me, and my children too for good measure."

Critically Tressilian surveyed the two children standing before him, identically cocky grins on their angelic faces. "These two were born corrupt. Now vanish, you little devils. Go hold up a stage coach. I don't want to see you again this afternoon."

With touching obedience, they scampered out, and Tressilian took Kristen in his arms once again. "But you have accomplished your aim too, haven't you? For you've reformed me, as you promised. Didn't I tell you from the first that I'd be finished with all those activities you objected to by the time I was thirty?"

"You're only eight-and-twenty," she replied softly. "But you always were precocious." Then, struck by the memory, she gazed wonderingly up at him. "Did you know then, that night by the ruins? That someday you would want—"

He shook his head regretfully. "I am nothing so clever as that, my love. I only knew I couldn't let you go entirely. And finally I find I can't let you go at all."

His arms tightened around her as if to make good on that threat. But unease teased at the edges of her happiness. Finally, breathlessly, she broke away. "Don't you have something to ask me?"

In an instant he was on one knee before her, holding her hand and gazing up to her, his eyes dancing with laughter and love.

"Lady Killeaven, you must be aware that during the years of our acquaintance my true affection and admiration for you have deepened into a devotion I can only call love, though mere words cannot truly describe the passion I feel for you. I know only that I cannot call myself complete till I can call you my own, so my darling, I beg you, do me the honor of becoming my wife."

Kristen brushed that ebony lock back, her caress lingering on the rapid pulse at his temple. "You are very adept at this, your grace. You must have had a deal of practice."

"Well, I have," he said in a normal tone, resuming his seat beside her. "Months worth. Every night I dream that speech, and every night I wake up before I hear your answer."

"Oh, am I interrupting anything?" Becky chirruped from the doorway. She ignored Kristen's fervent affirmative and plumped down beside her former fiancee. "You see, Kristen, I told you he would turn up. Thank you for my ring, by the way," she added to Brendan, extending her little hand to exhibit a sapphire set in white gold and surrounded by diamonds. "It was only fitting that you procure it for me, considering that in all the time we were betrothed you never did grace my finger with a token of your great love. You can be sure Daisy Grey took note of your lapse."

"But sweeting," Tressilian said reasonably— never a successful course with Becky— "you would have had to return it anyway, and what would I do with a slightly used betrothal ring" It's not the sort of thing I'd pass on to my next fiancee."

Becky shot Kristen an arch look. "She should be proud to wear it, whoever she might be, that is. For it would have been the symbol of True Love. But that's of no matter. You do think it's tasteful, don't you, Kristen? I know Daisy will be green with envy, but she will surely say that there aren't enough diamonds."

Kristen felt her own silly twinge of envy. "You have exquisite taste, Brendan."

"Devil a bit," Tressilian said with a grin, as usual interpreting her cool observation. "Jon's had it picked out for weeks. Had to be sapphires, to match Becky's eyes. Had to be white gold, to match her skin."

"How romantic," Becky sighed, pressing the ring to her cheek.

"You know, I never realized that all that romance sounds like rubbish when someone else says it. You see," he added as Kristen gave way to laughter, "how you have ruined me. No, Becky, my only role in this was to procure it from Ombier's— and to pay for it, of course," he concluded sotto voce to Kristen.

"Well, I thank you anyway. For everything."

"And I thank you, my darling girl." He took her hand and pressed a kiss on the palm, then closed her fingers over the kiss. He held her fist in both his hands, and asked tenderly, "Happy?"

Becky gazed down at their entwined hands, smiling sadly. "Entirely. Happy?"

"As soon as Jon is well."

Becky gave him a quick, hard hug. "He will be," she whispered. "I promise, I will give him all sorts of reasons to live."

"If you can't do it, no one can. For you have certainly made your first intended husband happy— I think." Tressilian kissed his onetime fiancee's cheek and released her.

Kristen was touched by the obvious affection these two shared, at least now that she knew of their masquerade to persuade Kristen of Tressilian's worth. And their conspiracy had been successful, for Kristen felt only the slightest jealousy seeing him kiss another woman. She could not doubt his love, and his intent to remain faithful. Now she had only to trust him and give him reason to live up to that trust.

She was the next recipient of Becky's overflowing emotions, and indeed, Kristen felt her own eyes sting with tears. "I'm sorry I was so horrid, dearest," she whispered as their tear-damp cheeks touched. "I thought you were hurting Brendan, but I was so wrong."

"I forgive you," Becky said handsomely, pulling away in a flurry of laughter and fine muslin. "I shan't even expect an apology, because when you were so hideous to me, I knew it meant you loved Bren, and all my efforts on behalf of True Love were justified. Speaking of true love," she added, her hand on the doorknob, "Lady Destain told me the most amusing on dit about your rejected swain, Stamberly. Oh, Bren, I do love how your eyes flash when he's mentioned. You look very dangerous—"

Kristen felt Tressilian's arm encircle her and turned longingly. "Really, Becky, we aren't in the mood for gossip today."

"But you will laugh so at this," Becky promised, blithely ignoring the earl's scowl. "He was found wandering along South Audley Street the other night, soaked to the skin. Isn't that odd? For I recall there wasn't a trace of rain— I remember thinking how sad it was that Kristen might die on such a lovely night."

Kristen shivered again, but Brendan drew her closer into the circle of his warmth. Sighing gustily, Becky continued, "Stamberly caught the most desperate ague from his exposure, and the woman who rescued him had to take him home and nurse him back to health."

"I'm glad he's on the road to recovery," Kristen interposed, then cast a quelling glance at Tressilian, who was looking dangerous again. "Well, I am, Brendan, even if you haven't it in you to be sympathetic. But Becky, this isn't the least bit amusing."

"That's because you keep interrupting me, so that I cannot explain it properly."

Obligingly, Kristen closed her mouth, and Tressilian sighed and traced her lips with a gentle, rough fingertip. "What a lovely mouth you have. I have dreamed so often about—"

"Brendan!" They both looked up to see Becky standing rigid, her hands on her hips, like an outraged Duenna. "You'll have time for that and more when I am gone."

Tressilian let his breath out. "Proceed, Becky. Quickly."

In a rush, Becky cried, "Stamberly was so grateful for her intercession he has become her cicisbeo!" Goaded by their impatience, she added, "Elise Winterleigh's ciscibeo! Don't you see how perfect that is? The Tory paragon and the tarty—"

"We get your point, sweetheart. And you are right, it's a fitting punishment for the dull dog. I'll give you two to one he's married to that odd little daughter of hers by year's end." Tressilian gathered Kristen into his arms and whispered, "I shall be your only devoted swain now, so you'd best make the most of it."

"Well, I can see you two have other things to talk about." Becky flung open the door and advanced through it with great dignity. An instant later her curly head invaded the room again. "Oh, Bren, I've decided to call my novel 'Love's Labor Won.' It's a play on the Shakespeare comedy— "

"'Love's Labor Lost,'" Tressilian finished with remarkable restraint. "Very clever. Go write a chapter or two now."

As Becky vanished again, this time for good, Kristen echoed faintly, "Her novel?"

"This whole scheme was," Brendan murmured, tilting her chin up and dropping a light kiss on her mouth, "all in the way of literary research, you see."

Literary discussion exhausted, Kristen gave herself over to another kind of converse. Through a haze of longing she felt his lips leave hers and trace a fiery trail to her ear. "Brendan, wait," she moaned. "I must tell you—"

His body tensed against hers, then his hands dropped from her back, setting her free. He leaned back against the cushions, studying her expectantly. "Yes?"

Shyly, she ducked her head from his questioning regard. "I trusted you. I want you to know that I didn't feel jealous— well, hardly at all— when you kissed Becky."

He looked disappointed, but rallied to take her hand and kiss each fingertip. "I do love her. But it's nothing you need fear."

"I see that now. And that is what I have admired most often in you—and lamented most often!— that you have such a generous heart. You give it so freely."

"Ah, well, Becky is the sister of my heart, then, as Jon is the brother of my heart. As Nick and Corey have always been the children of my heart."

"And I? What am I?"

Brendan tilted her head up, and she went lost in his fathomless gaze. "You are the owner of my heart. And you must take good care of it, for I told you I have given it irrevocably, and shan't ever accept it back."

With unconscious sensuality, Kristen unbuttoned his wool coat and slipped her hand under the fine lawn of his shirt till she felt his chest warm and sinewed. His heart— her heart— pulsed an insistent if erratic pattern against her touch. She took his mouth in a bold kiss and felt his pulse accelerate under her hand. Breathless, she whispered, "Oh, I do love you, don't I?"

He was tense again, his chest rising against her hand with a suspended breath. "We shan't know for certain until— until you tell me you will be my wife forever."

Forever. Kristen rested her cheek where her hand had been, his warmth touching her through the thin fabric of his shirt. She heard the unsteady beat of his heart, felt the unevenness of his breathing, now slowing, now speeding. Loving Brendan, she would never again live an orderly life. He would bring her intensity and passion, disrupting the quiet tenor of her days— and her nights. His instinctive gallantry would enflame her, for her complacency, she feared, wouldn't last through a single devastating smile aimed at another lady, and his carelessness would drive her mad. And when he left her for the sea, as she knew he would, the pain and anxiety would nearly kill her.

But she looked up then to see the tense set of his too-beautiful face, and she was obliged to caress his hard jaw until he relaxed into a rueful smile. Only I can give him peace, she thought, and only he can give me love. The rest did not matter.

"Of course I will marry you," she said simply, and gave herself over to the chaos of his love.

# ABOUT THE AUTHOR....

Alicia Rasley combines several careers: She raises her sons, teaches writing at a state university and in workshops throughout the country, writes software user manuals, leads writing discussions on a computer bulletin board, edits short story anthologies for a small press. In her spare time, she writes romances.

Her latest Regency, GWEN'S CHRISTMAS GHOST (written with Lynn Kerstan), was Zebra's 1995 Holiday Special, and, won the Romance Writers of America 's Rita award for Best Regency.

Other Regencies (all Zebra books) include:

LESSONS IN LOVE, romance's first "braided novel," a computer-driven collaboration with two other Regency writers, Lynn Kerstan and Julie Caille.

POETIC JUSTICE, a mystery-romance which centers on a villainous rare-books curator and his quest to discredit Shakespeare. This was nominated by Romantic Times as Best Regency Novel of 1994.

A MIDSUMMER'S DELIGHT, nominated for the 1994 RWA Rita award for Best Regency, which uses a historical setting for a modern dilemma—a young woman who takes on so many responsibilities she loses herself.

A ROYAL ESCAPADE, a Lancelot-Guinevere remake, with a Russian princess sent off to marry a dissolute royal duke, thus cementing an international alliance against Napoleon. This was nominated for both the Regency Plume's Award of Excellence and Romantic Time's Best Regency Novel Award in 1993.

And the novellas "THE WILDER HEART" in Zebra's 1993 Valentine anthology (just out on audiotape), and "HOME FOR CHRISTMAS" in the 1993 Christmas anthology.

She lives in Indianapolis with her attorney husband and their two sons.